TALES OF PANNITHOR

ASCENT OF THE GOBLIN KING

BY ROB BURMAN

Tales of Pannithor: Ascent of the Goblin King by Rob Burman
Cover image by
This edition published in 2023

Zmok Books is an imprint of

Winged Hussar Publishing, LLC
1525 Hulse Rd, Unit 1
Point Pleasant, NJ 08742

Copyright © Winged Hussar Publishing/Mantic Games
ISBN PB 978-1-950423-11-8
ISBN EB 978-1-958872-19-2
LCN 2022932311

Bibliographical References and Index
1. Fantasy. 2. Goblins. 3. Action & Adventure

Winged Hussar Publishing, LLC All rights reserved
Published under agreement with Mantic Games
For more information
visit us at www.whpsupplyroom.com

Twitter: WingHusPubLLC
Facebook: Winged Hussar Publishing LLC

Rob Burman

For my own little goblins: Harrison and Cameron.

The world of Pannithor is a place of magic and adventure, but it is also beset by danger in this, the Age of Conflict. Legions of evil cast their shadow across the lands while the forces of good strive to hold back the darkness. Between both, the armies of nature fight to maintain the balance of the world, led by a demi-god from another time.

Humanity is split into numerous provinces and kingdoms, each with their own allegiances and vendettas. Amongst the most powerful of all is the Hegemony of Basilea, with its devout army that marches to war with hymns in their hearts and the blessings of the Shining Ones, ready to smite those they deem as followers of the Wicked Ones.

Meanwhile, the Wicked Ones themselves toil endlessly in the depths of the Abyss to bring the lands of men to their knees. Demons, monsters, and other unspeakable creatures spill forth from its fiery pits to wreak havoc throughout Pannithor.

To the north of the Abyss, the Northern Alliance holds back the forces of evil in the icy depths of the Winterlands. Led by the mysterious Talannar, this alliance of races guards a great power to stop it from being grasped by the followers of the Wicked Ones. For if it ever did, Pannithor would fall under into darkness.

In the south, the secretive Ophidians remain neutral in the battles against the Abyss but work toward their own shadowy agenda. Their agents are always on-hand to make sure they whisper into the right ear or slit the right throat.

Amongst all this chaos, the other noble races – dwarfs, elves, salamanders, and other ancient peoples – fight their own pitched battles against goblins, orcs and chittering hordes of rat-men; while the terrifying Nightstalkers flit in and out of existence, preying on the nightmares of any foolish enough to face them.

The world shakes as the armies of Pannithor march to war...

Tales of Pannithor Timeline:

-1100: First contact with the Celestians
  Rise of the Celestians

-170: The God War

0: Creation of the Abyss

2676: Birth of modern Basilea, and what is known as the Common Era.

3001: Free Dwarfs declare their independence

3558: Golloch comes to power

3850: The expansion of the Abyss
  Ascent of the Goblin King
  Tales of Pannithor: Edge of the Abyss

3854: The flooding of the Abyss, the splintering of the Brotherhood, and Lord Darvled completing part of the wall on the Ardovikian Plains.
  Drowned Secrets
  Nature's Knight
  Claws on the Plains
  Pious

3865: Free Dwarfs begin the campaign to free Halpi – the opening of Halpi's Rift.
3865: The Battle of Andro;
  Steps to Deliverance
Several weeks after *Steps to Deliverance*
  Hero Falling
  Faith Aligned

3866: Halflings leave the League of Rhordia
  Broken Alliance

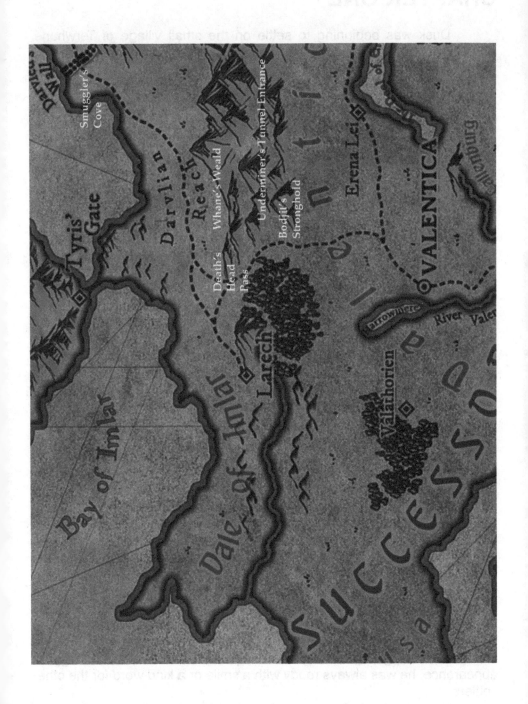

CHAPTER ONE

Dusk was beginning to settle on the small village of Terwhane. Echoes of laughter drifted gently through the air as children ran and danced between the small huts. Some chased other infants while others pestered the livestock left to roam about the settlement. Wisps of smoke rose from homes while simple meals were cooked inside, the delicious smells occasionally stopping the young ones as they dashed past.

Outside the tall wooden walls of Terwhane, a sharp holler went up from a grubby group of farmhands returning from a hard day's work in the field. Their greeting was met from a guard on top of the gate, who quickly signaled to a boy below to crank the pulley and let the men in. They entered through the gate laughing and joking, eager to get back to their homes and sample the meals they could smell drifting on the wind. Occasionally, their sons or daughters would run up to give them a hug before disappearing back into the maze of huts, giggling as their fathers tried to tickle them or ruffle their knotted hair. While they walked, the large wooden gate behind them eased back into position and the guards cast a vigilant eye back, away from the village.

Terwhane was really no different to many of the settlements and villages dotted throughout the countryside of Pannithor; it was made up of groups of families and friends that had collected together, not only to share resources, but to share protection too. Over the years, the settlements had grown until they were large enough to build defenses and protection against some of the horrors that roamed the land. Although life was hard, compared to the lords and ladies living in the cities of the Successor Kingdoms, it was *their* life - and they were determined to live it to the fullest.

In the center of the settlement, there was a hut larger than the others. It wasn't brightly decorated or particularly ornate. Instead, a magnificent orc's skull nailed over the entrance was the only indication that this was the center of Terwhane's power and the home of their leader, Brynn. His great grandfather had killed that orc and foiled a raid back in the mists of Terwhane's past - or at least that's what he liked to tell the children around the fire at night. He would boom with laughter as they screamed when he roared like the orc.

At that moment, Brynn strode out of the hall and into the settlement, preparing for his evening stroll. Brynn was a thickset man, his hands rough from years spent working in the fields, before he was chosen as Terwhane's leader. Like his hands, his face had been battered by his time in the elements, giving him a harsh complexion. But despite his haggard appearance, he was always ready with a smile or a kind word for the other settlers.

He walked with an ease that belied his strength, casually greeting those that gave him a wave. Although he didn't call it a patrol, Brynn liked to walk through the village like this every night. He would check on those returning from the fields or quietly enquire about the harvest, all the while making mental notes about what needed to be done the following day or prepared for the months ahead. Infrequently, he would be stopped by youngsters, asking him to pretend to be an orc and chase them through the makeshift streets. Each time, he would theatrically roar and lunge toward them before breaking into a hearty chuckle when the children squealed and dashed off into the shadows.

He always ended up by the large gate, ready for his update from the leader of the day watch. Even in a small settlement like this, it paid to have watchers around the clock – although attacks on Terwhane had been infrequent. When they had been raided, the chaos had been swift and bloody. Brynn slowly pulled himself up the ladder and onto the post above the gate.

"How goes it, Tam?" He clapped the leader of the day watch on the shoulder.

Outside of the settlement, it was unlikely Tam would have passed muster for a guard. His armor was a ragtag mix of items pulled together from trips to the larger cities for supplies. A dented iron helm leaned awkwardly to one side, and his bronze breastplate had clearly been expanded several times to account for his increasing gut. Despite his appearance, Tam was fiercely loyal to Brynn and Terwhane. When the marauders did come, Tam fought with the ferocity of a snow troll, and some loose fitting armor didn't stop him protecting the place he called home.

But tonight, Brynn could see that something was troubling his friend. He slowly drew away his hand and followed Tam's gaze. Beyond the fields of wheat and barley growing outside the gates, a dark green wood sprawled across the horizon. Known as Whane's Weald, the dense trees provided a perfect hunting ground to supplement Terwhane's livestock and crops.

"Something wrong in the Weald?" asked Brynn. Tam snapped his glare away.

"I can't be sure," replied Tam with a grimace. "I can't shake the feeling that *someone* has been watching me all day."

The pair returned their eyes to the Weald. Brynn squinted against the dwindling light. The ancient trees loomed in their vision, the slight breeze making the canopy rise and fall as though the trees were moving toward them. Brynn shuddered.

"There," hissed Tam and pointed to the Weald. Brynn strained his eyes but could see nothing. "Something is moving in the trees." Tam began edging toward the horn on his belt, ready to warn the settlers of an incoming attack. Before he could raise the alarm, Brynn lightly touched his hand.

"Just wait... I see it too. Don't be too hasty." In the distance, an object was clearly crashing and charging through the undergrowth. Brynn felt his friend's hand tightening around the horn. The pair kept their vision locked toward the bushes. Then, in an explosion of leaves and branches, a large stag burst through the treeline and charged into the field. It ran for a moment before stumbling and collapsing to the ground, exhausted. A wave of relief swept over Brynn, and he realized that both men had been holding their breath.

"It was just a deer," roared Brynn with a laugh. A few of the farmers below stopped and looked up at their leader before shaking their heads with a grin. "You're getting paranoid in your old age." Tam playfully punched him in the gut in response.

"Old age? You're three years my senior."

"Come on, it's time for the night watch to take over. Let's get you inside, old man." The hearty laughter of both men traveled over the walls and into the fields beyond.

Past the crops and toward the Weald, the stag shuddered and gasped its final, panicked breath, a small, black, and ugly arrow sticking out its side.

* * * * *

"What did you grogging shoot it for, you snoz?" asked an irritated, high-pitched voice, followed by the sharp crack of something being struck.

"There's good meat on a stag! I haven't had anything decent to eat in ages," came the whiny response.

"It charged right out into the fields. They could have seen us."

Far away from the eyes of the human village, two goblins stood bickering just inside the treeline of the Weald. Both were dressed in filthy black rags, with small dark hoods covering their green heads, apart from two slits where their large, green ears poked through. Standing roughly chest-height compared to a man, the diminutive creatures were dwarfed by the ancient woodland around them.

They moved with furtive, quick gestures, constantly glancing around them as though expecting someone to strike them. One goblin was rubbing his arm, where a vivid bruise was starting to form.

"Sorry, Grogger, I didn't think."

"That's your problem, Klup, you never grogging think." Grogger sighed with frustration as he dropped the stick he used to swipe Klup. He didn't understand why Bung had sent him on this scouting mission with Klup. He was perfectly capable of spying on a bunch of humans on his own. He'd done it loads of times before.

While Klup continued to rub his arm and whine slightly, Grogger turned his attention to the human settlement. His large ears twitched as he strained to hear if the alarm was being raised or if there were shouts of angry voices. As he concentrated, his large, pointy nose detected the tantalizing smell of food wafting across the fields. Without realizing, he began drooling at the thought of food. Klup was right, the clan hadn't eaten properly in ages.

A wicked grin spread across Grogger's face. Perhaps he and Klup could quickly grab that stag and make themselves a meal? After all, Bung wouldn't know what they were doing. Maybe they could tuck a bit of meat away for provisions, or even take some back to Bung and pretend they found it. Imagine how pleased he would be with a little extra meat for his fat belly?

Grogger was just about to tell Klup to drag the carcass into the wood when two mawbeasts came charging past him, spinning him around and knocking him into the dirt.

"I told you to tie those two up," he rasped. Grogger watched in horror as the wild animals burst through the treeline and thundered straight toward the dead stag. The creatures resembled a mix between a wolf and a lion; their shaggy manes were knotted and filthy, smeared in blood and food from their massive, gaping mouths. They snarled and snapped at each other as they dived on to the carcass. If the humans didn't hear them, they would probably smell the stinking beasts, thought Grogger.

"They must have slipped out the rope," whined Klup, apologetically. He nervously bounced from foot to foot. "Bung is going to kill us," he added with a nervous moan.

Grogger glowered at his assistant. Had Bung sent Klup on purpose to make him fail the mission? Had he wronged Bung in some way? He desperately wracked his brain to think of some slight he might have made against their temperamental and vindictive boss.

In the field, Grogger could hear the growls and grunts of the feasting mawbeasts. The sight of them eating caused his own stomach to grumble almost as fiercely. Grogger bit his lip while watching the human settlement. Yes, it was getting dark, but surely they would see this? He half-expected to be grabbed by the clumsy hands of a human guard at any moment.

He was about to leg it back into the forest when a devious thought popped into his wicked little mind.

"You'll have to catch the mawbeasts," said Grogger as he stabbed Klup in the chest with a green claw.

"Why me?" replied Klup in that nasal whine of his.

"You were the one that didn't tie them up properly. You said it yourself."

Grogger smirked to himself. This was perfect. If Klup caught the mawbeasts, then their cover wouldn't be blown. If he got eaten by the mawbeasts, then there wouldn't be anyone around to mess up his mission. And surely if the animals had eaten the stag and Klup, then they'd be too lethargic to gobble him up. He could just tell Bung that Klup had been devoured after falling off his mount. It happened all the time. No one would ask too many questions.

"Okay, Klup. We'll draw sticks for it. That seems fair, right?" Grogger scrabbled around on the woodland floor for a couple of thin twigs. He selected two suitable candidates before clutching them tightly in his little green hand and offering them to Klup.

"You first," he said, innocently. Klup nervously reached over and selected a stick. Realizing it was the longer stick, Grogger quickly snapped it with his sharp thumbnail before Klup could wrench it from his tight grip. Klup groaned as he produced the smaller half of the twig. With a grin - and making sure he kept his grip on the hidden remnants of the first stick - Grogger produced the second, now longer twig.

"Looks like the gobs have chosen, Klup. Here, I've got some more rope in my pack." Grogger threw the moldy rope heavily at his associate. Klup caught it with a moan, before trudging off toward the mawbeasts.

Grogger congratulated himself on a well-plotted and executed plan. In fact, he was half hoping - more than half, probably - that the mawbeasts would leap on Klup ravenously as soon as they saw him. In the quickly dimming light, Grogger's sharp eyes grew large in anticipation, and his tongue quickly darted over his jagged teeth while Klup neared the mawbeasts. He almost felt like shouting to surprise the animals further.

With Klup only a few steps away, the first mawbeast's head jerked up and it let out an ominous growl. Disturbed by the noise, the second beast lifted its bloody jaws from the carcass and glowered at Klup. *Any second now*, thought Grogger with a sense of glee. Klup was gently patting the air in front of him and making cooing noises to the beasts. Grogger sniggered to himself under his breath, but his excitement quickly turned to disappointment.

The mawbeasts stopped growling and just watched Klup getting closer. Cautiously, he tied one end of the rope around the first creature and quickly captured the second too. *Stupid beasts*, thought Grogger. Even they couldn't get things right. Klup turned and gave Grogger a goofy wave.

In a flash, Grogger snatched up his bow and shot an arrow straight through Klup's neck. There was a look of surprise on his face before the scent of fresh blood sent the mawbeasts wild. They dived on Klup, quickly ripping him to shreds.

Grogger shrugged. Sometimes one had to take matters into their own claws. He'd wait a moment before approaching the creatures though. They might have developed a taste for green flesh. Sitting down, he kept one eye on the village and the other on the feast in front of him. Hopefully there might even be some stag meat left for him - if not, he could always make the most of whatever was left of Klup. His stomach growled hungrily again.

CHAPTER TWO

The sound of children screaming startled Brynn awake. He was scrabbling for his heavy axe when the screams quickly turned to laughter. They were just playing, he thought, and relief washed over him. Pulling his hand away from the axe, he delicately brushed his wife Lucille's hair with a finger instead. She stirred slightly and unconsciously shrugged him away, perhaps thinking his light touch was that of an insect.

He lay still for a moment, staring at Lucille's long, auburn locks. It wasn't just her hair that glowed with a fiery essence. Since he'd been a boy, Lucille had captivated him. Her passion for life was intoxicating, and not a day went by that he didn't thank the Shining Ones that she'd chosen him - a big, brute of a man with a nose that had been broken more times than he could count. If anything should ever happen to her... with a shudder, he shook the thought away.

Brynn realized why his thoughts were taking a darker turn. Something about that stag the day before was playing on his mind. In the night, he had been plagued with visions of the animal being chased by ominous creatures. Yet every time Brynn tried to catch a glimpse at the pursuers, they melted into the shadows of the Weald.

Recently, travelers had spoken of more attacks by the almost mythical Nightstalkers. These hideous beasts could supposedly materialize out of thin air and rip a village to shreds. The ghostly beings were trapped lost souls, desperate to find a way back into the material realm, according to the traveling bards that occasionally visited. And that normally meant a lot of bloodshed. Orcs or Varangur warriors he could handle with axe and shield. But ethereal monsters? Brynn shuddered again.

Clenching his jaw, Brynn quickly rose from the furs of his bed and began to get dressed. He had to get a closer look at that stag.

"Where are you going?" asked Lucille, sleepily.

"Just a walk. You get back to bed. You need your beauty sleep." With a nimble grace for someone his size, Brynn just managed to dodge the fur blanket thrown by Lucille.

"There's not enough sleep in the world to fix your ugly nose. My mother always wished I'd married an orc," came the amused reply.

"I thought your mother was an orc?" This time, Brynn quickly ducked out the hut before another projectile came his way.

Walking through the settlement, he couldn't understand why the stag had unsettled him so. The familiar sounds of the blacksmith's hammer, the cries of livestock, or the shouts of other villagers failed to put his mind at rest.

Before he realized, he was at the village gate. Tam gave him a cheerful wave from the top of the defenses.

"Anything to report?" asked Brynn.

"Nothing, really. Farmhands left for the fields at first light. They reckon the harvest will be good this year."

"What about the Weald?" Brynn subconsciously turned toward the trees on the horizon. Tam raised an eyebrow.

"Something on your mind?"

Brynn grimaced. This was ridiculous. He'd seen the stag. Nothing was chasing it. No shadowy monsters had burst from the wood. It was just a deer. So why couldn't he shake this feeling of dread? His grandmother had always said she was part druid. Perhaps the icy fingers of magic had finally begun creeping toward Brynn.

"Fancy a closer look at that stag?"

"I thought you would never ask," replied Tam. "Anton, you're in charge."

"But... but," replied a scrawny teenager standing next to Tam.

"You'll be fine, lad. Just shout yer mam if Abyssals come charging over the hill." Tam clumsily clambered down the ladder and thumped onto the ground with a grunt. "I'm sure this here armor is shrinking. Open the gate then, Anton!"

Slowly, Anton opened the defenses, and the pair began walking toward the Weald. As they walked, Brynn waved to the workers in the field. Tam was right, the harvest did look good this year. The farm work was hard, but everyone had a smile on their face, safe in the knowledge that even with a harsh winter, they would have enough to see them through. Meanwhile, Tam took the opportunity to complain to Brynn about some areas of the defenses that needed strengthening. They were complaints Brynn had heard numerous times before, but he nodded eagerly as Tam rambled on.

As they neared the Weald, Brynn eyed the brooding trees with mistrust. He'd never liked the wood. Yes, his grandmother had told him to respect the place. Even said she had a vision of the Green Lady in there once. But Brynn couldn't trust it. Too many places to hide. Too many shadows that the sun never pierced. He would only hunt in there when times were desperate and only as a last resort.

"Where was the stag?" Tam's question wrenched Brynn from his thoughts.

"It was near that oak, I reckon." He pointed toward a large, gnarled tree on the outskirts of the wood, and the pair trudged onward. Around the edge of the Weald, long grass obscured the ground, so Tam began slashing at it with an old sword.

"Careful, the forest spirits will be after you," joked Brynn, uneasily. Tam grunted and carried on chopping the grass.

"I can't see anything. It must have fallen around here though."

Brynn turned back to face the village and checked his bearings. From here, he was struck by how small it looked. How fragile. Each of those homes represented a family he was responsible for. Mouths he had to make sure were fed. But compared to the might of the Weald, Terwhane shrank to insignificance. Like it could be swept away at any moment. Brynn cursed himself for the morbid thoughts. What was wrong with him today?

"Here! I've found something." Once again it was Tam that dragged Brynn from his own thoughts. He quickly walked over to Tam and followed the point of his sword. Blood was smeared on the grass, but there was no body to be seen.

"Where's the deer?" asked Brynn.

"Follow the blood, I guess." The friends followed the traces of blood and recoiled slightly as they saw the trail went into the Weald.

"I was hoping we wouldn't have to go in there today," sighed Brynn and subconsciously reached toward his axe.

"Want to get more men?"

"For a stupid hunch about a dead stag? We'll never hear the last of it. Come on, let's get this over and done with."

Brynn began striding toward the wood, and Tam quickly followed.

"Probably just a wolf," said Tam, hopefully. Brynn only grunted and readied himself to enter the Weald.

As soon as they stepped over the boundary, it was like entering a different world. While the early morning sun had shone brightly across the fields, when they stepped cautiously into the Weald, they were cast into a murky twilight. Even the temperature dropped somewhat, as the sun's warming rays failed to piece the dense canopy.

Thankfully, the trail of blood was clearly streaked across the green leaves and barks of the trees.

"Why would anything drag the carcass in here?" asked Tam as he stumbled over a knotted tree root. Brynn just managed to grab his arm before he hit the mud.

"Think I'd be more scared to eat in here than out there."

From amongst the gloom, they saw what was left of the stag. Brynn approached it cautiously and gave it a kick with his boot. Only a few strips of meat were left hanging from the broken bones.

"This was no wolf," muttered Brynn to Tam, who was inspecting a nearby bush.

"We have bigger problems," replied Tam, darkly. Using his sword to move aside some undergrowth, he revealed a small broken body, covered in blood.

"Goblins," growled Brynn.

CHAPTER THREE

Grogger had spent the return journey to the clan rehearsing his story about the unfortunate death of Klup.

"And then he fell off the Mawbeast and onto the ground. I tried to bash the grogging animal, but it wouldn't stop. Eventually it was just too late." One of the mawbeasts turned toward him when he said 'grogging animal,' and he bashed it on the nose with his bow.

"Oi! Don't you spoil my story." The trip back to the cavern from the Weald had been uneventful. The mawbeasts were fairly well-behaved after filling their bellies, and Grogger had even managed to scavenge a few strips of venison before they gobbled it all. He patted his knapsack where a few pieces of meat remained hidden.

"Who's that?" screeched a voice when Grogger approached a seemingly innocuous boulder. From out of nowhere, a goblin leapt out and viciously jabbed a spear in Grogger's general direction. The spear was actually a crude knife strapped to a long broom handle. Like Grogger, the goblin was dressed in dirty black rags but had the addition of a dented, rusty helmet strapped to his head. It constantly dropped over his eyes and obscured his vision.

Grogger tried to rein in the mawbeasts, but not before the one he was dragging along had bit through the spear. The other goblin howled in frustration and began hitting the mawbeast with the remaining broom handle. Grogger's mount growled angrily, frustrated at not being able to join in the action.

"It's me, Grogger," he replied quickly, hoping the situation wouldn't escalate. Goblins had a tendency for quick tempers and ill-thought violence. Something Grogger was keenly aware of but considered himself too intelligent to indulge in.

"Which Grogger? There's loads of 'em. Can't expect me to recognize them all." The guard was tussling with the mawbeast, who had now grabbed the broom.

"Split-tooth. Grogger Split-tooth. And I know there's only one Grogger in this clan!" He shook his head in frustration. How dare this grogging fool not know who he was. He was Grogger, the clan's best scout. The one who had helped them find this cave in the first place.

"Never heard of him." The guard was scrabbling backward up the rocks away from the advancing mawbeast. Grogger struggled to keep hold of the rope securing the animal, and it was almost unseating him. "You'll just have to wait out here while I make some inquiries."

"Make some inquiries?!" shrieked Grogger. "I'll give you all the grogging inquiries you need!" With that, he let go of the mawbeast's rope. Howling, it leapt toward the guard, snapping its gaping jaws hungrily and forcing the terrified goblin to desperately clamber further up the rocks. Grogger shot him a wicked grin before kicking his mount and steering it toward the mouth of the cave.

"You can't go in there!" screamed the guard, in between the snarls of the mawbeast.

"Maybe you'll remember my name next time," shouted Grogger as he disappeared down into the darkness.

The small opening of the cave quickly turned into a network of complicated tunnels that crisscrossed underground. The goblin lair was a bewildering maze of tunnels dug into the hard earth, which often led to nowhere. Once a goblin tribe had found a suitable location to call home, they would immediately begin frenzied tunneling to create all the required stores, living quarters, workshops, and prisoner cells. Unfortunately, the goblins' argumentative and skittish nature meant they would often abandon a tunnel they had previously started, or purposely ignore the advice of other goblins, and start digging in a completely different direction before realizing they weren't getting anywhere or crashing into a group of other goblins coming the other way.

Despite the seemingly random nature of the tunnels, Grogger knew exactly where he was going and headed onward. Although he wasn't nervous about traveling above ground - unlike some of his kind - he always preferred to be in the gloom, surrounded by the sounds and smells of other greenskins. Goblins were small, inherently nervous creatures, and even he felt there was something comforting being among so many others of his kind.

At first, he didn't see many other goblins; but the deeper he went into the cavern, the thicker the press of bodies became, as others rushed about whatever secretive task they had to complete. Some were carrying food; others were dragging along sorry-looking, often half-dead, prisoners – a mix of mostly humans and the occasional dwarf. The majority of goblins, however, were carrying digging equipment, ready to start a new excavation. The tunnels were alive with the sound of constant chattering and bickering.

Occasionally the walls would be rocked by the sound of distant explosions from the workshops of the Banggits and Gadjits. The collected goblins would stop for a moment and stare upward - terrified of a cave-in. When the ominous rumbles subsided, they would carry on as though nothing had happened until the next boom caused them to pause.

Eventually the number of goblins became too thick for Grogger to squeeze his mount through, and even the risk of being eaten by the tempestuous beast didn't seem to clear a way. He quickly dismounted and tied the mawbeast's reins around a nearby ceiling support. Let someone else take care of it, he thought.

With that, he carried working his way deeper into the lair. It was slow going, and Grogger became increasingly frustrated. So much so he began bashing anyone that got in his way with his bow. Often it wasn't clear that

Grogger was the culprit, so the injured goblin would spin around and start accusing anyone close to them. Numerous fights broke out behind Grogger as he pushed further into the caves, causing him great amusement.

Eventually the narrow, claustrophobic tunnels opened into a large hall. Carved into the rock itself, the gigantic opening was supported by a haphazard web of struts and supports. Clumsy wooden scaffolding desperately clung to the walls as though it might lose its grip at any moment. Dirty, ripped banners emblazoned with the insignia of the clan's leader, Bung, hung from many of the scaffolds. Grogger snorted in disgust at the crudely drawn insignia of Bung grinning manically and wearing a large crown. *As if that fat snoz could become king*, thought Grogger. Meanwhile, across the walls and ceiling, goblins armed with stolen tools swarmed everywhere, constantly fixed the straining supports. Grogger didn't even bother to look up when the frequent screams of falling goblins echoed through the chamber.

In the center of the hall was a raised mound of earth - the traditional spot for a clan's leader to hold court, eat, sleep, and relieve themselves. In fact, the only time a goblin leader would leave the safety of the mound was when they, reluctantly, rode into battle. Grogger's keen eyes could see Bung was up there now, berating a goblin about some misdemeanor - imagined or otherwise.

Bung was flanked by two large trolls - Og and Ug. These lumbering brutes were three times the size of a goblin and covered in thick, rippling muscles. Their huge upper bodies made them look like moving boulders, and they had the wits to match. The pair had been Bung's bodyguards since Grogger could remember, and they kept the leader safe from potential assassination attempts by rival clans and even his own followers. The trolls stood gormlessly beside Bung's makeshift 'throne' - an old chair Bung had nailed some spears to - and watched everything with complete disinterest.

Grogger neared the throne and caught the high-pitched shrieks of Bung. Although he was slightly bigger than a typical goblin - both in height and girth - Bung had a reedy, squeaky voice that gave him an inferiority complex. He would often talk through a large, hollowed out frostfang's horn when addressing the gathered crowd, thinking it made his voice sound deeper and more imposing. If anything, it just accentuated the squeakiness of it.

"I don't care if you say it wasn't! This meat tastes like it was poisoned," said Bung, jabbing a finger toward the cowering goblin and waving a chunk of fatty meat around with the other hand.

"It's the same gore meat you ate yesterday, your mightiness," replied the goblin and prostrated himself on the floor. "And you are very much alive today. Thanks be to the gobs."

"Well it didn't taste poisoned yesterday, you grogging liar! Are you trying to kill me? Who are you working with? My brother, Drung? He has always been jealous of me!"

"But, oh strong-voiced one, you killed Drung when-"

"Don't correct me! These plots take a long time to make up. He could have told you to do it before he died."

"But... I... the meat... is," stuttered the nervous goblin.

"Og, sort this out!" shouted Bung. The boulder-sized beast came to life and lumbered to the unfortunate goblin, dragging a massive bone club behind it. With an almost graceful swing, it brought the club round and struck the cook full in the chest. A sickening crunch echoed around the hall before the goblin was lifted upward and thrown across the room. The body landed with a wet thud amongst a group of gathered goblins, who immediately broke out in jeers and clapping. Og grunted and returned to his master's side.

Please don't let that be me, thought Grogger.

"Anyone else to see the Great Bung?" asked the diminutive tyrant, while taking a great bite from the hunk of meat. Grogger nervously stepped forward.

"Grogger, your hungriness," he said and bowed so low his nose touched the floor. "But before I begin, I thought your cleverness said the meat had been poisoned?"

Bung stopped eating with a mouth full of food. "Did I?" he replied, spitting chunks everywhere. He seemed to think for a moment. "No, no. That was my beer that was poisoned. This gore meat is delicious." He took another bite.

"Of course, my most cunning leader. How foolish of me." Grogger watched as Bung stuffed more meat into his mouth.

"Well don't just stand there gawping, Gruggy. What is it?"

"Grogger, my-"

"I'll call you what I want Gruggin. Or do you want to explain it to Og?"

"Of course not, your wiseness. Grogger, Gruggy, Groggle... it matters not to me." Grogger squeezed his fists in frustration. One day, they would all know his snozzing name. "I bring news of the human village near here and-"

"Oh, yes. Didn't I send you with someone else? Clop? Clip?"

"Klup," rumbled Og. Grogger stared in bewilderment at the troll.

"I was just about to say that," snapped Bung. "Klup. Where's he?

Grogger breathed deeply and put on his most dejected face. "He fell off his mawbeast and onto the ground. I tried to bash the grogging animal-"

"Right, he's dead then, fair enough," interrupted Bung. "What about this village?"

"Their defenses appear basic at best, and the harvest looks good."

"Plenty of food then?" asked Bung as he stuffed the remaining meat into his mouth.

"Plenty, your bloatedness."

"The gobs have smiled on us indeed," grinned Bung, with gristle leaking down his chin. "We'll attack the humans in two moons. Ready the troops!"

"Most wise, your wickedness," said Grogger and turned to leave.

"Oh, and Groggle!" Grogger's skin prickled. "You can lead one of the regiments in the battle. Seeing as you know so much about the village."

"But, I'm just a scout," moaned Grogger, urgently. "I've got no skill in battle. Surely it would"

"I hope you're not disagreeing with me, Groggin! Maybe you'd like to explain to Og?" The large beast stirred and tightened the grip on its club.

"Of course not, your craftiness. A wise decision." Grogger stomped off, muttering angrily under his breath.

CHAPTER FOUR

"Listen!" Brynn called out to try and calm the assembled crowd, but they refused to quiet down.

"What about the crops?" asked a voice.

"Should we protect the livestock?" asked another.

"Listen!" he tried again with more steel in his voice, holding up his hands for emphasis.

"Let's go to their cave and attack them, before they attack us!"

"This wouldn't be happening if we had offered more tributes to the Shining Ones," bellowed one lone voice.

Brynn sighed. He had toyed with the idea of not telling anyone about the goblin. After all, just because they had found one dead goblin, it didn't mean there would be an attack on the village. The stag and the, admittedly very close by, body could have been a complete coincidence. But he was reminded of his father's old saying: 'where there was one goblin, there were a hundred more hiding behind you with a bow aimed at your back'.

After finding the little green corpse, he had hurried back to the village with Tam, gathering the fieldworkers as they went. They had kept asking questions, but Brynn explained that everything would be clear once they got to the village hall. He didn't want panic to blossom immediately. Unfortunately, Tam whispered to his cousin about the goblin, and the rumor spread like wildfire. What started as a lone corpse quickly escalated to Brynn and Tam fending off an entire horde of angry goblins. By the time they arrived at the hall, it was a full blown disaster.

"The Wicked Ones have sent the invaders," shouted someone.

"Where will we hide the children?" cried a somewhat hysterical voice.

Brynn rubbed a hand over his face. He'd never seen the village like this. There was something odd about a goblin attack. Marauding orcs, vicious wildmen from the north, even Abyssals... people knew how to handle them. They knew what the battle plan would be. Yes, it would be a tough fight - and they would lose some people - but there was a clear strategy of defense. But with goblins, it all went mad.

He always thought it was something to do with the folktales surrounding the small green creatures. Whereas tales of vicious orcs or rampaging Varangur were used to scare grown men heading into battle, tales of goblins were used to scare children.

Don't go into the woods. There are goblins there.

You must not leave the village at night. That's when the goblins come out.

If you don't eat your food, a goblin will gobble it up... and then eat you!

All the threats. All the warnings. It created an exaggerated sense of terror. When adults heard there was a goblin attack coming, it took them back to those cold, miserable winter nights with the wind howling and strange noises outside their home. Every creak, every bump, was a potential goblin preparing to creep down the chimney and slit their throat. Goblins were the shadowy monsters that haunted their childhood. And that caused panic, even in adulthood.

"Please," Brynn tried once again, but the hall was lost in a cacophony of terrified voices. Frustrated, he grabbed his axe and banged it loudly against the wooden floor. No one stopped.

"Everyone, be quiet!" he roared and hammered the butt of the axe so hard it smashed through the wooden floor. This time, the room fell silent.

"We do not even know the goblins will attack," he quickly put up a finger to a farmer that was about to interrupt, "but we should be prepared in case they do. We have faced far more terrifying foes than a bunch of fairytale rabble, and this will be no more different than fending off orcs or northmen. In fact, I expect it will be much easier."

Brynn knew that was a white lie, but he just needed everyone to clear their heads and calm down while he thought of a plan. The truth was he had never faced a goblin assault. In fact, it had been a generation since Terwhane had fought off any goblin invaders, and Brynn had been just a boy then. He had a vague memory of being told to hide in the meat cellar below his house when the goblins came. When he eventually came out, he recalled the sobs of parents and noticing some of his playmates were missing. He never had the heart to ask where they went.

When he was older, his father told him about the attack, and the memory still chilled Brynn. Back then, the goblins had come without warning on a moonless night. Covered in filthy, black rags, they were almost impossible to spot as they swarmed across the fields and slammed against the fences surrounding Terwhane. The first many of the villagers knew of the attack was when a bizarre mining machine smashed through the gates before crashing into a house and catching fire. With the gates gone, the attackers quickly flooded the streets.

The first homes were the worst hit. Most people were still asleep when the goblins entered their houses, armed with wicked blades and knives. Those who had not been woken by the destruction of the gates were alerted by the desperate screams of their neighbors. Alarm bells began to toll and the villagers hurriedly mounted a defense against the goblins. The fighting was fierce, but as more residents gathered arms, the goblin attack started to falter. Without the element of surprise, the nervous creatures quickly lost their nerve. They soon fell to arguing among themselves about who was making the most noise and was responsible for waking the people up. When their numbers dwindled, the onslaught collapsed completely, and the remaining goblins disappeared as quickly as they had arrived - taking whatever spoils and prisoners they could carry.

Brynn shook the thoughts away and faced the crowd.

"The big advantage we do have is they probably don't know we found the body. Which means we can be prepared for whatever comes." Several heads nodded in agreement, and Brynn felt a sense of hope blossoming in his chest. "Tam will explain what we do next."

Tam stepped forward, and Brynn rejoined the crowd. A few of the villagers patted him firmly on the shoulder. They would get through this, thought Brynn. They would prevail.

* * * * *

I'll never get through this, thought Grogger.

He was standing just inside the treeline of the Weald. Not too far from where he had killed Klup, in fact. He hoped no one had accidentally stumbled across his body while waiting to launch the attack. Every time he heard a shout or raised voice, he expected it to be someone calling for his head. Then again, it had been several moons since Grogger killed Klup, and he hoped an animal would have made short work of the body.

After giving his report to Bung, the goblin clan had exploded into a hive of frenetic activity. Biggits - the commanders of a goblin force - had stomped around the caves, rounding up any 'volunteers' they could to join the makeshift army. Crude weapons were thrust into the claws of any goblin unlucky enough to get in their way and then herded outside ready to march to Terwhane. Grogger had a human dagger given to him and was told he would be leading a regiment of goblins armed with rudimentary melee weapons.

Bung wasn't a particularly well-liked or wealthy goblin leader, so his army was a ragtag selection of goblins armed mostly with swords, spears, and bows. He didn't have the influence or gold to build the mighty, if somewhat unpredictable, catapults or enough food to encourage a giant to join their ranks. Instead, Bung relied on sheer weight of numbers to overwhelm the enemy. If he threw enough goblins at a problem, eventually they would overcome it.

With the army rounded up, they had begun the march to Terwhane. Grogger had hoped to try and escape during the journey, but Ug the troll had been watching him the whole way. Every time he looked over his shoulder, the stupid, lumbering beast had been watching Grogger with those beady, cruel eyes. Once, when he'd been pissing against a tree, he looked over to see the annoying troll glaring at him. Grogger cursed the stupid troll.

And now here he was. Hiding in a wood and most likely only moments away from death. He looked along the ranks of his regiment and, once again, saw Ug watching him. Grogger gave the troll a wicked smile.

"Grog off," he muttered under his breath and quickly turned away when he saw the troll snarl. Surely he couldn't have heard him? Keen to distract himself, Grogger looked over at the village. The sun was beginning to set over the fields, and the previously bright autumn day was falling into twilight. His keen eyes spotted candles being lit in several of the homes. Grogger thanked the gobs that he and Klup clearly hadn't been spotted. The humans were totally unaware of the imminent attack.

While Grogger was congratulating himself for being such an incredible sneaky scout, a small goblin ran up to him panting.

"You're Grogger, right?" he gasped.

Finally, thought Grogger, the clan was starting to learn his name. They were beginning to recognize him and give him the respect he deserved.

"Yes, of course I'm Grogger, you grogging idiot." He stood a little straighter and raised his long, green nose a touch higher.

"Oh, good," replied the messenger. "I've already spoken to six other goblins before I found you. Someone said you died on the way here."

One of Grogger's regiment gave a little snigger.

"Bung says you need to lead the charge on the right flank."

"What?!" shrieked Grogger. "I'm a scout, not a grogging biggit. I haven't got a clue what I'm doing. Tell Bung he can stuff the grogging-"

Grogger stopped sharply when he realized Ug was barreling toward him, smacking any goblins unfortunate enough to get in his way. Grogger tried scrabbling backward, but other goblins in his regiment got in his way.

"What I was about to say," began Grogger, with Ug towering over him, "is to tell Bung he can stuff the grogging... humans... into... erm... a mawbeast's mouth... because I am ready to command these troops."

Grogger watched Ug carefully. After what seemed like an age, Ug grunted and tramped off to rejoin a couple of other trolls. Grogger resisted the temptation to stick out his tongue while the monster's back was turned.

His mind racing, Grogger quickly surveyed the flank he had been so unceremoniously put in charge of. Along with his own regiment of goblins armed with swords, known as a rabble, he had a regiment of archers called spitters, a small troop of fleabag riders, cavalry mounted on mawbeasts, Ug and his trolls, and that was it. The majority of the army was on the left, near where Bung was meant to be leading the charge. What the grog was he meant to do with this lot, he pondered?

A sharp blast on a horn disturbed Grogger's thoughts. He looked around to see where the sound was coming from.

"That means you're meant to charge," said the messenger helpfully.

To Grogger's left, dozens of goblins broke cover from the woods and began charging down the hill toward the village.

"You're meant to charge now," said the messenger with a smile.

Grogger watched as the rest of the army closed in on the village and made a quick prayer to the gobs.

"Charge," he mumbled, without much conviction. No one moved.

"You'll probably have to shout louder than that," said the helpful messenger. Grogger hoped he would be the first to get killed.

"Charge," said Grogger a touch louder and started jogging toward the village. He heard movement behind him and realized the others were following. How the grog was he going to get out of this mess?

CHAPTER FIVE

The villagers had spent the past few days preparing for the goblin attack. Weapons had been sharpened, bows had been fixed, shields had been hastily made, and anyone strong enough to swing a blade had been fitted for any old armor they could find. Whatever crops they could harvest were now stored in the village hall, along with some livestock and those who could not fight - mainly the elderly and children. They were as ready as they could be, thought Brynn.

"It's time!" shouted Brynn and thrusted his axe into the air. "Open the gate!"

Although the plan to defend Terwhane was simple, Brynn was confident it would work. From what he knew, goblins weren't known for their strategy when it came to combat. They would rely on their strength of numbers and the element of surprise. He expected them to attack at night and to charge from the safety of the Weald. All they had to do was make it look like they didn't know the goblin raid was coming and then, at the last minute when it was too late for the goblins to retreat, form up outside the settlement and take the brunt of the charge. Archers would be ready at the gate and could pick off as many goblins as they could. After the tales of the previous attack, Brynn wanted to stop the invaders outside the village. The chaos of them flooding the houses would make it harder to track them down and drive them off. Better to stop the assault before they even reached the gate.

Now with the goblins quickly advancing down the hill, Brynn was confident the plan would work. The greenskins were acting exactly like he had predicted.

Anton pulled on the ropes and slowly the gate creaked open. Once it was wide enough, Brynn marched through, followed by the men and women ready to fight to protect their village, quickly forming into a long line. They quickly formed up into a long line near the gate. Those with shields and swords stood at the front and prepared for the goblins to crash against them. Behind them were villagers armed with spears or farming equipment they could use to pick off the attackers.

"Get ready!" bellowed Brynn and dug his feet into the dirt to get a better stance.

Even in the dimming light, Brynn could see there were hundreds of goblins charging from the woods, along with a few lumbering trolls and cavalry featuring some sort of filthy-looking wild creature, ridden by goblins that appeared to be struggling to stay mounted. These must have been what he had heard tales about, the goblin's ferocious 'pets' – the mawbeasts. He thanked the Shining Ones there were no catapults or other war engines. He doubted the village would survive an onslaught from war machines.

Most of the force was on the left and was already closing in on Terwhane. The cavalry would hit them first, but the others wouldn't be too far behind. The smaller right flank, however, appeared to already be faltering. They were cautiously coming down from the Weald with what appeared to be little appetite for combat.

At a loss without the element of surprise, huh? thought Brynn with new-found confidence.

The goblin cavalry was now so close that Brynn could hear the roars of their beasts. Their massive maws snapped with each howl. After a few more moments, they were finally close enough for Brynn's surprise.

"Now!" he roared.

Villagers to his left and right started pulling on large ropes. Slowly, with plenty of grunts and groans, sets of large hidden spikes rose up from the fields, directly in front of the charging goblins.

Driven by the momentum of the charge down the hill from the Weald, it was too late for the goblins to halt the assault. The first cavalry slammed into the spikes and were impaled on the sharpened stakes. Those few mawbeasts that did manage to stop threw their riders to the ground and then began running wildly around. Seeing what was happening to the cavalry, the foot troops closest slowed their charge but were quickly carried forward by the hordes of goblins following behind, and many more were skewered. A ragged cheer went up from the villagers.

The initial charge was now in complete chaos. Without their riders, many of the mawbeasts were now out of control and had started to attack the goblins or eat the bodies of those on the spikes. Any that had managed to stop in time were picking their way carefully through the defenses or were hacking away at the wood to create a path. The momentum of the charge had been completely lost.

"Fire!" shouted Brynn, and archers began sending a stream of arrows toward the attackers. In this light, it was tough for the villagers to see, but Brynn nodded in satisfaction when he heard the occasional scream of a dying goblin. Anything that could help thin the remaining numbers would be useful when they finally made contact.

In the distance, a troll was making short work of the spikes. With each swing of a massive boulder, the defenses exploded into splinters, and a goblin occasionally went flying too. Slowly, the mighty fiend cleared enough of the stakes for the attackers to start swarming through again. Now the fight would begin in earnest.

"Hold fast!" thundered Brynn. "This is it!"

All they had to do was hold the line long enough for the goblins to lose their nerve and retreat. Brynn knew it only had to be a matter of time. The greenskins were visibly already shaken and it wouldn't take much to break them completely. Clearing his mind, Brynn readied himself for the attack.

The first goblin came toward him screaming and wildly waving a rusty blade in the air. Brynn roared and swung his axe, sending the diminutive warrior flying. More quickly followed, and Brynn had to switch to quick chops with his axe to keep up with the assault. He used his shield to block the clumsy thrusts of the goblins or simply bashed them over the head with it. Occasionally a villager would thrust a spear out from behind him to take out an enemy Brynn had missed. To begin with, he shouted his thanks; but soon, the attacks came too thick and too fast for him to thank each one.

Already his muscles burned and sweat dripped from his brow. But the line was holding. Even the troll was being kept at bay by quick jabs of spears from behind the shield wall. It roared in frustration as its body was criss-crossed with wounds.

Brynn thanked the Shining Ones the plan was working. He took a moment to survey the battle. Goblins were still pouring through the broken spikes, but their numbers were dwindling. The only unknown factor was the goblins on his right. They were still coming down the hill but with little enthusiasm. Brynn hoped they would just turn and run, and then the fight would be won.

* * * * *

Grogger watched in horror as the left flank descended into absolute chaos. The previously solid line of goblin warriors had descended into a wailing, chaotic mob. Some were still impaled on the spikes, others were slowly but surely being cut down by the humans. Numerous fighters were trying to retreat but continued to be pushed forward by the remaining goblins not sure what to do. Those who weren't trying to leg it were wildly thrashing their rusty blades about - causing as much damage to their fellow goblins as they would to any potential enemy.

With the madness surrounding him, Grogger had to admire the organization of the humans. When the goblins had flooded down the hill, they hadn't panicked or started yelling and running away. They had simply formed up and stood firm in the face of overwhelming numbers. Each had a clear part to play in the defense of the settlement and performed it with an almost ruthless efficiency. Grogger was reminded of the clockwork contraptions he had once seen in the workshop of a goblin gadjit. Each human worked together, rather than just trying to protect their own back. The result was almost spellbinding.

With no other options, Grogger had just carried on jogging down the hill, although he noticed the half-hearted battle cries of his flank had quickly fallen silent. He wanted to retreat, but he knew Ug and his trolls would be waiting for him, keeping his ever-watching eye on the goblin. He had to do something. He had to come up with a plan before it was too late!

"Halt!" he screeched at the top of his voice. The goblins closest to him slowed - mainly in confusion at the unusual command. They were more used to hearing 'run away' or 'leg it'. A few goblins carried on running past him.

"Stop, you grogging idiots!" he shouted again. This time, the majority stopped, although a few carried on heading toward the main fight. "That'll teach them for not listening," he muttered.

With everyone stopped, Ug stomped toward Grogger and growled. "Wait... wait! I've got a plan. I've got a plan!" he screamed, desperately. Ug stopped but glowered darkly at Grogger. Now he actually had to come up with a plan. Grogger clambered to the top of a nearby rock so he could see the gathered troops. He prayed to the gobs it didn't make him an easy target for archers.

"What are you doing?" hissed a goblin nearest to him.

"Trying to keep me, I mean *us*, alive."

The right flank had now completely ground to a halt. In the distance, Grogger could hear the shouts and screams of other goblins continuing to attack the village, providing them with a welcome distraction.

Ug and his trolls were grunting in frustration at the delay, while the pack of fleabag riders was having difficulty controlling their unpredictable mounts. Grogger grimaced as one rider was thrown into the dirt by an unruly mawbeast, which quickly set upon his master and began eating him. He had only had a few moments to put his plan in place before they all went wild. Ignoring the screams of the unfortunate rider, a plan began forming in Grogger's mind.

With the remainder of the goblin force now engaged with the villagers, the humans were too busy to keep an eye on Grogger and his flank. The humans were fighting outside the main gate to the settlement, and Grogger cast his mind back to the scouting trip. There was no other way in, but the fence was simply a circle. If the villagers were busy fighting at the front, perhaps they wouldn't notice a smaller force going around the fence and attacking from the other side? A wicked grin spread across his face.

"Oi, you!" he pointed at the leader of the fleabag riders. "Take your scruffy pack and go around the fence. If we get them from the front, you can sneak round the back and get them from the other side. They won't see you coming until it's too late."

Grogger smirked to himself at the brilliance of his plan.

"Piss off," responded the troop leader.

"Yeah, grogg off," came another cry. Grogger stopped smiling and wildly scanned the gathered crowd to see who else had shouted.

"You're not the grogging boss," said a particularly weak-looking goblin armed with a bent butcher's knife. Grogger shot him a menacing glance, and the rebel went and cowered behind another fighter.

"Bung put me in charge of the right flank."

"Well, who's in charge of the left flank then?"

"There he is," said Grogger and pointed toward the main fight. As one, the green noses of the goblins swung toward where he was pointing. They were just in time to see a strong-looking human chop the head off a slightly larger goblin wearing a plumed helmet. In response, there were numerous groans of despair from the goblins, and Grogger was sure he heard more than one throw up.

"Guess that puts me in charge of both flanks, then," said Grogger smugly. He looked at the leader of the mawbeast cavalry and smiled. In response, the rider reluctantly nodded and gave a quick whoop. The pack legged it toward the right side of the settlement, keeping to the fields of crops and away from the spikes directly in front of the gate. Grogger hoped they would not just run away.

"Right," he shouted to the archers. "You stay here and keep shooting at the humans. But make sure you stop when we start fighting. I don't want to get shot by my own grogging troops."

"We can stay here and not do *any* fighting?" asked one archer, eagerly.

"Just try and stick as many humans as you can before we reach them. When we start fighting, you stop shooting. Then you can run back to the woods for all I care."

A cheer went up from the archers, and they began notching their arrows.

"Ug, you and your trolls can go in the front. You can smash those shields out the way," commanded Grogger. This was starting to feel good. Ug paused for a moment before grunting at the other trolls and moving forward. Grogger was keen to have those big idiots at the front to smash the wall – and hopefully be the target for the humans' arrows, rather than the goblins.

Grogger hoped the cavalry would be coming around the side of the settlement by now. It was now or never.

"Charge!" screamed Grogger as he jumped down from the rock. He ran as fast as he could toward the enemy and was pleasantly surprised when he heard the others following him. The trolls blundered past him to lead the attack. He was starting to believe this actually might work.

The small arrows of the archers soared overhead. The majority missed their mark, but enough found their target. Grogger chuckled at the shouts from the humans. However, with Grogger charging toward them, the villagers on the right had started to shift position, ready to take the secondary assault. Although they hadn't suffered many casualties from the initial attack, Grogger could see they were tired. Most were slick with sweat and blood. They were holding their weapons heavily beside them and were struggling to draw breath, which was even better for the goblins' plan, Grogger grinned with the thought.

More arrows struck the humans, and Grogger hoped his archers would not get too carried away and keep shooting. He was only a few steps away now and almost directly underneath where the arrows might fall. He prayed to the gobs the archers remembered the plan and those riders actually turned up.

When the fleabags still hadn't shown up, he cursed the cowards; but it was too late to change the plan now - they were about to engage the enemy. Roaring loudly, Ug thundered straight at the humans, swinging his heavy club as though it weighed nothing. With a deafening clang, it smashed into the shield wall and scattered the defenders. Another troll entered the fray, swirling a great rock before him. Each blow was met with a sickening crunch as bones gave way under the immense force. Finally, a third troll casually wheeled a massive, rusty broadsword through the enemy troops. Although it had been blunted long ago, the sword was still devastating. It cracked legs and arms as though they were twigs. Everywhere it touched, humans fell crying to the ground. The villagers desperately slashed and hacked at the trolls, but it was no use. Driven wild by battle lust, the trolls could feel nothing, and their regenerative powers healed the wounds almost as quickly as they formed.

Now it was Grogger's turn to enter the fray. He jumped on the chest of a defender that was crumpled on the floor, his legs broken by a troll. Grogger gave him a quick smile and plunged a dagger into his throat. But he didn't have too long to celebrate. A spear whistled past his head, and Grogger only just managed to duck out of the way. He wheeled around desperately and saw a nervous-looking woman gearing up to stab him again. Grogger dodged under another blow and slashed at her legs. She fell to the ground, screaming. He was about to slash her throat when Ug's club crashed into her, crushing her chest.

Grogger looked around him. He could see that many of the humans were huffing and puffing with exhaustation. But even though they were starting to tire, most were still stronger and more muscular than the puny goblins. Eventually they would triumph, and Grogger's body would be food for crows. He nervously looked around and prayed to the gobs that the cavalry would not just abandon him.

* * * * *

Near the gate, Brynn grimaced as he felled another goblin. The attack seemed endless, and as soon as he killed one goblin, another two took his place. In a brief moment of respite, he heard the roar of trolls to his left and his heart sank when he saw the devastation they had caused. Friends he had shared drinks and broken bread with lay crushed and trampled. The shield wall had been broken, and goblins swarmed between swords and spear, hacking and slashing at any that got in their way. Meanwhile, the trolls were unstoppable, and they were getting closer to the gate.

"To me!" roared Brynn. "To me!" The villagers surrounding him formed up once more, with Brynn at the center. They needed to stop the trolls... and fast. Just waiting for them to attack wasn't going to work, the villagers had to take the fight to them. Brynn was sure that with the trolls gone, the goblins' resolve would weaken and the attack would end.

"Focus on the trolls," he shouted. "We can win this!" Shouts and cheers from the villagers eager to seek their revenge on the beasts that slaughtered their neighbors rang up through the crowd. The villagers gathered around Brynn turned to face the new threat from their left. Stop the trolls and this would all be over. They would win and save the village. This would all fade to a bad memory he could tell his grandchildren about.

"Cha-" Brynn's rallying cry was cut short by shouts from the archers on the wall. Then he heard the howling and the hammering of paws. Before he could turn, the ragged-looking goblin cavalry crashed into their rear. Small spears tore through the ranks while the mawbeasts snapped and clawed at anyone the spears missed. It was mayhem.

The archers on the walls panicked and began firing into their own troops, often missing the goblins and hitting those they were trying to pro-tect. Brynn's shouts were drowned out by the snarls and screams swirling around him. A heavy feeling flooded Brynn's heart as he considered for the first time that they may not win.

In a panic, Brynn realized he hadn't seen his wife Lucille since the battle began. She had been one of those armed with a spear. Seemingly safe from attack, or so Brynn had thought, he had told her to keep to the rear and near the gate. But now he couldn't remember if she was on his left or right. He prayed to the Shining Ones she wasn't one of those facing the trolls. Ignoring the chaos behind him, he powered forward, quickly booting a goblin in the face that ran up to him screaming.

"Lucille! Lucille!" Another goblin charged at him. Fuelled by a rising anger, Brynn scooped the diminutive foe up in his large, worn hands and crushed its throat before slinging the body aside.

Then he spotted her, and his heart sank. She was backed up against the fence surrounding the settlement, fending off goblins on her own. During the fight, she must have picked up a sword and was now swinging it at any leering, vicious goblin that came close. She was sur-rounded by bodies, both goblins and humans.

"Lucille!" he shouted again, and this time she saw him. She raised her hand to give him a wave, and then the unthinkable happened. One of the trolls slammed into her, knocking her down. Her sword flew from her hands, and she began scrabbling desperately for any weapon she could find. But it was too late. Holding its massive broadsword in both hands, the troll plunged it down through Lucille's skull, and she went limp.

Brynn's blood turned ice cold and his knees began to buckle. He blinked away tears, but the horror was rapidly replaced with a burning an-ger. A fiery rage that blocked everything but the vision of the troll killing Lucille.

He had a vague recollection of Tam shouting for him to stop, but there was no point. He knew what he must do. With an almighty roar, he pounded toward the troll. The dim-witted beast was too slow to avoid the powerful swing of Brynn's axe, and it powered through the rudimentary breastplate of the troll, straight into its chest. The armor fell broken to the ground, but the troll remained standing. Blinking at Brynn, it slowly pulled out the axe, looked at the weapon, and then lobbed it away. Brynn gasped in horror when the axe wound immediately began to heal. The troll roared in Brynn's face, covering him in thick, stinking spittle, before punching him square in the chest with a massive fist. Brynn fell backward and hit his head on the ground, dazing him for a moment.

This wasn't what was meant to happen, he thought.

* * * * *

This was exactly what was meant to happen, thought Grogger. What a grogging tactical genius! Of course Bung had been right to put him in charge. He clearly recognized Grogger's brilliance. Of all Bung's failings - and they were numerous - he knew that Grogger was a born leader.

He ducked a spear thrusted lazily toward him by a grogging human and thrusted his dagger into yet another victim. He'd lost count of how many he had killed now. Probably almost as many as the trolls, he thought smugly.

His attention was briefly caught by a commotion near the fence. A big human was trying to kill a troll but quickly got swatted away. All men looked the same to Grogger, but there was something about this one. He squinted to get a better look and grinned when he realized who it was. It was the leader of the village. He recognized him from the scouting mission. He had seen him shouting orders and bossing the other humans around. Unlike Bung though, he hadn't had to hit or whip anyone, and the villagers seemed to listen to him, so he must be important. If Grogger could kill him, then he would be hailed as even more of a hero. Grinning, he ran over toward his next victim just as the human leader was struggling to pull himself up. The man groaned as he shook his head, his arms reaching out almost blindly to search for a weapon that was not there. Grogger could see the human was struggling, although he was amazed he could even move after being hit in the chest by a troll. Eventually Grogger saw the man had picked up a sword and was clumsily swinging it around in front of him.

"Come with me," Grogger said to a couple of other goblins as he neared his target. Now that the man had picked himself up, Grogger was no longer so confident about taking him out. The trio of attackers leapt in front of the man and brandished their crude weapons while sniggering. Three against one seemed pretty good odds, even if the human was back on his feet.

The human stopped when the goblins jumped at him. They dodged in and out, poking and prodding a mix of blunt swords and spears made from rusty knives. Somehow, their target managed to parry their ungainly attempts. Eventually one of the goblins sprang too close and the man made a wicked slash across its throat. It fell to the floor with a high-pitched, desperate scream.

Grogger cursed the Shining Ones as his stupid grogging ally gasped its last breath. Perhaps he needed more goblins to take down this big human? Before he could give merit to that thought, the leader thrust his blade forward. Grogger let out a panicky yelp, grabbed the other goblin next to him, and used him as a shield as the blade plunged through and got tangled in the goblin's dirty, tattered robes. Sensing an opportunity, Grogger sprang forward and slashed his dagger across the wrist gripping the sword.

The human howled as the weapon cut into him, causing the blade to fall from his grasp. As he reached down to recover the sword, Grogger leapt in once more, slashing a wound across the man's thigh. The human leader recoiled, anger seething across his clenched teeth and furrowed brows as he glared at the goblin, and Grogger danced around him, cackling and jabbering.

With a loud laugh, Grogger stepped aside from a clumsy strike from the human. By the gobs, these humans were slow. He slipped under another punch and jabbed his dagger into the human's soft belly. In response, Brynn gave a sharp gasp and stumbled backward. Grogger quickly barreled into him, and the momentum sent them both to the ground. Before Brynn could gather himself, Grogger scrambled on top of Brynn's chest and looked into his prey's eyes with a manic grin.

"No one bests the mighty Grogger! This village is mine," he said in high-pitched common tongue, then viciously drove his dagger into Brynn's chest again and again.

CHAPTER SIX

Grogger strutted through the ruins of the human village with a smug, self-satisfied grin on his face. The village was in havoc. The night sky was lit by flaming homes, goblins were bickering over the spoils they had looted from homes, and screams drifted through the haphazard streets. Bodies - those of humans and goblins - were dotted everywhere, and greenskins scrambled over them looking for valuables.

After the leader had died, the villager's defenses quickly fell apart. Some had been inspired by the death of the bossy human to retaliate with a greater ferocity, but others had been too shocked to put up much of a fight. The goblins, on the other hand, had taken full advantage of the wavering humans. Some that had started retreating returned to the battle with a new-found confidence, increasing the numbers once more and making it even easier to overwhelm their remaining enemy. Even Bung, the clan leader, had charged down from the safety of his viewing spot in the Weald to join the fray. Grogger, meanwhile, had danced through defenders, slashing and cutting with his dagger while screaming at the top of his lungs that he had killed the human leader.

With the goblins busy taking out the remaining villagers, the trolls had quickly turned their attention to the large gate guarding the settlement. Armed with their heavy weapons, they had made short work of the wooden structure, and it gave way after only a few blows. With the gate gone, the goblins had flooded the village and all was lost.

Now Grogger was joining the looting and gathering up whatever he could find. As usual, it was chaos as the goblins were making a frantic dash to collect as many spoils as they could carry. Grogger was worried he would miss out on the best finds when he spotted some with armfuls of trinkets or books running from the now abandoned huts. He was keen to find himself a nice, sharp dagger. The clan, including Grogger, was meant to take the valuable finds back to the cave, but it was hard for the goblins to overcome their naturally selfish nature, and many would stash away their favourite treasures.

He snickered to himself when he spotted some goblins being grabbed by Bung's most trusted allies and *encouraged* – with the occasional vicious kick or punch – to add their loot to a large pile in the center of the village. Eventually the pile would be hauled back to the clan's cave by the prisoners captured in the assault. So far, the spoils of war consisted of weapons, shields, armor, and, most importantly, food.

Grogger was just eying up a nice pot lid that he thought could double as a decent shield when his sharp ears caught his name being shouted somewhere. It sounded like dozens of goblins were chanting, "Grogger! Grogger! Grogger!"

This is it, he thought, they've recognized my contribution to the fight and want to reward me. With that, he dashed off toward the source of the shouting, his heart beating with a sense of excitement. Perhaps Bung himself wanted to reward him? Promotion to chief scout and never forced to fight again. His small chest swelled with pride as he turned the corner of a house, ready to greet his adoring crowd.

"Here I am, Grogger the-"

His fleeting sense of pride was quickly dashed when he saw a small group of goblins carrying the leader of the fleabag riders on their shoulders and chanting. Grogger's claws shook with indignation. They thought that useless rider was him! The Great Grogger! The one responsible for them destroying the humans in the first place. The goblin who had come up with the brilliant plan and killed the village leader. Grogger realized he was grinding his teeth in frustration.

"Oi!" he screeched, but no one looked over. "Oi! You grogging idiots, that's not Grogger! *I'm* Grogger!"

This time, the fleabag rider turned around and spotted Grogger. He shot Grogger a wicked grin and then stuck two green fingers up, before joining in with the chanting. Grogger shook with rage and drew his dagger. He would show them who Grogger was. But before he could march over and chop that smirking idiot's two fingers off, a small cough from behind disturbed him.

"Grogger?" asked a voice. Grogger exhaled, relieved someone knew the true Grogger. The actual Grogger that helped Bung's useless rabble claim their biggest victory yet. Maybe they could help him deal with the flagrant case of mistaken identity. He turned and saw the small, nervous-looking messenger that had spoken to him before the battle.

"Yes, *I'm* Grogger," he replied.

"Oh good, I asked about ten other goblins before I found you," explained the relieved messenger. "Someone said you must be dead. In fact, most said you must be dead."

"What? You *just* spoke to me before the battle! Don't you recognize me? I'm the one that helped us with the fight. We're inside this village because of me!"

The messenger looked over Grogger's shoulder toward the chanting and pointed at the fleabag rider.

"I thought it was him? He was the one that led that brave flanking charge and broke their nerve."

"It was my idea though!" screamed Grogger. "I came up with the plan. I killed the... ah, forget it. What do you want?"

"Bung wants to see you."

Grogger's face fell. Being summoned to see Bung was never a good thing, and he was not in the mood to deal with that fat, grogging imbecile. Maybe he should just kill the messenger and pretend he never received the demand.

"Tell Bung he can shove his request-"

Grogger stopped when a large shadow loomed over him from behind, followed by an ominous growling.

"Ug's behind me, isn't he?" whispered Grogger. In response, the messenger nodded eagerly. "As I was about to say. Tell Bung he can shove his request... straight into... my... erm... claws, because I will be right there!"

Before he could turn to greet Ug, he was unceremoniously scooped up by the troll and held by the scruff of his neck.

"Ah, Ug," he struggled to utter, "I didn't see you there."

With a grunt, Ug tucked Grogger under his sweaty, stinking armpit and started stomping off toward their destination. Before Grogger turned the corner, he spied the fleabag rider waving at him.

Why me? thought Grogger. *Why does this always happen to little old me?*

After a few moments, they arrived at a larger home toward the center of the village. Grogger recoiled slightly as he saw the big human's decapitated head above the door. Grogger spied some young humans staring at it and howling with grief. They were quickly rounded up and forced away by some goblins armed with spears.

Grogger was just wondering where all the prisoners were being kept when Ug dropped him to the ground. He landed heavily but thought better of complaining to the troll. Instead, he dusted himself off and entered the hut, with Ug following closely behind.

Inside the hut, Bung was sitting on a large bed wrapped in fur blankets. As usual, he was eagerly stuffing his face with food, although Grogger couldn't tell what it was. A pile of more food - consisting of hunks of meat, half-eaten potatoes, and what looked suspiciously like the occasional human leg - was balancing precariously on the end of the bed. Bones and strips of nibbled flesh littered the floor. Og the troll was standing on one side of the bed, and Ug shoved past Grogger to stand on the other. The beast grunted to Bung, who looked at Grogger and frowned.

"How dare you disturb my dinner!" he roared, bits of detritus spilling from his gawping gob.

"You sent for me, your nastiness," replied Grogger and bowed as low as he could.

"Did I?" said Bung, while eyeing Grogger, suspiciously. "Perhaps you're here to poison my food!"

Bung began spitting food onto the bed.

"Og!" he screeched. "Kill the intruder!" Og stirred and glowered darkly at Grogger, snarling.

"It's Grogger, your cunningness," he said, panicking. "You sent a messenger and Ug to fetch me. I regret that it disturbed your meal."

Grogger resisted the temptation to say that Bung spent most of his time eating, so any conversation was likely to disturb the fat fool. Instead, he continued to keep his eyes to the floor, ready to dash out the hut if Og made a move.

"Ah, Groggin! I remember now. You're the one I so wisely put in charge of that flank." Grogger bristled at the sound of his name being mangled once more. "You executed my plan perfectly. Such a good idea I had to tell you to charge second and send those fleadbag riders round the back. This is why I'm boss, Grozzer. Always thinking."

Always scoffing, thought Grogger with a sly smile.

"Yes, of course, your smartness. I couldn't have done it without your tactical brilliance. Thank the gobs for your genius."

Feeling a little more confident, Grogger threw up his claws as though he were praising the gobs, then slowly raised his head to look at Bung, who had started eating again.

"Seeing as you can follow my clever commands," started Bung, although Grogger was having trouble understanding him between the mouthfuls of food. "I have something else for you to do. A new mission that I'm sure a goblin of your simple talents can handle."

"Another scouting mission?" asked Grogger. In all honesty, he was quite relieved. The thought of having to help haul back their spoils from the raid was enough for Grogger to consider any chance to escape. But he was surprised Bung wanted to attack another village so soon. Normally the clan would feast on whatever food they had captured until they ran out and only then, when necessity demanded, would they be forced to assault somewhere else. This cycle would continue until, eventually, the clan failed in an onslaught and they no longer had enough food to support the hungry mouths. Then it would be broken apart by in-fighting and squabbling, and the goblins would drift off to join other clans or start their own.

"Not quite," mumbled Bung, his mouth still full of food. "My spies have reported there's a captured wiz not too far from here, and I want you to rescue it."

Grogger's now confident demeanor faltered slightly. A wiz? That was the last thing this clan needed. A wiz was the term used to describe a goblin that could tap into the wheel of magic. Currents of magical energy swirled across Pannithor, but only some felt their call. While ancient races like elves had an innate ability to sense the currents, goblins weren't natural magic wielders. Those that could harness it were treated with suspicion by the other goblins. This mistrust wasn't necessarily unfounded, because a wiz could pose a potential threat to a clan. While an elf mage or human wizard would spend countless years studying the wheel of magic, once a wiz felt the pull of magic, they would go into a frenzy. They would attempt to learn as many spells as possible, not caring about their own safety or that of others. A wiz usually hoarded magical books, parchments, potions, or artifacts and experiment with them without having a clue about what they were doing. It was not uncommon for a wiz to blow themselves up, along with a large portion of their clan during one of these experiments. The thought of getting wiped out in a ball of magical energy sent a chill down Grogger's spine.

"A wiz?" he asked. "Are you sure that's wise?" Grogger immediately regretted the question.

"Are you calling me stupid, Goggin? Are you saying I am unwise?!" Bung was spitting food everywhere as he screeched. He threw the fur blankets off and scrambled across the bed toward Grogger, scattering food as he went.

"I want a wiz!" he screamed and punched his fists into the bed like a petulant child. "And you are going to get me that wiz!"

"Of course, your wiseness." Grogger had to think carefully here. "But why now? Your clan has survived without the dangers of magic so far, and your cunning foulness has led us to lots of mighty victories. A wiz can be *unpredictable*."

Bung rolled off the bed, stomped over to Grogger, and then poked him in the chest with a flabby claw.

"Because this victory has shown the clan can get even larger! We can conquer bigger places than this puny village. Towns! Cities! Nothing will be safe from the mighty Bung. So I need to make the army stronger, and for that I need a wiz. All that magic blasting about can destroy walls and stuff like clicking a claw. We'll be unstoppable."

Grogger gave a sickly smile to his boss.

"Absolutely, your unstoppableness. But a wiz..."

Grogger was cut short when Bung slapped him across the face. Instinctively, he reached for his dagger, but stopped when he heard the rock-like growls of Og and Ug.

"I want a grogging wiz, and if you can't get me a wiz, then what's the grogging point of having you around? Og, kill him!"

"Wait, wait, wait!" screeched Grogger before Og could march over to him. "Of course I can get you that wiz. Not a problem. I just might need some help, that's all."

"Oh, I've got you some help," sniggered Bung, and he gave a short, sharp whistle. Two goblins entered the tent, and Grogger let out a groan. One was the leader of the fleabag riders that Grogger had last seen giving him two fingers and the other was a goblin carrying all-manner of high explosives from bombs to rockets packed with gunpowder.

"Meet Gritter Fingernipper, fearless fleabag rider, and Klunk Blackclaw, the banggit."

Grogger could handle Gritter, it was Klunk he was worried about. In terms of danger, a banggit was second only to a wiz in terms of destructive power. While a wiz would become obsessed with anything magical, a Banggit lived their life to find items with explosive power. Their claws - if they had any left - were constantly stained black from handling gunpowder, while their skin was covered in blisters from burns. Grogger just hoped Klunk would blow himself up so he didn't have to deal with him.

"And Ug will be going with you too, just to keep an eye on things," added Bung. The troll looked slightly surprised at this command and glowered at Grogger in response.

"Oh, thank you, your malevolence. Having Ug with me will make it *so* much easier to get the wiz," replied Grogger, sarcastically. "Now, I'll just need to know where the wiz is and who has captured it."

"All on this map," said Bung. "Og, chuck him the map."

Og reached over to a small table and passed Grogger a crumpled piece of stained parchment. He quickly unraveled it, and his face fell when he saw the note about the captors.

"Eurgh, scalies," whined Grogger.

CHAPTER SEVEN

"This is the stroke of luck we needed," laughed Furna, the female salamander's eyes blazing momentarily. "It's almost time to head home!"

She couldn't hide the excitement from her voice, and coils of thick, smoky vapor rose from her gaping, toothy jaws as she laughed. The thought of getting back on the open sea sent a warm feeling coursing through her fiery blood.

"To the Three Kings," chorused the gathered salamanders, shouting the name of their homeland.

Even the name conjured up sweet memories for Furna. She had spent most of her life on the sea, after sneaking aboard a ship destined for Basilea when most would consider her to still be a hatchling. Despite her young age, she showed a natural affinity for sea-faring life and had quickly become popular amongst the crew, acting as their lucky mascot until she was old enough to start earning her way. Now as captain of her own ship, she had a thirst for adventure, which caused her crew to follow her command, no matter where they sailed.

Recently that devotion from her crew had been pushed to its limit, after their ship had been wrecked. Many months ago, Furna had overheard a tale in a tavern about an orc captain that had been captured by the Basilean navy. After paying a few coins to a drunken Basilean sailor, she learned about one of the rumoured treasure troves of Captain Greenclaw, the notorious orc marauder. Keen to return to the Three Kings with a hull bulging with booty, Furna and her crew had set off with the wind in their sails.

But that is where things went wrong for the salamanders. A freak storm battered their cutter, causing the waves to toss it around like a plaything. Despite their best efforts, the ship had been wrecked and what remained of the crew had been washed up on the shores of the Ardovikian Plain. Stranded.

Furna had initially struggled to rally the crew – and a few had threatened to go off on their own – but she offered them a plan. They would work as mercenaries for a while and gather enough gold to buy a small ship and return home, perhaps even with Captain Greenclaw's treasure aboard too. If she were honest with herself though, it was because she hated the idea of returning to the Three Kings with her tail between her legs aboard the ship of another corsair. Her pride was hurting far more than any injuries she received in the shipwreck, and she wanted to sail back with her head held high. The only problem was, human lords were happy to hire the salamanders as muscle to settle a petty land dispute, but they were proving more reluctant to sell them a decent ship at a reasonable price and they needed more funds.

Despite the fact they had been ashore for so long, Furna still wore the garb of a typical salamander sailor - a black tricorn hat, trimmed with gold and emblazoned with a symbol of the Three Kings. She wore the hat with pride, even refusing to remove it while bathing. Across her scaly chest, two holsters held a pair of flintlock pistols, given to her by the previous captain of the ship. She guarded them closely and kept them spotlessly clean. In combat, she often preferred to use a cutlass, dangling at her waist, rather than risk damaging the pistols.

The other salamanders were in similar garb, but with the occasional bandana, instead of a hat, and one of the salamander's traditional obsidian blades, rather than a cutlass. Unlike the sailors of other species, the salamanders chose not to wear heavy, wool peacoats and thick, bell bottom trousers. It wasn't anything to do with fashion, but merely practical. With the swashbuckling antics of a crew, the red-hot scales of the salamanders and their fiery blood had a tendency to set the clothing on fire. As dramatic as it was for the enemy to see a flaming salamander charging toward them, it also meant the sailor would spend a lot of their earnings on new clothing.

Furna stopped revelling with the crew for a moment and cast her gaze over to a sorry-looking goblin gagged and tied to a tree. This was the reason they finally had something to celebrate. This were their way back to the Three Kings. The puny goblin's robes were tattered and splattered with dirt. Its wild eyes swiveled as it struggled against the ropes and shrieked into the dirty rag shoved into its mouth. Furna threw a small rock at its head.

"Quiet," she said, with a hissing lilt that was common for salamanders when speaking the common tongue. "None of your stinking little green pals are coming to your rescue. You belong to us now."

She wasn't sure if it understood, but the goblin stopped shrieking, and its wild eyes settled on Furna for a moment. It glared at her with an intensity that caused the salamander to feel a small shiver, despite her hot blood. She wrenched her gaze away and attempted to laugh it off. The goblin was crazy, nothing to worry about.

She was right about it being a stroke of luck though. A few days ago, they had been approached by a hedge witch while traveling on the road. She told the salamanders that her home was being raided by an invisible creature, and that each morning she would find her herbs and potions ransacked. Although she explained she wouldn't be able to pay the salamanders, her garden was full of dragon's scale, a warming herb that could be boiled into a brew to help keep the chill away during cold nights or adventures to the frozen north. Desperate to delay the ominous cooling of their blood, Furna had agreed, and the salamanders followed the hedge witch home.

At first, they assumed she was crazy because the salamanders had seen nothing. But on the third night watching the house, Furna had spotted movement on the roof. She gave a sharp hiss to her first mate, Rorsha, and pointed to the roof. He nodded and prepared to spring the trap. After a few moments, they were greeted by an unusual sight. A goblin dressed in robes covered with crudely drawn stars and moons struggling under the weight of potions, herbs, and books, clambered out a window, chuntering to itself. It saw Rorsha too late to avoid a sharp crack over the head from a cutlass and was quickly sprawled across the floor.

Furna sensed an opportunity as soon as she saw the odd-looking greenskin. On their travels, she had heard the magical academies in Valentica were keen to study the impact of magic use on non-humans. The wealthiest colleges would pay considerable sums for live subjects and, if she recalled correctly, a goblin wizard was particularly rare. She had heard that most died in battles or simply exploded due to their own incompetence. As such, a college would be particularly keen to acquire this specimen. There would probably be a bidding war.

The hedge witch wanted to kill the goblin there and then, claiming its blood would hold healing properties but Furna insisted they take the creature instead. The hedge witch agreed and, in lieu of payment for their help, she gave them enough dragon's scale brew to last several weeks.

Furna took another sip of the brew and could feel the warming liquid trickle down her throat. She didn't know how the hedge witch made it, but the potion had an intoxicating effect, which explained the raucous conversation of the salamanders gathered in the clearing. They would have to be careful about how much they drank. But that was a problem for another day, now they could enjoy the warmth of the campfire and revel in each other's company. It had been a long, hard road to get where they were, but now the end was in sight.

"How long until we get to Valentica?" asked a burly salamander called Shalesh, who was the ship's cook. Even without a ship to call their own, he still captured and cooked their food while traveling on the road. Although he had run out of the spices and herbs of the Three Kings long ago, Furna still appreciated his attempts to remind them of home through his hearty cooking.

Being reminded of the Three Kings was something she certainly appreciated at the moment. The normally fiery blood of the salamanders had begun to cool after being away for so long, and it could only be fully restored by bathing in the island's volcanic pools. The more days that passed since the shipwreck, the sharper the pull to return home had become.

"A few weeks, unless we can find transport," replied Hr'zak, the navigator, while tracing a claw across a battered map. "Although we may struggle. There's a lot of anti-human resentment coming from the Successor Kingdoms recently. I doubt anyone will pick up a band of roguish - but good looking - corsairs like us."

"Weeks?" groaned Rorsha. "In that case, I just hope we can find more of this." He took another swig of the dragon's scale and beamed. "It's like Kthorlaq's Tears back home, but it doesn't get you as drunk."

He let out a loud belch, and the salamanders broke out in raucous laughter.

"If you hatchlings didn't drink so much, perhaps we would get home sooner," replied a gruff salamander sitting on his own. His scales were a darker shade of red than the others, while his body was patterned with old wounds and a chunk of his tail was missing. A dirty eye patch covered his left eye. Berusk was an aging salamander that had served on many ships in his long life. But due to his age, his body cooled more quickly than the younger members of the crew, and he felt the desire to return more keenly than them. Once the call came, it had been a tough few months for Berusk, which didn't help his already grumpy nature. Throughout their time on land, he had taken to complaining almost ceaselessly about the weather to Furna. She would just grit her teeth and nod once more, while he muttered about the 'chill winds' coming from the north. Furna knew he was struggling, but his complaining had started to irritate some other members of the crew.

"If you didn't slow us down so much, perhaps *then* we could get home sooner," retorted Rorsha.

Despite his age, Berusk leapt to his feet, growling. "Come here and say that, hatchling."

"Why? Did you struggle to hear me, ancient one?"

Berusk drew a large sword, which immediately roared into flame, caused by the salamander's fiery essence. Flickering shadows danced around the camp after being brought into life by the blazing blade, and the trees almost seemed to back away from the surging fire.

"Enough!" shouted Furna. "You two squabble like scorchwing chicks. Berusk, put your sword away. Rorsha, stop teasing the old one, he's killed deadliers foes than you with that blade... and without it too."

Before Berusk sheathed his blade, Furna saw the goblin was completely still and eyeing the weapon intently. It had a strange wonder in its eyes. When it spotted the salamander looking, it quickly went back to swiveling its eyes around in a mad gaze. Perhaps it wasn't as mad as she thought. She turned her attention back to Berusk and Rorsha.

"It's like being with a couple of ghekkotah." There were sniggers around the camp. "Look, it's just a few more weeks and then we can all get home. In the meantime, let's thank Kthorlaq for this dragon's scale and have another sip. To fire..!"

"... and fury!" replied the rest of the group and held their cups aloft. Rorsha glared at Furna across the quivering flames of the campfire before downing his drink.

CHAPTER EIGHT

"For the hundreth time, I do not want to hear about the explosive nature of mawbeast dung," said an exasperated Grogger.

He cursed Bung for sending Klunk with him. He had to be the most boring and stupid goblin he had ever met. Even Klup was better than this. The small warband of goblins had been on the trail of the salamanders for six moons, and there had still been no sign of their quarry. Every night, Klunk would bore them with facts about things that caught fire, what objects created the biggest explosions, how you could change the color of the explosion with different ingredients, which spiky things Klunk liked to put inside bombs... the list went on.

"I can get you plenty of dung," said Gritter. "Mawbeasts pits are full of the stinking stuff. You'll just have to collect it and keep all your limbs intact."

The three goblins bobbed along astride three mawbeasts, while Ug the troll loped behind them. Grogger was amazed the hulking monster never seemed tired. Not even the weight of his enormous club slowed him down as they traipsed through mountain trails and woodland. Hidden in a cloak of shadows, Grogger knew where his companions were, but he also knew an unaccustomed eye would not be able to spot the figures dressed in all black. Well, except for Ug. The hulking giant's size, despite his ability to keep up with the mawbeasts, must have made him stick out even on a moonless night.

Now they were making slow progress through a woodland trail that appeared as though it hadn't been used for moons. Occasionally, Gritter would jump off his mawbeast and inspect the overgrown path for tracks. This consisted of him almost lying flat and sniffing the ground with his long, green nose while patting the soil with his claws. Grogger was convinced he didn't have a clue what he was doing, but at least it kept him quiet for a while.

The massive trunks loomed ominously over the path, and Grogger expected centaurs or fawns to leap out at any moment. Every crack of a broken branch or rustle of the leaves sent his claw twitching toward his dagger. But the attack never came. Then again, perhaps being captured by beasts of nature would be a sweet relief to the inane chatter of Gritter and Klunk.

"What about troll crap?" asked Gritter with a smile. Grogger rolled his eyes.

"I hadn't even thought of that," replied Klunk. He pulled on the reins of his mawbeast and turned to face Ug. "Do you think-"

Ug replied with a rumbling growl.

"Ah, no, yes. I shouldn't ask." He gave his mawbeast a kick and quickly caught up with Gritter.

"Just let me know when he goes for a crap," whispered Klunk out the side of his mouth. The pair made conspiratory sniggers.

Suddenly, Grogger's sharp ears picked up some more laughter. But rather than the high-pitched snarking of his companions, this was much deeper and there were several different laughs at once. He halted his maw-beast and held up his claw to stop the others. Klunk crashed into him.

"Shhhh, you grogging snoz," snapped Grogger.

"Who you calling a snoz?" replied Klunk. "I should blow you sky high for-" Grogger wheeled round and slapped Klunk across the nose.

"Shut up," he hissed. "There's someone else in the woods."

This time, the three goblins stopped to listen. Even Ug seemed to be straining to hear whatever had alarmed Grogger. More laughter crept through the trees along with raised voices. Gritter's eyes grew wide with fear.

"Let's leg it," he whispered. Although Grogger had just been considering running in the opposite direction, he couldn't be sure what they had heard. However, he could be sure that if Ug caught him making a run for it, or he returned to Bung empty-handed, then his little green neck was likely to be crushed.

"Wait here," said Grogger. "I'll go and look. Could be some beardies for us to kill and cook." At the mention of beardies, otherwise known as dwarfs, the other goblins, and even Ug, appeared to relax slightly. They had often come across dwarfs while digging the numerous tunnels that made up the clan's home and were used to dealing with this common foe.

"If you hear me screaming, come and rescue me. Don't run off."

Grogger wrapped his black hood tighter around his face and crept off the side of the path.

"If we hear him screaming, we're definitely running off," Grogger heard Gritter mutter, nearly out of earshot.

Despite the almost pitch black of the woods, Grogger's keen eyes picked out every potential root that may trip him up or branch that could slap him in the face. He slid through the trees like a shadow, only stopping occasionally to listen for the laughter that had caught his attention back on the path. After a while, he spotted a campfire dancing in the distance and started creeping ever closer.

He spotted large, bulky forms sitting around the fire. These definitely weren't beardies. They spoke in short, bark-like sentences, with the occasional hiss. Grogger shuddered when he realized these must be the salamanders they were looking for. He had never fought a scaly, although he had heard some of the goblins from other clans describe how salamanders breathed fire, turned into a raging inferno, and even had weapons that burst into flames. Grogger had never believed a word of it, but he could smell the acrid wisps of smoke curling from their toothy jaws, and he caught the occasional glint of their flaming eyes. Now, he wasn't so sure.

He tiptoed closer to the campfire to see how many salamanders they would have to deal with and to, hopefully, get a glimpse of the wiz they had been sent to rescue. A pair of the scaled beasts were having what looked like an argument in the center of the clearing. Their barks were louder than the sounds Grogger had heard before, and one in particular looked like it was spoiling for a fight. The angry one drew a sword, and Grogger recoiled in horror when it set alight. The roaring flames lit the clearing, and Grogger was convinced the salamanders would spot him. He pressed himself against a tree and prayed to the gobs he wouldn't be spotted. However, with the woods now well lit, Grogger could pick out the twenty or so salamanders around the campfire. As he scanned the camp, his nervous heart leapt when he saw a filthy-looking goblin bound and gagged at the base of a tree.

Grogger began wracking his brain to come up with a plan. He didn't fancy his chances of taking on the big lizardy things in a direct fight, even with Ug on their side. And the thought of being on the receiving end of those flaming swords sent a chill down his spine. They would have to carefully track the salamanders and wait for the perfect moment to snatch the wiz from under their scaled snouts. It wouldn't be easy. The scalies were likely to be on their guard and keeping a close eye on the wiz. Perhaps, he thought, Ug could take out one and then... his thoughts came to an abrupt end when an almighty explosion shook the woods around him, followed by the sounds of rockets whizzing into the air before exploding with a small pop. The sky lit up with greens and blues, casting odd shadows around the woods.

"Klunk," he hissed.

The explosions clearly caught the attention of the scalies. They all snapped their heads toward the sparks dancing through the sky. Some were smiling and watching the show with a sort of dumb, glazed stare. Even Grogger had to admit it was a magnificent display. The lights scampered and wheeled across the moon in captivating patterns.

"Who wants a closer look?" Grogger heard one of the creatures hiss. Several of the others nodded.

"Guard the goblin, Berusk," commanded what appeared to be the leader, and she set off through the woods with the remaining scalies in tow.

As they stomped past him noisily, Grogger scrambled around the tree to avoid being spotted. Once they were all gone, he turned his attention back toward the camp. That snoz Klunk had provided him with the perfect opportunity. There was just one guard left in the camp... although it was that angry one with the flaming sword.

Slowly, Grogger sneaked around the perimeter of the clearing, keeping as close to the treeline as he could. The guard was sitting with its back to the trees, muttering and hissing under its breath, but it was watching the wiz closely. Grogger was now so close, he could feel the heat coming off the scaly beast. He just needed to distract the guard for a moment while he grabbed the wiz. He felt around on the floor for a pebble and smiled when he found a suitable rock. Taking aim, he threw the stone at the creature, but it pinged off its thick hide without effect. The captor didn't move a muscle.

Grogger slid his tongue across his sharp teeth while thinking what to do next. His eyes darted about the clearing looking for something he could do to distract the guard long enough to grab the wiz and leg it. However, while he was thinking, he noticed the guard's grumbling chatter had stopped and had been replaced with heavy, regular breathing. Grogger listened for a little longer and realized with excitement that the stupid grogging scaly had fallen asleep! This was going to be easier than he thought.

With nervous glances around him, Grogger emerged from the trees and walked slowly toward the wiz. At any moment, he expected to hear the shouts of the returning salamanders, but nothing came. Nearing the salamander guard, the heat became almost unbearable, and Grogger could feel the sweat running down his head and dripping off his long nose. He was half tempted to run back to the trees, but he knew he would never get another opportunity like this.

As he rounded the guard and the log it was sitting on, Grogger got a good look at the captive. The goblin was slightly smaller than himself and was pinned against the tree with their eyes closed. They were dressed in a filthy, purple robe; but underneath all the grime, Grogger spotted small stars and moons sewn into the fabric. He had heard wizzes had a taste for the theatrical in their clothing, but this was something else.

As Grogger was about to reach out to touch the wiz, their eyes snapped open in fear, then grew wide with realization when they must have seen that Grogger was another goblin. They immediately began moaning and struggling against their restraints.

"Shhhhh," hissed Grogger and put a claw to his lips, but the wiz continued to struggle. "You'll get us spotted."

Grogger approached the wiz and started pulling at the ropes wrapped around the captive. His sharp claws picked and pulled at the tight knots, but it was slow work, particularly with the wiz continuing to wriggle and squirm. Suddenly, the wiz fell still and their eyes grew wide in horror as they focused on something behind Grogger.

Grogger flinched as he heard the roar of the salamander's sword catching fire behind him. Once again, the clearing was lit by a fiery orange glow, and Grogger knew this was the end. Unless... he ripped the gag from the wiz's mouth.

"Do some grogging magic!" he screeched.

"With pleasure," said the wiz with a smile. The wiz started muttering under their breath and their eyes rolled back into their head. A wind began swirling around Grogger, and he had to quickly grab onto the ropes to avoid being blown away. The wiz's eyes flashed green, and a sharp wind blasted toward the salamander, knocking it backward and onto the ground.

"That was meant to be a fireball spell," said the wiz with a confused grimace.

"Let's just get these ropes off," replied Grogger. This time, he reached into his belt to pull out his dagger and began hacking away at the ropes. They quickly began falling away, and the wiz pulled out their hands before rubbing them together to get the feeling back.

"Quick, that scaly is getting up again," said the wiz, matter of factly.

"I'm going as fast as I can," snapped Grogger, and he grinned when the last rope fell away. His jubilation was brief, however, when he felt an intense heat behind him. Grogger whirled round, brandishing his dagger and prepared to face the salamander. It towered above the goblins and growled under its breath as it swung its sword from side to side and stamped toward the greenskins.

"Now would be a good time to use that fireball spell," hissed Grogger.

"Hmm... I just to need to remember if its *infurnus* or *infernolis*," replied the wiz, small sparks spitting from their claw with each magical word. "I wish I had my books with me."

But it was too late. The salamander roared as it lifted the flaming sword above its head and prepared to strike Grogger. Then, over the sound of the roar, a loud whistling suddenly filled the night sky, and Grogger looked up just in time to see a large rocket trailing through the air with a blue trail of sparks behind it. The rocket struck the tree above them with a loud explosion, followed by an almighty cracking and crashing sound. An enormous branch - scorched by the explosion - fell straight on the salamander's head, knocking it to the ground. It let go of the sword, which immediately stopped burning and returned to cold, black obsidian.

"Was that you?" asked a shocked Grogger.

"Let's just say for the sake of argument that it was," replied the wiz.

"Who cares? Just leg it!" screamed Grogger, and with that, the pair dashed into the shadows of the wood.

Grogger and the wiz ran through the woods as quickly as they could. This time, there was no need to be quiet, and Grogger was keen to get back to his small warband as quickly as possible. If only for the comfort of having Ug to fight against the salamanders, instead of him.

He could hear the blood pounding in his ears as he ran. Each knotted and gnarled tree seemed to twist into the shadowy form of a salamander, ready to strike. More than once, Grogger reached for his dagger, convinced he was about to be ambushed. Using brief, frantic glimpses of the moon through the dense treeline, he navigated his way back to the path where he had left Klunk, Gritter, and Ug.

However, his heart fell slightly when they crashed through the treeline and onto the overgrown path. He stood there, panting, struggling to catch his breath. The gang was nowhere to be seen.

"They grogging legged it," he groaned.

"We can't stop for long," said the wiz behind them. "It won't take those scalies long to realize I'm gone, and they're going to be angry."

"Shut up, I'm thinking," snapped Grogger. Without the mawbeasts, it would take moons to get back to Bung, and he didn't fancy their chances of outrunning the salamanders. Perhaps if they stuck to the woods, it would be harder for the salamanders to follow them? Grogger was just about to head back into the woods when he was disturbed by a sharp hiss.

"Psssssst, is that you Grogger?" came a voice from the trees. Grogger quickly recognized it as Klunk.

"Yes, you grogging idiot. Who else would it be? Now come out, we need to get moving."

Gritter, Klunk, and Ug emerged from the dark of the trees, along with the mawbeasts.

"Good distraction," said Grogger, nodding at Klunk.

"What?"

"The explosions and stuff. It distracted the scalies long enough for me to grab the wiz." Grogger pointed proudly toward the rescued captive.

"Distract-what?" asked Klunk, a look of confusion across his face. "We didn't do anything at all. Just wait here quiet as... something that's really quiet."

"A mawpup's fart," suggested Gritter, a little too eagerly.

"Yeah, but we don't stink like a mawpup's fart," replied Klunk. "More like a worm. Yeah, a worm's quiet and they don't smell. We waited here like worms."

Klunk nodded and smiled at Grogger, clearly satisfied with his train of logic.

"Who you calling a worm?" hissed Gritter and reach towards his weapon.

Grogger waved his claws in irritation to shut the pair of chattering fools up.

"What were all the explosions and stuff about then?" Grogger was becoming increasingly frustrated by this idiot.

"Oh, that?" Klunk looked a little nervous. "You saw that, then?"

"They could probably see that back at Bung's cavern," snapped Grogger. "Of course we grogging saw it and heard it!"

"Right, well you see, I noticed that Ug was going for a crap and-"

"You mean to tell me, that wasn't meant to be a distraction?!" screeched Grogger and jabbed a claw at Klunk's chest.

"Not exactly. More of an experiment, than a distraction," replied the banggit with an awkward smile.

Grogger blinked in amazement. Just when he thought Bung had actually sent him with some useful assistants, he was reminded they were all complete imbeciles. Still, the job was done, and now they just had to return back to Bung.

"Just stop talking. We need to get moving. Those scalies will be on our trail soon. Mount up!"

"Scalies?" moaned Klunk.

"It's getting light soon," said Gritter. "We can't stay on the path for too long, we'll be too easy to spot."

"I know a cave not too far from here. We can hide there," replied the wiz.

"Lead the way, wiz," said Grogger.

"My name is Kackle Flashzap!" replied the wiz, proudly.

"Of course it is," sneered Grogger. He hated the ridiculous names the wizzes would give themself. As soon as they realized they could use magic, they felt the need to adopt a more grand-sounding name.

Grogger climbed onto his mawbeast, while Gritter and Klunk did the same.

"What about me?" asked Kackle. Grogger thought for a moment. There wasn't enough room for two goblins on the back of a mawbeast, and they were grumpy enough carrying one. A little smile crept across his face. "Ug, perhaps you could assist?"

The troll grunted and scooped the wiz up before tucking him into his sweaty armpit.

"Wait a minute!" screeched Kackle.

"No time to argue. Ug give our new ally some encouragement," said Grogger. Ug quickly obliged and squeezed the wiz until he pointed in the correct direction. Grogger flashed them all a quick smile of satisfaction and pulled on his mawbeast's reins.

CHAPTER NINE

With the light show seemingly over, Captain Furna and her crew returned to the clearing. They hadn't been able to find the source of the fireworks but she had never seen anything like it. Although she had heard the wizards of the Successor Kingdoms would often put on spectacular shows of magic that lit up the night sky, it was never something she had been able to see for herself. Behind her, the other salamanders laughed and jostled each other, cheered by the fireworks and the dragon's scale brew still coursing through their hot blood. However, when they returned to their camp, the laughing quickly stopped as the crew surveyed the scene around them.

Berusk was lying prone on the floor, a large, smouldering branch beside him. But, most worrying of all, the wiz was gone, and all that remained was a bundle of ropes on the floor. Furna dashed over to Berusk.

"What happened?" she asked, shaking him slightly to bring him back to his senses. The older salamander struggled to focus on her for a moment but eventually replied.

"Goblins," he growled.

"What in Kthorlaq's name happened here?" Furna tried to contain the anger in her voice. She wasn't angry at Berusk. She was angry at herself for drinking too much of the dragon's scale brew and not being more cautious. She shouldn't have left him on his own. He was getting old, and the cold was starting to seep into his bones. It made him more sluggish, less agile. Furna cursed under her breath again.

"One of the critters came out the wood while you were all watching the fireworks," replied Berusk, gruffly. He was sitting in the dirt and nursing a large bruise on his head from where the tree branch had struck him.

"One goblin managed to knock you out?" said Rorsha, with a chuckle. "Your age is getting the better of you, ancient one."

Berusk growled loudly, and Furna had to press hard on his shoulder to stop him from launching at the younger salamander. Smiling, Rorsha shook his head and moved away to lean against a tree. He casually played with a small obsidian dagger, which occasionally burst into flames.

"You've got to admit, it seems unlikely one goblin could take you out, old friend. Were you poisoned? Shot?"

Berusk shifted awkwardly in the mud and paused for a moment.

"The branch hit me. Knocked me out cold. Think one of those blasted fireworks must have hit it. Last thing I remember was an almighty bang, and then it's all black until you came, Captain."

Furna gave him a smile. She could see he was embarrassed by what had happened. Berusk's agility may have waned over time, but his pride was as fierce as ever.

"It's my fault Berusk, I shouldn't have left you alone."

She clapped her claw around Berusk's and pulled him back to his feet. He wobbled unsteadily for a moment before grunting and firmly planting his feet on the ground.

"No more dragon's scale brew unless it's absolutely necessary," Furna shouted to the camp. "We can't afford to be sloppy."

The gathered crew nodded their agreement, although Furna spotted Rorsha quickly taking a swig of something from his hip flask. He shot her a winning smile before taking great interest in the tree he was leaning against.

"What are we going to do without that wizard?" asked the chef, Shalesh. "That was our way home!"

"Ha!" laughed Furna, humorlessly. "You think a couple of goblins can outsmart us? They can't have got too far, and we've tracked harder prey than them before."

She hoped her lack of confidence wasn't reflected in her tone. The truth was, she had no idea how they would find the goblins in this wood, and time was running out for them to find a ship and get back to the Three Kings. Furna could almost hear the tribal drums beating in the shadow of the volcanoes. Still, this was no time to panic the crew. She had to keep a level head.

"Hr'zak! You're the best at tracking I've seen. Let's find these greenskins and crush their puny, little necks."

"Yes, Captain," replied the navigator.

"Berusk? Which way did they go?"

"Like I said, Captain, I blacked out when the tree hit me, but I seem to remember we saw a path to the north earlier today. If I was them, I'd be heading to that."

Furna nodded in agreement.

"Grab your stuff and let's go."

The crew spent a few moments stuffing their knapsacks and slinging them across their broad, scaled shoulders. When they were ready, Hr'zak checked his compass, and they set off north, with the navigator leading the way.

The moon had disappeared over the horizon, making the woods almost pitch black. The salamanders were forced to use their flaming swords to light the way, but it was slow going; they regularly tripped and stumbled over hidden roots or fallen branches. Furna cursed the wood for their lack of speed. She knew that each moment spent among the trees was another chance for the goblins to increase their distance.

Looking around the gloomy surroundings, she wondered why some of her kind joined the cause of the Green Lady and pledged allegiance to the Forces of Nature. The thought of spending a lifetime under a canopy of green, rather than sailing across the open seas, gave her an uneasy feeling. She hated not being able to see the stars and having to rely on Hr'zak's compass. It was like having one of her senses cut off.

She was snapped out of her melancholy when a twig slapped her across the face.

"Sorry, Captain," replied the hulking mass of Shalesh in front. He was struggling to squeeze his mighty frame through the undergrowth and slowing them down even more.

"Just hack the damn branches out the way!" shouted Furna in frustration.

"Are you sure that's wise?" asked Berusk, cautiously. "These trees are ancient, Captain. They may have a voice, and they will tell of what we've done."

"I don't care. After today I never want to see a tree again. Cut them down!"

The crew replied with shouts, and Furna was greeted by the harsh sound of branches being hacked and slashed. The flaming swords of the salamanders left scorch marks on the trees they had cut, and the smell of burning followed them on their journey. She ignored the quiet groans and whispers that swirled around them as they cut their way through the woodland. It was just the dragon's scale brew, she told herself. Just the dragon's scale brew.

Her head swiveled around as she heard panicked shouts from behind.

"What's that?" she asked Berusk.

"I did say we should be more careful," he grunted.

Furna pushed her way back down the line of salamanders and was greeted by a scene of utter confusion. Two of her crew were leaping up to try and reach another salamander that was dangling from a branch high off the ground and screaming.

"What in the Three Kings is happening here?" boomed Furna.

"The tree, it's crushing me," wailed the trapped salamander. "Get me down! Please!"

"Don't just stand there! Cut him down. Hack it to pieces, if you have..."

Furna's command was cut short by a booming bellow that echoed through the wood. It roared through the branches and caused the leaves to tremble. Furna turned her head from side to side as she heard the trees creak and groan, as if they were moving.

"Please, just get me down," continued the desperate captive. But before the crew could start cutting, there was a loud snapping noise, and the salamander's lifeless body fell to the ground with a thud. Furna stared in horror as the bark of the tree shifted to reveal two piercing blue eyes that were looking straight at her. The glowing eyes cut through the dark wood like a beacon, and Furna nervously saw more springing to life around her.

Another branch snapped out and pierced a crew member through its chest before lifting them off the ground and up into the treeline. Under her feet, Furna could feel the roots beginning to move, as though the trees were preparing to pull themselves out of the soil and start chasing them.

"Run!" she yelled. Furna turned back and crashed through the undergrowth. Occasionally, she would have to duck as a branch appeared to swing toward her or leap over a root that raised awkwardly from the dirt. She heard the cries of her crew that weren't so nimble and hoped they had not been scooped up like their unfortunate crewmate. But there was no time to think about that. She had to get to the path. At least then they wouldn't be completely at the mercy of nature. Desperately, she continued to run. The adrenaline caused her fiery blood to boil, and black smoke billowed from her snout.

One of the crew members running alongside her was suddenly tripped by a tangle of roots. Furna skidded to a halt and turned back to help her, but it was too late. A pair of willow trees with blazing blue eyes scooped up the legs and arms of the salamander and began to pull. Furna averted her eyes at the awful sound of her crewmate being torn asunder. Wiping tears from her eyes, she sent a prayer to Kthorlaq and charged back through the undergrowth to catch up with the others.

She leapt over another root and crashed out from the greenery into the back of Berusk, who was waiting on the clear path.

"How many?" she asked, as two more of the crew emerged from the dark of the trees.

"With you three, we're just missing Krat'lk, Ralz, and Tulsk," replied Berusk. "Did they make it?"

Furna shook her head sadly.

"In that case, we're all here," he sighed. "I warned you not to mess with the trees."

"Remind me to listen to your cryptic warnings about whispering trees a bit closer next time then," growled Furna.

Now she was out of the woods and onto the slightly clearer path, she could tell the glimmer of sunlight spreading through the cover. In the growing light, she saw her crew was all breathing heavily, and many had fresh scars caused by rogue branches. Some were even bleeding, and their broiling blood hit the cold earth with a sharp hiss. She eyed the menacing treeline uneasily, waiting for more attacks.

"Give me some good news, Hr'zak," she shouted. The navigator was kneeling on the ground and using his flaming blade to light the path. He turned toward Furna and stood back up.

"I have good news *and* bad news, Captain," he replied. "I've found goblin tracks, so we can follow them."

"I take it that's the good news?"

"Indeed. The bad news is they're mounted on what look like large dogs, judging by the prints, so they're going to be much faster than us."

"They'll need to hide soon though," said Furna. "The sun's coming up, and they prefer to travel in the dark. We can use that to catch up to them. Let's keep moving everyone!"

"One more thing, Captain..." Hr'zak raised a claw. "They appear to have a troll with them."

Furna sighed and put a claw to her head. She looked out onto the path and consider how in the Three Kings they would deal with a troll.

* * * * *

Grogger and the goblins had ridden through the night to Kackle's mysterious cave. The wiz had constantly protested about being carried under Ug's arm until Grogger got so bored of his whining that he asked Ug to put the gag back in his mouth. After that, Kackle was forced to point in the direction they should head, a slightly dejected look on his grubby face.

Eventually, with the light just peeping over the horizon, they came to a cave entrance hidden among some thick bushes, and Kackle nodded eagerly. The small group pushed through the vegetation and into the dark cave. Grogger tried to hide his relief at being away from the rising sun. They quickly tied their panting mawbeasts up and walked further into the hollow. Grogger nodded to Ug to drop Kackle. He fell to the floor with a bump and immediately wrenched the gag from his mouth.

"I should blast you into the sky," he screamed at Grogger. "No one treats the great Kackle Flashzap like that!"

Grogger rolled his eyes.

"Put the gag back in and tie him up with the mawbeasts."

Ug grunted and reached toward the wiz.

"No! No! Wait, there's no need for that. I should be saying thank you for rescuing me."

"Don't thank us, thank the great Bung when you meet him," said Grogger, sarcastically.

With the wiz now quiet, Grogger took a moment to look around the cave. The thing that hit him first was the stench. Piles of bones were scattered around the place, and the walls had a clammy-looking moss that crawled everywhere. But rather than being the abandoned cave of some monster, Grogger quickly spotted books and empty bottles scattered across the floor. He also saw the odd scorch mark on the ceiling. In the corner sat a large, battered cauldron above a small but now extinct pile of kindling, and near it was some moldy hay that had been collected together like a bed.

"Is this where you *live*?" Grogger asked Kackle.

"Yes, since leaving my clan," he replied with a dejected note in his voice.

Although goblins preferred to live in large clans, it wasn't uncommon for a wiz to live outside the communal cave. Their magical experiments were so unreliable that it simply wasn't safe for them to put all the other goblins at risk. Instead, they were often forced to live in neighboring caves or even small huts far enough away so that when they did, inevitably, open up a portal to the Abyss or accidentally summon a fire elemental, only the wiz paid the price. However, it was unusual to find a wiz out on their own, completely cut off from the tribe.

"What clan?"

"The Furbiters," muttered Kackle.

"That was old Graf's tribe, right?" asked Gritter, while throwing some of the bones toward the mawbeasts. They dived on them hungrily, snapping at each other as they crunched and gnawed on the remnants.

Grogger eyed Kackle suspiciously.

"Heard they got wiped out when some fish folk sent in a load of water elementals and flooded the tunnels. Only Graf and a few others made it out alive."

"Yes... fish folk," mumbled the wiz.

"Something you want to tell us?" said Grogger. Kackle walked over to his bed and sat down with a bump. He held his head in his claws for a moment before replying.

"We were getting short on drinking water because the tribe had been using the only water supply in the cave to crap into, which was making us sick. So Graf asked me to summon some new water out of the ground. I thought it wouldn't be too hard. On a raid, I'd found a book written by one of the fish folk's mages. It was in a mix of elvish and something else, so I could make out most of the words, and there was a spell about making water."

A stillness settled around the cave, even the mawbeasts had fallen asleep after the long ride and a few morsels of rotten meat. Kackle continued his story.

"Normally I would do my spells in my hut, but Graf wanted the water straight away, so he asked me to get my books and start the incantation. I started chanting and everything was going good. I had found a small spring under the cavern and the water was drawn up to me, spouting through tiny cracks in the floor. Problem was, it kept coming... and coming. Graf asked me to stop, but I hadn't read the bit about stopping the spell, so I just turned to the next page that mentioned water. Again, I started the incantation but I could tell something was wrong. The trickle was getting bigger and bigger, until it looked like a huge wave, just before it crashed against the rocks. Graf was screaming at me to stop, but it was the most impressive thing I'd ever conjured, so I carried on, just to see what might happen."

Grogger had a sinking feeling that he knew what was coming next, but he wanted to hear it from the wiz. This is why he didn't trust the grogging magic users. They were a danger to everyone around them.

"Eventually the water did stop, but the wave was massive... and that's when it started roaring. Two arms raised up from its side and it began smashing everything. I'd accidentally turned the spring into a grogging water elemental. I quickly uttered a teleportation spell, but not before hearing Graf say he was going to kill me. I've been hiding out here ever since."

Kackle threw his claws in the air and flopped back onto the bed, dramatically.

"And that's why I told Bung a wiz was grogging dangerous," said Grogger, pointing at Kackle. "You've wiped out one clan! What's stopping you doing the same to ours? We're leaving you here."

"No, no, please!" replied Kackle and scrambled over to Grogger on his hands and knees. He pawed at Grogger. "I can't stand being here on my own. I want to be part of a tribe again. That's why I told you this, so you would know I'll never do anything like that again. Goblins aren't meant to be out on their own. You've got to take me back! I can't be alone anymore. Those scalies will find me again!"

Grogger recoiled slightly from the groveling wizard.

"No chance, I'm not risking it. If Bung wants you, he can come and get you himself. I'm not drowning in my own grogging cavern."

A low growl filled the cave. Grogger turned toward Ug.

"Oh, come on! You must see that he's dangerous? Bung doesn't know what he's doing."

In a flash, Ug stomped across the floor and grabbed Grogger around his neck. Kackle backed away to his makeshift bed.

"Kill him! Kill him!" shouted Gritter and jumped up and down clapping. "I'll take the wiz back and get all the credit."

"Okay, okay," squeaked Grogger, pawing desperately at the troll's thick finger. "We'll take him back! We'll take him back!"

Ug dropped Grogger to the floor and thudded back to his seat. Coughing, Grogger rubbed his neck and took in large gulps of air. He scowled at Gritter.

"Kill him?" he wheezed.

"I meant you kill Ug," he whispered, while covering his mouth and eyeing the troll nervously. Grogger rolled his eyes. He would have to watch that one. Perhaps a little accident on the way back to Bung?

Goblins fall off their mawbeasts all the time, thought Grogger, remembering what had happened to the hapless Klup.

"The thing with the water elemental was a long time ago," muttered Kackle. "I know what I'm doing now. I've been studying." He pointed to the various books around the damp cave. "Since I left Graf, I've been stealing as much stuff as I can and even reading some of it."

Grogger looked at the grubby-looking wiz. The thing with Graf had been many, many moons ago. So the fact Kackle hadn't blown himself up in the meantime showed that perhaps he did have some control.

"Prove it," said Grogger. Kackle leapt up excitedly and grinned. He rushed over to a pile of musty scrolls and started throwing them around, muttering under his breath.

"Nothing explosive or fiery," added Grogger and noticed Kackle's shoulders droop slightly. "Just something simple."

Kackle continued foraging and eventually pulled out a small scrap of paper.

"Have you ever had your future told?" he asked Grogger.

"Grogg off. It's not possible," Grogger replied with a snort.

"What if I told you I knew you would rescue me?" A mad glint entered Kackle's eyes.

"You were cowering like an orcling when I found you. There was no way you knew we were coming to rescue you."

"Just let me show you," said the wiz. He began searching for more trinkets and artifacts among the piles of what looked like rubbish. Gritter sidled up to Grogger.

"If he's doing magic, I reckon I'd rather wait outside the cave," whispered Gritter.

"Me too," echoed Klunk. The pair walked out the entrance, sniggering slightly. Ug watched them go, gave a grunt, and went to join them.

If I get blown up in a wiz's cave, I'll haunt them all, thought Grogger.

"Here we are!" shouted a jubilant Kackle. He scampered over to Grogger and sat in front of him. In his claws he had a bundle of what appeared to be the teeth of a large, reptilian beast called a slasher. These mighty creatures were sometimes captured by the most powerful and successful goblin leaders before being ridden into battle. Grogger wondered how Kackle had managed to get hold of so many teeth.

Kackle popped the teeth in a small, chipped cup that had been carved from the horn of an animal, and he began to rattle them around. Then he started coughing and snorting before spitting a large phlegmy ball of spit into the cup. Again he shook the cup. Finally, he used one of his sharp nails to rake a cut across his left palm and squeeze a few drops of blood into the cup. This time, he shook the cup more violently and whispered a few words under his breath. Grogger noticed the cave got even gloomier, and the smell of sulfur tickled his nostrils. He started to worry Kackle was messing with spells used by the warlocks of the Abyss, but before he could stop him, Kackle shouted some gibberish and threw the cup down, violently. The wiz grinned at Grogger and then slowly lifted the cup back up to reveal the split contents.

Kackle tapped each tooth with a claw before looking at Grogger. He shook his head and tapped each tooth again before casting a wary look at Grogger.

"This... this can't be right," mumbled Kackle. "I need to try again."

"What's it say?" asked Grogger. Despite his skepticism, he was interested in what the wiz had seen in the teeth.

"Nothing. Nothing. I must have said something wrong." He grabbed the small scrap of paper and started scanning the words.

With a frustrated growl, Grogger slapped the piece of paper away and pinched Kackle's ear.

"What do they say?"

Wriggling under Grogger's grip, Kackle shifted nervously. His eyes leapt from the teeth and back to Grogger before he replied.

"The teeth have spelt... 'king.'"

Grogger twisted Kackle's ear harshly.

"You're a lying snoz! Tell me what they really say!"

"King! King!" shrieked the wiz. "They say king!"

Grogger looked nervously toward the entrance of the cave in case the other goblins were listening.

"Do the spell again," he whispered.

Kackle gathered up the teeth and cup, then repeated the spell. This time, Grogger definitely caught the smell of sulfur and thought he heard a rippling laughter echo round the cave.

"Same again. They say 'king.'"

"Oh no! Please don't do another fireball spell. My clothes almost caught fire! Aaaaaaaaargh! Make sure you stay out there! It's not safe in here!" Grogger shouted toward the entrance. He heard Gritter say something about moving further away.

"What does it mean?" Grogger whispered to Kackle.

"There is only one way to be sure," he replied. "You must see the vision yourself."

"I am not letting you cast a spell on me! I don't want to be melted or teleported to the Abyss. You've got no idea what these spells say." He pointed quickly to all the various items dotted around.

"It's not a spell, it's a potion. I made it for Graf once. It's how he knew he would be a powerful lord."

"Didn't show him that water elemental though," snorted Grogger. "Is it safe?"

"Of course," said Kackle with a sickly smile.

"Quickly then, before the others wonder what we're doing." Then he turned back toward the entrance.

"AAAAAAAAR! My ears are burning," Grogger screeched as loudly as he could, then nodded quickly at the wiz. Kackle shot up and began rummaging around the room. He stopped for a moment to click his claws, and a flame ignited underneath the cauldron. Grogger couldn't help but be slightly impressed.

Kackle began tossing seemingly random items into the cauldron, and Grogger heard the bubbling intensify. Soon, it began to give off a sickly green glow, which illuminated the slick, wet walls with an unnatural light. Grogger watched with increasing interest as Kackle threw more ingredients into the filthy pot. As each hit the luminous brew, it would briefly erupt into a green flame before disappearing beneath the broiling concoction.

The stench was overwhelming to Grogger's keen nose, and he almost felt his legs buckling underneath him. Again he detected the slight hint of sulfur. He cursed himself for not asking where Kackle had found this grogging spell. He saw Kackle throw what looked like a mawbeast jaw into the cauldron and then begin to stir frantically with a large metal ladle. A loud pop caused Kackle to jump backward. Grogger was about to ask what was happening when a green flash erupted from the cauldron and briefly illuminated the cave. In the light, Grogger was sure he saw a demonic shadow behind Kackle, who had a feverish, mad grin plastered across his sweaty face.

"It is ready," cackled the wiz, bouncing from foot to foot as he laughed.

Grogger approached the brew with unease and gazed into the swirling green mixture. It bubbled and trembled as if alive. Grogger recoiled when a skull momentarily rose to the surface before being sucked back down beneath the murk with a slurping noise. He eyed Kackle with suspicion.

"Are you sure this will work?" Kackle appeared completely distracted and carried on laughing. Grogger leapt at the wiz and flashed his dagger toward the sorcerer's throat.

"Are you *sure* this will work?" he asked again, pressing the dagger a little harder. Kackle stopped giggling and eyed the blade nervously.

"I assure you, this will work, Grogger. Remember the signs."

Grogger carefully lowered the dagger, keeping his eyes locked on the wiz. He sniffed the air, and his mouth twisted into a grimace. He looked again at the bubbling, stinking brew.

"And I definitely have to drink it?"

"Oh, yes," chuckled Kackle and walked over to a nearby table, covered in mold, where an assortment of scorched parchments and filthy potion bottles sat. He rummaged through the piles before producing a scum-encrusted cup and returned to the cauldron. Carefully, he dipped the cup into the pot, and Grogger noticed he was cautious not to get the mix on his hands. As the container hit the surface, it was greeted by a peculiar hissing noise, and Grogger's keen ears caught the sound of laughter once more. Perhaps it was just Klunk and Gritter outside, he told himself, with little comfort.

After a moment, Kacle removed the now full cup and handed it to Grogger. A waxy, nervous smile spread across Kackle's face, and he nodded eagerly. Grogger almost wretched when he sniffed the brew.

"If this kills me, I will haunt you to the end of your days," he growled. And with that, he tipped the contents into his mouth. He quickly swallowed the thick, viscous liquid before he could taste too much, but even the aftertaste almost caused him to throw it all back up. Grogger screeched in pain as the scalding hot mix slowly moved down his throat. He grabbed the side of the cauldron for support and gritted his teeth. He didn't want Gritter and Klunk to come inside and investigate what was going on. His claws trembled as he gripped the metal pot tighter. He noticed that Kackle was watching him intently.

Grogger could feel the liquid begin to settle in his stomach, and he braced himself for the worst. He took in a deep breath and clutched the cauldron with both claws. He waited. And waited. And waited some more, expecting that at any moment he would begin to see visions or at least feel something. But nothing happened. He let go of the cauldron and marched over to Kackle, who was backing away into a pile of papers. Grogger grabbed the wiz by the scruff of his dirty collar.

"Nothing is happ-"

Suddenly a bright green light erupted from Grogger's mouth. His spine arched in agony as it felt like a thousand hot needles began pricking him at the same time. Kackle's robes fell from his grasp as his claws trembled uncontrollably. He cast a terrified look toward Kackle and tried to ask for help, but all that emerged was a strangled, gurgling sound. Grogger's knees buckled, and he fell to the grimy floor of the cave. His body was wracked by spasms while an acrid-smelling smoke drifted from his ears. In the brief moments of lucidity when his mind wasn't reeling from the pain, he realized that this was the way he would die. Kackle had tricked him into drinking some sort of poison. Gritter must have paid him. Or it was all a trick by Bung. He cursed them all and hoped the gobs would strike them down.

Then, just as quickly as the pain had started, it vanished. Grogger stopped twitching and lay still for a moment, staring at the scorch marks on the ceiling. He wasn't dead! But that wiz soon would be.

He tried to lift himself off the grime-covered floor, but before he could reach for his dagger to gut Kackle, painful visions flashed through his reeling brain.

A mighty goblin army... screams of animals... a forest in flames... the broiling depths of the Abyss... a door bursting open... a vast fleet of strange ships... dwarfs fighting dwarfs... himself stood triumphant atop a mountain of skulls, goblins knelt around him...

Grogger's breath came in rasping gasps as his body continued to twitch slightly. Kackle approached him cautiously.

"What did you see?" he asked.

"My legacy..." gasped Grogger before more visions tormented his mind.

Him surrounded by mechanical contraptions... a massive maw-beast... Bung's corpse... a singing dagger...a pair of silver gauntlets... a glittering city of bronze... more goblins... thousands of goblins... a sea of green, chanting his name... a crown... his crown!

When the visions stopped, he clutched Kackle's claw.

"You were right," he rasped.

"Tell me everything," replied Kackle, smiling.

In between slight spasms, Grogger repeated what he had seen to Kackle. The wiz nodded eagerly and made some scribbles in an old, leather-bound book. The pair spoke in conspiratorial tones and would occasionally stop to listen if the other goblins were re-entering the cave.

"How do I make it all come true?" asked Grogger, when he had finished explaining.

"Sounds like you need to deal with Bung first," replied Kackle.

"I'd never get close enough, and if I did, then Ug and Og would beat me to death."

"In the visions, you had an army, correct?"

"Yes," snapped Grogger, irritated at the question.

"Then perhaps you need an army to overthrow Bung?"

"Where the grog am I going to get an army from?"

"I know where to find someone who could help!" An excited tone entered Kackle's voice.

"Graf? There's no way he would help you. He would kill you."

"Not Graf. Magwa!"

"Magwa? Ha!" Grogger snorted, dismissively. "They told me about him when I was a gobling. There's no way he's still alive. He must be ancient by now."

Grogger paced around for a moment, thinking about the wiz's words. Goblins didn't have many heroes or legends - mostly because they tend not to live long enough to develop a legendary reputation - but Magwa was one of the few. Grogger had to admit, that he almost admired Magwa. In the tale he had been told, Magwa was a runitsh but ordinary goblin that had been bossed around like most others. The clan leader, whose name Grogger couldn't remember, seemed to delight in abusing the smaller goblin, constantly torturing him mentally and physically. Being told this as a small gobling, Grogger could sympathise with Magwa's plight, although he doubted he would have had the courage to leave the clan, like Magwa did.

Magwa roamed the plains, scavenging whatever food he could find and trying to hide from his would-be pursuers. In one cave, Magwa stumbled across a female mawbeast and her pups. The mother had been injured in a fight and was limping badly, which meant she wasn't able to attack Magwa, but he also realized she wouldn't be able to get the food required for her pups. This part of the story always seemed unrealistic to Grogger, because no goblin would ever choose to help, but Magwa started hunting to feed himself and the pups. Grogger assumed it must have been because Magwa worked out that having a loyal pack of mawbeasts at his side could prove useful After all, the plains are a dangerous place for a lone greenskin.

No matter the reason, Magwa kept on feeding the pups while the mother recovered and, over time, he developed a bond with the beasts. As they grew, he began to take them hunting with him and they would return to the cave to share the spoils. Grogger guessed it was the closest Magwa could get to being back in a clan, and the mawbeasts provided some welcome protection for the diminutive goblin. Magwa formed a friendship with one mawbeast in particular, who was the runt of the litter. The other creatures would snap and claw at their brother whenever they had the chance, and Grogger thought Magwa must have seen similarities with himself. So, whenever possible, Magwa made sure he gave the runt extra meat and broke up any fights when Jo'os, as Magwa called him, was clearly getting hurt. All this kind behavior made Grogger feel uncomfortable, but he liked this bit of the story, because Magwa's cunning plan was about to pay off!

Under Magwa's care, Jo'os grew stronger and stronger. The previously weak mawbeast developed thick, rippling muscles and massive jaws that could snap bones like twigs. The creature grew three times the size of its siblings, and they would cower whenever he growled or barked. The runt had become the alpha, and wild mawbeasts roaming the plains quickly began to join the pack. Any that attempted to attack or bite Magwa were quickly pounced upon by Jo'os, and the remaining beasts quickly realized that Magwa and Jo'os were the leaders of the pack. Perhaps, if Grogger were king, goblins would consider him to be the leader of the pack?

With the mighty Jo'os and a small warband of mawbeasts at his side, Magwa sensed an opportunity. He could finally get revenge on all those that had bullied him. He tore through the tribe's cave like a wildfire, and the mawbeasts made quick work of any that tried to stop them. Eventually they arrived at the heart of the clan. The leader begged for mercy, but Magwa's appetite for leniency had vanished long ago. With a whistle, he ordered Jo'os to devour his tormentor piece by piece. The other goblins were forced to watch, guarded by Magwa's horde of mawbeasts. Grogger chuckled to himself as he recalled this part of the tale. It was always his favorite bit. When he was little, he would make chomping noises while listening to the story.

Goblins are quick to adapt to the shifting landscape of power within a clan, and Magwa was quickly promoted to leader. After that, he roamed the land with a mighty pack of mawbeasts and hundreds of goblins under his command. But as far as Grogger knew, no one had seen Magwa for many, many moons. The thought of Kackle knowing him seemed preposterous, it not an outright lie.

"They're both still alive," started Kackle. "I've heard it's something to do with a prod he stole from an elf drakon herder. His wounds heal quicker when he has it, and it works on Jo'os too."

"Forget Magwa, tell me more about that prod," replied Grogger, with an interested gleam in his eye.

"I wouldn't recommend stealing anything from Magwa. Jo'os tends to be very protective from the stories I've been told."

"But, if he dies fighting or something, then perhaps I can get the prod, right?" asked Grogger. He was determined to get his claws on that magical artifact.

"Sure", answered Kackle, cautiously, "but the most important thing is that Magwa still has his mawbeasts. They would be the perfect start to any army... *boss.*"

Grogger's head flashed up when Kackle called him boss. It had such a wonderful tone to it. A tone that fitted someone of Grogger's reputation. Up until now, he had never thought about being a biggit, let alone a king... but it made sense. He wasn't like the others. He was cleverer, more tactical, more cunning, even sneakier, and he didn't lose his temper needlessly like all the other lesser goblins.

"What do you want?" he snapped, when Klunk coughed from outside the cave, disturbing his grand thoughts.

"Are you alive? Is it safe to come back in?" Cautiously, Klunk edged into the cave. Grogger noticed Gritter was giving him the occasional push.

"Yes, we're alive and it's safe... *for now.*"

Gritter shoved past Klunk and sat down on a rock, smirking.

"So can he do magic then?" asked Gritter.

"Oh, yes," replied Grogger, and his mouth twisted in a devious smile. "He can *definitely* do magic."

CHAPTER TEN

"They were definitely here," said Hr'zak, sniffing the air inside the damp, gloomy cave. He gave an involuntary shiver as a breeze swirled round the lichen-covered walls and wrapped his cloak closer around his shoulders. Thunder boomed outside the cave, and occasional flashes of lightning lit up the cave with an eerie blue light. "Whole place stinks of goblins."

The salamanders had been on the trail of the greenskins for hours. Despite taking short rests and only stopping when absolutely required, they could never catch up with the mounted goblins. There was a growing sense of frustration among Furna's crew, brought on by the fatigue of their pursuit and the longing to return home. As the chase went on, that desire became more desperate, and the salamanders were becoming hot-headed and ill-tempered.

"What in Kthorlaq's name is this?" asked Shalesh. He was staring in disgust at the contents of the cauldron. The cook picked up a stick from the cave floor and dipped it into the gloop. At first nothing happened, until it suddenly erupted in a green flame. The fire crept up the stick unnaturally until Shalesh dropped it in shock. The stick sat on the surface for a moment, still flaming, and then disappeared into the liquid with a slurping sound.

"This was the wizard's home," said a smaller salamander called Igne, standing in the corner of the cave. She was rifling through scrolls and papers scattered across the floor. Back when they were on the ship, Igne had told Furna that she had trained as a mage priest back in the Three Kings, but learning the ways of magic couldn't compete with the swashbuckling stories she heard whispered among the acolytes in the temples. Eventually she ran away to become a sailor, but often her training came in useful during the exploits of Furna and her crew. She held up some papers to show the others.

"They are incantations written in elvish and dwarfish. Think I even saw a few books that had the holy seal of Basilea. The goblin was just collecting spells. I doubt it could even read some of this stuff." Igne was about to look for more spells when she noticed Rorsha about to pick up a massive, horned skull.

"Don't touch that!" she shouted, and a booming peal of thunder shook the cave. Rorsha froze with his claw about to clutch the skull. Igne moved to stand beside Rorsha and produced a dagger from her belt. Carefully, she pointed at markings on the skull.

"That's a molloch's skull," she explained. Mollochs were one of the most terrifying demons spit forth by the despicable Abyss. Huge, lumbering beasts larger than a troll, their eyes burned with a malevolent fire; they only cared about one thing - sending more unfortunate souls to spend an eternity of torment in the depths of the Abyss.

"The markings carved on the skull are written in Abyssal script. It is most likely cursed."

Igne muttered a prayer under her breath and smashed the skull with the butt of her dagger. A ghostly roar echoed around the cave, followed by another thunderous boom. The former mage priest shuddered slightly.

"Be careful what you touch," she said to Rorsha, coldly. The first mate nervously looked around before crossing his arms tightly across his chest.

"We'll stay here a while," said Furna.

"Have you gone mad?" retorted Rosha with a look of disgust. "This is no place to rest."

"Show some respect!" shouted Furna. Her voice bounced off the walls. She regretted snapping at Rorsha and wasn't sure if it was this ill-setting or the cold that was starting to give her the chills. She tried to calm her ragged nerves. "Would you rather we all spent more time in *that*? Our blood is already chilled."

Furna pointed toward the hammering rain outside and, as if on cue, a crash of thunder filled the cave.

"Of course, Captain," huffed Rorsha.

"Perhaps you can learn some more manners while taking the first watch?"

Rorsha looked like he was about to protest but decided against it and stomped off toward the entrance. Furna spotted him taking a quick swig from his flask. She hoped it wasn't more dragon's scale brew. That damned drink had already caused enough problems.

"Right," said Furna with a clap of her claws, "let's get that stinking cauldron outside and light the fire. Get some warmth in here!"

Two of the crew grabbed the cauldron roughly, and a drop of green gloop splashed on the floor. It disappeared with a hissing noise, leaving behind an acrid smell.

"Be careful with that," whispered Igne. The salamanders nodded and carefully disposed of the cauldron without another spillage. Furna walked over to Igne, who was busy lighting the fire. The wood roared into unnaturally large flames. The captain wasn't sure if it was something Igne had done or the remnants of the goblin's magic.

"Anything in here that might say where they've gone? The storm will make it hard even for Hr'zak to find the trail again."

"I'll look, Captain, but it's not easy to find clues amongst all this." Igne spread her claws to indicate what seemingly appeared to be rubbish spread around the cave. "Rather than trying to learn the art of spellcasting, a goblin wizard just collects whatever they can find and hopes for the best. It can often be quite dangerous." Igne pointed to the scorch marks on the ceilings and walls.

Furna clapped her crewmate on the shoulder and gave her a toothy smile.

"I'm sure you'll do your best."

"I always do, Captain."

With the warmth of the fire spreading through the cave, Furna was starting to feel like her old self again. The cold not only slowed her movements, it could also dull her thoughts too. After spending so long in the freezing rain of the storm, Furna was worried she could currently be out-smarted by an orc. She looked around the cave at her crew and could see they were also struggling after the long trek. A night in the cave - even if it was grim - would do them good. They could attack the pursuit tomorrow, after a decent night's rest. Her gaze paused on Berusk. It looked as though he was shivering, and that was not a good sign for a salamander. She sat on a rock beside him.

"Are you alright, Berusk?"

"Never better, Captain." He tried to smile, but Furna could hear his sharp teeth chattering. She reached into a pouch on her belt and produced a small flask.

"Here, take a swig. It'll warm you." Furna tried to hand him the dragon's scale brew, but Berusk weakly pushed it away.

"I don't need that. Just give me a moment by the fire and I'll be fighting fit."

Furna had to admire Berusk's pride, but one day it would be the death of him. A salamander of his age couldn't risk having their blood cool too much, because even the volcanic vents of the Three Kings may never warm it again. She pressed the flask into his claws.

"That's an order, Berusk," she said, kindly.

Berusk nodded in response and took a long swig of the brew. The effect was immediate. His teeth stopped chattering and his eyes glowed with renewed energy. He went for another pull on the flask, but Furna quickly snatched it away. Berusk hissed and snapped his teeth angrily before shaking his head as though waking from a slumber.

"Sorry, Captain," he said, quietly. Furna patted him on the leg.

"We'll get home soon, I promise. The goblins can't have got far in this weather. Igne's a clever one, she'll find something."

Berusk gave an embarrassed cough.

"If I start to slow you down, you must leave me," he said quietly. "As much as I want to see the Three Kings again, I don't want your safety to be at my expense. Just promise you'll take my bones back to drop in the volcano."

Furna shook her head.

"We've already lost too many on this voyage, and I don't want to lose any more. You're many seasons older than me, Berusk, and I'm sure you've got plenty of seasons left. We *will* make it home in time."

"Found something!" shouted a jubilant Igne, lashing her tail from side to side with excitement. Her scales seemed to glow even brighter when she was happy.

"Told you," said Furna to Berusk with a smile. "No more of this talk about not getting home. You're depressing enough already."

The old salamander gave a short snort of laughter, and a wisp of thick smoke crept from his nostrils.

"You hatchlings bring out the worst in me," he huffed, quiet for a moment, but a smile crept onto his craggy face. "Thank you, Captain. It's been an honor to be part of your crew."

Furna nodded and headed over to Igne.

"Tell me it's good news," she said.

"It's a map, or at least I think it was a map. Looks like old dwarf etchings showing a nearby fortress in the hills."

She handed the grubby parchment to Furna. Without Igne's teachings, she couldn't understand the markings around the side, but she recognized the practical runes of dwarf script. It appeared to show the surroundings, including the cave they were in and the forest they had traveled through to get here. She noted with a sharp snort that some of the trees had evil glares. Perhaps the dwarfs had fallen foul of them too?

Not too far from the cave, the dwarfs had clearly marked a hold or garrison. And she immediately spotted what had caused Igne's excitement. Scrawled next to the garrison in almost illegible common script was a single word. Furna looked at it a few times in confusion, before asking: "What's a 'magwa?'"

* * * * *

Not too far from the cave, Grogger was looking suspiciously at the seemingly abandoned dwarf fort. The ancient structure had been carved into the hillside itself, making it seem almost as though it was growing from the rocky hill. A large entrance, big enough for a regiment of dwarven soldirers to easily pass through, was the most striking feature of the fort. It was carved into the shape of a huge dwarf's head, and its mouth would have once held a massive gate. Grogger shivered at the thought of having to walk into a giant dwarf's mouth. He considered sending Gritter in first... just to be safe.

The fort must have once been a grand and imposing sight, but it had long fallen into disrepair, and pieces of rubble littered the surroundings. One eye on the mighty head had collapsed, making it look as though the dwarf was winking at any would-be visitors. Great clumps of ivy grew around the top of the dwarf's head, like a bizarre green wig, and the rubble strewn across the bottom gave the dwarf jagged, unnatural teeth. The once glorious fort was a shadow of its former self, and Grogger wondered how long it must have been abandoned.

A storm rumbled in the distance, and Grogger didn't fancy staying out here on the open plains. On the other hand, he didn't like the idea of going into the fort either.

Grogger had managed to convince Klunk, Gritter, and, most importantly, Ug that this little detour was required to try and recruit Magwa into Bung's army. At first, they'd been skeptical about the idea of Magwa being alive, let alone joining Bung. But, somehow, Grogger and Kackle had persuaded them it was worth a shot. Grogger could still feel Ug's beady eyes watching him at all times. If only there was some way to get rid of the troll, he thought, but that was a problem for another time; now he just needed to find Magwa.

"You're sure that's where he is?" Grogger asked Kackle.

"Well, this is where I heard he was."

Gritter was sniffing the air with his long, green nose. His nostrils flared with each sharp inhale.

"Definitely getting a whiff of mawbeasts," he said.

Grogger had noticed that their mounts had been unusually quiet as they got closer to the fortress. Even a loud boom of thunder behind them didn't seem to spook the beasts. They just kept their eyes fixed on the entrance and occasionally gave a low growl. A flash of lightning suddenly lit up the area with an eerie blue glow, and Grogger was sure he saw someone watching them from the eye of the ancient dwarf.

"Lead the way then, Kackle," said Grogger, gesturing forward with an open claw. Kackle grimaced slightly but shuffled toward the fort. As they got closer, Grogger noticed the crumbling stones of the fortress had goblin writing scratched across them. Over and over again, '*MAGWA STILL LIVES*' was crudely etched into gray rock. Some letters were as tall as a goblin, while others were almost illegible.

"Guess this is the right place," whispered Klunk with a nervous tone in his voice. Another crack of thunder made all the goblins jump. Even Ug seemed on edge. Wind blew through the openings of the old fort, whistling through the mouth and eyes of the massive dwarf. It almost seemed like the whole place was groaning. A long, pitiful moan that spoke of years of abandonment and neglect.

Grogger debated turning back. Perhaps this whole thing was stupid? After all, he was basing all this on the magic of a potentially mad wiz. He'd never trusted magic before... but something about those visions had seemed so real. Occasionally, they would still flash across his mind, causing his body to spasm slightly. And the one that kept coming back so clearly was him wearing that glittering crown surrounded by goblins as far as he could see.

He was also intrigued by Kackle's tale about Magwa's magical prod. As preposterous as the story sounded, he certainly liked the idea of a magical artifact that healed his wounds and seemingly gave him a longer life. Since Kackle had brought up the legendary goblin's name, Grogger had been trying to work out how old he must be. When goblins talked about Magwa, it was like a distant memory; a story passed down by their ancestors. Everyone had heard the story of Magwa and Jo'os. Magwa must be decades, perhaps even centuries, old. Grogger's eyes lit up at the thought of that prod, and it gave him the courage to press into the fort. He could be king forever!

Grogger dismounted from his mawbeast and clambered over the teeth-like rocks that had fallen into the entrance. The moaning wind seemed to grow louder as he neared the top, and Grogger suppressed a shudder. He tried to tell himself it was caused by the cold and not fear. As he was about to descend into the dark of the dwarf's gaping mouth, he turned back to make sure the other goblins were following him. He was disappointed, although not surprised, to see they were all just watching him. When he caught their gaze, they all looked around them as though they hadn't noticed he was glowering at them.

Grogging cowards, he thought, and he scrambled into the pitch-black fort. Another rumble of thunder bid him farewell.

He tumbled down the rocks and into a large, cavernous hall. Thankfully, his sharp eyes could see in the murky dark, and he stopped for a moment to gather himself. At one point, the hall must have been as grand as the carved entrance. It towered above him, and on the ceiling, Grogger could make out huge chandeliers that had once held thousands of candles. Now they just swayed in the wind that crept through the open doorway and made an ominous creaking sound when they moved. Grogger could also make out impressive carvings that criss-crossed the roof. Most showed dwarfs heading to battle or fighting their enemies. Each of the dwarfs wore intricate armor and carried rune-etched hammers and war axes. Grogger grimaced when he saw some carvings that showed these impressively armored dwarfs slaughtering goblins. Each of the greenskins had been given a dumb expression - even the decapitated heads bore the same, foolish grins. Grogger turned away in disgust. He hated the arrogant beardies.

The ceiling was held in place by rows and rows of mighty pillars that spiraled up into the gloomy heights. A few were damaged and surrounded by rubble, and Grogger hoped there were still enough to hold up the hillside above them. Even in the dark, Grogger could see that many of the pillars had 'MAGWA STILL LIVES' written on them in an erratic scrawl. Doors led off from the great hall, and he assumed these would lead to barracks, an armory, and other rooms the dwarfs needed when required to prepare for war. Some of the doors were smashed, leaving a gaping black void that even Grogger's keen eyes couldn't pierce. He would wait for Ug before exploring too far.

However, perhaps the most striking thing inside the hall was the stench. The whole place had a musty, animalistic smell that even Grogger recognized as that of a mawbeast. He looked around the floor and saw it was littered with cracked bones and dusty piles of dung. It was smeared over tattered rugs that had been ripped or chewed. But none of the crap looked fresh. It was all dried up, and as Grogger walked, it crumbled under his boots. It didn't look like any mawbeasts, or any goblin for that matter, had been here for a while; Grogger cursed Kackle for the wrong informa-tion.

He was about to leave and reprimand the wiz when a low growl echoed through the hall. At first, Grogger thought it was the rumble of thun-der outside, but it continued to grow in volume. He desperately scanned around the room and began backing toward the fallen rocks at the en-trance. He shouldn't have come in alone. He cursed Kackle again. Then, as quickly as it had begun, the growling stopped.

"Who's that?" asked a voice. Although it spoke in goblin, the voice sounded different somehow. It was deeper than a typical goblin voice and sounded slower and more tired too; unlike the normally skittish chatter of a greenskin. Grogger scanned the hall, and toward the rear of the grand room, he thought he spotted a pair of red eyes, accompanied by much bigger yellow eyes nearby.

"My name is Grogger," he replied, nervously. His reedy voice echoed around the walls, and even to him, it sounded scared. Grogger gave a cough before trying to sound more confident. "I'm looking for Magwa."

He was greeted by a low, slow laugh, which was definitely coming from the direction of the red eyes. The grim laugh traveled around the hall and sent a chill down Grogger's spine.

"Come closer," said the voice. "Let me see who wants to find the legendary Magwa."

Despite his instincts, Grogger crept slowly toward the voice, while keeping one claw on the handle of his dagger. As he neared the mysteri-ous voice, he picked out the shape of a grand throne at the rear of the hall. Sitting on the throne was a small goblin, and Grogger caught his breath when next to it he saw the outline of the biggest mawbeast he had ever seen. Outside, there was a crash of thunder, and a flash of lightning briefly lit the room.

Grogger recoiled at the fleeting sight of the monster and guessed it must be the infamous Jo'os. It was at least three times the size of a normal mawbeast. A shaggy black mane of thick fur spilled across powerful mus-cles, and scars were etched across its body. But what horrified Grogger the most was the gaping mouth, full of razor sharp teeth. Although some were cracked and damaged, he was under no illusion that the beast could easily rip him apart in an instant. Grogger desperately wanted to turn back, to run to safety outside the fort and make sure Ug was here to protect him. Then again, he wasn't sure Ug could even tackle this horror.

Another flash of lightning lit the hall, and this time, Grogger took the opportunity to inspect the goblin lounging in the large, ornate throne. He was smaller than Grogger and wearing a battered, rusty helmet with a tatty blue crest adorning the top. His hands were covered by large, leather gloves - the type used by mawbeast handlers to tame their wild beasts. But what surprised Grogger were the wrinkles etched across his face. Grogger had seen these lines on the old humans he had fought in the past, but never on the face of a goblin. His skin also appeared to be faded, like paper that had spent too much time in the sun. Rather than the vibrant green of Grogger, it was a more pale hue.

"I'll ask again... who wants to find the legendary Magwa?" The aging goblin spat the 'legendary' like an insult. Grogger edged closer before he spoke but quickly stopped when Jo'os began growling. "No closer until I know who you are."

"My name is Grogger Split-tooth, from Bung's Red Claw Tribe." Against his better judgment, he bowed slightly to Magwa and was greeted by a mirthless laugh.

"Look at this, Jo'os, he treats me like a lord." Magwa chuckled and ran his gloves through Jo'os' thick mane. Grogger was surprised to hear the gargantuan beast purr like a mawpup.

"Of course, a goblin so great-"

Magwa drew his glove away sharply and snapped his head toward Grogger.

"Great? Great! What's so *great* about being Magwa? What's so *great* about watching those around you die of old age? What's so *great* about seeing countless litters of pups come and go? What's so *great* about barely remembering how you became the legendary Magwa in the first place?"

Magwa's voice held a bitterness that Grogger hadn't heard in a goblin before. He sounded old and tired. This conversation definitely wasn't going the way he planned, and he constantly eyed Jo'os, expecting the animal to spring on him at any moment. Slowly, Magwa raised himself out of the throne, and Grogger's eyes grew wide when he saw Magwa reach for his prod and use it like a walking stick. He held tightly onto the prod as he approached Grogger, while Jo'os padded behind him. After slowly staggering down from his throne, Magwa reached Grogger and glowered intently at him.

"Do you know how old Magwa is, Grogger Split-tooth?"

Grogger paused for a moment while he tried to think of the best answer.

"There's no need to try and flatter. Magwa can almost see the thoughts running through your tiny head." Magwa tapped Grogger sharply on the head with his prod. A sharp electrical current passed through Grogger, and he gave a small, involuntary jolt. Magwa leaned in closer to Grogger and his reeking, stale breath washed over him like a wave of rotten fish.

"The honest answer is, Magwa doesn't know either. Sometimes Magwa sits here for hours, hidden in the dark, and tries to work it out, but Magwa only has so many claws."

Magwa held up his gloves and giggled. Grogger saw they were covered in teeth marks and small rips. Magwa gave another unhinged laugh and shuffled back to his throne. Jo'os walked up to Grogger and started sniffing him. Grogger had heard the best thing to do with a wild mawbeast was to not show fear and remain completely still. If you ran, the animal would think you were prey. He clenched every muscle in his body and closed his eyes while Jo'os snuffled around him.

Suddenly, Grogger's body began twitching with painful spasms as he suffered another vision. This time, he saw himself holding Magwa's prod, and Jo'os stood next to him. Magwa was nowhere in sight. He fell to the floor in agony and was vaguely aware of Jo'os growling at him and nudging him with his muzzle. He writhed around on the dirty, filth-encrusted floor for a moment, expecting that at any moment Jo'os would take a bite. Instead, Magwa gave a sharp whistle, and Jo'os plodded back to his resting place beside the throne. When Grogger eventually stopped shaking, he realized Magwa was clapping and laughing.

"Magwa may be old, but Magwa hasn't seen anything quite like that. Are you sick Grogger Split-tooth? Magwa is not sure what it feels like anymore to be sick. Perhaps you could enlighten Magwa?"

Grogger grunted and cautiously stood back up. He tried to brush the crusty mawbeast dung off his clothes but quickly gave up.

"I'm not sick. I suffer from... *visions*," answered Grogger. He knew how ridiculous that must sound. However, Magwa stopped laughing and stared at his visitor.

"And what do the visions tell you, Split-tooth? Did they tell you to seek the legendary Magwa? Is that why you have disturbed us?"

"They tell me that I will be king. The greatest goblin king ever."

This time, Magwa did laugh. A long, shrieking wail that soared around the hall like a banshee.

"We have a king with us, Jo'os. A king! If only we had known, we could have made this grand hall more fitting for royalty." Magwa waved his prod around, and Grogger noticed small sparks flying off it as it moved. What the grog was that thing? Jo'os just yawned and appeared to go to sleep.

"Do you know how many goblins Magwa has met that thought they would be king?" asked Magwa with a sneer. "Every ambitious biggit thinks they've got what it takes to become a king. And you know what happens to them all? *Dead!*" Magwa screamed the last word.

"Magwa has outlasted them all! Magwa has watched as they were decapitated, stabbed in the back, crushed by catapults, blasted apart by cannons, torn limb from limb by dragons... Magwa thinks you get the idea. The life of a king is a short and painful one. And here you stand, in our home, and tell Magwa *you're* going to be king. If anyone should be king, it should be Magwa!"

Grogger eyed Magwa warily. He had previously been terrified of Jo'os, but perhaps the old goblin was more dangerous than the mawbeast. His mood swings changed faster than the wind. For a moment, Grogger wondered where the other mawbeasts were. All the legends told of Magwa's great horde of mawbeasts that followed him and Jo'os around, but there were no signs of any other life besides the two before him. Bracing himself for the worst, Grogger tried a different approach with Magwa.

"A king needs subjects, and you appear to be lacking any followers, *great* Magwa." This time it was Grogger's turn to spit the word 'great'. "Just you and your pet alone in this tomb."

"Pet? He's my friend. My only friend! How the grog dare you, you little snoz," screeched Magwa, waving his prod around again. The air in the fort became thicker, like just before a storm. Grogger prepared for the worst. At least, he thought, if Jo'os swallowed him, he'd go down whole and probably wouldn't feel much pain. He closed his eyes and waited. After a few moments, he noticed the air pressure had returned to normal and a different noise had replaced Magwa's mad wails. Grogger realized with revulsion that Magwa was *crying*. Huge, choking sobs that shook his frail body. Occasionally he would blow his nose loudly on an old piece of tapestry across the back of the throne.

"You're right. You're right!" wailed Magwa. "No one follows Magwa anymore. No one *cares* about Magwa anymore. Only Jo'os." The old goblin reached out tenderly and patted the furry monster.

"You're the first visitor Magwa has had in many, many moons. The first to come looking for Magwa too. Most come for shelter, and Jo'os gets to have a little snack." Magwa slumped back into the throne with his short legs drooped over one of the ornate arms and his head resting on the other.

"How old are you, Grogger Split-tooth?" asked the old goblin, almost kindly.

Grogger shrugged, surprised by the sudden change in tone. Age was an unusual concept to a goblin. Most were just happy to make it to the next moon. It didn't matter how many there were, as long as they saw another.

"What a luxury, not to care," said Magwa, the words barely above a whisper. Magwa sat up on the throne again and pointed to some of the writing scratched onto a pillar. "Every moon, Magwa writes a new one. And even in a grand hall like this, Magwa has almost run out of space." Magwa's voice rose to a crescendo and echoed eerily around the abandoned hold.

"A goblin shouldn't have to live this long," he muttered. "Magwa knows our kind just wants to see another moon. But when you've seen as many moons as Magwa has, you grow tired. Each moon is a curse. A reminder of all the others you've seen rise and fall. So Magwa sits in here, in the dark, hoping to never see its silver light again. But it taunts Magwa, peeping through the cracks. Seeping through the smallest gaps. Clawing at Magwa's eyes, even when they are forced shut. And so Magwa writes again, 'Magwa *still* lives.'"

Grogger blinked, now convinced the old gob had gone mad, and he wondered why Kackle hadn't said anything about the fact Magwa was clearly unhinged. Grogger sensed an opportunity.

"Why not end it?" Grogger braced himself for another outburst but, instead, Magwa responded with a hollow laugh.

"Oh, don't think Magwa hasn't thought about it, but then what would happen to Jo'os? He's nothing without me."

Grogger looked at the heavyset, muscular mawbeast and wasn't convinced. Jo'os could probably take on a slasher and come out on top. Instead, Grogger guessed that even at Magwa's age, a goblins' natural desire for self-preservation was hard to shake off.

"What happened to all the other mawbeasts and goblins?" asked Grogger. He was genuinely curious about how the senile old snoz had ended up like this.

"Dead, of course, and when you've seen so many pups die, it becomes too much to watch the light fade time and time again. So, when the last one joined the Great Pack, Magwa decided it would just be Magwa and Jo'os. As for Magwa's kin, who cares? They were never part of the pack."

Magwa absentmindedly grabbed an old bone from the side of the throne and began gnawing at some stale meat. He picked a bit off and threw it to Jo'os. The great beast snapped it up while in midair and quickly gulped it down. As the pair were distracted, Grogger eyed the old 'prod' that Magwa had used all these years. Up close, he could see the intricate elvish lettering that swirled around the delicately carved staff. Occasionally, the writing was interrupted by small displays of leaves and flowers. The staff was finished off with two glittering silver prongs. Now and again, an arc of lightning would pass between the points. Even to Grogger, it was clear it was no simple drakon prod. He decided to try and find out more, if only to make sure he knew how to use it.

"What about the prod? How long have you had that?"

"Why do you ask?" replied a suspicious Magwa. He subconsciously grabbed the prod and held it tight across his chest. Jo'os let out a low growl.

"Just saying it doesn't look like a normal mawbeast prod, that's all."

"It's none of your business what it is," snapped Magwa. "It's Magwa's! That's all you need to know."

Grogger held up his claws to try and calm the situation. Speaking to Magwa was like trying to stay balanced on a chariot being pulled by particularly unruly mawbeasts, and almost as dangerous. Grogger was about to push his luck when Kackle's voice came drifting down the fort.

"Boss, the sun's coming up, and we'd rather be in there than out here when it does."

It was only then Grogger noticed the first thin rays of daylight creeping in through the gaping entrance.

"Another moon passes," said Magwa's voice, wearily. "Tell your friends they can sleep here until the sun falls, and then Magwa wants you all gone. Leave Magwa and Jo'os alone."

With that, he slowly eased himself up and stalked out through a door behind the throne. Jo'os padded silently alongside him.

Kackle and the others approached.

"All going to plan?" whispered Kackle.

"Not quite. Right. We'll stay here for the day and then move on when the moon's back up. I don't think Magwa will be joining us."

Grogger had one more desperate plan. He didn't care about the grogging old goblin. He just needed that prod. So, he'd wait for the senile git and his pet to go to sleep, and he'd swipe the staff from under their noses.

"Let's get some sleep," said Grogger, barely managing to suppress his cunning grin.

CHAPTER ELEVEN

"Are you sure this is the place?" Furna asked Igne. She held up a claw to bring the crew to a halt behind some small boulders. Overheard, the sun beat down, and Furna relished the opportunity to bask in its rays. She closed her eyes for a moment and felt the heat wash over her scales.

After spending some time resting in the wiz's cave, Furna thought her crew looked healthier and more prepared for the task ahead. The orange glow had returned to their eyes and smoke billowed from their open mouths when they laughed. It was almost possible to forget that calling to return home. But occasionally, she could see their eyes drift to a faraway place as they remembered the red-hot volcanoes of the Three Kings. They would fall silent for a moment before snapping out of the daze and joining back in with the laughter.

The only one that still worried her was Berusk. Even for him he was unusually sullen. Throughout the journey to the cave, he had kept to the back of the crew and didn't speak to anyone. He would occasionally just mutter to himself and slash his tail in frustration at some unknowable slight. Furna just hoped the cold hadn't taken hold in his blood, then even dragon's scale brew wouldn't be able to keep him going.

Hr'zak looked again at the scruffy map Igne had found before passing it to Furna.

"I'm confident this is the place, Captain, but I've still got no idea what a magwa is."

"In that case, let's make sure that this time we're on our guard," said Furna and eyed her crew, carefully.

Furna looked over at the old dwarf fort and was sad to see how it had fallen into disrepair. She had met plenty of her dwarfs on her travels and, although they were often more sullen than Berusk, she had an admiration for their amazing talents with building and engineering. The great stone dwarf head must have once been a sight to behold.

"There's something outside the fort," hissed Igne.

The salamanders instinctively ducked down and pressed themselves closer against the boulders. Furna scrabbled in her belt for her telescope and quickly pressed it against her right eye. Scanning over the entrance, she couldn't see a thing. Suddenly a flash of movement caught her eye. She moved the telescope to try and catch the object again, but it was too fast. Eventually it stopped, and she caught her breath when she saw a mawbeast gulping down a stray rabbit. Another mawbeast jumped into view and began pulling at the small carcass. The two beasts began fighting, leaving a third mawbeast to sneak up and finish off the meal.

"This is definitely the place," said Furna with a toothy grin. Her tail slapped the mud in anticipation. Furna looked up at the sun, shielding her bright eyes. It had passed its highest point and was now starting to drift downward. They had a few hours before nightfall, and she preferred to tackle the goblins in daylight, while they were likely to be sleeping.

"We"ve got to be quick," Furna told the gathered crew. "It's still light, so the goblins are probably going to be asleep. If we get in there now, we can catch the greenskins napping. I'll take a small crew, the rest stay out here. If we don't come out, then come in all guns blazing."

Furna quickly looked over her crew. A few goblins wouldn't pose much of a problem. The last time with Berusk and the tree branch had been a fluke, so there was no need to go into the fort mob-handed. Plus, with a smaller party, they'd make less noise and could hopefully slit their little green throats before they even knew they were there.

"Hr'zak, Berusk, and Shalesh, you're with me. Rorsha, you keep an eye on the rest out here."

"Yes, Captain," came a chorus of voices.

"Igne, anything in your magic training to help with those maw-beasts?"

Igne gave a confident nod and began chanting. The words rose up and down, reminding Furna of the sound waves made when they crashed against the shore. While chanting, Igne quickly pressed her claws together in different patterns, and soon, the air around her began to shimmer. The wisps of smoke around her mouth moved in unnatural ways, and her eyes burned with the fires of the Three Kings. Finally, with a loud shout, she thrust her claws toward the mawbeasts. Furna quickly grabbed her telescope and watched the animals. She expected to see them burst into flames or get struck by lightning. Instead, nothing appeared to happen.

"Igne, are you sure-"

"Just wait, Captain."

Furna carried on watching the beasts running around outside the fort entrance. Suddenly, they stopped and fell to the ground in unison.

"Are they dead?"

"Not dead, just sleeping," answered Igne, panting slightly. It appeared that casting the spell had exhausted her.

"Are you okay?" asked Furna.

"Just a little out of practice, so I don't know how long it will last either. You better be quick."

"With me!" shouted Furna and ran toward the fort, accompanied by her chosen party. They covered the ground between the boulders and the entrance in no time. Pressing a claw toward her scaly lips, she approached the three mawbeasts. She recoiled at the stench of the stinking animals. Their thick manes were knotted with blood and gore. Furna could see ticks and fleas scurrying through the matted mess as though it were a forest. They were breathing heavily through those massive jaws, and Furna shuddered at the sight of the razor sharp teeth. Those mighty, powerful jaws would easily be able to crunch through their thick, scaly skin. She gave one a small kick. It snuffled slightly but didn't wake. The sight of them repulsed her, and she felt a boiling rage build inside her gut. The goblins had ruined her plan to get home. They should have been on their way to Valentica now to sell the damn wiz and get the money for the ship. Instead, she was stuck in the middle of nowhere, and every day spent away from the Three Kings was another day that risked the lives of her crew; she hated putting them in danger. She hated spending another day on land. She hated the damn greenskins.

"Slit their throats," she hissed.

"What?" asked Shalesh. "They're asleep."

"I don't want them waking up while we're inside," replied Furna, tightly. "Slit their throats. That's an order."

"Yes... Captain," came the muted response.

Furna turned her attention toward the dark, gaping mouth of the fort. Behind her, she heard blades being drawn, followed by a sound like meat being sliced by a butcher and thuds as the corpses hit the dirt. Furna strained to listen for any sort of noises inside the fort. She leaned her head and paused for a moment. She caught a loud, rhythmic growling that reverberated out the dark. It was a monstrous noise that almost sounded like the heavy growls of a dragon. What in Kthorlaq's name was in there? Was that the 'magwa'? What sort of hideous beast could make such an awful noise?

* * * * *

Grogger tried shoving his claws over his ears, but it was no good. Ug's snoring was as loud as the mining drill on a mincer. The noise was so deafening, Grogger was surprised it didn't shake the whole fort to pieces. He looked over at Gritter, Kackle, and Klunk and was amazed to see them fast asleep on the remains of what must have once been a grand dining table. They were huddled together, clearly missing the press of bodies in the communal sleeping space of the tribe. They twitched slightly as they slept. When one of them nudged the other, they would receive a small, instinctive kick or shove. Even sleeping, the goblins bickered.

Still, Ug's snoring rolled through the fort like the engine of a dwarf's steel behemoth. A massive, mechanical beast that seemed positively quiet compared to Ug. Grogger picked up a small rock and lobbed it at the troll. The lumbering monster stopped for a moment, and Grogger breathed a sigh of relief. He settled down on Magwa's throne again and tried to go to sleep. Grogger closed his eyes for a moment and was almost immediately disturbed by Ug's infernal snoring. If anything, it had got louder. Grogger ripped away the moth-eaten dwarf tapestry he was using to cover himself and realized it was pointless to try and sleep.

Then again, while the others were sleeping, this could be the opportunity Grogger had been waiting for to swipe Magwa's magic prod. Although he had come to convince Magwa to join his army - well, once he had an army - the old gob was clearly one mawbeast short of a pack, and he doubted he would be much use as an ally. That prod would prove far more useful!

Grogger was hatching his plan to kill Magwa in his sleep when a flash of movement caught his eye near the entrance. He squinted slightly against the fading sunshine leaking through the opening as he tried to look more closely. There! There it was again. Something was peeping over the broken 'teeth' of the dwarf's mouth and looking inside. Grogger was just about to wake Gritter up and complain that he hadn't secured the maw-beasts properly when one of the shapes leapt gracefully over the rocks and into the fort. It was quickly followed by three more large shapes, which caused Grogger to catch his breath in alarm. It was the salamanders!

"Scalies! Scalies!" he screeched and dived off the throne.

Grogger ran over to Ug and kicked him in the head to wake him up. The thick-headed troll awoke with a start. His eyes took a moment to focus, but they quickly locked on Grogger and he gave a growl. Grogger leapt aside from a clumsy swipe of Ug's massive, boulder-like hand.

"Not me, you grogging snoz! The scalies are here. They want Kackle back."

Ug processed the information for a moment before springing up and grabbing his massive club. He issued a loud roar that caused small particles of dust to fall from the aging ceiling. Now Grogger felt a little more confident. He had counted four shapes moving over the rocks, and he was sure Ug could deal with at least two of those. That just left the other two.

Kackle, Gritter, and Klunk ran over to join Grogger and Ug.

"What's the plan?" asked Gritter. There was an edge of panic to his voice.

"Let Ug deal with two of them," answered Grogger. "Me, you, and Klunk will fend off the other three. Kackle... think of something *magical!*"

"I could blow the room up," replied Klunk, helpfully, and produced a very large looking bomb from the sack on his back.

"Not while we're in it, you snoz!" answered Grogger. He was about to add another snide comment, but it was too late, the salamanders were upon them.

Ug bellowed and charged toward a pair of the attackers, swinging his massive club. The pair ducked underneath the arcing weapon just in time and began dueling with the troll. Despite his size, Ug was surprisingly nimble and blocked the blows of their obsidian swords with relative ease. When the blades did manage to cut his skin, the wounds would quickly heal, thanks to his regenerative powers. Each time he was nicked, Ug would give a grunt of pain, but the swings of his club would become more furious.

With Ug occupied, Grogger screeched at Gritter and Klunk to team up against one of the creatures. One was armed with a sharp-looking blade that Grogger really did not like the look of. *Better they deal with that*, he thought.

The trio danced around each other with weapons at the ready. Only armed with a crude spear, Gritter resorted to parrying the blows and tried to keep a safe distance. Meanwhile, Klunk would dart in and slash away at their foe with a small dagger. It was pointless though, and the salamander simply stepped aside each time the goblins came close. With each dodge came a small laugh and smoke would billow from the salamander's nostrils.

That left Grogger to deal with the awful monster he'd faced in the woods on his own, which Grogger thought was a terrible injustice. Armed only with his dagger, Grogger was forced to dodge the swings of the heavy, obsidian sword. For a moment, Grogger wondered why the salamander hadn't set the weapon on fire, like before. A small mercy, perhaps. He rolled under another potential death blow and jabbed his dagger into the salamander's leg. The puny blade scraped harmlessly across its thick scales and it grunted in amusement at Grogger's squeal of frustration.

"Do something!" Grogger screamed to Kackle. "Don't just stand there like a golem!"

Grogger slid under another vicious slice and tried to stab into his enemy's side, but the blade just pinged off without causing harm.

"Can you do something to make me stronger?" screeched Grogger while leaping backward.

"Ah-ha! I've got it," shouted Kackle.

"I don't care if you've got it, just do it!" panted Grogger.

Grogger caught sight of Kackle as he rummaged around in his robes and eventually produced a small scroll with neat, human writing on it. Grogger tried to see what it said and was fairly sure it said 'strength'. Or 'death'.

"Wait, what will that do?" asked Grogger, but it was too late.

Kackle took in a deep breath and steadied himself. Holding out a claw at Grogger, he began reciting the words on the scroll. Grogger recognized some of them as elvish, and was alarmed to hear Kackle struggling to form some of the trickier words. However, something was happening, because a red glow was forming around Grogger's outstretched claw. When Kackle shouted the final word, the glow formed into a massive red fist and shot toward Grogger. Kackle closed his eyes as the spell was unleashed.

The glowing fist smacked straight into Grogger and, for a moment, he was bathed in an unnatural red light. He didn't have much time to consider what had happened because the salamander jabbed at him with his terrible, black sword. Grogger jumped over it and made a desperate stab toward his attacker. However, rather than sliding harmlessly off the aged scales, this time it made a vicious-looking wound, which immediately drew blood. The hot liquid hissed as it dripped on the cold floor of the fort. Grogger grinned at his foe's grimace of pain.

"Do that for the others!" Grogger shouted to Kackle.

Soon red, glowing fists were hurtling toward the other goblins. A couple missed their target and harmlessly disappeared into the ceiling. But eventually, he managed to hit Klunk and Gritter. Kackle looked over at Ug and shrugged, probably not wanting to waste his energy if Ug didn't need the help. He was still managing to keep the two salamanders at bay and, as if to prove the point, the troll delivered a bone shattering backhand to one of the attackers. The salamander flew backward and smashed its head on one of the columns holding up the ceiling.

The fight with Klunk and Gritter wasn't going so well, however. Both goblins were covered in small knicks from the salamander's rapier. Gritter stabbed toward their foe with another clumsy attempt and was greeted by a hard kick in the face, followed by the distinct sound of teeth cracking as the goblin hit the ground hard. The salamander marched forward to deliver the killing blow but was disturbed by the loud crash of a door banging open at the back of the once grand hall.

"Who disturbs Magwa's sleep?" came an ear-splitting cry.

When Magwa burst through the door of his sleeping chamber, he looked horrified to see the scalies fighting with the goblins.

"This is Magwa's home!" screeched the old greenskin. "Magwa should have killed you when you entered, Grogger Split-tooth. This was a trap! A trap to kill Magwa."

Grogger panicked. He was no longer sure if the scalies were the real threat or the mad Magwa. In response to the intrusion, Magwa banged the prod on the floor, sending sparks of lightning up towards the ceiling and causing Grogger to wince. He ducked under another strike and briefly looked around at the salamanders. They hadn't understood Magwa's shrieks but surely the magical energy and a grogging big beast must get their attention? He grinned slightly, as he considered that Magwa might provide just the distraction he needed to slip away unnoticed. However, before he could leg it, Magwa started shouting again.

"Magwa orders you to kill it!" Magwa screamed at Jo'os and pointed at the nearest salamader.

Jo'os crossed the space between him and the salamander in a flash. The gigantic mawbeast sprang at the foe and knocked him to the ground, just before he could slice through Gritter's chest. His rapier went skittering across the floor and into the shadows. Jo'os leapt onto the scaly's chest. He began pounding at the mawbeast's side, but it was no use. It was like a hatchling slapping against the thick hide of a rhinosaur. Jo'os' stinking breath came in excited gasps, and globs of drool dripped onto his prey's face. Then, with a final growl, Jo'os opened his gaping jaws and closed his mouth around the salamander's head. Jo'os gave one savage twist and ripped its head clean off before gulping it down whole. Blood sprayed across the dusty, dirty floor.

"This *Magwa's* home!" shouted the old goblin in clumsy common tongue.

* * * * *

Fury raged in Furna's chest at the death of another member of her crew. She ignored another potentially deadly swiped from the troll and charged at the goblin with the prod, screaming. Raising her sword, she prepared to send the damned greenskin back to whatever pit he crawled from. She was surprised by the almost disinterested look of her target, but it didn't matter, she had to get revenge for Hr'zak.

The goblin casually lowered his magical prod and jabbed it in Furna's direction. Great forks of lightning erupted from the prongs and crackled toward her. The hall lit up with an unnatural blue light that caused the shadows to shift and move ominously. The bolts of lightning quickly enveloped Furna, and she writhed in agony as the magic raced and skipped across her thick scales. Her muscles twitched and contracted while the current passed through her. She heard the goblin let out a shrill laugh that almost drowned out the crackling energy of the lightning. He shot again.

Furna gritted her teeth and tried to ignore the pain. Dropping her sword, she reached with shaking claws to one of the pistols strapped across her chest. At first she hoped to shoot the goblin that was attacking her, but with the lightning coursing through her body, she wasn't confident of hitting her target. Instead, out the corner of her eye, she noticed the massive monster ripping chunks of flesh from Hr'zak's corpse. She was disgusted at the strings of meat hanging from the monster's bloody jaws. It had to die. It had to pay for killing Hr'zak. Furna struggled against the lightning and tried to take aim; her claw trembling in agony.

* * * * *

With one scaly dead and another two out of action, Grogger was feeling more confident of their chances of survival. Although, despite his newfound confidence, the big salamander he was facing wasn't giving up. Grogger's breath came in rasping gasps as he dodged and evaded more potentially lethal strikes from his assailant. He just hoped the mad old goblin would shoot this salamander next, because he was growing tired.

As he dodged another blow, Grogger spotted the salamander bathed in lighting had somehow produced a pair of pistols and was beginning to take aim. Normally he would be too busy being concerned about protecting himself, but he could see the advantage of keeping Jo'os alive, particularly if he got that prod and Jo'os followed his every command. Also, he wasn't sure what would happen to the already unhinged Magwa if he saw his only friend get shot. He didn't want to be on the receiving end of that lightning.

Grogger threw his dagger at his assailant to distract him. The salamander easily swatted the attack away with his long, thick tail, but it was enough time for Grogger to run at Jo'os. The goblin bashed into Jo'os just as a crack of gunfire echoed around the dusty hall. Grogger half expected to feel the bullet strike him at any moment. The pair tumbled forward, with Jo'os snapping at him angrily, annoyed that Grogger had disturbed his meal. When they finally stopped, Grogger gasped in horror when Jo'os pinned him down with one of his fearsome claws.

This is what I get for trying to help someone, thought Grogger bitterly and closed his eyes, ready for the end.

"Jo'os no!" shouted Magwa. "Here!"

The huge mawbeast gave one last snap at Grogger then bounded off toward his master. Grogger breathed a sigh of relief, but this was no time to relax. There were still two scalies to deal with. He quickly jumped up and surveyed the scene. His former attacker had taken the opportunity to run to the stunned attacker and was helping them get back up. Grogger could see they were moving unsteadily to her feet, but their eyes burned with a bitter rage. Ug was stomping toward his sparring partner and was preparing to make the finishing blow while the salamander was slumped against a column. Gritter and Klunk were now hiding underneath the large dining table they had previously been sleeping on. Kackle was leaning against a pillar and breathing heavily. Clearly the spells had taken more out of him than he expected. Finally, Magwa was running his claw through Jo'os' blood-encrusted mane and saying what a good boy he was, almost as if they weren't in the middle of a battle of life and death.

Grogger was about to command them all to kill the remaining scalies when he heard shouts from the entrance. He looked over and was alarmed to see more salamanders leaping over the boulders and running at them. A gun cracked loudly and a bullet pinged off a column that was alarmingly close to his head.

"More grogging scalies!" screamed Grogger, followed by the sound of another pistol being fired. He looked over to the salamander that had been helped from the floor and was horrified to see them smile. The fight had turned against the goblins. Grogger scooped his dagger from the floor and dashed over to Magwa.

"Is there another way out?" he panted, desperately.

"Of course there's another way out! Do you think Magwa is a snoz? Follow Magwa!"

Magwa and Jo'os ran off behind the throne and through the large oak door that led to Magwa's sleeping quarters. For a moment, Grogger just considered leaving the other goblins and Ug to deal with the new salamanders, but there was a definite advantage in having more allies on his side - just in case something went wrong and he needed some bodies between him and the scalies.

"Follow Magwa! Follow Magwa!"

The goblins didn't need asking twice and sped toward the crazed legend. Ug was clearly more keen for a fight and bellowed in frustration, before smashing his club on the floor a few times. The heavy blows caused one of the supporting columns to shake, and Grogger noticed with keen interest large pieces of masonry tumbling from the ceiling.

"Come on, Ug, you grogging oversized orc!"

The insult snapped Ug out of his battle rage and he glowered at Grogger, a simmering anger behind his beady, little eyes. Then, with one last stamp of his feet, he jogged over to Grogger and followed him through the door. The troll only just managed to squeeze his massive frame through the opening.

Once inside the room, Grogger slammed the door shut and threw the bolt across to lock it. He was surprised to see that Magwa's bedroom was little more than a storage room. A makeshift bundle of dirty old tapestries tucked in the corner was clearly where Magwa and his pet slept, but the rest of the small room was stripped bare of whatever used to be kept in here. The goblins and Ug were tightly packed into the small space and Grogger felt an instinctive ease at being pressed in against so many bodies. His sensitive nose picked up an almost rotten, earthy smell that caught in the back of his throat, and then he noticed Magwa point to a small hole in the ground. With a groan, Grogger realized that Magwa slept in something he'd heard of called a 'water closet,' and his 'escape route' was the sewer.

"We're never going to escape down there," whined Grogger, looking at the small opening. "Ug won't fit!"

"Do you doubt Magwa?" The old goblin suddenly pointed the prod at the toilet.

"No…" squealed Grogger, terrified that the lightning would rebound around the room. But it was too late, a bolt of energy cracked from the prod. It was followed by an intense flash and the sound of crashing rocks.

"I'm blind!" screeched Gritter. Grogger clouted him around the ear.

"Don't be a snoz," hissed Grogger. He looked toward the hole and was relieved to see a much larger opening in the floor. Magwa had a self-satisfied grin on his face.

Grogger pushed past the others to peer into the darkness. The smell of hundreds, if not thousands, of years of dwarf sewage overwhelmed him, and he almost toppled into the hole.

"This is the only way out?" he asked reluctantly.

"Trust Magwa," came the reply.

Even in the gloom of the sewer, Grogger would see the impressive structure underneath the fort. It was almost as big as a tunnel mine and was held up by intricately carved marble columns. A small trickle of water coursed through the center of the tunnel, and Grogger realized there must be an underground stream somewhere that the dwarfs had diverted to clear the sewage. Gritter suddenly pushed him aside and jumped down the hole.

"It's like a road down here," came his echoing voice. "Beardies even have to show off when they're crapping."

Kackle was the next to leap down the opening.

"Guess all that ale has to come out at some point," he chuckled.

Klunk was about to jump into the hole when Grogger quickly grabbed his arm.

"Wait! I have a plan to stop the scalies following us."

"Do I get to blow something up?" replied a hopeful Klunk.

"What's the biggest bomb you've got?"

A large, slightly manic grin spread across Klunk's face.

"The biggest?"

"The biggest!"

Klunk's eyes grew wide with excitement.

* * * * *

Outside the room, the salamanders were preparing to assault the goblins. Rorsha quickly ran to Furna.

"What happened, Captain?"

"Well, we've found out what a magwa is," she replied with a grimace. She was still a bit unsteady on her feet, forcing her to lean on Berusk for support. "Good news is, I think he's got something even more valuable than the wiz. We've got our ticket home!"

She gave Berusk a brief nod and then forced herself to stand tall. Furna hoped her crew wouldn't notice her knees wobbling and the involuntary spasms in her tail as the remaining electricity traveled around her body. Out the corner of her eye, she spotted the remains of Hr'zak and felt her blood boil. She slapped her tail on the floor angrily and black tendrils of smoke billowed from her nostrils. Furna could feel the rage coursing through her.

"Captain?" said Igne, meekly.

"What is it?" snapped Furna and immediately regretted her response when she saw the smaller salamander recoil slightly. Igne gave a small, nervous cough before continuing.

"The map that wiz had, there are also plans for this fort." Furna tried to calm her frustration. She didn't care about plans. She wanted to kill those goblins! Sensing the captain's annoyance, Igne quickly carried on. "Well, if I'm reading them right, they're currently stuck in a water closet. There's no way out."

"Well done," said Furna with a grin. "To me! Let's get those filthy gobs!"

In Kthorlaq's name, she would not let those damn greenskins escape.

Furna ducked when she heard the lightning crack inside the water closet.

"What are they doing in there?" she muttered to herself. "Igne, are you sure that's just a water closet. There's no way out?"

Igne inspected the plans again.

"No, just a water closet with a sewer. No exit."

She held up the plans and Furna paused for a moment. It dawned on her what the goblins were doing.

"They're escaping down the damn sewer! Quickly, get in that room and stop them!"

Despite his age, Berusk was the first to reach the door. He kicked the door so viciously, it smashed open, came off its hinges, and tumbled into the room. Furna shoved past and charged in, pistols drawn. Her eyes grew wide in horror when she saw the room was empty and a large hole had been blasted into the floor. The goblins had gone.

She was about to order the salamanders down the hole when she heard a strange fizzing sound coming from under the broken door. Furna kicked the door aside and was greeted by a curious sight. Underneath was what looked like a large metal ball, made from random bits of metal hammered together. At the top of the ball, a long piece of rope was growing shorter by the moment as a sparking flame traveled up it toward the ball. Finally, scrawled on the front in common script was the word 'ka-boom'. Furna's face fell.

"Get out! Get out!" she bawled, backing out the small, stinking room. "Get out as quick as you can! This whole place is about to blow."

The salamanders ran as fast as they could, but it was futile. Just as they made it to the entrance, a blast from the makeshift bomb threw them forward and knocked them to the ground. Chunks of the fort crashed down, and through the cacophony, Furna could make out the awful screams of her crewmates as they were crushed by the collapsing roof.

She rolled into a ball, tucking herself up with her tail wrapped around her, like a youngling inside an egg before it hatched. She was quickly covered in a thick layer of dust and she prayed to Kthorlaq that she wouldn't be the next to have her fire extinguished by the infernal explosion.

After what seemed like hours, but must have only been moments, the deafening noise of falling masonry stopped. It was quickly replaced by moans of pain and cries of anguish as those that survived spotted the remains of their crewmates.

Furna gave a cough, and dust erupted from her mouth.

"By Kthorlaq's name, I'm going to kill those damned goblins, if it's the last thing I do," she growled.

CHAPTER TWELVE

Grogger ached. It seemed like they had been walking through the sewer for days, but it just kept going on and on. Although the smell didn't appear to be getting any less potent. Gritter and Klunk kept asking to stop, but Grogger wouldn't risk it. He was convinced the salamanders would have been killed in the blast, but he couldn't be sure. He wanted to make sure he was as far away from the fort as possible.

The sewer itself was continued on the slight downward slope, and Grogger assumed it was to help the flow of water. Small glowing gem-stones in the ceiling gave off a dim light and led them further down the tunnel. Even this far away from the fort, the carvings were still ridiculously elaborate. Grogger hissed when he saw one illustration showing a goblin having his head stuffed down a toilet by a dwarf. Stupid grogging beardies. He kicked some water in frustration and almost lost his balance.

"How long is this grogging tunnel?" he asked Magwa. The old goblin was hobbling along in the front, with Jo'os loping alongside him.

"It has been some time since Magwa came down here, but Magwa does not think it is longer than a moon's walk to the exit."

"A moon's walk?!" shouted Gritter. "That's it. I'm stopping." He thumped down on a small ledge running alongside the tunnel.

Grogger was about to tell him to keep moving when a wave of fatigue washed over him. He suddenly realized how tired he was, and he wondered if it was the after-effects of Kackle's spell wearing off.

"Okay, okay! You're weaker than an orcling, Gritter. Everyone take a break and then we'll carry on."

The goblins came to halt and sat along the ledges. Jo'os began lapping at the water running through the old sewer, and Grogger realized how thirsty he was too. He dipped his dusty claws into the clear water, scooped some up, and then gulped it down greedily. He didn't care that it was an old sewer. It must have been centuries since a dwarf last sent a crap sailing down here. He leaned back against the wall and closed his eyes for a moment. He was so tired.

Grogger woke with a start when he heard someone splashing toward him. Instinctively, he reached for his dagger, prepared to strike whomever it was. He quickly stopped when he saw it was Magwa. The old goblin was staring at him.

"Do you really think you will be a king, Grogger Split-tooth?" he whispered. Grogger nervously glanced at the others to see if they had heard. Magwa kept staring at him. Then, slowly he moved to sit beside Grogger.

"Magwa wanted to be a king once," he sighed. "A great king, with Jo'os at Magwa's side. The greatest goblin king that ever lived. But Magwa was never meant to be a king."

"What happened?" asked Grogger, genuinely curious about the older goblin's past.

"Magwa gathered many, many followers and even more maw-beasts. The pack was magnificent. So many beasts. So many beasts to follow Magwa."

Magwa began making a low, wailing noise, and Grogger thought he might be crying again. Then he realized he was howling like a mawbeast. It echoed ominously down the sewer and sounded more like the moans of a ghost than the howl of an animal. Perhaps Magwa was more like a ghost, thought Grogger. An old goblin from a different age that was forced to watch everyone else disappear into the mists of time. Further down the tunnel, Jo'os joined the howling. Rather than the low moan of his master, this was a deep-throated bellow that drowned out all other noise. Suddenly the pair stopped and, even in the gloom, Grogger spotted a far-away stare on Magwa's face.

"The pack grew and grew. We tore through the land. Goblin and beast, all following Magwa. No one could stop us. Magwa was the *Great* Magwa! Greatest goblin king ever. But everything has to die one day... apart from Magwa.

"We had destroyed so many villages and the pack was growing. But as the pack grew bigger, we needed more supplies. More armor. More weapons. More food. Magwa decided we should raid a human town. The scouts said it had too many soldiers, that the walls were too thick, but who could stop the Great Magwa and his magnificent pack? Magwa knew the town would fall."

The old goblin fell silent and closed his eyes. For a moment, Grogger thought he might have fallen asleep. He was about to give him a nudge when he started speaking again.

"The humans were ready for us. They had been preparing. Strong men on horses rode through the pack, slashing and stomping the maw-beasts. Their hooves cracking the skulls of Magwa's pups. Magwa watched and listened to the howls. The pack was so big, but the humans were too strong, too clever. Magwa was no king. Magwa was a fool. A fool without a pack. Magwa the Great Fool."

Grogger couldn't remember hearing stories about Magwa losing a great battle. In goblin legend, Magwa was always seen as a hero, sur-rounded by a swarming pack of angry mawbeasts. But that wasn't the Mag-wa he saw now. The legend was too tired and too old. Wrinkles tugged at his fading skin, and Grogger noticed his claw trembled slightly as he held the magic prod that had seemingly cursed him to this long life. No goblin should be forced to live this long; killing him and taking the prod would be a mercy, Grogger considered darkly.

"Can Grogger Split-tooth be a better king than Magwa?" asked the mad old goblin.

"In the vision, I am the king that unites the goblins," he replied, with a confidence that surprised himself. Magwa grunted and gave a short nod.

"You saved Jo'os, so Magwa will help you. Magwa will join the great king, Grogger Split-tooth." Magwa began to tap his chin with a claw. "You will need many more goblins to be a king, Grogger Split-tooth. And Magwa knows just where to find them. It is time the underminers left their tunnels!"

"The whats?" asked a bemused Grogger. He was about to ask more when Magwa tapped the prod to his forehead, and Grogger was immediately overwhelmed with a vision.

Tunnels... long tunnels that stretched further and further into the earth... pale goblins... mighty tunnels burrowing forever... the roar of a beast... a goblin with a blood-soaked beard... the pale goblins surrounding Grogger.

Grogger's body twitched slightly from the after effects of the visions. He wiped some drool from his mouth.

"Where... where do we find them?" he stuttered.

"Magwa knows," replied the former king with a manic grin.

* * * * *

Furna was furious. She could feel the rage building in her gut and spreading through her entire body. Her claws shook with the anger surging through her red-hot blood. Her tail swished from side to side to relieve some of the tension. It only got worse when she looked over what was left of her crew. Luckily the cave-in hadn't killed anyone, but they were covered in deep cuts and mean-looking bruises.

She knew that, ultimately, she was annoyed at herself. The crew had trusted her as captain, and she had failed. So many of them had died because of her poor decisions. First the shipwreck, then the forest, and now this madness.. She wasn't fit to be a captain anymore. She had put the crew in danger, and now they were at risk of never making it back home. Furna gave a loud cough to gather the attention of her crew. They all looked at her expectantly.

"I have made some grave errors as your captain," she said softly. "You have all served under my watch to the best of your abilities, but I have failed you. I am not fit to be captain of such brave souls. Such courageous sailors, each and every one of you. I will step down as captain and let Rorsha take command."

She saw the first mate's eyes lit up. *This was clearly the moment he had been waiting for*, she thought ruefully. The opportunity to command his own crew. He gingerly pulled himself up from a log he had been resting on and approached Furna.

Amongst the rubble of the ruined fort, she had somehow managed to find her tricorn hat. It was dusty and torn in places after the explosion but, despite its tattered appearance, she knew its significance as the symbol of captaincy. Slowly she pulled it from her head and prepared to hand it to Rorsha. She hoped he would do a better job than her. As the first mate approached, she held out the hat and felt her heart sink. How had it come to this?

Suddenly, with a loud snarl, Berusk slapped the hat out of her hand and onto the mud.

"What are you doing, old one?" snapped Rorsha as he drew his blade. It roared into fiery life, causing shadows to dance around them. Berusk ignored the younger salamander and turned to Furna.

"So you're giving up?!" he shouted. "A few goblins get in your way, and this is your answer?!"

"The captain has spoken Berusk," spat Rorsha. "Recent events have proved she can't handle the responsibility anymore."

Berusk roared and leapt at Rorsha, knocking him to the ground.

"Responsibility? Don't make me laugh, Rorsha. How would you know anything about responsibility? At the first sign of trouble, you have to take a pull on your dragon's brew. You're like a human sucking on its mother's teat."

This time, Rorsha growled and dove toward the older salamander. Berusk casually grabbed Rorsha's water container from his belt before delivering a vicious kick that sent him sprawling to the ground again. Berusk popped open the container and gave it a sniff.

"Smells like this water has gone off," he growled and began pouring the oily, black liquid into the dirt.

"You old bastard!" hissed Rorsha, his tail lashing in the mud. "The cold has got into your blood. It's sending you crazy. I should put you out of your misery. It will be a blessing for you to receive Kthorlaq's embrace!"

Berusk ignored the jibes and turned to Furna.

"I've served in many crews and seen many captains lose their nerve, but they never give up. So what if the goblins escaped? So what if you lost the ship? So what if you're losing crew members? It's not about what's happened, it's about what you're going to do about it. A captain's life will never be easy, so you've got to make the tough decisions. Do you honestly think Rorsha is ready to make those tough decisions?"

The younger salamander had pulled himself back up and spat loudly. The spit landed near Berusk's feet and hissed as it hit the earth.

"My first decision would be to leave you behind, ancient one. I've said before, you're slowing us down," said Rorsha.

"I'm still faster than you'll ever be, hatchling," growled Berusk. "Next time I'll snap your neck, instead of snatching your little comfort bottle."

The pair began circling each other, swiping their tails in the dirt and kicking up dust.

"Stop it, both of you!" shouted Furna, causing the rivals to pause. "Berusk, you're right. As captain, I got us into this mess and, as captain, it is my responsibility to make sure we get out of it too. I need to get us a ship."

Rorsha gave a grunt of frustration.

"Your time will come, Rorsha," said Furna. "Once we're back on a ship, I'll hand over to you. Then you can get us home to the Three Kings.

Until then, it's up to me to bear the burden."

Berusk gave her a smile before bending down to pick up the dusty tricorn hat.

"Captain?" he said and handed it to Furna. In response, Furna nodded and firmly placed it on her scaly head.

"What's the plan then, *Captain*?" asked Rorsha. Furna detected more than a hint of bitterness.

"Same plan we had before. We go after those damn goblins. You saw what that prod did. If we can get that, it doesn't matter about the wizard. We can sell that and get enough gold for five ships."

The gathered crew nodded in agreement.

"Igne, have you still got the plans?"

"Yes, Captain," she replied and eagerly produced the tattered plans from a pouch on her belt. Furna gave her a wink.

"Please tell me those plans say where the sewer leads to."

"There is a note about Death's Hand Pass," she replied, "but it's on the other side of the hills. It's going to be a long walk."

"Well, we better get started," stated Furna. She noticed Rorsha was eying her keenly and walked over to him. Furna clapped him around the shoulder.

"Your chance to lead won't be long in coming," she explained. "Just have patience."

Furna strode off to ready the crew, but out the corner of her eye she noticed Rorsha try to suppress a shiver. She stopped a moment and carefully watched her first mate. His eyes were fixed on the dragon's scale brew as it seeped into the mud. For a moment, she considered questioning him, but there wasn't time. They had goblins to catch!

CHAPTER THIRTEEN

After what had seemed like hours, the goblins finally emerged from the sewer and into a small valley. The water from the tunnel trickled into a small stream that ran off into distance. Either side, rocky hills rose up to touch the moonlit sky. Patches of dead grass were scattered haphazardly between the gray rubble. Grogger eyed their surroundings cautiously, expecting a salamander to leap out at any moment. A sudden movement caught his eyes on the left slope, and his claw reached for his dagger. When he saw it was just a group of rabbits, he breathed a sigh of relief.

"Gritter, go and rustle us up some grub," he said and pointed at the animals.

"Yes, boss," came the reply, and Gritter began stealthily creeping toward the rabbits. There weren't many creatures that could outsneak a goblin. Even Grogger's sharp ears couldn't detect Gritter's delicate footfall. Grogger's stomach growled hungrily as he thought of eating those meaty morsels.

He took his mind off the rabbits by thinking about Gritter's response. He had called him boss without even thinking. Even during the skirmish with the salamanders, the goblins had listened to his commands, and it seemed as though Ug was giving him less hate-filled stares too. The more he thought about it, the more that the visions from Kackle must be true. Yes, there was a difference between becoming king and commanding thousands of goblins, compared to this ragtag bunch, but it was certainly good practice.

In his heart, Grogger guessed he always knew he was destined for great things. He could even remember back to his days as a gobling in the woods of the Mammoth Steppe. Grogger had vague memories of crawling from the spawning pool deep underground and quickly creeping through the dark to find his way to the surface.

From that moment, his life was a dangerous one – fully of death and tragedy. Grogger quickly banded together with the other goblings. They were all tiny creatures, roughly the size of a human hand, and they all had the same goal in mind: survive to see the next moon. It was something that had driven Grogger, and every other goblin, throughout his life. An almost obscene level of self preservation. Once he had banded together with the other goblings, his next task was to escape the tunnels of the goblin caves. An instinct told them all to get out as quickly as possible to avoid the twisty maze of nasty creatures, like bats, giant millipedes, trolls and adult goblins, which would happily gobble up a newspawned gobling.

Grogger's swarm of goblins quickly grew to hundreds, and they would group together for safety. The horde worked their way through the caverns, but some would occasionally wander off in a different direction, never to be seen again. Grogger had heard of older goblins discovering passages full of gobling bodies that had died when they failed to find a way out.

Most goblings don't want to lead, but Grogger had relished the opportunity. He was bigger than most, so he had pushed through to the front and strode through the tunnels like he owned them. Of course, he had lost a few followers along the way - even thrown a couple into the gaping maw of a rogue mawbeast they encountered - but they emerged from the cave triumphant.

From there, they scurried into the nearby woodland, ready to forage for whatever food they could find. Grogger was still the biggest, so the goblings followed him wherever he went. As the days went on, a simple language began to form in their minds - remnants of the black magic used by Garkan to create the greenskins all those centuries ago - and Grogger quickly realized he could boss around the small goblings to find food for him, or build a shelter when it rained. Grogger was king of the goblings.

However, his reign was short lived. While he had been the biggest and strongest fresh out the spawning pool, the others quickly overtook him. Although he was never the runt of the litter, some of the other goblings soon realized they could push him around, and his leadership was eventually toppled. The gobling king was dethroned.

The experience left a bitter taste in the young Grogger's mouth, but he was determined not to let it stop him. After seeing that he couldn't win by brawn alone, Grogger learned to use his brains. Even as a gobbling, he knew he was different from the rest. More sneaky. More intelligent. More cunning. And so many of his enemies found they would accidentally fall and trip into a ravine, or they might eat a poisoned mushroom by mistake, some occasionally woke up with a sharp stick stabbed between their shoulder blades.

"A bird must have dropped it," came the explanation from Grogger, and the other goblings would nod sagely before looking to the sky nervously for more falling sticks.

Of course, each time one leader died, another large gobling would take their place, but Grogger didn't mind. They would all treat him as their friend, because he was so much cleverer than they were, which meant he still received the benefits of leadership without actually having to do any of the shouting. He could just sit back and relax as they mysteriously fell into a river and drowned... after tying rocks to their own legs.

Eventually, the time came when the goblings grew to full maturity, and the call to return to the clammy caves where they were spawned became stronger. By now, Grogger's kin had decreased to a few dozen, and he had to be more careful about the accidents that befell anyone that disagreed with him. They worked their way back to the cave, and Grogger was careful to stay amongst the pack - even a fully grown goblin was a tasty snack to plenty of animals that lived in the forest.

Arriving at the cave, Grogger was amazed at the sheer number of greenskins. They must have numbered hundreds, even thousands. Everywhere he looked, the goblins were frantically carrying out whatever task they had been given. Grogger and his small pack drew mocking glances from those in the cave. While the other goblins were dressed in the rags and armor they had stolen from raids, Grogger's gang were wrapped in fur or even large leaves they had foraged from the woodlands. Eventually, they were spotted by a biggit and dragged into the center of the cave to meet their new leader. And that was how Grogger's life under the leadership of Bung had begun. He couldn't even remember any of the goblings that had grown to maturity with him. He didn't even know if they were still alive. In truth, he didn't really care.

What those years in the woods had told him was that he had a knack for leading, and he had always felt like he was meant for more – something in the back of his mind that slowly, but persistently, nagged away at him as he went about his daily duties. He guessed that was why he had been so quick to believe Kackle's premonition. It was because, deep down, he had always suspected he was special. Had always known he was destined for greatness.

Grogger was suddenly snapped out of his thoughts by Gritter returning with a clawful of dead rabbits. A couple were still twitching as he tossed them into the middle of the group. In a flash, Jo'os leapt onto the pile hungrily, his massive toothy mouth gaping open.

"No! Jo'os, no!" screeched Magwa. Grogger watched intently to see if the massive beast would follow his master's command. The animal issued a low growl and snapped his jaws a few times before backing away, tail between his legs and head hung toward the ground. Grogger almost couldn't believe it. Jo'os could easily overpower them all, apart from Ug - although even then, Grogger doubted the mawbeast would go down without a fight - yet he followed Magwa's commands like a pup. Once again, Grogger realized that despite his desperate need to get his clutches on Magwa's staff, he wasn't sure what he could do about Jo'os.

"You first, Grogger," said Magwa and pointed at the rabbits. The statement caught Grogger off guard. Once again, it was almost like they were treating him like the boss. He nodded and grabbed one of the still twitching rabbits. Bending the head backward, he plunged his small, sharp teeth into the fur and greedily gulped down the warm flesh.

"Nice catch, Gritter," he grunted between mouthfuls. "Everyone, help yourselves."

The other goblins and Ug dived on the remaining rabbits. Grogger spotted Jo'os eyeing them as they devoured the morsels. The mawbeast licked its lips and Grogger shivered. He hoped Magwa was going to feed him soon.

"Jo'os, fetch!" shouted Magwa and tossed a limp rabbit into the distance. Jo'os let out a yelp and bounded into the darkness. He returned a moment later with the rabbit carefully held in its mighty jaws and dropped it at Magwa's feet while wagging his short, stumpy tail. Magwa picked up the carcass and threw it again. This carried on for a few minutes until Jo'os became bored and hungrily began ripping the rabbit apart while hiding behind a large rock.

"Does he always do what you say?" asked a curious Grogger.

"Mostly he listens to Magwa," came the answer. "Or he gets a quick zap." Magwa banged the staff on the ground and sent a few sparks of lightning shooting into the sky. The mad old goblin let out a shrill laugh.

"And not just Jo'os that does what he's told when Magwa gives them a zap!" He carried on laughing. The high-pitched wail echoed around the valley and, for a moment, Grogger was scared someone would hear. Then, as quickly as he had started, Magwa came to an abrupt stop. The valley fell into an eerie silence. Keen to break the silence, Grogger remembered their conversation from the sewer.

"Tell me about the underminers, Magwa. You said they could help me?" He had lowered his voice to a whisper, keen that the others didn't hear him. Apart from Kackle, they were still under the impression he was rallying more goblins to Bung's banner. He just had to wait until he had more on his side before letting them know about his plan.

"An old tribe. Perhaps as old as Magwa." Again, there was a touch of sadness in the goblin's voice when he spoke about time.

"How come I haven't heard of them?"

"The underminers are very secretive, and they hardly ever come above ground. Magwa heard their tunnels stretch all the way to the Abyss. They just keep digging."

Grogger recoiled at the mention of the Abyss – the great wound on the face of Pannithor from which all-manner of demonic horrors constantly filled out into the world above. He didn't fancy finding a bunch of Abyssals waiting for him down a dark tunnel.

"If they never come above ground, where do they get all their food and stuff from? Only so long you can stay in a tunnel."

"Plenty of food underground, if you know how to get it. Magwa has seen the giant worms they breed. Mouths as big as a mawbeasts', and teeth just as sharp. They raid the beardy tunnels while riding the worms and, if they find no food, they eat the worms."

Grogger recoiled at the thought at having to eat worms all his life. Yet, despite himself, he found he was becoming more curious about the mysterious underminers.

"In my vision, I could hear machinery. Is that how they dig the tunnels?"

"They have huge drilling machines, with drills the size of your troll. Machines the size of a beardy's stomping machine. Perhaps bigger. They're powered by the black rocks stolen in the raids. They can dig faster and further than anything Magwa has seen."

"How do you know so much about them?" Grogger jumped as he

heard Kackle ask the question. He looked up to see all the goblins, and even Ug, were listening to Magwa.

"Magwa was…" the old goblin paused and grimaced. "Magwa was captured by them. The underminers don't like strangers, and Magwa went into the wrong tunnel. They grabbed Magwa before Magwa could shout to Jo'os for help, and Magwa dropped the staff."

Grogger didn't like the sound of this one bit. Was the mad, old goblin trying to get revenge on the underminers by going back there?

"How did you escape?"

"Jo'os tracked Magwa down." The mawbeast padded over at the mention of his name and nuzzled against his master. "He was howling at the cave entrance, and Magwa howled back. The underminers didn't care about a howling, little goblin. But they soon cared when Jo'os came roaring through their tunnels. So many dead! All to save Magwa."

He patted his leathery glove against the size of the gigantic animal.

"Doesn't sound like they will be happy to see you," said Grogger, sarcastically. "Jo'os kills a bunch of them, and then you expect them to welcome us with open claws? You're madder than I thought." He gave a frustrated sigh and started picking his teeth with a rabbit bone.

"Do not call Magwa mad," he hissed with a menace that Grogger hadn't heard since they were back in the old fort. "Times are changing. Can you not feel it, Grogger Split-tooth? The beardies dig ever further for their golden rocks. The chittering rats swarm through our tunnels. Even the humans dig for precious gems. The underminers can no longer hide in their caves. They can't survive on their own. Slowly but surely they will be pushed out and then wiped out. But if they join a new clan – a more powerful clan – then they can survive."

Grogger eyed Magwa warily. He didn't really trust his new companion but, if he ever hoped to take over Bung's clan as his own, he would need bigger numbers. Perhaps the underminders could help him snatch the advantage?

"Fine," huffed Grogger. "How far are they from here?"

"No more than two moon's walk, perhaps three if your troll slows us down."

Ug growled, and Grogger wondered if the troll may have struck Magwa without his mawbeast guarding him so closely. As he was wondering if he could somehow persuade Jo'os to kill Ug, he noticed the first streaks of sunlight creeping over the top of the desolate valley. He didn't want to be out in the open like this during the day, just in case those grogging scalies had actually survived and somehow managed to follow them. Halfway up the hill, he spotted a small cave.

"Let's get some rest there and head out tonight," he said and pointed at the cave. With the light slowly leaking into the valley, Grogger couldn't escape the fact he felt like eyes were watching him. He nervously looked around and could see nothing, but there was still that niggling doubt itching away at the back of his brain. He didn't want to be out here much longer.

"Quickly then, you bunch of snozzers. Let's get some kip."

And with that, they scrambled up the barren hillside and into the cave.

* * * * *

"Does the map say anything more about this Death's Hand Pass?" Furna asked Igne. The smaller salamander was struggling to keep up with the long strides of her captain. They had been walking down a mountain trail through the night and well into the day, desperate to catch up with the goblins. Furna knew that desperation was leading her to push the crew harder than ever before, but she had taken back command, and now it was down to her to get them home. It was down to her to rise above the challenges they were facing and lead her crew. It was her responsibility.

"There are some runes, but they're dwarfish," answered Igne. "I never really learnt much about the dwarfs. My own fault for stowing away on your ship."

Furna chuckled quietly.

"And never a day goes by that I don't thank Kthorlaq that you did."

"Doesn't sound like a pleasant place though. Why don't we ever need to find anywhere like Peaceful Valley?"

The pair laughed before Igne studied the map again.

"There is a human farmstead not too far from the pass. Should we stop there before pursuing the goblins?"

"We haven't got the time, Igne. The greenskins had the advantage of being able to head straight down that sewer, while we've been forced to take the scenic route."

Furna had to admit that the scenery around them was breathtaking. Although the trail they were walking clearly hadn't been used in a long time, it was clear to see it winding through hills that crested up and down. In the distance, large snow-capped peaks seemed to stretch to try and touch the sky, while above them, eagles soared before occasionally diving down to catch their prey. Throughout the journey, they had made regular stops to fill up their water pouches at clear mountain streams that cascaded down moss-covered rocks. Although it would never compare to the humid jungles of the Three Kings, Furna was enjoying the trek, despite their desperate situation.

There was a small cough behind them, and Furna turned to see Berusk had caught them both up.

"You mentioned something about runes?" he asked. "I've been around my fair share of dwarfish ships. I might know a thing or two."

Furna nodded to Igne, who passed Berusk the map. "Worth a go," she muttered.

Berusk studied the runes intently for a moment, whispering under his breath. Occasionally he would grunt in frustration. Eventually, he thrust the map back into Igne's claws and shrugged.

"Perhaps I only know dwarf cursing?" he spat. "I can't make any of it out, apart from one bit about a curse and death."

"Oh, good," sighed Furna. She looked ahead to where she assumed the pass must be and suppressed a shiver when she saw the clear blue skies were turning to an angry gray in the distance. "How long until we get there, Igne?"

"I reckon it will be nightfall, if we carry on at this pace."

Furna eyed the brooding clouds once more. The words 'curse' and 'death were never a good combination. She just hoped the goblins had even less warning than her.

CHAPTER FOURTEEN

A small, pale-skinned goblin with larger than normal eyes, colored black rather than the typical red of a greenskin, scurried deeper and deeper into a network of tunnels. Unlike the tunnels of a typical goblin lair, these were carefully held up by thick columns to support the massive weight of the ground above constantly pressing downward. Other small, pale-skinned, almost white goblins, swarmed around the columns, covering them in a thick paste of watery mud. They chittered constantly in a high-pitched tone, snapping at each other occasionally when the mud slopped on the feet or face of a neighboring goblin.

The small goblin sniffed the air constantly, its large nostrils twitching as it detected the correct way through the myriad tunnels. Occasionally, it would stop to let a large drilling machine rumble past a tunnel that crossed his route. The goblin was forced to cover its large, sensitive ears as the deafening engine of the machine roared past, driven by grinning goblins that kept pushing the throttle well beyond its safe speed. Other goblins desperately clung onto the side, whooping and hollering as the drill picked up more and speed. The jubilant shouts would often be drowned out by a scream, as one unfortunate rider fell under the gigantic wheels of the construction. Only to be followed by roars of high-pitched laughter.

Further and further the goblin went, passing crude pens packed with large, pink worms that gnawed relentlessly at their cage, until eventually it reached its destination. The large tunnel opened into a grand chamber that dwarfed even the biggest cave of most goblin clans. In the roof of the hall, large bats, the size of dogs, ducked and swooped as they caught any insects foolish enough to let their guard down. The small glowing tails of the bugs would be snuffed out whenever a bat hit their target.

The goblin pushed through the throng to make his way to the center of the massive cave. Carved from the rock itself was a large mound, with steps winding around it. It dashed up the steps until it arrived, panting, at the summit. Catching its breath, the goblin immediately prostrated itself on the floor in front of a large, ornate throne carved from the same rock as the mound. Chiseled into the throne were delicate skulls and names, covering almost the entire surface of the large seat.

"There are overworlders in the valley, your majesty."

"I see," hissed Grukhar Rockcrusher, queen of the underminers. Compared to the weedy goblin prostrating itself in front of her, Grukhar was a head taller, with wiry, strong muscles running up her exposed arms. As the goblin watched, she turned an overly large, ornamental mining pick between her hands. Most of the undernourished underminers would have struggled to even lift the pick, nevermind play with it so casually.

"Go on, tell me more," she snapped, with a hint of irritation.

"Yes, yes, of course." He eyed his queen nervously as she glowered down from the throne. It wasn't uncommon for those who brought bad news to receive the pick between their eyes. Up on her seat, Grukhar was a commanding sight. Along with the large pick casually turning in her hands, Grukhar wore a crown carved from the skull of a dwarf. The grizzly piece still bore the eye sockets of its former owner, which now held two red gems, while the top had been smashed to give a crooked ring. The queen's impressive ears, covered in piercings, stuck out from the crown and held it in place.

However, it was her belt that tended to draw the eye of most visitors to her pedestal. Strapped around it were dozens of beards she had cut from the dwarfs she had captured. Some were covered in grime, after being on the belt for years, whereas others still had the gleam of fresh blood. It was almost impossible to count the number that formed a makeshift skirt around her legs. Tearing its eyes away from the grisly sight of the beards, the goblin carried on.

"There were seven of them. Five of our kind. A field troll and the *muncher.*"

Grukhar sat bolt upright at the mention of the muncher.

"Are you sure that's what it was?"

"Yes, yes," answered the goblin. "It has returned."

"Where are they now?" Grukhar's voice had a tone of excitement.

"The dead place."

Grukhar's face broke into a wily grin, and she burst out laughing.

"Oh, this could not be more perfect. Make sure they have a warm welcome as they travel through the valley. If they survive, bring them to me."

"Of course, my queen." The nervous goblin began slowly shuffling backward.

"Oh, and please make sure they don't escape," she said with an icy tone. "You know how annoyed my pick gets when goblins fail me." With that, she broke into a wailing laugh and her subject made a hasty retreat down the steps.

* * * * *

Grogger's sleep was suddenly interrupted by the horrendous noise of Ug's snoring. He must have been tired if he managed to sleep through that all day. He stretched and rubbed his eyes before jumping up with alarm when he realized the cave was brightly lit by moonlight. They had overslept! He cursed himself for not forcing anyone to stay on watch. Now they had wasted most of the night by sleeping.

"Wake up, you snozzers!" he shouted. "You've all let us sleep for too long."

The others woke up with a start and looked around with confusion.

"Look lively, we need to get moving." Everyone grabbed what meager provisions they had and prepared to set out. Grogger turned to Magwa.

"Right, lead the way."

The old goblin was clearly suffering after sleeping on the cold floor of a cave, rather than his former home. Grogger saw he was leaning heavily on the prod and using it to aid his slow movement. Occasionally, he would grab onto Jo'os for support. The powerful beast didn't appear to care as his master tightly clenched clumps of fur.

When they left the cave, Grogger realized the valley looked a lot different to the previous evening. A thin mist was drifting just above the stream, and it seemed to drown out the soft trickle of the water. The whole place had a hushed, almost expectant feeling to it. His sharp eyes scanned the neighboring hillside before he rushed to catch up with Kackle.

"Do you feel anything *wrong* with this place?" he asked the wiz. The mist continued to swirl around them.

"Wrong, how?" Grogger saw Kackle was now nervously looking around them.

"I keep feeling like someone is watching."

The sound of some pebbles trickling down the hillside made them both jump. Grogger squinted to see if he could spy any movement, but the mist obscured his vision.

"Just keep an eye out," said Grogger and ran to catch up with Magwa. The older goblin was making slow progress, and the clang of his prod hitting the ground was one of the few sounds echoing through the hills.

"What did you say this valley is called?"

"Magwa doesn't know. It has been a long time since Magwa was last here."

Grogger sighed in frustration at the senile old snoz. This time, he walked over to Gritter and Klunk who were walking together.

"Something's not right here. I can feel it."

"What do you mean, boss?" asked Klunk.

There was that word again. Boss! Grogger felt himself swell with ambition, but this wasn't the time to dwell on it. His skin prickled ominously.

"Just looks like some old hills to me," responded Gritter.

"Do you not feel it? My ears are twitching."

Grogger was startled for a second time as more small rocks tumbled down the hill. He tried to tell himself that it was just rabbits disturbing the loose earth. But he couldn't shake the impression that something terrible was about to happen.

"Just be prepared for anything," hissed Grogger.

As they had been walking, he saw the landscape had changed slightly. Whereas before the rocks were irregularly dotted around the hills, now they were grouped together in patterns. Grogger approached a row of four stones that were half his height. First, he noticed they were all perfectly cut to be the same height, and then he hissed in horror as he saw runes carefully etched into each one. They weren't rocks. They were gravestones! He groaned when he saw they were surrounded by dozens of similar sized graves. He could feel himself starting to panic and ran back to Kackle.

"It's a grogging beardy graveyard. That senile old snoz is leading us right through a grogging graveyard!"

"So what? The only good dwarf is a dead dwarf, right?" Grogger grabbed Kackle by the scruff of his dirty robes and pressed his large nose in the wiz's face, his eyes darting constantly.

"You're telling me, you can't feel anything? Your magical senses aren't tingling or whatever they do?"

"Well, I never really had any sort of magic sense... it just sort of *happens*."

Grogger groaned in frustration and pushed Kackle away. This time, he ran back to Magwa. He tried to tell himself he was being irrational. That there was nothing to worry about, but since he started to have those visions, he was sure he could *sense* danger better than before, and now his senses were screaming at him that something wasn't right.

"Can't you move any faster?" Grogger resisted the temptation to start pushing the older goblin.

Jo'os stopped and began growling. A low rumble that somehow managed to cut through the blanket of mist.

"What's wrong, Jo'os?" asked Magwa.

"Oh, so you listen to the mawbeast, but not me?" said an exasperated Grogger.

"Shhhh... do you hear something?" Magwa was cupping a claw around his ear and tilting it to the side.

"I have been saying there's something out there! We are surrounded by grogging gravestones, and now there's someone following us."

"Shut up," snapped Magwa and pointed into the distance. Grogger was about to give him a piece of his mind when he followed Magwa's finger and saw where he was pointing. A figure was approaching them through the mist. It looked too small to be a salamander, but Grogger didn't want to take any risks.

"Weapons at the ready, everyone." He was pleased to hear the sound of everyone following his orders. This bossing others around stuff was starting to come naturally, almost like when he was a gobling leading the other useless idiots through the tunnels. However, he quickly spun around when he heard the unmistakable noise of Klunk lighting the fuse of one of his bombs.

"Why are you lighting a grogging bomb? Have you got the brain of an orcling?"

"Sorry, boss," replied Klunk, miserably. He licked two fingers and used them to pinch out the crackling flame.

From the mist, the figure kept coming closer until the group recognized the unmistakable shape.

"It's just a goblin," said Gritter, cheerfully.

"Bit of a weird looking goblin though," answered Klunk. "It's got funny black eyes and its skin's a funny color."

"Still, nothing to worry about. Hey! Don't worry, we're goblins too!" shouted Gritter. The mysterious goblin stopped and produced an ornate horn from a bag at its side. Even from this distance, Grogger could see it was the hollowed out horn of a frostfang, covered in strange scrawls.

"Grukhar sends her regards," screeched the goblin and pressed the horn to his lips. It let out a mournful tone that set Grogger's teeth on edge. The noise echoed unnaturally around the valley, as if it was getting louder and coming from different locations. Around them, the mist appeared to be getting thicker too. It coiled around their legs like a snake and grasped up toward their arms and face.

"This might be a problem," whispered Magwa out the side of his mouth.

"Oh, *now* it's a problem?" replied Grogger.

The sound abruptly stopped, and the unknown goblin scuttled back into the mist. For a time, the group stood still in complete silence, just waiting for something to happen. Even Jo'os fell silent. Grogger found himself clutching his dagger harder and harder, until the knuckles of his claws turned white.

A low moan broke the pregnant silence. In the distance, where the goblin had vanished, Grogger saw another shape heading toward them.

"Is that the goblin coming back?" asked Gritter.

Its movements were shambling and jerking, not like the furtive gestures of the hornblower. It carried on moaning as it got closer, but the mist obscured its face.

"Oi! You snoz, grog off!" shouted Gritter. The shape issued a low moan, but this time, it was greeted by other groans around them.

"This is definitely a problem," sighed Magwa and banged his prod on the ground. Sparks crackled through the mist.

It was almost possible to see the stranger in front of them and, through the mist, it did appear to have the outline of a goblin, but its ears were drooping and the shuffling walk was like nothing Grogger had seen. Then it quickly became clear why. The mist began to clear, and Grogger saw with horror it was a zombie goblin. Its eye sockets were empty, and a swollen tongue dangled limply from its gaping jaw. Part of its ribcage was exposed, and Grogger saw that animals had been nibbling away at its flesh. It gave another low moan and appeared to pick up speed as it saw the living creatures. The undead monster was joined by another shambling goblin... and another.

"Un... un... undead goblins," stuttered Kackle.

"Not just goblins," replied Gritter solemnly and pointed toward one of the gravestones. Grogger recoiled as he saw the living corpse of a dwarf pulling itself from its grave. It dawned on him that this was probably the location of a fierce battle between dwarfs and goblins from ages ago. Something unnatural had preserved the corpses, and now they were coming back to life. Coming back to life to kill him! A sudden boiling rage surged through Grogger. He was going to be king. King of all the goblins! And he wasn't about to let a load of shambling, brainless zombies stop him.

"Don't just stand there, let's get 'em!"

Grogger's shout snapped them all out of confusion, and they sprang into action.

Magwa gave a shout and shot of blast of energy toward the nearest zombie dwarf, which exploded in a shower of rotting flesh. The old goblin cackled maniacally and sent more blasts of magical energy into the mist. Wherever the blasts landed, they sent limbs and heads flying into the air, clearing the fog for a moment - which only revealed more zombies to deal with.

While the undead goblins wore tattered rags, the dwarfs had been buried in ceremonial armor. The elaborate breastplates were carved with detailed illustrations, but they weren't just for decoration. Grogger cursed as his dagger slid harmlessly across the silver plate of a dwarf reaching out for his throat. He shoved his attacker backward so hard that it stumbled and fell. Seeing his opportunity, Grogger leapt forward and plunged his dagger into the zombie's forehead. It immediately went limp, but Grogger had no time to relax because another dwarf, complete with knotted beard, was shambling toward him. He was about to leap at the next attacker when a small, fizzing bomb shot past his ear and landed right in front of the zombie. In a blinding flash, the undead dwarf was reduced to a smoking pile. Grogger spun around.

"Watch where you're throwing those things!" But Klunk didn't hear a word, he was laughing wildly and lighting more and more bombs. As each one exploded in a burst of vibrant color, the impact reduced its target to dust. The problem was more enemies kept coming.

Gritter had scrambled on top of a large rock and was jabbing his spear at any zombies that came close. Even from where he was fighting, Grogger could hear that each stab was greeted by a wet, sucking sound when plunged into the face of a moaning monster. A dwarf with a large, white beard reached up at Gritter and Grogger saw its mouth gaping open, which allowed worms and insects to slither and scurry out of the body where they must have taken nest.

"Stop messing about up there," shouted Grogger. He struggled to make himself heard over the background noise of groans and Klunk's incesent explosions.

First the bombs and now this fool balancing on a grogging rock, thought Grogger and quickly dispatched another grasping horror that came too close.

Gritter tried to stab down but lost his footing and shoved the spear through the zombie's beard, where it got tangled. Grogger watched while he tried frantically to pull it free, but it was stuck fast. After one final attempt, the weapon slipped from his claws, sending the stricken dwarf tumbling backward. The brainless creature struggled to right itself as the spear got caught between its legs.

The incident had left Gritter weaponless on top of the rock. Perhaps sensing his weakness, zombies had begun to crowd around him. Undead goblins and dwarfs alike grasped toward his fresh flesh. Without his spear, Gritter resorted to viciously kicking down at the foul things, but it was doing no good, realized Grogger. They would just tumble back and return, more eager than ever to sink their teeth into his warm flesh.

"Help!" screeched Gritter to no one in particular.

As Gritter continued flailing around, Grogger decided that enough was enough. Although he was too busy to offer assistance – and didn't like his chances against all those undead – he knew just the troll who could help.

"Ug!" he screamed. "Help Gritter!" A loud bellow indicated that Ug had heard his cry.

So far Grogger was impressed, or rather relieved, to see that the zombies had posed little threat to Ug and his enormous club. Every swing of the heavy weapon sent enemies flying. He didn't even appear to be bothered about aiming, as far as Grogger could see. Thankfully, the zombies were so stupid, they just kept shuffling straight forward, directly into the path of his deadly blows. After Grogger called to save Gritter came, Ug made one last swing - spilling zombies onto the dirt - before setting off to follow Grogger's command. An undead dwarf in rusty armor stumbled in front of Ug, arms outstretched and moaning mournfully. Grogger was about to shout and tell the stupid beast to watch out, but the troll almost casually picked up the enemy by its head and squeezed it until the skull cracked and sent rotting gray matter oozing over the troll's massive hands. Ug then tossed the lifeless corpse aside and carried on toward Gritter. Grogger felt his stomach recoil in disgust.

The zombies appeared to be too preoccupied with desperately reaching up at Gritter to notice Ug's approach. Behind them, he gave a sharp kick to an undead goblin flailing its one remaining arm around. The impact sent it sprawling onto the floor, where Ug quickly dispatched it with a heavy stomp. Its head exploded with another sickening squelch that caused Grogger to gag.

Grogger realized with a sense of relief that the commotion had caught the attention of the half a dozen zombies that were clawing at Gritter. In fact, even a couple of undead that had been approaching Grogger spun their sightless eyes at Ug. The slack-jawed, groaning monsters shambled toward the troll. Ug gave a roar and swung his mighty club once more, seemingly unphased by the fight so far. The zombies didn't stand a chance, much to Grogger's delight. Under the devastating impact of the trunk-like club, the attackers were sent sprawling, and Grogger had to duck underneath a wayward limb that went speeding over his head. Meanwhile, the other zombies were quickly mushed into a decaying mess by Ug.

"Thanks, Ug," beamed a clearly grateful Gritter, but the battle was far from over.

The once peaceful valley had descended into madness around Grogger. Moans appeared to come from all angles, blasts of lightning from Magwa's prod tore through enemies, while the ear-splitting booms of Klunk's seemingly endless bombs could probably be heard from back in Bung's cave.

Although it wasn't all bad, realized Grogger. In between slashing and chopping his would-be killers, Grogger was impressed to see Jo'os leaping between the zombies, ripping off limbs and heads with a twist of his mighty jaws. He was amazed to see that even Kackle was managing to cast mostly correct spells. He watched as one group of zombies erupted into flames, before another had their head removed by a well-aimed blast of lightning.

Grogger was about to congratulate the wiz, but before he could shout, Kackle pulled out a moldy-looking scroll and began chanting in a language that Grogger couldn't understand. A chill wind appeared from nowhere and whistled through the valley. Kackle's voice rose to a dramatic crescendo, which Grogger could just about hear over the rushing wind. The chanting was met by an odd throbbing sound that hurt Grogger's ears, although the odd sensation quickly stopped when a shimmering purple light appeared before Kackle and started spinning in an ever-increasing circle. Inside the shape, Grogger could see an inky darkness, and nearby zombies started being sucked into the void by an invisible force.

A shout of celebration caught in Grogger's throat when he spotted something terrible in the portal. A pair of horrific creatures, with mouths filled with row upon row of sharp teeth, emerged inside the gloom and began clawing at any zombies that got too close, before dragging them into the yawning void. Grogger started to panic when the monsters appeared to be attempting to creep their way out but, thankfully, with an ear-splitting 'pop' the portal vanished, along with the awful monstrosities and any zombies unfortunate enough to be grabbed.

Grogger breathed a sigh of relief and continued hacking and slashing away at the undead.

* * * * *

Hope and anxiety warred in Furna's heart as the sky was lit by shimmering colors and the hillside shook with explosions. That had to be the goblins. But who were they fighting?

"Sounds like a war going on down there," said Shalesh.

"It's got to be those goblins," snarled Furna. "Come on, this is our chance!"

The salamanders had been marching almost constantly for the past two days, but Furna could feel it within the others – the thought of finally getting their claws on the greenskins spurred them onward. She broke into a jog, following the sounds of combat, and while the others were close behind, she felt Igne try to grab her attention from her right.

"I've got a bad feeling about this," she said, in betweens pants of exertion. "There's some old magic here. Can't you feel it?"

"I don't care what sort of magic is down there. We can end this, right now!"

"Captain, I..."

"I know, Igne, but this might be our last chance to capture them. Who knows where they'll end up if they get through this valley?"

As they neared the battle, an unnatural mist swirled around them. It dulled the noise of fighting, but occasionally the fog would be lit by strange colors from what she assumed must be the spells or weapons of the goblins.

"Seriously, I have a very, *very* bad feeling," whispered Igne.

In the distance, Furna spotted a cluster of shapes walking toward them. It must be the goblins. She drew her cutlass. Although she was still sore from the blast she had taken from the goblin's magic prod, her desire to be rid of the greenskins reduced the pain. She gave the weapon a few test swings and nodded with satisfaction.

"Weapons ready!" she hollered and heard the crew preparing for battle.

The shapes kept coming. There was something odd about their shambling gait, but Furna assumed it was down to the fact they too would be tired from their journey. Gritting her teeth she charged, closing the distance between them in a matter of moments.

As she neared, the mist cleared, and she realized why Igne had sensed something awry. Instead of the goblin's gang, Furna was greeted by the sight of five undead goblins. She recoiled slightly at the decaying flesh hanging limply from their bones as the living dead stumbled toward them.

"What in Kthorlaq's name have those goblins done now?" she muttered to herself.

Thankfully, she had fought the undead plenty of times in her past. Once, she had come across a ship that was crewed by an entire fleet of zombies. Despite their rotting brains, something compelled them to keep sailing round the Infant Sea, desperately searching for whatever it was they had been looking for. Still, the main thing was to not let them outnumber her. On their own, they were as useless as a hatchling; but in a group... well, that was when things got nasty.

"Stick together and go for their heads!" she roared and ran to the nearest attacker. With an easy sweep of her cutlass, she plunged the blade through the jaw of a zombie and straight into its brain. The horror went limp. She quickly pulled her weapon back out and decapitated another enemy that was reaching toward her. Its moaning head fell on the floor and carried on groaning for a moment before falling still. Two more emerged from the thick mist and hungrily gnashed their remaining teeth at Furna. She pulled a pistol from its holster and quickly shot them both in the face, showering their last teeth across the ground.

Around her, the other salamanders were fighting against more hordes of the undead. Flaming obsidian swords cut through the zombies almost as easily as they sliced through the mist. However, it seemed that no matter how many they defeated, more were pulling themselves up from the dirt around them. This was just slowing them down. They needed to find those damn goblins.

"Press on! Press on!" she hollered and charged into the fog. Ahead, she could just make out more shapes through the mist. A zombie pulled itself up through the mud and reached at her leg but was quickly dispatched by a blast from her pistol. She was almost out of ammo, but it didn't matter. When she found the goblins, she wanted to make sure she was up close so she could see the light fade from their smirking faces. Finally, she came to the heart of the battle, and the sight caused her to catch her breath slightly.

There were packs of undead dwarfs and goblins everywhere, spilling out of graves or digging themselves out of the ground. More and more seemed to be flooding into the valley from all directions. Groans filled the air around them. However, she was pleased to spot the goblins they were hunting among all the chaos. Although she was surprised to see they appeared to be coping with the onslaught of undead. One of the goblins appeared to be barking orders in its high-pitched, native tongue. No matter, she thought, even with the zombies, they had finally cornered the goblins. With a roar she charged into the fray.

* * * * *

Grogger heard the roar and looked over to Ug, assuming it must be him. However, the troll was busy pounding zombies into the ground. Grogger was surprised to see what looked like a smile on Ug's face, almost as if the troll was enjoying the attack. Next, he scanned around to see if Jo'os was responsible for the noise, and his heart immediately skipped a beat. Charging into the valley were the salamanders. He ducked instinctively as one of their pistols cracked, and he saw the head of a nearby zombie reduced to pulp.

His mind raced. How had the scalies found them? How had they escaped the cave-in? And, most importantly, how in Garkan's name was he going to escape? Now he had to escape a horde of zombies and a bunch of angry scalies. With a petulant stab, he drove his dagger into the head of a clumsy undead dwarf that had stumbled too close. If only there was a way to use the zombies against the scalies. However, he didn't have time to think as he spotted what he assumed to be the leader of the salamanders barrelling toward him. He looked around desperately for Kackle - hoping the wiz could cast the power boosting spell from back in the fort - but he was cowering behind a gravestone and occasionally sending blasts of magical energy into the zombies. Now it was too late, and the salamander was upon him.

Grogger ducked just in time and the cursed scaly's blade swiped harmlessly over his head.

"Can you even understand me, stupid goblin?" barked his attacker in the common tongue as Grogger blocked a wicked rapier slash with his dagger. Grogger stuck out his tongue in response.

"I'll take that as a yes. I just want you to know that you have caused me and my crew a lot of misery. I will relish the chance to put my blade through your skinny throat."

Grogger leapt backward as another vicious blow hurtled toward him. His foot got caught on the body of a dwarf and he stumbled, sprawling onto the mud. The salamander's eyes gleamed, and she thrust her blade straight toward his throat. In a flash, Grogger grabbed the corpse of a near-by goblin and pulled it on top of him. The blade pierced the rotting flesh and stopped mere inches from Grogger's neck. He breathed a sigh of relief and thrust the body away before rolling out the way of another potentially lethal blow. His breath was coming in desperate, short gasps.

"You're panicking, little one. Not so easy without that magic prod is it?" She thrust downward again, almost as if she were toying with him now. Grogger's eyes darted this way and that, desperately looking for a way of escape. He scrambled backward to hide behind a gravestone, panting heavily. His foe followed him, laughing. Suddenly, as she stepped onto the grave, a rotten hand burst through the mud and grabbed her ankle. The salamander tried to pull it free, but the grip was like iron. She stabbed down, but the grip held fast. Grogger peeped over the top of the gravestone.

"You understands? Stupid scales?" asked a grinning Grogger in broken common tongue. "You not kill Grogger." With that, he scrabbled up the hillside, sending loose stones rolling down toward his assailant. The mist was beginning to clear, and he needed somewhere to hide. Nearby, he spotted what looked like a large building and legged it.

He heard the salamander roar in frustration and looked back just in time to see a decaying dwarf's head emerge from the grave. Grogger grinned and stopped to watch, hoping that the zombie would somehow best the salamander that dared to attack him. Black smoke billowed from her mouth as she rained blows into its moaning mouth. Eventually, its head was a fleshy pulp, and the previously vice-like grip fell away. Grogger groaned and turned to dash toward the building, while the sound of the pursuing salamander crept dangerously close behind him.

In the back of his mind, Grogger wondered what was happening to the other goblins, but he didn't have time to care about them. His most important objective now was to stay alive. He approached the building, and he realized with a shiver it was a gigantic mausoleum. The large stone structure was decorated in elaborate carvings of dwarfs, many of which had been desecrated at some point in time. The stone head of what Grogger assumed must be a dwarf king loomed over the top of a gaping, dark entrance that was guarded by a set of large iron gates. Grogger ran over, hoping to find safety inside. He stopped when he saw they were held together by a rusty padlock and recoiled at the charnel stench of the mausoleum. Carefully, he approached, holding his sleeve over his sensitive nose. Deep in the shadows of the interior, he could sense something heavy padding around. Suddenly, something slammed against the gates, sending the already nervous Grogger scuttling backward. Inside the gloom, Grogger saw the unnatural glow of two large red eyes. His nervous face broke into an excited grin. He grabbed a rock and stood as close as he dared to the mausoleum, ignoring the hungry snuffling behind him.

"Oi! Scales! Up here."

Grogger eyed the salamander and licked his lips. She must know it was a trap. She *had* to know it was a trap. But he could see the anger surging through her. He could also hear the growls under her breath as she weighed up her options.

Come on you stupid lizard, he thought and gave her another wave.

Down in the valley, he could hear occasional shouts and the crack of pistols echoing through the hills. There was no time to worry about that now, it was just him and this blasted scaly.

With a gleeful sense of anticipation, he saw the salamander shake her head – perhaps clearing those last thoughts of doubt – and charge up the hill.

"There's no escaping this time," she bellowed.

"We see," replied a grinning Grogger and smashed the rock down on the padlock. It bounced off harmlessly. His smile fell away and was replaced by a look of panic. He brought the rock down again, but nothing happened.

"Whatever trap you had planned doesn't appear to have worked," laughed the salamander. "Time for you to die."

Grogger whined in frustration as he tried again to break the lock. This time, the rock skidded out his claws and tumbled down the hill. He looked at the salamander running toward him and knew this was it. Nowhere else to run. The future goblin king. Dead on a hillside. He just hoped he wouldn't come back to life as a zombie. At least let him rest easy.

The iron gates flew open as the creature inside slammed against them. Grogger was knocked sprawling and cursed as the padlock thumped into the back of head. Shaking the shock away, he quickly scurried out of the way, because he knew what was coming. Inside the mausoleum came a mighty roar, followed by the heavy stomps of something moving.

* * * * *

Furna covered her face, fearing the goblin had let off some sort of explosion, but the roar quickly brought her to her senses. She looked up to the entrance to see the head of a gigantic undead beast emerging from the darkness. Furna felt a sickening lurch in her stomach as she realized just what was heading toward her. In life, it had been a slasher, one of the great monsters forced into combat by the goblins. The large reptile was dragon-like in appearance, without the wings, and it swung a huge spiked tail from side to side as it stumbled out onto the hill. Normally, a slasher was a terrifying sight to behold on the battlefield, but this was something else. Its scaly skin had rotted away in some areas, exposing the skeleton underneath, and its skull was partly showing, which only helped to emphasise the massive fangs lining its powerful jaws. The slasher hungrily snapped its teeth together and focused two unnatural, glowing eyes on Furna. It let out a long, rumbling roar and stomped toward her.

Before turning to escape back down the hill, Furna's blood boiled as she saw the infernal goblin sticking his fingers up.

"Time for scales to dies," he screeched and began clapping.

Furna hissed in response before quickly sheathing her cutlass and starting to run. Behind her, she could hear the clumsy pursuit of the undead slasher as it slipped and slid on the loose dirt. Back down in the valley, the number of zombies had reduced significantly, but the remaining goblins and her crew were still busy dealing with those left.

"We're turning the tide," said Shalesh as she approached.

"We've got bigger problems!" she shouted while splashing through the stream at the bottom of the valley. She quickly punched a zombie that lurched too close as she neared her crew.

"What could possibly be worse than this?" asked a panting Berusk, while decapitating a shambling goblin. A mournful bellow answered Berusk's question.

"*That*," replied Furna.

CHAPTER FIFTEEN

Grogger listened as the slasher stomped down the hill, and he smiled, smugly. He was about to run back to gather up his gang when he sensed something from inside the mausoleum. Almost like someone calling to him. He carefully approached and peered into the dark.

"Hello?" he asked. There was no response.

He waited a moment, just in case his voice had attracted any nearby zombies. No movement came, and he ventured into the mausoleum. The walls were lined with stone carvings of dwarfs, and each had runes underneath that Grogger couldn't understand. Inside, it stunk of rotting meat, and Grogger saw piles of bones, almost as if someone had been feeding the slasher; but his eyes were drawn to the tomb in the center of the room. The stone lid had been removed and was smashed on the floor nearby. Grogger approached cautiously, expecting an undead hand to slowly rise from the tomb at any moment.

Eventually he plucked up enough courage and peered over the top of the open casket. Inside was the skeleton of a dwarf, dressed in intricate golden armor. Upon his head was a large crown, encrusted with precious gems, no doubt mined from the nearby hills. However, the stately appearance of the corpse was spoiled by a crude knife that had been plunged through his head. At least that explained why he wasn't moving, Grogger realized with a sigh of relief.

The dwarf was clutching a sword. It caught the light in unusual ways, and Grogger found himself almost hypnotized by its appearance. Running up the length of the sword were intricate swirls of arcane text that Grogger vaguely recognized as the language of the Abyss. He was puzzled about why a beardy would be holding a blade that belonged to the Abyss, although he had heard that some dwarfs went mad and began worshipping that infernal place.

Without realizing what he was doing, Grogger reached out to grab the blade. He could feel the pressure inside the mausoleum grow as he tightened his claw around the weapon. The patterns on the sword began to glow red, and an intense shooting pain fired up Grogger's arm. He screamed in agony and tried to let go, but his grip grew tighter around the hilt. His eyes rolled up into their sockets, and Grogger began to experience another vision.

A dwarf lord... eyes gleaming red... taking the sword from a hideous demon... the dwarf surrounded by gold and more dwarfs with red eyes... Grogger holding the sword... fighting a dwarf riding a giant brock... Grogger plunging the sword into his chest.

He snapped out of the vision and looked down at the sword. The runes were glowing green and the pain had stopped. Carefully, he pulled the weapon toward him. He was surprised by how light it felt, and he was sure it had shrunk slightly, making it easier for him to wield. He gave a few experimental swings and lunges before nodding in satisfaction. Outside, he heard the roar of the slasher, and he realized he needed to gather up the other goblins.

Leaving the whispers of the mausoleum behind, Grogger scrabbled down the hillside, rocks and pebbles tumbling behind him. He was pleased to see the mist was definitely clearing now and he could see far clearer; and then he noticed with satisfaction that the slasher was shambling straight at the scalies. Meanwhile, the goblins had grouped near Ug and were fending off a small horde of zombies. They looked exhausted. For the first time, Grogger saw that Ug was struggling to swing his giant club. Instead, he was relying on short jabs and punches to keep the undead at bay. Kackle looked the worst. His face was completely drained, fatigued from the amount of spells he had been required to cast. He was leaning against a rock and breathing heavily. He almost looked as bad as some of the undead goblins.

Grogger ran toward them, stopping quickly to stab his new sword into the head of a zombie that got too close. The blade almost seemed to sing as the runes glowed brighter, and then it tore through the monster's rotting eye socket.

"Where have you been?" panted Gritter when Grogger neared them.

"Dealing with our scaly problem," he replied and pointed at the slasher. The roars of the creature had attracted the remaining zombies who were swarming toward the salamanders. The rest of the valley was littered with corpses, now completely devoid of life. Grogger thought this was how it must have looked all those years ago during the original battle.

"Nice dagger, boss," said Klunk. "Where did you find that?"

"None of your business," snapped Grogger. Despite only just finding the weapon, he felt weirdly protective over it. He quickly shoved it into his belt, and the runes stopped glowing. Grogger spotted Magwa eying the sword keenly.

"We need to get out of here while we can. Magwa, lead the way."

The old goblin looked like he was about to protest before changing his mind and giving a short nod.

"This way," he said and pointed with the prod.

Before they disappeared into the mist, Grogger gave one last look at the salamanders and couldn't resist a snort of laughter. The slasher was almost upon them, followed by a stream of zombies. That would be the last time they would see the scalies. He stuck a finger up in their general direction, and with that, he ran to catch up with the others.

* * * * *

"To me! To me!" roared Furna as the slasher closed in. The crew grouped around their leader.

"Shouldn't we just retreat?" asked Rorsha. "This isn't our fight."

"The undead have got our scent now. If we run away, they'll just keep following us, pushing us further back. We need to get through this valley. Weapons ready!"

And with that, the slasher was upon them. Furna ducked a vicious swing from its huge, spiky tail. Pieces of decaying flesh slid off the appendage as it whirled around. Despite its shambling movements, the smell of fresh flesh had driven the undead horror into a battle frenzy. It roared in frustration and swung the tail again, this time spilling zombies everywhere.

Furna quickly loaded one of her pistols and carefully took aim between the slasher's eyes. In the echoing valley, the gun sounded like cannon fire when she pulled the trigger. The bullet flew true but pinged harmlessly off the slasher's thick hide. She sighed and realized that would have been too easy. Instead, she put the pistol away and drew her cutlass.

The slasher was now snapping hungrily at Shalesh and some other members of the crew. They were just about managing to keep it at bay with desperate parries from their obsidian swords. Each time they hit the slasher, chunks of flesh would fall to ground, but the creature carried on undeterred.

Furna's mind raced. She had to do something. The salamanders were already tired, and it would only take a slight lack of concentration for the slasher to find its target. She looked over at the beast and saw that some of its skull was exposed on the top of its head. It was moving around too much for her to shoot it with a pistol, but if she could get on top of it! Furna loaded her pistols and took aim.

The first shot hit the slasher in the snout and it roared with anger.

"Hey! Over here!" she shouted. The creature reared upon her, but it quickly turned back toward Shalesh. Furna grunted and fired again. This time, the bullet hit just below the slasher's eye. Its head snapped around to Furna, and its milky, undead eyes focused straight on her.

"Great. Now I've got its attention," sighed Furna before shouting again. "That's right, you overgrown ghekkotah. Come and get me!"

The slasher bellowed fiercely and charged. Despite its decaying limbs, Furna was surprised by its turn of speed. She rammed the pistols back into their holsters and scanned the surroundings for something that would help execute her plan. To her left she saw a gravestone that was bigger than all the rest. In fact, it was roughly the size of a salamander and was most likely the grave of an important dwarf general that died during the battle. With the slasher closing down the gap between them, Furna sprinted to stand in front of the stone slab.

"Over here! Here I am!"

Furna stood her ground as the slasher charged. She hoped this plan would work. The undead beast picked up speed as it crossed the valley. Again, Furna was surprised by its agility and hoped she was fast enough to get out of the way. As it got closer, her nostrils filled with the slaughterhouse stench of the slasher, and she became woozy. Furna shook her head to clear her mind, just in time to leap out of the way of the thundering beast. It slammed heavily into the gravestone, cracking the ancient monument and sending stone showering everywhere. As Furna had hoped, the impact had temporarily dazed the slasher, giving her the chance she needed. Drawing her cutlass, Furna ran at the monster. She ducked a lazy swing from its tail and leapt onto its back. Perhaps sensing what was about to happen, the slasher began bucking like a wild rhinosaur, but Furna had spent years on the sea. Her legs held firm while she fiercely plunged her weapon into the exposed skull, and she smiled when she heard a satisfying crunch within. The slasher gave a huge convulsive jerk when the cutlass pierced its brain, throwing Furna to the floor. Dazed from the fall, Furna couldn't move quickly enough as the mighty corpse of the slasher fell straight on top of her and the world went black.

* * * * *

Grogger could feel his entire body aching. It felt like they had been moving through the valley for an age. They had started off at a decent pace - keen to put as much space as possible between them and the salamanders - but when they realized no one was following them, they had dropped to a shambling walk. The moon was almost setting, and Grogger wasn't keen on being out in the open. Around them, the mist had cleared completely, allowing Grogger to see the barren scrubland that ran up the hillsides. They hadn't seen more undead since leaving the salamanders, so Grogger thought it was time to get some answers. He caught up with Magwa.

"What the snoz happened back there?"

Magwa gunted in response.

"Was that a little welcome party by your friends?"

"Magwa didn't know about the zombies," he answered, moodily.

"That weird little goblin said something about Grukhar. Who the grog is Grukhar?"

The old goblin shrugged slightly.

"Magwa thought Grukhar would be dead by now."

"You're not answering my questions," snapped Grogger.

"She is the queen of the underminers. Master of the Depths. Tunneller Supreme."

Magwa raised his arms dramatically as he spoke each new title.

"See, I grogging told you they wouldn't want to see you again!" snapped Grogger.

Grogger buried his head into his hands and began groaning.

"But you are the great Grogger, are you not?" hissed Magwa under his breath. "The one that told Magwa what a great king you will be. The one to unite us all." Magwa gave a bark of laughter. "Not everyone will join as quickly as Magwa. You need a test."

Grogger wanted to slap the old snoz, but Jo'os was loping along beside them. Then again, perhaps Magwa was right. If Grogger could get a tribe like the underminers to join him, then how hard could it be to force everyone else?

"You said we were two moons away. How do we find them once we're there?"

Suddenly, Grogger could sense movement all around them. Everywhere he looked, small, pale-skinned goblins were emerging out of hidden holes, armed with crude-looking picks and hammers. They glowered menacingly at Grogger and his small gang.

"Magwa thinks they have found us."

Out of one hole emerged who Grogger assumed must be Grukhar. She was sitting on a rickety wooden seat that was being carried by four other goblins. She gave them a vicious prod with her pick when they almost dropped her, causing her to lose her composure slightly. Grukhar quickly regained her almost regal stature as the chair was carried toward Grogger.

"I am surprised you escaped, old one," she sneered at Magwa. "And you have more allies this time."

"Magwa brings you a king!" he shouted and pointed at Grogger with a flourish. Grogger glanced over to Ug nervously, expecting to see the usual angry stares from the troll, but he was surprised to see Ug was barely paying attention. Gritter and Klunk meanwhile were gazing at him, open-mouthed.

"A king?" laughed Grukhar, raucously, rocking the chair and almost causing the goblins to drop it. She gave them another vicious jab. "I see no king here. Just a scruffy bunch of grogging overworlders that are in my territory. Tie them up!"

Groups of underminers started swarming down the hillsides.

"What do we do, boss?" asked Gritter.

"Nothing... for now," replied Grogger while a pair of underminers roughly started binding his claws together. Jo'os was growling and snapping at anyone that came close.

"Muzzle that monster!" roared Grukhar, almost standing in her chair. "Muzzle it!"

"Control Jo'os," hissed Grogger to Magwa. "Just do what she says, until I come up with a plan."

Magwa began making soothing noises and stroking the mawbeast's bloody snout. He motioned to a pair of nearby underminers to pass him their rope and, almost tenderly, began wrapping it around Jo'os' mouth. The creature's growls turned to whimpering.

"It won't be for long," said Magwa, gently.

"Now, tie the old one up," screeched Grukhar.

"Magwa is too old to cause trouble. Look, Magwa needs a stick to walk." The old goblin motioned toward his magical prod. Grogger admired the wiley goblin; if he could keep the prod, then escaping would be easy. His admiration was quickly shattered by the peels of high-pitched laughter from Grukhar.

"Do you think we're a bunch of goblings, *Magwa*? Oh, we know who you are now. We know all about your great beast and magical staff. We know about the *legendary* Magwa! Grab his prod and tie him up like the rest. What sort of stupid snoz would fall for a trick like that?"

A nearby underminer tried to snatch the prod, but a short blast of energy sent it flying backward. The underminers roared with squealing laughter. Then, they laughed even more when the unfortunate victim began writhing around in dirt while electricity raged across its skin. After a few moments, its skin began to blister and burn. Eventually it stopped moving.

"Stop messing around!" screamed Grukhar. "Magwa, throw the prod on the floor."

Reluctantly, Magwa carefully placed the prod down. A pair of underminers wearing thick gloves gingerly approached the magical artifact. They snapped and bickered about who was going to try and pick it up first.

"Just grab it!" shouted a frustrated Grukhar. "The prod *might* kill you but I *definitely* will."

The arguing underminers looked at each other and slowly reached out. One closed its eyes as it finally clutched a glove around the prod. However, this time there were no blasts of energy. The pair held the weapon aloft and the gathered underminers let out a ragged cheer.

"I always hoped you would come back one day, Magwa," sneered Grukhar as her minions approached with the prod. She recoiled in horror when they shoved it toward her, batting them away with her pick. "I don't grogging want it! Carry it back underground and bring them too."

Grukhar gave her transporters another vicious whack, and they slowly turned around, barely managing to keep the rickety throne straight.

A particularly thin and weedy-looking underminer smirked at Grogger and tugged the ropes tied around his wrists.

"Time to go home," he squeaked and dragged Grogger down a rough tunnel carved into the hillside. Once they were all inside, a large boulder was rolled over the entrance, and they were quickly plunged into darkness. Even for Grogger, the inky blackness made it difficult for him to see. He could just about make out the goblins surrounding him, along with Ug's lumbering shape, but the rest disappeared into black. The underminers, on the other hand, seemingly had no difficulty seeing and were chatting merrily about their new captives.

"Reckon we'll eat 'em?" came one reedy voice.

"Lot o' meat on that troll," answered another, and Grogger heard the smack of lips.

Ahead of him, Grogger heard someone stumble and hit the ground heavily. The line stopped while a few vicious kicks were delivered to the unfortunate individual.

"It's the wiz. I think he's dead," came a shout. Grogger strained his eyes to see what was happening. He heard a few more kicks, followed by some mumbling. Suddenly, a fireball roared from Kackle's outstretched claws and incinerated an underminer that was about to deliver another wicked kick. In the dancing light of the burning goblin, Grogger saw the tunnel ahead delved ever deep into the hillside. Either side of him, thick pillars held up the roof of the passage, disappearing into the distance. From his brief glimpse, there were no side tunnels, just a straight path down. He risked a desperate look behind, but his heart sank when he saw there was no way out behind them. The only way was down.

Grogger heard more mumbling and saw a small nimbus of light growing around Kackle's claws again. He was amazed the wiz could still conjure any magic after the fight with the zombies.

"He's casting another spell!" came a panicked scream. Some of the other underminers started legging it down the tunnel.

"Knock him out! Knock him out you useless bunch of snozzers," came an irate cry from Grukhar. An underminer - clearly keen to earn the respect of his leader - ran forward and bashed Kackle over the head with the handle of a hammer. Kackle went limp, and the growing light around him immediately flickered out and plunged them back into complete darkness once more.

"Any more funny business," echoed Grukhar's voice from up ahead, "and I'll just kill the wiz right now. I mean it!" Her voice rose to a high-pitched screech.

"No more funny business," replied Grogger and let himself be dragged further into the cavernous tunnel. His normally cunning mind raced as he pondered how they could escape. But with each step, he felt their situation become more desperate. This wasn't how it was meant to be, he thought, and spat on the floor.

CHAPTER SIXTEEN

Furna grinned as the wind whipped around and the salt water splashed onto her scales. The cold water evaporated with a sharp hiss each time it hit. Above, a small number of scorchwings circled, occasionally swooping down to catch unwanted fish thrown over the side of the ship by ghekkotah pulling in small fishing nets. Their almost tuneful cries moved up and down in time to waves.

Ahead was nothing but the open sea, her favorite place to be in the world. She gazed at the blue horizon, contemplating the clawful of adventures she had already had and the adventures she would no doubt have in the future. Her attention was caught by something in the distance. A large object was bobbing along the ocean on their portside. She squinted against the bright sunshine, but the thing refused to come clearly into view.

"Captain!" she cried. "Captain!" She didn't want to panic, but something about the sight sent a chill running up and down her tail. For the first time, she noticed she could no longer hear the scorchwings, either. She looked to the skies and saw they had scattered. Nervously, she returned her attention to the portside.

A mighty claw clapped her on the shoulder, and Furna was relieved to see it was Captain Trusk. The mighty tyrant, a species of reptile that grew to almost the size of an ogre, towered above her, and she could feel the bristling power underneath his grip. Trusk was unusual for his kind. Although some tyrants would join the crew of the ship, not many took on the role of captain, instead preferring to work below decks or get stuck in during the horrifically brutal boarding actions.

Trusk shot her a winning smile, revealing a mouth full of golden fangs. Long ago, Trusk had decided the best place to keep his gold was inside his prodigious jaws. What had started as a few teeth was a now glittering display of precious metal.

"You called, little Furna?" She almost felt stupid now. The object was probably nothing. But she still couldn't shake the cold shiver creeping up her scales.

"There's something out there," she whispered, still feeling awkward.

"Speak up, girl. I've been too close to too many cannon to put up with whispers," bellowed the captain. Furna coughed and pointed out to sea.

"There's something on the horizon."

Trusk followed her claw and squinted.

"You've got better eyes than me," he chuckled and reached into his belt before quickly producing a battered telescope. He held it up to his left eye, pressing it hard against a thick, vicious-looking scar that zig-zagged down his face. Trusk gave a grunt. "Have a look for yourself."

He thrust the telescope in her claw, and she nervously peered through it. It took her a moment to find the object, but eventually it came into view. She was greeted by the sight of a broken-looking frigate, heavily listing in the water. No sails were raised and the ship, if she could call it that, appeared to be made from random scraps of wood nailed together. She could only see it from the rear, but it was like nothing she had ever seen.

"Ship on the portside," roared Trusk. "Full speed ahead!"

Cries of 'aye, aye, Captain' and sharp whistles echoed down the deck, and Furna heard the sails whipping as they caught the wind.

"Let's take a closer look, shall we? About time I got another tooth."

"Captain, are you sure? There's something not right with... whatever that is."

"Furna, you ain't been at sea long, but eventually you'll learn a sailor's instincts. And my instincts are telling me there's something good on that ship. You'll see."

"But, Captain..."

"No buts," he snarled, almost viciously, before correcting himself. Then more gently, he added: "Look, if you're worried, keep the telescope and let me know if there are any problems. You're our little good luck charm, so I'm sure you'll spot any danger."

Furna nodded, annoyed that she had troubled the captain and worried he would think she was too nervous for a life at sea. Trusk gave her a wink and strode off to grab the ship's wheel.

"I said full speed!" he boomed. "I've seen ghekkotah eggs hatch faster than this thing. Get a move on."

Gripping the telescope tightly, she trained it back toward the ship. Was it her imagination, or was it beginning to turn toward them? Now she could start to see along its side more clearly. The construction was so ramshackle, she assumed it must have been damaged in a previous attack. Perhaps the crew had attempted to patch it up before giving up and leaving the hulk stranded somewhere. It had probably been drifting on the currents for months, if not years. Even as she watched, a few pieces of moldy-looking wood fell into the waves.

She trained the telescope on the deck. A flash of movement caught her eye but was gone in an instant. Furna sighed and pulled the telescope away from her eye.

"Get a grip," she growled to herself. "Now you're imagining things."

Without the distraction of the telescope, she caught a strange sound being carried over the waves. It was a sort of rhythmic banging that was slowly picking up speed. She tilted her head, keen to see if it was coming from below decks. Furna turned back toward the captain and wondered whether she should mention the noise. But he was too busy laughing with the first mate and talking about which tooth he would get replaced next.

Once again, she turned her attention back to the ship. Now there was no doubting it, the ship was slowly but inexorably turning toward them.

A few cannons peeped out from gunports along the starboard, and Furna was convinced she could see lights flickering through tiny windows. But surely nothing could be aboard the wreck? She was amazed it hadn't already sunk below the depths. The banging noise was definitely getting louder and faster, she was sure of it. Furna looked around at the other members of the crew, but none appeared to have noticed, or they were too busy tackling the sails.

Suddenly, black sails unfurled from the masts of the mystery ship and billowed outward as the wind caught behind them. Now there was no mistaking the vessel was turning toward them. Furna heard shouts from the captain, telling them to prepare to fire. The vessel was one of the strangest she had seen. The bow of the ship ended in a large, metallic point that rose above the water. Furna couldn't understand the design, as its height wouldn't help it to cut through the waves any faster. Then her stomach leapt with horror as she realized the true nature of the mechanism. It was a drill!

The clanking and banging noises she had heard reached a crescendo, and the metallic point started to spin. With each rotation it gained speed, going faster and faster until it almost seemed to be pulling the ship behind it. The whirring nose crashed through the waves, scattering spray with each terrible turn.

"Evasive action!" hollered Trusk. The ghekkotah and corsairs of the crew desperately heaved at ropes to try and change their course, but it was too late. After moving to meet the seemingly stranded ship, the wind was no longer in their favor, and now the horrendous ship was powering straight at them, its own sails billowing with a strong wind behind them.

It was close enough now that Furna could see orcs flooding the deck, armed with wicked-looking axes. They screamed and shouted in their filthy tongue, and Furna was glad she couldn't understand their cruel language. Small goblins scampered up the ratlines, desperately trying to repair damaged parts of the sails, which flapped loosely in the wind. Occasionally they would lose their grip and fall into the sea, or crash onto the deck below. Each time this happened, it was met by vicious whoops of joy from the orcs and their fellow goblins scurrying among the ropes.

Furna's ship was painfully turning away from their pursuer, but it wasn't enough. The deafening roar of the mighty drill drowned out the shouts of both crews, and it slammed into the hull, almost knocking Furna into the sea. It tore through the wood, hurling huge chunks into the sky before they splashed down into the waves below. Some flew past Furna, crushing her fellow crewmates that were rushing onto the deck. She ducked when another piece hurtled over her head and knocked a ghekkotah screaming over the portside. The churning drill continued its terrible journey, pulling the two ships closer and closer together until, all of a sudden, it stopped.

Everything grew quiet, apart from the moans of the crew that had been hit by stray pieces of wood and the lapping of the waves against the side of the ship. Then the orcs began to chant. It was a low, guttural grunt that started quietly and grew to a roar that was almost as loud as the drill. Furna had never faced anything like it. She was stupefied by fear and nearly didn't notice the huge wooden plank slamming down onto the deck. Somehow, she managed to roll out the way before almost being knocked overboard by the primitive construction.

"To arms! To arms!" shouted Captain Trusk, and Furna's world turned to madness. Sailors from down below began running onto the deck, rapiers and cutlasses at the ready. She heard the crack of pistols and spotted a few orcs that were stepping onto the boarding plank fall into the crisp, ocean waves as the shots hit home. Overhead, she spotted the goblins firing over small grappling hooks that ripped through the masts before being dragged back to catch on the ruined material. As soon as they were secure, shrieking greenskins started sliding down the ropes, ready to hack at the sails to stop any chance of escape.

"Furna! Furna!" over the chaos, she thought she could just hear the captain calling her name.

* * * * *

"Furna!" With a start, she opened her eyes, looking around her surroundings in a blind panic. A familiar shape loomed over her.

"Trusk?"

"Trusk? Haven't heard that old sea lizard's name in a long time." Through the daze, she recognized Berusk's voice. "What's got you thinking about Gold Fang?"

Furna realized she was lying on a makeshift cot of hay. She tried to sit up, but the world began spinning wildly. With a groan, she laid back down.

"Must have been a dream... or more accurately a nightmare."

"Ah, the blood runner?" asked Berusk, softly.

"The blood runner."

"I always forget you were there," he replied. "You can't have been at sea too long then. Wet behind the scales."

"Eight months," she said, before a shooting pain in her head stopped her short. She closed her eyes again.

"You were shouting in your sleep."

"Nothing too embarrassing, I hope." She smiled, weakly, but her eyes remained closed.

"Just the usual. Saying I'm a better sailor and that I should have been captain," chucked Berusk.

"You're only saying that because I can't hit you."

Furna grunted and struggled to sit up. Berusk reached over and, almost gently, eased her into a sitting position. With a sigh, she slowly opened her eyes. Weak beams of sunlight cut through a poorly thatched roof, but it was enough to cause her to wince with discomfort. Her cot was on the floor of a small storage room. Bags of grain were piled up to one side, and a mouse carefully picked its way through the stores, nibbling occasionally at a small morsel. Berusk was sitting next to her, using a bag of grain as a seat.

"Thought we'd lost you," he said.

"The slasher!" Furna shouted, as if only just remembering the terrible beast. She fought feebly to lift herself.

"Long gone," replied Berusk as he placed a claw delicately on her chest. Furna relaxed a little.

"What happened?"

"You decided it was a good idea to surf it," he laughed. "But it did the trick. You killed that stinking beast, then it fell on top of you. Knocked you out cold. You've been like this for three days. We went looking for help and stumbled across this place."

"And the crew?" A nervous look flashed across her face, and her tail lashed against the ground.

"We all made it. Must have fought a hundred damned undead, but we didn't lose anyone. A lot of bruises and scratches, but we're all present and correct. I made sure we left no one behind. We've lost too many as it is."

"Thank you," replied Furna, and she clutched his claw. "What about the goblins?"

"Ah, that's not such good news. Rorsha followed the tracks, but he said it was almost like they disappeared into the rocks. Reckoned they'd vanished."

"Vanished?" Furna paused and hoped too much dragon's scale brew wasn't playing tricks on his mind.

"There may be an answer to that though. Come with me." Berusk stood up, slowly. Furna could hear the creaking of his joints, and she wondered just how long he had been sitting by her side. He offered her a claw. After momentarily trying to pull herself up, she swallowed her pride and grabbed it, gladly. Berusk grunted slightly as he heaved her onto her feet. For the first time, she noticed how filthy her clothes were, covered in dark bloodstains. She smiled slightly as she thought how Trusk wouldn't have even let her on the deck in this state. Now she was expected to lead her own crew looking like she had just gone ten rounds with an ogre. Carefully, she picked up her pistols and cutlass, and very gingerly managed to tie them around. Each small movement sent shooting pains up and down her body.

Slowly but surely, she shuffled away from her cot, and Berusk opened a battered-looking wooden door, spilling light into the room. Furna turned away slightly as her senses screamed in agony. But, not wanting to seem weak to whatever was waiting on the other side, she gritted her teeth and slammed her tail against the floor, kicking up a cloud of dust. Out the corner of her eye, she saw the mouse dart back into the safety of the grain bags.

"Let's go," she huffed to Berusk and prepared to march out the door, head held high.

"Captain, are you forgetting something?"

Furna was holding her tricorn hat. It looked battered, most likely after the incident with the slasher. She dusted it off slightly and placed it, gently, on her head before striding outside.

The remaining crew members were lounging around on the grass. Some were playing dice, others were picking at portions of their meager supplies, and many were clearly nursing some nasty wounds. At the sight of Furna, they immediately leapt to attention and saluted.

"Captain," they chorused, cheerfully.

"At ease, at ease," she said, trying to smile and hide the agonizing spasms coursing through her body. "Stay with me," she whispered to Berusk, who gave a small nod in reply.

Furna went to each and every crew member to make sure they were okay. She could see the tiredness in their eyes, but they all put on a brave face, saying their wounds were just scratches or that they would be home soon. It tore at Furna's heart. Finally, she came to Rorsha, and for a moment, he just stared at her.

"I thought Kthorlaq may have taken you," he said, flatly.

"I bet you've been trying on my captain's hat!"

"Not my color." Rorsha smiled wickedly. "Good to have you back though, Captain."

"And even better to be back... I think." She winced slightly at another shooting pain. "Now, where in the Three Kings are we?"

For the first time since leaving the storeroom, she looked around properly. Ahead were a small number of round brown buildings, each with a thatched roof that rose to a small point. A trail of white smoke emerged from the top of one, while the others appeared to be abandoned and some had doors that hung off the hinges. Surrounding them were fields as far as the eye could see, however only one appeared to have any crops growing in it, and even those appeared unusually small. Many of the other fields were covered in the remnants of rotting plants. A decent-sized barn loomed over the smaller buildings, and Furna heard the braying of animals inside. Simple farm equipment and a rickety-looking cart leaned against the dark brown wood of the barn.

"Nice place," she said to Berusk with a smirk.

"Be nice," he replied. "Humans aren't often this friendly."

"Humans?"

Furna shot him a concerned look, but before Berusk could answer, a thin, stern-looking man emerged from one of the buildings. He wore peasant's clothes but had the unmistakable posture and stride of a soldier. A thick, black beard covered his gaunt face, which only helped his bright eyes look even keener. Furna was never sure how to age a human but, judging by the deep wrinkles that crossed his brow, she guessed he was getting on in years. Drawing himself up, he marched over to Furna and her crew. Despite his age, she was surprised that he strode over to them with a powerful grace. She was even more surprised when he stopped and saluted.

"I guess you must be the captain?" He said in clipped tones.

"Yes, sir," she eyed him carefully. He had the unmistakable bearing of a military man, despite the ragged appearance. She also assumed he had once held a rank, judging by his tone. "And I guess you were once a captain too?"

"Captain of the Basilean 4th Battalion at Arms. Although it seems like a lifetime ago."

"Takes a captain to know one," she held out a claw for a handshake. It was a human custom she never quite understood, but it seemed to be the convention in these situations.

"Indeed, ma'am," he replied and thrust his hand into hers before pounding it with a powerful motion. "Rowan Bossesus, at your service, Captain."

"Please, just Furna," she said with a smile. "Only the crew have to call me captain. And I assume I must have you to thank for taking care of this motley lot while I was... *resting*."

"I didn't lift a finger," he laughed. "It was all my wife, Mary. If it was up to me, I would have told you all to sod off. Soldiers don't mix with bloody sailors." Furna saw the amused glint in his eye and she grinned. They had only exchanged a few words but, unusually for a human, she already liked Rowan.

"I better tell the wife you're awake. She's been worried sick about you. Mary! Mary!"

From behind one of the buildings, Furna heard a bucket being dropped and a string of curses. Then, who Furna assumed must be Mary, stomped around the corner. She was much smaller than Rowan, with a coarse mane of blonde, unruly hair. Her thin face must have one been very beautiful and still contained a certain grace that even Furna could admire. Large green eyes, which must normally have been pretty, were squinted in a scowl, and her full lips were set into a furious grimace. Mary's simple apron was splashed with what Furna took to be milk.

"Row, you bloody idiot. I split the bloody milk, you daft sod. I just washed-"

"The captain's *awake*, Mary."

With that, it was like a spell had been severed. Mary's face broke into a grin and her eyes lit up. She raced over to Furna and eagerly began shaking her claw. Her small hands were dwarfed by Furna's powerful talons.

"Pardon my Ophidian, we don't often have guests. And my husband only understands soldier talk." She shot him an angry look.

"I believe I need to thank you for caring for my crew."

"Oh, it's no trouble. No trouble at all!" Furna noticed that Mary was staring at her intently. "I've never met salamanders until now, you know. I mean, I met a ghekkotoe in the court of the Golden Horn once, but that's not the same, is it?"

"Ghekko*tah*," corrected Berusk.

"Oh, pardon me. Ghekko*tah*, of course. I've been in the bloomin' country too long, thanks to *him*. Lost all my air and graces, then replaced it with bloomin' crop names and harvest schedules."

Furna laughed at the pair. Strangely, she hadn't felt this good in months, as she did now watching the couple bicker.

"And you, Rowan, have you met our kind before?"

"Yes," he said, somewhat crisply. "Fought alongside some of your lot at the Battle of Carn's Bridge." A distant look entered his eyes.

"Carn's Bridge? My clutchmate fought there. Third Legion Kthorlaq's Chosen," Berusk chipped in, eagerly. "He said you almost held the bridge, despite the odds. Told me he never saw men fight so bravely against the Abyssals."

Rowan inhaled deeply, and Mary touched his arm delicately.

"A generous compliment."

"I didn't mean any disrespect-"

"None taken. I still think we *could* have secured the bridge. If only they had let me send-"

"Now, now, Rowan. The captain has just woken up. She doesn't want to hear your war stories. You'll send her straight back to sleep again." Despite the jest, she smiled warmly at her husband, and he nodded slowly.

"Once I get going," he sighed and rolled his eyes while Mary patted his arm.

"Berusk tells me we've been here for three days causing you trouble," said Furna. "Unfortunately we don't have much, as you may have heard, but if there's any way we can help to say thank you."

Rowan and Mary exchanged glances.

"Actually, we may be able to help each other," said Mary, cryptically. "But look, you must be famished. Come inside the house and you can have something to eat and we can talk a little bit more."

"Please, don't make a fuss. I'm happy to stay out here with the crew."

"I *insist*," stated Mary in a way that quickly stopped any further debate. Furna turned to Berusk and shrugged before Mary grabbed her claw and almost dragged her inside the house. Despite the simple appearance outside, the home was homely and warm inside. The single room was bigger than her private quarters on the old ship, with a small wood burner in the center, a rustic dining table and chairs. A small kitchen was tucked against a wall, and Furna could smell something delicious bubbling away in a large pot on a decent-sized stove. Opposite the kitchen was a comfy-looking bed that took up an overly large portion of the available space. Mary noticed Furna looking at the bed.

"There were some comforts I wasn't willing to give up when we left Basilea," she said with an awkward smile.

Above the bed, the Basilean crest hung on the wall, and Furna noticed an old, but remarkably well-polished sword and shield leaning against a small set of drawers.

"Would you like a drink? Tea, perhaps?"

Rowan let out a small laugh.

"She's a sailor, Mary. We'll need to crack out something stronger." He walked over to the drawers and pulled out a bottle of rum. He blew the dust off and popped open the cork.

"I was given this by my brother, after he joined the Basilean Navy. Told me it was strong enough to drop an orc."

Rowan grabbed a couple of slightly dirty glasses and poured himself and Furna a generous slug of bronze liquid. He gave it a sniff and coughed slightly.

"Think even my blood might turn to fire after this!" he knocked it back and poured himself another.

"Please, take a seat," said Mary and pointed Furna to one of the available chairs.

"Honestly, there's really no need to make a fuss." Furna sat down and removed her hat as a mark of respect.

"I won't hear another thing about it," replied Mary. "Now, let's get you something to eat!"

She bustled over to the stove and filled a bowl with a hearty-looking stew before passing it to Furna. Grabbing a spoon, Furna quickly gulped it down, and before she knew it, the bowl was empty.

"Guess I was hungrier than I thought!" she said with a smile. Using her long snake-like tongue, she licked the remnants from her scaly lips, failing to acknowledge the surprised looks from both Rowan and Mary. "Now, I'll try that rum!"

Furna knocked back the rum. She felt the warming liquid trickle down her throat. It wasn't quite the same as the dragon's scale brew, but it certainly helped to restore some of her lost warmth. Rowan quickly poured her another and made sure he filled the glass to the brim.

Finally, Mary sat down opposite Furna. She glanced at her husband nervously before speaking.

"Berusk explained you've been having some problems with goblins," she stated. Rowan grunted slightly.

"They're a damn plague," he snorted. He looked like he was about to continue before Mary shot him a glance.

"That's right. We've been tracking a small group of goblins for a while now. We captured one of their wizards and were planning to sell it for... erm... research at one of the colleges of magic. They pay a lot for live subjects to study. But some of its little stinking pals came and rescued it. We need the money for a new ship, you see."

"Sounds like you've gone through a lot. Couldn't you have found another way to raise the funds?" asked Mary.

"It's become… *personal*. Some of my crew have died while pursuing the greenskins." Mary nodded and gave Furna a sympathetic smile.

"Hard to let go when you've lost people," added Rowan. A distant look briefly crossed his face.

"Berusk mentioned the tracks disappeared into the mountains?"

"Yes. It was almost like they vanished," answered Furna. "Guess if they've gone, we're back to square one. Assume you don't need any help on the farm?"

She tried to smile at her joke, but the truth was far more painful. They had lost the goblins and their chance of returning home soon. A shiver shot up her tail as she thought of more months spent away from the Three Kings. She doubted Berusk and some of the other older members of the crew would make it home. Furna just wanted to break down and cry. She had failed as a captain, and her crew would suffer as a result. She considered heading to the ports to try and find some other salamander corsairs that might be heading home, but the chances were thin, plus it would take an age to reach them.

She didn't fancy spending too much time in the big cities, either. Lord Darvled, a powerful human in the Successor Kingdoms, had been gaining more power over recent years. He made no secret of his hatred for the other races of Pannithor and was championing the Lands of Men as the true rules of Pannithor. Although he was initially dismissed as small-minded, each incursion by marauding orcs or attacks from the demonic Forces of the Abyss ensured his voice grew louder and his opinions less obnoxious. And now that sentiment was being picked up by plenty of others too. She just knew that spending too much time in somewhere like Stirlmarket or Slateport would lead to tensions between the humans and her crew.

Suddenly, Mary reached over and gently placed her hand over Furna's claw.

"It can't have been easy for you," she said warmly, "but all might not be lost. And we might be able to help each other."

"How?" asked Furna. She realized she must have been unable to hide the desperation in her voice.

Rowan poured himself another drink and knocked it back.

"We know where your damn goblins have gone," he said gruffly. "Since we moved here, the bastards have been terrorizing us. Why do you think all the other houses are empty? They all up and left. We came here with other former soldiers from my battalion but, eventually, they couldn't stomach it. It has been anything but the peaceful life we expected. As soon as the crops were ready to harvest, the goblins would descend on us like damn locusts. Stripped the fields bare and then took off back into the mountains."

"Surely you fought back?" asked Furna.

"Oh, we tried! But for every single goblin we killed, another ten seemed to take its place. We wrote to the local lord for help and asked if he could send troops, but he didn't care. Out here, people are left to fend for themselves. Now we just lock ourselves and the livestock away at night. Hoping the goblins don't come."

"Couldn't you build defenses?"

"That all costs money, and we've hardly had enough crops to feed ourselves, nevermind take it to market." Rowan thumped the table angrily. "It wasn't meant to be like this! No wonder the damn lord sold us the land so cheaply."

"I hate to ask... but why don't you move back to Basilea?" asked Furna and noticed Rowan's nostrils flare.

"This is meant to be our *home*," replied Mary before her husband could say anything. "All that's left for us back in Basilea is bad memories for Rowan. We wanted a fresh start. At first, we were happy to fight for it, but you can only fight for so long."

Furna looked at Rowan and Mary, and she realized how tired they both looked. Dark bags clung to their eyes, and Mary's hands trembled slightly. Furna wasn't sure what it was, but she felt determined to help the couple. If they couldn't get home, perhaps this could be the crew's final good deed before their fires died.

"How can we help?" she asked. Furna saw a flash of hope on Mary's face.

"This time, we'll take the fight to them!" said Rowan sternly. "I found an entrance to their damned caves."

"You want to go *into* the caves?" Furna was starting to regret her potentially hasty offer of help.

"If we go in during the day, they'll all be sleeping. They won't see us coming. We get in. Find your wizard goblin. Kill the leader and get out. Without the leader, we'll have some time to rebuild while they squabble among themselves to find a new one. The current one's a nasty piece of work, and I doubt they'll find anyone as bad."

"Even with my crew, I'm not sure there are enough of us."

"There's a village not too far from here. They're just as sick of being victims of the goblins as we are. I'm sure they'll have men willing to fight."

"Willing to fight alongside salamanders?"

"Willing to fight alongside anyone if it gets rid of the damned goblins. Even if they believe Darvled's nonsense, you're the lesser of two evils."

Furna rubbed a claw against her scaly chin. This was madness. Perhaps going to a port wouldn't take that long? One of the busier trade hubs was bound to have corsairs? Suddenly, Mary grabbed both her claws and gave her a pleading look, stopping Furna in her thoughts.

"Please! We're desperate. You're our last chance. After this... after this... I don't know." Mary's voice trailed off into a whisper.

Furna had never seen such desperation and something echoed

with her own, seemingly lost, situation.

"What's the plan?" she asked and hoped this wouldn't be another decision she would regret.

CHAPTER SEVENTEEN

The goblins had been dragged deeper and deeper into the tunnels until eventually they arrived in a central hall. It was like nothing Grogger had ever seen. The awe-inspiring space was lit by gigantic glowing stalactites that hung from the ceiling, which finally allowed Grogger to see what was around him. However, he didn't have long to take it all in before he was rudely shoved into a small, rusty cage. The door was slammed shut and locked by a giggling underminer.

"What's the plan, boss?" whispered Gritter to Grogger through the bars of his neighboring cage. For once, Grogger wasn't really sure what to say. Alongside him, the other goblins were being forced into other cages that lined the wall of the massive cave. Even Ug was squeezed into a cell toward the end of the row. Grogger spotted Kackle's unconscious body being lobbed unceremoniously into his prison. Looking around his small cage, Grogger grimaced in disgust when he noticed the floor was covered in thick, dark blood. It was fresh too, which meant the last prisoner must have been recently killed. His mind raced while he considered how they were going to get out of this situation.

Around them, some underminers were unenthusiastically tucking into a sloppy sort of white mush. Grogger was reminded of the time he saw Ug sneeze. They were scooping it from bowls made from hollowed skulls and slowly putting it into their mouths. Even from this distance, Grogger could smell the vomit-like stench wafting from the makeshift bowls. With each mouthful, the large eyes of the underminers bulged even further, and many quickly rammed a claw against their mouth to stop them immediately throwing it back up. Once finished, the goblins clutched their scrawny bellies as it looked like terrible cramps bent their bodies in two.

"Worm gut stew," said Magwa.

"Is that how she plans to kill us?" replied Grogger, trying to cover his nose from the awful stink creeping from the food.

Grogger was disturbed by a loud clanging noise at the end of the row of cages. He pressed his head to the bars to see what was happening. Grukhar was walking toward him while banging her pick on the cages. The sound reverberated around the cavernous space. Eventually she stopped at Grogger's cage and banged her pick dangerously close to his nose. He quickly leapt backward to avoid the blow but slipped on the blood and whacked his head on the rear bars. Grukhar responded with a cruel shriek of laughter.

"The king has fallen!" she roared and laughed again. When none of the other underminers laughed, she turned on them viciously. "I said, the king has fallen! Look, he has actually fallen over."

This time, her subjects responded with raucous laughter. Grogger saw a few rolling around in the dirt and holding their sides as they guffawed loudly. Even the ones forcing the worm guts down their throat stopped for a moment to join in with feeble giggles before going back to throwing up, noisily. Grukhar nodded in satisfaction. Even Bung wasn't this bad, thought Grogger.

"How come I never heard of you if you're a king then?" she asked and poked her pick through the bars. Grogger didn't respond.

"There ain't no kings under here, only queens," shrieked Grukhar. "So when your queen asks you a question, you grogging respond!"

"Yeah, you grogging respond," echoed a couple of thin goblins behind her. Grukhar wheeled round to stare at them.

"No one asked you, snozzers!" She raised her pick as though she were about to strike them.

"He's not a king yet," came a weak voice from another cage. Grogger realized it was Kackle.

"I thought I said to gag the wiz?" Grukhar's eyes were wide with fear. After Kackle's brief display of magic in the tunnels, Grukhar was clearly scared of what else he might be capable of.

"You said to knock him out," answered a nearby underminer, helpfully. This time, Grukhar did unleash her anger on the hapless goblin. She leapt on her victim before raining down blows with her pick. Eventually the goblin went limp and Grukhar stood back up, straightening her crown. A couple of underminers quickly dropped their bowls of worm gut stew and eagerly dragged the body away. Grogger caught them talking about whether they should cook the corpse.

"Yeah, you're right," said Grukhar. "I did say to knock him out, but I meant gag him too. Makes sense, right?"

The gathered underminers nodded in agreement while Grukhar strode over to Kackle. The wiz was still down in his cage, and his already dirty robes were now caked in filth. Grukhar bent down so she was close to his head.

"Look up there," she whispered, but still loud enough for Grogger to hear. "I've got a load of spitters ready to stick you full of arrows the moment you start muttering any spells."

Kackle managed to turn his head.

"Understood," he groaned.

"Now, tell me why he ain't a king *yet*."

"He has visions. Magical visions. They showed he's going to unite the clans."

Grukhar burst out laughing, followed by roars of nervous laughter from her followers.

"Unite the clans? I've got more chance of turning into a dragon!" She smiled with pleasure at her own joke. Some underminers clapped when she turned to look at them. Several backed away, as though they were scared she was about to turn into a dragon.

"Magwa can feel it too," came the old goblin's voice. "There is something special about this one."

Grogger was shocked to hear Magwa talking like this. There was a tone of respect in his creaking voice. Did they really believe he was going to be king, or were they just doing it to annoy Grukhar?

"What they on about, boss?" hissed Gritter. Grukhar hammered on the cages with her pick.

"Quiet, the lot of you! So you expect me to believe a mad old snozzer and a wiz that's probably crazy too?" She marched over to Grogger's cage and stared at him with wild, black eyes. Grogger held her gaze, determined not to show any weakness.

"How many beardies you killed then, king?" She ran her claw through the various gruesome trophies around her belt. "Each of these is a beardy lord or whatever they call themselves that I've killed with my own claws. Don't know how many other beardies and humans I've killed. Even found the odd ratty sniffing about and killed them too. That's what a queen does. Kills stuff. Lots of stuff. So, how much stuff you killed, *king*?"

Grogger held her gaze, cooly.

"It doesn't matter how much *stuff* I've killed before. The most important thing is who I'm going to kill next," he replied, slightly surprised at how calm he sounded.

"And who's that?" Grukhar narrowed her eyes.

"You," he growled.

Grukhar howled in anger and tried to grab Grogger through the bars of his cage. He casually leaned out the way as she scrabbled desperately to get him in her clutches.

"He even sounds like a king now!" said Magwa, shrieking with laughter. His high-pitched hysterics were joined by the muzzled grunts of Jo'os. Grogger thought he even caught the low rumbling of Ug laughing.

"Shut up! Shut up!" screamed Grukhar and stomped her foot. Magwa carried on laughing. "Shut up or I'll just shoot the wiz."

The cavern fell into an uneasy silence. An underminer nervously tiptoed up to Grukhar.

"Your majesty, perhaps we should just kill them now anyway?"

Grukhar began trembling with rage. The scalped beards wobbled on her belt. The underminer quickly melted back into the crowd, despite a few attempts by others to push it back to Grukhar.

"We're not going to kill them now," she answered quietly. "We're going to have a little bit of *fun* with the king and his loyal subjects."

She turned to the gathered crowd.

"Open the pit!" she screeched and was greeted by rapturous applause. Immediately the cavern broke out into cries of: "Pit! Pit! Pit!"

"What the snoz is the pit?" hissed Gritter.

"I doubt it's good news," sighed Grogger.

Toward the center of the cavern, at the foot of the mound leading to Grukhar's throne, the crowd parted to reveal a slight depression in the cave floor, which the underminers enthusiastically gathered around. Grukhar quickly skipped up the steps to her throne. There was an unhinged grin on her face that grew as she neared the top. Once seated, she eagerly pulled a large lever. Grogger felt the floor shake slightly as the depression began to split apart, revealing a gloomy-looking hole. The charnel stench that rose from the chasm was overpowering, forcing Gritter and Klunk to each hold their nose, although the underminers didn't seem to notice.

"Bring our guests closer!" shouted Grukhar. For the first time, Grogger realized there were rusty wheels on the bottom of each cage. Underminers quickly grouped round the cages and began pushing or pulling them to the edge of the pit. Jo'os threw himself wildly against the side of the cell, while Ug reached out with his mighty hands to crack the skulls of a few underminers. It wasn't enough though. Slowly, but surely, they edged closer to the pit. Just when Grogger thought they were about to be thrown in, the underminers stopped and disappeared back into the crowd. The cages of Grogger's gang teetered dangerously on the edge.

Grogger strained his eyes to see what was in the pit, but all he could see were bones. Bones, he noticed, that were mainly goblin-sized. Grukhar thrust her pick into the air and the crowd fell into pregnant silence.

"Great *king*!" she smiled at her own joke. "Your subjects have gathered to watch a special test of strength that I hope will entertain and please your majesty."

There were forced titters of amusement from the underminers.

"But which of your subjects would you like to see die first?"

Grogger pondered the question. He certainly didn't fancy facing whatever was in the pit. At least not until he knew what it was. He momentarily considered throwing Gritter into the pit, but the goblin appeared to have changed his tune since previously saying Ug should kill him. Magwa and Kackle probably wouldn't even survive the steep fall into the pit, and Klunk was useless without his bombs. That left Jo'os and Ug. Even though the mawbeast was the biggest and most vicious he had ever seen, he couldn't be sure it would survive with the makeshift muzzle around its neck.

"I'm waiting! Give me an answer, or you'll be heading into the pit!"

"Throw the troll in," answered Grogger, and Ug roared in anger.

"You heard the king, the troll has been chosen." Underminers quickly gathered around Ug and slowly heaved the heavy cage into the gaping hole. The cage cracked against the hard rock walls before landing heavily on the bare floor and smashing open. Shaken by the impact, Ug slowly pulled himself free of the shattered prison. He glared up at Grogger and growled. In response, Grogger shrugged and mouthed, 'sorry.' The situation had left him with very little choice, and he just hoped that Ug's tiny brain would be able to comprehend that.

With a shake of his head to gather his senses, Ug approached the walls of the pit and tried to clamber up. The attempt was useless, however, as the walls were slick with damp and mold. His thick fingers simply slid away from the slick rocks.

"Release Grum!" bellowed Grukhar. This time, the underminders began chanting "Grum! Grum! Grum!" in an increasingly excited fever pitch. Several goblins ran to a pair of ropes on the far side of the pit and began struggling to pull them backward. Grogger strained his eyes to see what was happening in the dark expanse before him. At the back of the pit, he could make out some sort of large portcullis that was slowly opening. An ominous bellow erupted from behind the portcullis.

"Grum! Grum! Grum! Grum!"

"What's a grum?" asked Gritter.

"I think we're about to find out," replied Grogger, while nervously watching the portcullis creep upward.

The gate was shaken by something slamming against it. The underminers pulling on the rope almost lost their grip as another slam battered against the metal. Now Ug stopped trying to pull himself out of the pit and turned to watch the portcullis opening. Two, large gray hands emerged underneath the barrier and threw it upward. The goblins holding the ropes went flying as the rope went slack. Some underminers stopped chanting for a moment to laugh at their misfortune. One poor soul was laughing so much that it tumbled into the pit, which caused even more merriment.

The goblin in the pit desperately started scrabbling up the walls. It pleaded with the others to throw down a rope so it could escape, but they just responded by laughing or throwing rocks at it. Grukhar laughed loudest, as she leaned on her throne to get a better glimpse of the action. Another roar came from the pit, and the crowd fell deathly silent.

"Here we go," whispered Grogger.

A figure burst from the gloom that was previously hidden by the portcullis, and Grogger caught his breath. The creature was a head taller than a troll and covered in thick, almost rock-like skin. Even in the dim light of the stalactites, Grogger could see its gray skin was covered in moss and lichen. It flexed its muscles before pounding its fists together. Small bits of skin flew off with each blow. Down its spine, large rock-like bone protruded through the skin to make jagged spikes. Its face wasn't that dissimilar to a troll, but it had a far more pronounced jaw that jutted out like the underhang of a cliff. When it roared, Grogger glimpsed teeth that glowed like the stalactites and stalagmites of the cavern.

"A deep cavern troll," stated Magwa, almost in awe. "Magwa thought they were extinct."

"I wish they were extinct," whimpered Klunk. "At least we know what a Grum is now."

At first, Grum focused on Ug, but then the frantic movements of the goblin clawing at the rocks to escape caught its attention. In a surprising turn of speed, it stomped over to the terrified pale-skinned goblin. It grabbed the struggling underminer in one of its boulder-like fists before clamping its powerful jaws around its head and ripping it clean off. Blood sprayed all over Grum's face, and it dropped the limp body to the floor before stamping on it with a gigantic foot. The crowd erupted into cheers and applause.

For the first time since he had known Ug, Grogger saw that the troll was scared. Even its dull brain could work out that the chances of winning against Grum were exceptionally low. Now the troll began searching around in the dirt, looking for something to use as a weapon. Many of the aging bones simply crumbled to dust when he scooped them up. Swords and shields scattered across the floor were too rusty to provide any real protection. In frustration, Ug hurled a shield out of the pit toward Grukhar. It bounced harmlessly off the base of her throne and Grukhar nervously laughed it off. Instead, Ug settled on a large rock that could be used as a makeshift weapon before Grum charged in for the kill.

When Grum reached out to grab the troll, Ug batted his outstretched hand away with the rock. The blow knocked Grum slightly off balance, and Ug quickly followed it up with a crunching uppercut using the rock. The force of the blow would have been enough to knock any other creature's head clean off, but Grum just responded with an angry grunt. In response, Grum pulled back his head and delivered a furious headbutt to Ug's face. The impact sent Ug flying to the floor and shattered his nose. Dark blood immediately began streaming down Ug's face.

"Kackle, can you do anything?" asked Grogger, but he was greeted by an ominous silence. Nearby, Jo'os was slamming itself against the cage, oddly keen to join the fight against the cavern troll. Grogger's attention was drawn back to the pit as Grum roared once more and thundered toward the stricken Ug. But, just when Grogger thought it was all over, Ug scooped up a handful of dirt and lobbed it into Grum's eyes. Now temporarily blinded, Grum rubbed angrily at his face to clear the dirt while furiously stamping the floor. Sensing an opportunity, Ug slowly pulled himself to his feet and located his rock once more. With Grum's back turned, Ug raised the weapon and slammed it down on Grum's skull.

Klunk let out a cheer which quickly turned to a groan when the rock broke in two and fell harmlessly to the ground. Grum spun round and delivered a crunching kick to Ug's chest. Even from outside the pit, Grogger heard the sickening crunch of bones, and Ug was forced back down to the ground again.

"He's going to kill him," said Gritter with a terrified sob.

"And then he's going to kill us," added Grogger, sadly.

This time, Ug was quicker off his feet, but Grogger could see he was breathing heavily. Grum rubbed the final pieces of dirt from his eyes, and the two trolls began circling each other. All around the pit, the underminers were whooping and hollering with excitement. Grukhar was standing on her throne and clapping gleefully.

"End it!" she screamed. Grum briefly looked up from the pit before issuing a deep roar. Tucking his head down, Grum barrelled toward his foe.

Grogger winced at the thought of being hit with such force and was glad it wasn't him in the pit. However, we was surprised when Ug deftly stepped aside and stuck out a leg. Grum tripped and smashed into the side of the pit with an almighty crash. The underminers began to boo.

As Grogger was watching, he sensed something begin to pull at his attention. It was almost like a voice calling to him from somewhere in the cavern, and he recognized the call. He looked up and down the other cages to see if one of his gang was talking to him, but their attention was focused on the spectacle in the pit. Instead, he looked around the cave and his gaze paused on the sword he had found in the mausoleum. The underminers had left it in a pile of other weapons and detritus from their raids. Grogger also noticed Magwa's magical staff and the rest of his gang's stuff. The stupid idiots had just chucked everything to one side. However, what really caught his interest was the fact the patterns up and down the sword were glowing red once more. They shimmered with an unnatural light that lit the gloom around it. Grogger felt the blade calling to him. Felt its power. The language of the Abyss swirled around his ears. For a moment, he forgot everything that was happening around him while he listened to the tempting purrs of the weapon.

"The dagger can help," muttered Grogger and shook his head to clear the demonic whispers.

"What?" asked Gritter.

"I think my dagger can kill Grum!"

"Ha!" laughed Gritter. "There ain't no way that little thing can kill Grum. Look at him! The visions or whatever you've been having have sent you crazy."

"This wasn't a vision. It was... something else."

Back down in the pit, Grum was slowly heaving himself up from the fall, while Ug was searching around again for something to use as a weapon. This time, his large fist closed around a mighty leg bone. He swung it side to side to test its weight, then readied himself for another attack by Grum.

"I need to get out this cage and help Ug," said Grogger and rattled the bars of his tiny prison.

"Forget about Ug! He's as good as dead," replied Gritter.

"If Ug dies, we're all as good as dead. We're next for the pit, remember?!"

Grogger racked his brain about how he could get out the cage. He had nothing to pick the lock. Kackle might have been able to use magic, but his keen ears could still hear the labored breathing of the unconscious wiz. That left only one option. An absolute last resort.

"Klunk, have you got anything that could blow up this lock?"

Two cages to Grogger's right, the banggit dragged his attention from the awful spectacle of his pit and looked at Grogger.

"They took my bag," he replied with a frown. "It had all my best stuff in it."

"Anything else that could help?"

Klunk began fumbling in the pockets of his jerkin and hidden compartments in his sleeves. He produced a handful of tiny rockets, small round objects that looked like miniature bombs, some fireworks, and several pieces of flint. It was a miniature arsenal.

"Only these," said Klunk, miserably, "but these hardly make a sound, and the explosions are only one color. Pointless really."

Grogger shook his head in disbelief. The stupid snoz didn't realize that he had everything they needed to escape.

"Any of those a smoke bomb?" hissed Grogger. Although the underminers appeared to be captivated by the fight between Grum and Ug, he didn't want them overhearing his plan. Klunk held up a small, green ball.

"This will probably make some smoke, but the bang is crap." Grogger ignored the banggit's disappointed face.

"What about the lock?" This time, Klunk showed him what looked like a firework.

"This should do the trick."

"How many have you got?"

Klunk held up three claws.

Grogger's superior intelligence quickly calculated a snoz-proof plan that even Klunk's bungling couldn't ruin.

"Throw them down to me," hissed Grogger. "Magwa, I'll give you two so you and Jo'os can escape."

"What about me and Klunk?" whined Gritter.

"Magwa can get you out once he gets his staff back," snapped Grogger. "Anyway, back to my great plan! Klunk, when I say, throw that smoke grenade into the pit so it gives Ug some more time. Then I'll blow my door off while everyone is wondering what the grog is happening. Okay?"

Klunk nodded and threw the fireworks to Gritter, ready to pass to Grogger. For a moment, the mawbeast handler stared at the fireworks, and Grogger wondered if he was about to use them to escape himself. But, with a heavy sigh, he passed all three onward.

"This better work," muttered Gritter.

"It *has* to work," replied Grogger and handed the other two explosives to Magwa after pushing his into the lock of his cage. "What makes it explode?"

"Just pull the string," said Klunk. Grogger hesitantly did as the bangit said, watching as a grin spread across his face. "And now make sure you stand well back."

"Stand well back?!" shouted Grogger. "I'm in snozzin' cage!"

Green sparks erupted from the firework as it made a loud hissing noise. Grogger pressed himself into a corner of the enclosure. A few underminers turned to see what the noise was.

"Chuck the grogging smoke bomb!"

Klunk twisted the small ball and then lobbed it into the pit. It bounced off the sides and landed between Ug and Grum. Both trolls stared at the object with confused looks. Then with a loud 'crack,' the bomb exploded, and thick green smoke erupted from the ball. It instantly filled the pit and then began creeping over the sides and enveloping the gathered underminers closest to the grisly arena.

Meanwhile, Grogger closed his eyes and covered his head as the firework continued to spit and hiss. If this thing took his face off, he was definitely coming back to haunt Klunk. He cursed the grogging banggit and his grogging bombs. Suddenly, the firework exploded with a loud bang. Even with his eyes shut, the flash of the explosion hurt Grogger's eyes, and he could only imagine how painful it must have been for any underminers nearby. He heard a loud crash as something landed in the pit. After blinking several times, the bright spots in Grogger's vision disappeared, and he saw the door to his cage had been completely blown off. Klunk was clapping, happily.

"Magwa, wait until I'm in the pit, and then blow your door off too."

Edging around his cage to avoid falling into the pit, Grogger then ran to the pile of weapons. Everywhere else, the cavern had erupted into absolute chaos. The green smoke continued to rise from the pit, and underminers were pushing and shoving against each other to escape from the thick clouds. Grukhar screamed insults and curses while Grum thumped around the pit below, bawling in frustration. Ignoring the chaos around him, Grogger arrived at the stash of weapons. For a moment, his attention was drawn to Magwa's staff. He considered grabbing that and escaping from the underminer's cave, leaving Magwa and others to deal with Grukhar. But, he didn't like his odds of escaping on his own, and his chances of surviving outside the cave were likely to be even less.

Instead, his claw reached out to the blade, and as it got closer, he almost sensed the weapon singing to him. Strange words and laughter filled his ears. The dagger wanted to fight, it wanted to kill. Grogger gripped the weapon and the singing stopped abruptly. Instead, the glowing runes turned from red to green, and Grogger felt a strange sensation of fearlessness creep through his body.

Holding the blade tighter, he turned back to the pit.

"Here goes nothing," he muttered and ran straight toward the gaping chasm. Through the green clouds of smoke, he just saw the edge approaching and prepared to slide down on his backside. Unfortunately it was bumpier than he thought, and he tumbled down the rocks before landing with a crunch on the hard ground below. Thankfully, the dagger was still gripped in his claw.

Grogger quickly leapt up, just in time to see the smoke was finally starting to dissipate. Unfortunately, it also revealed Grum in all his terrifying glory, and he was rushing straight at Grogger.

CHAPTER EIGHTEEN

Grogger was paralyzed with fear. His small legs were wobbling, and his bony green knees knocked together as he started in horror at the mountain rampaging toward him. Grum's eyes were fixed on the diminutive greenskin, and they raged with an ancient fury. Grogger cursed himself for such a foolish mistake. He blamed the supernatural whispers of the sword and almost wanted to throw it away, but something compelled him to keep a firm grip.

Grum raised a massive fist in preparation to crush Grogger's skull. He tried to will his legs to move, but the sight terrified him. Instead, he closed his eyes and thanked the gobs that his end would come quickly, at least. However, as he tried to send his thoughts to the great goblin warlords and kings of the past, he sensed movement to his right.

Ug charged through the remaining smoke and slammed into Grum with incredible force, using the leg bone he found as an impromptu battering ram. The impact came from nowhere and knocked Grum to the floor with an almighty crash. In response, the cavern troll howled in anger. Grogger opened one eye and saw Ug looking at him. The troll grunted and gave Grogger a nod.

"Would you believe I'm here to help?" said Grogger with a shrug of his scrawny shoulders. His attention snapped back to Grum, who was hammering his gigantic fists into the dirt while he slowly pulled himself upward.

"Smash him in the face then!" Grogger commanded to Ug. The troll considered the command for a moment then grunted in approval. He strolled over to Grum, windmilling the leg bone as he went. The hefty weapon picked up speed with every moment, until it made a deep humming sound, like the engine of a machine. Grum tried to roll out the way, but his bulk was too cumbersome. The spinning club caught him directly under the chin and sent his head flying backward with a cruel snap. Grogger noticed pieces of the bone - and Grum's face - fly off and ping against the sides of the pit. Grum's yellow eyes rolled up into his skull and his body went limp, hammering his face into the floor with a thump. Grogger grinned with excitement. He had done it!

"Finish him off!" screamed Grogger.

Ug lifted the bone with both hands and prepared to deliver the finishing blow. He let out a deep cry and swung the weapon as hard he could. However, at the last moment, Grum somehow snapped back into consciousness. His rocky arm shot out and grabbed the club before it struck his head for a second time. Using the momentum of the attack, he twisted the bone before Ug could let go and sent the troll flying over his shoulder. Ug hit the pit wall head first and slumped to the floor. Grogger was alarmed to see he didn't appear to be breathing.

Overhead, Grogger heard two dull thuds, which he hoped were more of Klunk's fireworks freeing Magwa and Jo'os. Hopefully they wouldn't just run away and might come to help him in the pit. He could hear more shouts and screams from Grukhar. But now wasn't the time to think about that, he had bigger problems to worry about.

Grum had pulled himself back up and was glowering at Grogger. The cavern troll thumped one fist into the other a few times before pointing straight at Grogger. Just when he could feel himself becoming overwhelmed with fear again, the blade began to whisper to him. The shimmering green runes pulsated with an arcane energy as the whispers told Grogger to stand his ground.

Now is not your time, great Grogger.

Grogger returned Grum's deadly stare and slowly stuck out his tongue. He wasn't sure if the cavern troll even knew what it meant, but it still enraged the beast. He thundered straight at Grogger, thick globs of spit falling from his prodigious jaws. Grum raised his arm to smash Grogger in the face, but this time, he wasn't afraid.

Duck.

Grogger rolled under the blow at the last moment. He could feel the rush of air as the gauntlet-like fist passed just inches from his head.

Slice.

As Grogger rolled, he stuck out the blade to carve through Grum's right leg. The singing grew louder. Grogger quickly jumped to his feet and looked back at Grum. The lower portion of his leg was ruined by a thick wound. The edges glowed red like molten lava. Dumbfounded, Grogger simply stared in wonder at the damage he had inflicted. Grum also seemed confused. His dumb face looked down at the scar like he wasn't sure what it was.

Strike again.

Grogger let out a battle cry. In comparison to the roars and bellows of the two trolls, it seemed positively pathetic; but for Grogger, it felt good. He jabbed up Grum's torso and was delighted to see the blade slice through his foe's thick skin. Grogger twisted the blade and was pleased to hear a roar of pain. He didn't have too long to celebrate, however, because Grum casually swatted Grogger away and forced him backward.

Again!

The songs filled Grogger's ears and swelled his heart. Could everyone else hear the glorious calls? It was like Garkan himself was speaking to him. His claw trembled around the hilt of the dagger.

AGAIN!

This time it was a demand. Grogger dived forward and spun sideways to avoid a poorly timed uppercut from Grum. The giant troll overbalanced itself from the force of the missed attack, and Grogger sensed an opening. Turning back to face Grum, he gripped the blade and sliced down at the cavern troll's wrist. Terrified the weapon would simply bounce off

Grum's rocky skin, he was ecstatic as he saw the sharp edge slice through the wrist as though it were rotten meat.The severed hand hit the ground with a dull thud and, for the first time, Grogger saw what looked like fear on the creature's face.

Don't stop!

Grogger leapt again, this time hoping to hamstring his enemy. He prepared to slice Grum's knees but was shocked when Grum's foot connected with his chest. The blow was clumsy and ill-judged, otherwise it may have instantly killed Grogger. Instead, it sent him spinning backward, with furious pains racing through his body. Most troubling though, was the fact Grogger lost grip on his dagger. The singing stopped, instantly.

Clutching his chest, Grogger scanned the pit with nervous eyes. He gaze fleetingly paused on the limp body of Ug, and his heart fell when he realized no help was coming from that direction. A low rumble suddenly filled the pit, and Grogger was horrified when he realized it was Grum laughing. An awful smirk was plastered across the beast's face and, even more awful, was the fact that Grogger could already see the sliced off hand was beginning to grow back. He needed to find that dagger! Suddenly a voice cut through the chaos.

"Your dagger is near the gate!" Grogger recognized Gritter's reedy tones.

He quickly looked over to the gate and saw something glinting in the dust. He glanced back at Grum and saw the determined look on his gray, rocky visage. This would be a race that Grogger needed to win! He sprinted for the blade and tried to ignore the earthquake-like pounds of Grum's steps behind him. With each booming step from the cavern troll, it felt like the earth bounced under Grogger's feet, but he was getting closer. He reached out a claw to grab the dagger and could almost hear the singing again. The tip of Grogger's claw was just a hair's breadth away from the hilt, but it wasn't enough. With a sweeping motion, Grum stretched out and batted Grogger out the way. Surprised by the blow, Grogger was lifted off his feet and catapulted across the pit. He landed heavily in a pile of bones.

Groaning, Grogger lifted his head and was distraught to see Grum picking up the dagger. He looked up around the edge of the pit to see if help was coming from Magwa and Jo'os, but all he could see were the eager faces of the underminers. Occasionally, flashes of blue light lit the cavern, but the viewers didn't seem to care. His attention returned to Grum. The weapon was no longer glowing and wasn't burning Grum. Instead, the dull beast was simply staring at it with a confused expression. Grogger wondered for a moment if the troll could hear the singing.

Sensing an opportunity to escape, Grogger ran over to Ug. His whole body screamed in agony from the fight with Grum, but he didn't know how long he might have left. He was strangely relieved when he reached the great bulk of Ug to see that he was still breathing.

"Wake up you big snozzer!" he shouted into what he assumed were

Ug's ears. "We need to get out this grogging pit." There was no response.

But, just when Grogger was struggling to lift a rock to thump over Ug's ugly head, the troll let out an almighty groan. Slowly his eyes opened and eventually focused on Grogger's face... and then the rock.

"I wasn't going to kill you! I was trying to wake you up!" He lobbed the rock to the floor and gave the troll a lop-sided smile. "That's the only grogging thing that's trying to kill us!"

Grogger directed Ug's attention to the cavern troll and was slightly surprised to see it still staring at the dagger.

"What's that stupid snoz doing with *my* dagger?"

Grum lifted the blade to his ears, as though it was listening to something.

"It's talking to him too. I thought it only talked to me," said Grogger, rather petulantly.

Then, Grogger was perturbed to see the cavern troll casually lift up the blade and eat it. With a mighty gulp, Grum swallowed down the weapon and then returned its attention to Grogger and Ug.

"That was my dagger! You snoz! You grogging snoz! That was *my* dagger!"

Grogger felt a rage quite unlike anything he felt before. The cavern troll had taken away his special dagger. *His* dagger. Grogger couldn't believe the audacity of it. He no longer cared about saving his life or Ug's, for that matter, he just wanted that weapon back. He picked up a rock and lobbed it straight at Grum. It pinged harmlessly off his forehead. The monstrous troll bellowed in response.

"Now would be a really good time for you to get back up again," said Grogger, desperately shaking Ug. The troll attempted to stand but simply slid back down the sides of the pit again before giving Grogger an apologetic grimace.

Grum was stomping ever closer to them. Casually, he scooped up a rock, and Grogger knew the cavern troll was going to use that boulder-like block to bash his brains into a messy pulp. Without the dagger, it was pointless. He may as well let his attacker send him to oblivion. Just then, his ears picked up something. Although it was faint, he could hear the dagger singing again. The soft chanting filled his black heart with wonder, and a stupid smile spread across his face.

"Can you hear it, Ug? The gobs are singing to us!" Ug responded with a confused grunt.

Grogger looked over to Grum and was surprised to see he had stopped moving. Instead, he was clutching his stomach and moaning slightly. Grum let out an almighty burp, and Grogger noted trails of green smoke trailing from his mouth. He burped again and then...

Take cover.

... exploded.

Chunks of thick gray skin shot around the pit, crashing against the walls and floor. Some even shot out of the gaping hole and smashed into the watching underminers where they were met with a scream of pain. Grogger tucked himself against Ug, convinced one of the pieces would take his head clean off. However, when he didn't feel his fantastically intelligent brain being removed from his shoulders, he quickly straightened himself back up.

"All part of the plan," he said to Ug with a slightly manic grin. Ug rolled his eyes and grunted. "That was definitely the plan. The old exploding dagger trick."

Turning his attention away from Ug, Grogger looked at the spot where Grum had once stood. All that remained were a pair of smoking feet and, in between them, was Grogger's dagger. The runes glowed brighter than ever, and Grogger had to shield his eyes slightly as he approached. Cautiously, he grasped the hilt, expecting it to be hot, but it was exceptionally cool, even after the explosion. Holding the weapon aloft, he shouted up to the watching underminers.

"I am Grogger Split-tooth, killer of champions! And I am your KING!"

Outside the pit, the underminers fell silent. As one, they gazed upon Grogger and the smoking remains of the unbeatable Grum.

"What did he say his name was?" asked one underminer.

"Oh, come on! I literally just shouted it!" whined Grogger.

"Who cares. He's king now!" answered another. Around them, excited muttering broke out among the other goblins.

Their muttering was silenced by a furious scream from Grukhar.

"What are you doing? Get in that pit and kill him!" She pointed her pick down at Grogger, who was still rather foolishly holding the blade in the air, with a slightly stupid grin still on his face. "He's no king. He's a snoz!"

"He killed Grum," replied a particularly thin underminer.

"No one's ever killed Grum before," joined another. There were mutters of agreement from other underminers.

"I ain't ever seen Grum get hurt, let alone killed," added one, nodding enthusiastically.

"Of course no one has ever killed Grum before, you snozzers. He wouldn't be grogging alive if that had happened!" Grukhar was screeching wildly. "We can get another Grum!"

"There isn't another Grum," interjected one underminer, rather sadly before breaking into loud sobs. Another goblin delicately placed an arm around its shoulder.

"You don't need Grum!" shouted Grogger. "Join me, and you'll never need another Grum. I'll lead you out of this grogging cave, and we'll take over the world!"

"Don't you dare listen to him! Don't you grogging dare!" screamed Grukhar and stomped toward the edge of the pit. She swung her pick wildly as she walked and bashed any underminders that were foolish enough to get in her way. "He's not the king. He's a stupid snozzing grog!"

Grukhar leaned over the edge of the pit. Her eyes fixed on Grogger, and he saw the fury burning behind the large, black eyes. Grogger needed to do something about her before she caused any more trouble. Then he could get out of this awful cave. He considered commanding the underminers to throw her into the pit, so he could fight her. However, after the scrap with Grum, he wasn't confident of besting her. He eyed the beards around her belt and thought of all the beardies she must have killed. Even with the dagger, he wasn't sure he could beat her.

Suddenly, he was disturbed by a sharp crack of magic. A blue arc of lightning briefly lit the cavern and gave the underminers an eerie blue glow. There was a sharp scream, and the blackened, smoking corpse of an underminer toppled into the pit, almost hitting Grogger.

"Oi!" he shouted.

Around the pit, the crowd of watchers parted and Magwa appeared, followed shortly by Jo'os, who snapped and growled at those around him. The aging goblin pointed a trembling claw at Grukhar.

"Underminers, your *king* has spoken. Grukhar's reign is over."

Grukhar roared with maniacal laughter.

"Your king? Your grogging king?!" she looked into the eyes of the spectating underminers. "Who has helped the underminers to thrive? Who has helped dig our caverns deeper and further than ever before? Who has kept you alive?"

"Some of us alive," replied a quiet voice. Grukhar quickly cast furious glances around the crowd, and a goblin disappeared back into the press of bodies.

"Those that died were weak! It takes strength to be an underminer. Not some wannabe king with a fancy, glowing dagger." Her voice reached a frantic crescendo.

"*Magic* dagger," replied someone. Grogger thought it might be Klunk.

"Yeah, it makes stuff go boom," agreed an underminer. There were enthusiastic nods from the other goblins.

"Could make other stuff explode," added another. "Enemies 'n' stuff."

"Remember old Grum?" said one. "It made Grum explode." This was met by more nods, and Grogger was sure he heard some goblins crying while muttering Grum's name.

"Of course they remember Grum, you snoz!" shrieked Grukhar. "That *just* happened."

There were murmurs among the crowd, and Grogger could feel the atmosphere was on a knife edge. If he could just say the right thing, the crowd could turn in his favor.

"All Grukhar has done has shut you away in this cave, while all the other goblins grow strong. She's kept you weak. She's kept you starving. It's never been about keeping you safe, it's been about making her feel powerful. Join me, and you'll become stronger than ever before. Tougher than even grogging beardies."

Grogger looked across the faces peering over the pit. A ripple of hushed voices spread around the room. Many of the underminers were nodding in agreement, but an equal number were shaking their heads and pointing at Grogger. It wasn't working. They weren't listening.

"And... and... erm..." he searched desperately for something else to say. What in the gobs' name could these deranged goblins ever want? "And... and, I promise you... that... you'll never have to eat worm guts ever again!" He finished with a dramatic flourish.

This time, there was a wave of excited chattering that spread quickly throughout the cavern. He saw a few underminers hugging each other. Some were openly weeping while others were clapping.

"No! More! Worm! Guts!" he roared, for emphasis. This time, there was an almighty cheer.

"No more worm guts," came the reply.

"He can't promise that!" screeched Grukhar and flailed her arms around.

"No more worm guts," repeated the underminers and fixed their eyes on Grukhar.

"Worm guts make you strong! They get us through the long days." This time, there was a hint of desperation in her voice, and she began scurrying backward up the mound to her throne.

"No more worm guts!" the crowd all shouted and edged closer to Grukhar. She swung wildly at them with her pick, but the goblins kept coming. "No more worm guts!"

"You snivelling snozzers. He doesn't care about you. Your queen cares about you! The worm guts have helped us all survive! We've all suffered for the good of the clan."

Grukar scrabbled to her throne and climbed on top of it. More underminers gathered near her while Grukhar viciously tried to kick them away. Still, they kept coming. As one underminer clawed up to reach for Grukhar's grisly belt, she fell backward and pushed a small lever on the side of her dais, and a hidden compartment flipped open. Hunks of smoked meat, dried fruit, and other delicacies spilled out of the throne and onto the mound. Grukhar stopped and nervously stared at the pillaged items.

"I can explain!" she screeched, but it was too late. With cries of 'no more worm guts,' the underminers fell ravenously on the pile and started stuffing whatever they could into their eager little mouths. Scuffles broke out between the goblins as they desperately grabbed whatever food they could. Crumbs shot from their gaping mouths as they continued to chant.

"Grab her!" shouted Grogger from down in the pit. At first, the underminers were too busy trying to stuff their bellies, so Grogger shouted again. "Grab her!"

This time, they listened. The underminers swarmed toward their former leader. With sickening crunches, Grukhar plunged her pick into the skulls of those that came too close. The corpses tumbled from the mound but were quickly replaced by more furious pale-skinned goblins. Grukhar was quickly overwhelmed. Her pick was thrown to the floor and a group of underminers clasped her writhing body.

"I have no idea how that food got there," she said, but there wasn't much conviction in her voice.

"Throw her in a cage," roared Grogger, triumphantly, and his ears rang to the sound of his singing sword, now louder than ever, while the underminers chanted his name.

CHAPTER NINETEEN

Rowan strode confidently from his home and into the morning hazy sunshine, holding a gauntleted hand against the weak light. He was wearing the full armor of a Basilean man-at-arms. His white tunic had recently been washed, and he had spent the evening polishing the metal to a bright silver. He could feel the breastplate was loose, and it rattled against his body as he moved. Too many meager meals in the countryside, he considered wryly. Rowan and Mary had come here for a better life. Instead, they were scraping an existence off the land and the few animals that hadn't been stolen in raids by goblins or simply died through lack of food.

He looked over the 'troops' he had managed to round up and sighed. Along with Furna, he had spent the past few days traveling to nearby villages and settlements, trying to convince the inhabitants to join him in the quest to drive out the goblins. A few had simply asked him to leave because they were either too afraid or too selfish to join in the fight. At the time, he had noted bitterly, that these tended to be the ones with the best defenses or an abundance of crops and livestock. So much for Darvled's promise of humanity sticking together, he thought with a grimace.

Instead, it was often those like himself - the people that had been terrorized by the goblins or other marauders - that agreed to take up the call. Although he couldn't fault their courage, he could certainly despair at their lack of any actual training or proper weapons. A few had dug out rusty swords and shields - and there was even a crossbow or two among the gathered farmers - but most were armed with pitchforks, wicked-looking scythes, and other farming implements. He didn't fancy their chances of close combat inside the tunnels, but he needed all the help he could get.

While traveling from homestead to homestead, he had heard similar stories time and again. The farmers would just be getting on their feet when the goblins would arrive like locusts and strip the land of whatever they could find. The haphazard, chaotic attacks of the goblins often meant that something would be left behind, but it was never enough, and the farmers were forced to live on meager rations. It was something Rowan had plenty of experience with, and he sighed in frustration - both at his own predicament and of those gathered before him. Suddenly, he felt the delicate touch of Mary on his shoulder.

"Is this going to work?" she said in almost a whisper.

"We have to try something," replied Rowan, and his voice took on a more military tone. "The alternative doesn't bear thinking about."

With that, he rammed his gleaming helmet on his head and marched toward Furna, who was busy talking to her crew. Compared to the farmers, the sight of the towering, heavily muscled salamanders filled Rowan with a hint of hope. His mind briefly traveled back to the Battle of Carn's Bridge, where he had fought alongside a battalion of salamanders. He still remembered their flaming swords smashing through the ranks of the Lower Abyssals and casting them into the depths below the bridge. Their ancient battle cries had rang in his ears as they charged into hordes of demons, smoke billowing from their mouths and nostrils. It was like nothing he had ever seen, and he just hoped that even with what remained of Furna's crew, it would help turn the green tide.

He saluted Furna and his gauntlet clanged against the metal of his helmet.

"What do you think?" he asked.

"To our chances of surviving or you in that *resplendent* armor?" A smile tickled her scaly lips as she reveled in the word 'resplendent.' A few of the other crew members chuckled in response.

"Damn sailors," he replied.

"Stupid soldiers."

The unlikely pair beamed at each other.

Furna's crew had kept separate to most of the gathered humans. While drumming up support for this seemingly impossible mission, Rowan had remained cautious about telling his fellow men that they would be fighting alongside salamanders. Since Lord Darvled had begun rising to prominence in the Successor Kingdoms, a sense of mistrust toward the other races of Pannithor had spread like a weed. Everywhere it touched, doubt would blossom, and the realms of men would withdraw into themselves, nervously eying anyone that was not human. The 'Time of Man,' as Darvled liked to call it, was becoming the 'Time of Suspicion,' as far as Rowan was concerned.

Some villagers had eyed the salamanders warily when they arrived at Rowan's farmstead, and a few had even left, muttering under their breath about working with 'monsters.' However, most had greeted the sight of the salamanders with a sigh of relief. It was clear that Furna and her crew would help to even the odds against the goblins. For some, it was the first time they had met a salamander and there were curious, slightly furtive glances, at the crew as they casually lounged around waiting for the battle ahead. A few children - unencumbered by Darvled's insidious speeches - had been playing among the salamanders. Some took great delight in trying to touch their tails, then running away squealing when the salamanders whirled round with a pretend roar. Rowan gave a smile when he spotted Berusk, who he understood to be one of the older salamanders, growling at a couple of children that were attempting to set a stick on fire by poking it against his tail. With Berusk, he wasn't quite sure the growls of frustration were completely playful. He turned his attention back to Furna.

"Do you think we've got a chance?" he asked.

"Of heading into a goblin's nest, with only a few poorly-armed humans, one Basilean man-at-arms, and a crew of tired - but incredibly courageous, good looking, and well-trained – salamanders, and getting out alive?"

"Well, when you put it like that, I don't know why I'm even worrying," laughed Rowan, with a confidence he didn't really feel.

"The only thing that worries me is how we find our way in the tunnels," added Furna. "From what I've heard, goblin nests are like a maze, and I don't want to get stuck down there."

Rowan's face fell. The labyrinthine tunnels of the goblins were notorious, but he had hoped that by sticking together, the group wouldn't get lost in the confusing shafts. However, with Furna's fiery eyes burning into him, he had to admit that his plan - if he could even call it that - was weak.

"Captain, I might be able to help with that," came a voice, and Rowan saw a smaller salamander approach. Although she was mostly dressed in the same garb as her fellow corsairs, he spotted a few scrolls spilling out a pouch on her belt, and her claws bore strange rings bristling with odd gems or runes.

"Ah, Igne, I can always rely on you in moments like this," said Furna and clapped a large claw around her shoulders. "Come and put Rowan's mind at rest... *and mine.*" She added the last words with a whisper.

Igne coughed slightly, clearly not enjoying the attention she was now getting.

"Well," she started, "whatever that magical staff is that the goblin has leaves a sort of trail. I could feel something in the fort and then again when we fought them in the pass. I think that in the tunnels, I should be able to sense it and lead us in the correct direction."

"Assuming they haven't thrown the infernal thing away," came a growl behind them. Rowan turned to find another salamander watching them. He hadn't been introduced to this one, and Rowan had noted that he mostly kept apart from the others.

"If you have a better plan, then I'd like to hear it, Rorsha," snapped Furna with the hint of a growl.

"The only plan I care about is how you plan to get us home, *Captain.*"

Furna let her arm drop from Igne's shoulders, then pounded over to Rorsha. She went so close that her scaly snout almost touched his. Her voice dropped to a cold hiss and wisps of smoke curled from her nostrils.

"This *is* the plan to get us home, Rorsha. Once we have the wiz and whatever that magical staff is, we'll have enough to get a ship. Then you can take over and do whatever in Kthorlaq's name you want to. Until then, we stick to my plan."

Rowan watched warily as Rorsha's eyes blazed with anger and frustration. His hand slowly dropped to the hilt of his sword, and Rowan realized he was sweating. He noted, worryingly, that Furna's claw was edging closer to one of her pistols. Rowan bit his lip. If the salamanders started fighting among themselves, the gathered villagers would quickly lose confidence and head home. He watched nervously and hoped that no one else was witnessessing this tense exchange.

Rorsha slowly dropped his head and backed away.

"We stick to the plan then," he grunted and skulked off to sit in the shade beneath a small tree. Rowan relaxed, before realizing he had been holding his breath. Furna turned back to Igne with a sigh.

"Rorsha does have a point, what if they have thrown the staff away?" Furna whispered.

"Well, let's pray to Kthorlaq that they haven't," replied Igne.

* * * * *

Rowan eyed the yawning opening to the cavern system with suspicion and strained his ears to listen to any sounds of movement from inside. Traveling to the cave had taken longer than expected because Furna, quite rightly, insisted on sending scouts ahead to check for guards. However, the progress had been slow because the trail was dotted with boulders, cracks, and crevices where watchful goblins could be hiding.

As a result, the sun was now sliding toward the horizon. Rowan had hoped to enter the tunnels in daylight while the goblins were sleeping, but time was no longer on their side. He listened again and almost expected to hear the battle cries of the goblins as they charged out of the chasm.

He had fought goblins countless times before. The Basilean patrols were often called to protect outposts on the fringes of the Hegemony that were regularly attacked by greenskin invaders. Out in the open and across the battlefield, the goblins seemed almost comical. No matter the size of their force, they quickly fell apart when charged by the might of the Basilean army, and once proud ranks of goblins resorted to bickering and in-fighting as they turned on each other.

But here, standing staring into the dark, with a foul-smelling wind drifting from the inky black, he had to admit that he was feeling nervous. Numerous times on the march here, he had thought about turning back and calling the whole thing off. Was it really worth it? Putting his life at risk, along with the others trailing behind him? But then he thought of Mary and the life they had imagined together, away from the rigid rule of the Hegemony. He thought of the stories those gathered around him had told of the goblin attacks and how it had impacted their own hopes of a peaceful life. They had never expected life out here to be easy, but they had all thought they would at least have a chance of a new life. He set his jaw and glared angrily into the gloom. The goblins had to be stopped.

"How do you know this is the right cave?" asked Furna as she stood alongside Rowan.

"You see Nian over there?" said Rowan, and pointed at a scraggy-looking man armed with a wood axe. "The goblins took his six-year-old daughter."

"They steal children?" gasped Igne, standing near them.

"They steal anything," grunted Rowan. "Somehow the child gave them the slip as they were heading down into the depths, and this is where she came out. She told Nian, and he marched here with others from his village ready to take revenge. Only Nian made it back out."

Rowan looked at Nian and saw that he was muttering to himself and staring at the cave. He had never been the same. This was likely to be just one of the paths the goblins used to get down into their awful lair, although there didn't appear to be any recent tracks. He wasn't sure if that boded well or not.

"Can you feel the staff, Igne?" asked Furna.

Igne placed her claws on her temple, closed her eyes for a moment, and her breathing slowed. Her eyes abruptly snapped open.

"It's in there... and so is *something* else." She shuddered, involuntarily.

"Great, more surprises," replied Furna with a huff. "Reckon you can find the staff though?"

Igne hesitated a moment before giving a short nod.

"We're all yours then, Rowan. Lead the way, and Igne can give you guidance, if you need it."

Rowan turned to the rag-tag force and realized just how desperate they all looked. The salamanders stared at him with tired but determined gazes, while the humans simply looked tired. All had white knuckles from gripping their weapons nervously, and their eyes held a pleading gaze. There was no turning back, it was now or never.

"I'll head in first with Furna and her crew," hissed Rowan and hoped the sound of his voice wouldn't carry down into the goblin lair. "We'll use the flames from their swords to light the way and mark the walls as we go. Stick behind us and don't venture into any other tunnels, because you won't find your way out. If you've got daggers, axes, or short swords, then use those if we're fighting in the tunnels. A pitchfork or spear is no good in close combat. Hopefully they'll still be sleeping, so they'll be groggy and unprepared. So, we find the leader and kill it. I know you're scared, but this is our chance to strike back. To take back those lives we've all dreamed off!"

A few ragged cheers ripped quietly through the crowd.

"Here goes nothing," he whispered to Furna and was greeted by the roar of the salamanders' flaming swords igniting.

CHAPTER TWENTY

Grogger couldn't sleep. Each time he closed his eyes, the whispers from the dagger stopped him from drifting off. Lounging in Grukhar's throne, he casually stroked his new-found weapon. He had no idea what it was or where it had originated from, but he didn't care. He just remembered the way it had sliced through Grum's rocky limbs. Perhaps he no longer had to worry about stealing Magwa's prod? Then again, why have just one magical weapon when he could potentially have two? He smirked to himself. He could have a whole armory of magical stuff!

Around him, the underminers were still sleeping. On the floor of the cavern, they were huddled together closely for warmth. Occasionally one would accidentally lash out in their sleep, causing those around them to retaliate with their own kicks and punches, before settling back to sleep again. Nearer to him was his gang, sleeping around the base of the throne. He saw that Magwa clutched his staff tightly as he slept. Every now and then, small sparks of lightning would shoot off it and bounce along the floor before fizzling out. In the cages at the edge of the grand hall, he spotted Grukhar and recoiled slightly when he realized she was glaring at him, angrily.

He wasn't sure why he hadn't just killed her straight away. After the underminers had rebelled against her, they had simply thrown her in the cage and forced her to eat worm guts, while they shared her hidden food. Of course, Grogger had taken the lion's share, but he was happy to let the underminers have their fill. If only to stop them potentially turning on him too. They'd spent a few moons almost gorging themselves on Grukhar's hidden supplies, but now it was all gone. Grogger let out a small burp and considered whether it had been wise to eat everything so quickly. Although, it would be easy to just send out the underminers to gather more supplies. He was sure there would be plenty of human farms around here, which meant plenty more food. Grogger sniggered slightly. This being in charge lark was easy. He realized now why Bung had done whatever it took to hold onto power.

The thought of Bung reminded him of his goal. To raise an army big enough to take on Bung, so he could become the undisputed king. Looking around the sleeping goblins, he certainly had enough bodies, but he wasn't sure about weapons or war engines. He knew for a fact that Bung had plenty of those to go around, and he didn't fancy being on the receiving end of a rock thrower. Perhaps the underminers could build them, he considered. Staying here and bossing everyone a bit wouldn't be so bad. In fact, why even bother with Bung? He was in charge now, and perhaps that was enough. Even Ug seemed to be following his instructions. The once loyal bodyguard of Bung appeared to have come around to the idea of Grogger being in charge, which caused a thrill of excitement to soar through the goblin. If Ug thought he was boss, then anything was possible.

His thoughts were disturbed by a low growl. Grogger looked over to see that Jo'os had woken up and was grumbling at some unseen foe.

"A nightmare, Jo'os?" he asked and casually tossed the mighty mawbeast a bone. The animal caught it in midair and crunched it quickly. Grogger had noticed that the beast had started to behave differently toward him. It no longer looked at Grogger like his next meal and would occasionally even let him stroke his matted, filthy mane, while Grogger tried to ignore the jealous stares from Magwa.

Jo'os padded toward Grogger and nuzzled against his legs. Making sure that no one was watching, Grogger quickly rubbed his claws through Jo'os' thick hair.

"Who's a good boy? Who's a good boy?" Jo'os' back leg thumped against the floor and his eyes closed slightly. "Who's not going to eat Grogger, then?"

Jo'os' eyes abruptly shot open and he started growling again. Grogger snapped his claws back and shrank into the safety of his throne. After a moment, he relaxed slightly when he saw that Jo'os was sniffing the air and growling, rather than about to pounce on Grogger. The mawbeast swung its head from side to side while it tried to catch the scent of whatever it was that had disturbed it. Eventually, Jo'os stopped and fixed its gaze on one of the tunnels leading off the main cavern.

"What is-"

Before Grogger could complete the sentence, his body was wracked by spasms, and he toppled back into his throne, twitching as a vision raced through his mind.

Salamanders... humans... slaughtering goblins as they slept... fire everywhere... Grogger fighting... Grogger falling... dying... a cave of blood... his dagger clutched in scaly claws... a final song... his body...

"No," gasped Grogger in between fading spasms. "No! That isn't meant to happen. That isn't what I saw! I'm meant to be king! KING! Not dead in this grogging cave!"

His shouts disturbed some nearby underminers, who gave a few low snuffles before going back to sleep. Grogger gripped onto the throne and pulled himself unsteadily to his feet. He was so close, and now those snozzing scalies were going to ruin it all. Unless...

"Wake up! Wake up!" he screeched and stood on top of the throne. A few goblins started stirring, but a large portion remained fast asleep. He tried shouting again, but it had little effect. Suddenly a loud howl echoed through the cavern as Jo'os threw back his head and wailed into the air. This time, the goblins did wake up and looked around with alarm.

"What's up, boss?" asked Klunk. His eyes darted nervously from left to right.

"I-I mean we need to get out this cave," babbled Grogger.

"No we don't," replied Gritter. "We're safe in here. Nothing to worry about-"

Gritter was cut short when Grogger sent a stinging slap across his face.

"I tell *you* what to do," he hissed. "And if I say we need to get out this cave, we need to get out this cave."

Gritter rubbed his cheek gingerly. "Yes, boss."

"Why did you disturb Magwa?" The old goblin was slowly pulling himself up off the cave floor, and Grogger noticed he had scrawled 'Magwa still lives' in the dirt. *Mad old snoz*, thought Grogger.

"The scalies are coming," said Grogger, as he tried to control the rising panic in his voice.

"No chance, the-" Gritter stopped himself when Grogger raised a claw menacingly.

Grogger didn't want to tell them all about the vision. At least not all of it.

"Jo'os caught their scent and then... and then I had another vision that showed me them coming."

"And how did this vision end, wonders Magwa?" The old goblin was eying Grogger, curiously.

"It ended with us getting the snoz out of here," snapped Grogger. For a moment, the pair eyed each other menacingly. Magwa tightened the grip on his prod while Grogger wrapped a claw on his dagger. The air around them seemed to grow thick with magic. Eventually Magwa relaxed a little.

"As Magwa's *king* commands."

Grogger nodded and reluctantly pulled his claw away from the dagger. He looked nervously over toward the numerous tunnel entrances. Was it his imagination, or could he hear shouts echoing down the channels? Feeling a sense of panic threatening to overwhelm, he grabbed a passing underminer that was searching for any remaining food near the throne.

"What's the best way out of this grogging cave?" he hissed, barely managing to not break into a hysterical shout. The underminer looked confused by what was happening.

"Depends where you want to go. There are different tunnels that go all over the place. We like digging tunnels. My favourite tunnel is-" the underminer stopped and gave Grogger a weak smile before Grogger furiously pushed him away.

He desperately scanned the tunnels that lined the cavern walls, and a rising sense of panic threatened to overwhelm him. He realized he had no idea where the shafts went and, more importantly, he had no idea which one the salamanders and humans would be using. He shuddered at the thought of running up a path only to discover it was blocked by the scalies and their awful, flaming blades. Despite all these potential exits, he was trapped. Now he did begin to panic, and his breath came in short, ragged gasps. A preening laugh cut through the hubbub of the gathered goblins.

"It looks like our *glorious* leader has a problem," spat Grukhar and burst into high-pitched laughter once more.

Grogger tried to compose himself and *think*. Some underminers had overheard him telling Gritter the salamanders were coming and whispers were spreading. A few were already disappearing up tunnels or hastily grabbing whatever weapons they could find in the massive pile of rubbish. If Grogger didn't do something quickly, things might quickly get out of control. He looked over to Grukhar and reluctantly realized she might be the only way out of this mess. Grogger skipped down from the throne and squeezed his way through the throng of underminers to push toward Grukhar's cage. She gave him a mocking sneer and bowed slowly.

"My lord," she giggled.

"Is there a secret way out of here?" he hissed, trying to avoid the other goblins hearing what he was asking.

"A secret way out?!" she shouted to the goblins behind him and then broke into hysterical laughter again. Nearby underminers quickly turned their attention to the conversation.

"Why does he need a secret way out?" asked one.

"Do we need a secret way out?" said another.

"Who has got a secret way out?" cried a third.

"Have you got a secret way?" came another voice.

"I demand you tell me where the secret way out is!"

And with that, the underminers quickly started squabbling amongst themselves. Grogger rolled his eyes and let out an exasperated sigh.

"Not easy being leader, is it?" said Grukhar with a grin.

"I haven't got time for this," rasped Grogger and pressed himself against the filthy bars of the cage. "If I'm right, some very angry scalies are about to march through one of these grogging tunnels, and we need to get out of here."

"Why not fight them? We've fought beardies and ratties in here before."

"I need to stop what I saw, we're all dead if-" Grogger tried to stop but it was too late, he had said too much.

"Something bad happen in one of your visions, mighty king?" Grukhar was clearly relishing the opportunity to tease Grogger. He considered killing her right now, just to stop her babbling.

"Let's just say, it will be better for everyone, if we can get out of this snozzing cave quickly." Grogger paused for a moment and listened intently, convinced he could hear shouts coming from one of the tunnels again. Was it the underminders that had fled already, or was it the scalies on their way into the cavern? "Very quickly!"

"Why the grog should I help you?" asked Grukhar. It was a fair question, thought Grogger, and one he wasn't sure he had an answer for. However, in true goblin fashion, when he took Grukhar's throne, he should have killed her. The perfect way to stop a former leader trying to reclaim their power was to make sure there was no former leader. But something had stopped him. Something had made him put her in this cage.

"I didn't kill you for a reason," stated Grogger, "and I think this is the reason. You're meant to help us out of here."

"Me? Help you?" Grukhar spat viciously onto the floor.

"Let me put it another way. If I don't get out of here alive, then neither do you." He flashed her a wicked grin. Grukhar went silent for a moment and ran her pink tongue across sharp, yellow fangs.

"When you put it like that, it seems I don't have a choice."

Grogger fished into his pocket and produced a rusty key. He held it up in front of Grukhar's face.

"Don't make me regret this," he uttered before placing the key in the lock and turning it slowly. Throughout the process, he kept one hand on his dagger, just in case Grukhar leapt at him. The hinges of the door squealed in protest as it crept open, and Grogger braced himself for the attack. Instead, Grukhar waltzed out her prison and gave him a sweet smile.

"I'm at your command," she said and fluttered her green eyelids.

"There must be a secret way out of here," he rasped. "Somewhere that no one from the outside could know about."

"Of course there is, but I'm not sure you're going to like it."

"Just tell me where it is before I regret letting you out of the cage."

Huffing, Grukhar pointed at the pit, which had been closed since the battle with Grum.

"You must be joking," sighed Grogger.

"Through the back of Grum's pen, there's a tunnel that leads to the surface. It's well hidden and no one knows about it. Mainly because no one dared go past Grum to get to it, and he was too big to fit."

Grogger calculated what Grukhar's possible betrayal could be. Yes, she could get him in the pit... but then what? Grum was long gone. Yes, she might try and overpower him... but why wait until going in the pit to try that? His mind raced with all the ways he would try to trick himself if he were in Grukhar's position. His gaze never left hers while he racked his superbly cunning intellect.

"Open the pit," he shouted after a moment. "Open the pit!"

Underminers immediately ran over to Grukhar's former throne and pulled the lever to open the pit. There was a rumbling sound as the ground shuffled backward to reveal the gloomy depths below.

"If this is a trick, I'll get Jo'os to eat you... slowly. Starting with the feet."

Grukhar looked at him with mock shock plastered across her green face. She pressed her claws against her chest.

"Me?" she gasped. "I'm shocked you would even think that."

Grogger knew this was such a bad idea, but the remnants of that awful vision flashed through his mind. Him... lying dead on the floor of this awful place. He needed to get out of here! Quickly, he clambered up onto one of the cages, so he was visible above the panicking throng of goblins. He cupped his claws around his mouth.

"Everyone, listen!" he shouted as loud as he could. "Any moment now we're about to be attacked by scalies and humans."

There were cries of dismay from the underminers, and Grogger was sure he spotted a few faint in horror. Others simply darted up the tunnels to try and escape - not even caring what Grogger might have to say.

"You are more than capable of fighting them!" he shouted. This time, there were more horrified screeches and a larger portion of underminers disappeared into the dark, grabbing weapons as they went. Grogger growled as he let them go; they would provide a welcome distraction for the humans and salamanders.

"But there will be no fighting today!" he roared, trying to sound majestic. "Today... we run away!"

This statement was met by confused looks by the crowd.

"Did he say we're *all* running away?" enquired one underminer to his neighbor.

"No fighting?"

"We don't have to fight?" said one underminer enthusiastically.

The underminers erupted into sporadic applause as the realization dawned on them that they weren't about to be forced into combat.

"Let's see that grogging vision come true if no one's in the cave," hissed Grogger to himself with a grimace.

"Everyone into the pit! There's a secret exit down there!"

Underminers started throwing themselves eagerly into the gloom of the pit. Some even began singing an impromptu song:

Underminers like to run away,
live to run another day.
Dash as fast as you can go,
The ones that die are just too slow.

"After you," said Grogger to Grukhar and motioned down to the pit.

"Where's my pick?" she growled.

"You can have it when we're safe."

"I'll *need* a weapon."

"I'm sure you can improvise."

Grukhar grunted in frustration before flashing Grogger a hollow smile and leaping into the pit. Grogger quickly followed, the sound of his sword singing in his ears.

CHAPTER TWENTY-ONE

Rowan stopped suddenly and held up his hand to halt those behind him. Progress down the tunnel had been extremely slow. The light from the flames of the salamanders had constantly caused eerie shadows that played tricks on Rowan and the others. In the flickering flames, each limestone-encrusted stalagmite had taken on the appearance of a goblin ready to strike. Even now, Rowan heard one of the farmers cursing in frustration as his small sword clanged noisily off a rock.

What's more, the tunnel played tricks with sound and echoes. There had been numerous times when he thought he heard the charging of feet and braced himself for a horde of goblins to storm out of the darkness. But when they finally turned a corner, they were greeted by drips of water falling into a small pool. Rowan strained his ears again and was convinced that this time he could hear something coming toward them.

"Prepare yourselves," he whispered, and the echoes carried up the twisting tunnel behind him. He was pleased to hear the shuffling of feet and weapons being drawn. He waited and waited, but nothing came. Straining his eyes, he peered into the oppressive darkness beyond but, even with the flames from the swords of the salamanders, the gloom pressed on them relentlessly, making it impossible to see more than a few feet.

After waiting for a few more moments, he shook his head and decided they should move on. He pointed forward and set off into the inky murk. Behind him, he caught the grumbles of some of the villagers as they put away their weapons. The deeper they went into the cave, the more restless they became. Rowan couldn't blame them, but he needed them to concentrate instead of complaining about how much longer it was going to take. He continued walking and tried to ignore the hushed tones drifting down the tunnel.

Ahead, Rowan noticed that the flickering light of the flaming swords was being swallowed by hungry darkness. It no longer bounced weakly off the muddy walls of the tunnel and, instead, disappeared into nothingness. As they crept ever downward, he saw the shaft starting to open into a larger, yawning chasm. He pressed through the darkness and immediately felt the claustrophobic grasp of the tunnel give way.

The others spilled through behind him, and there were gasps of wonder... and dismay. They were standing in a mighty cave, packed with a forest of stalagmites that towered above even the salamanders. Rocky structures twisted up toward the ceiling and many were met by stalactites stretching down to greet them. Rowan shuddered slightly, even though there was a certain beauty in the rocky structures, it was almost like being in the jaws of a gigantic beast.

Unseen creatures whirled around the ceiling and occasionally flapped near Rowan and the others. Rather than see them, he could just feel a rush of air cross his face before it vanished back into the maze of stalagmites.

On his left, Rowan spotted a pool of calm water. The surface was like that of a mirror, reflecting the finger-like stalactites that hovered above it. In the orange glow of the salamanders' flaming swords, it almost looked as though it was on fire. A ghostly blaze among the stone trees. He thought he caught occasional movement beneath the glass-like water.

However, despite the natural beauty of the cavern, Rowan's attention was held by a troubling sight - numerous openings that indicated there were multiple tunnels stretching away from them. So far, they had been lucky because the tunnel they had followed had twisted along a singular path. This had surprised Rowan, after hearing numerous rumors and reports about the chaotic nature of goblin dens, but he had been equally relieved that their progress had been simple, though slow. Now with the prospect of multiple paths ahead of them, his heart fell.

"Make sure someone marks the entrance we just came through," he hissed behind him. "I don't fancy getting lost down here."

As he surveyed the cavern ahead of them, Rowan's stomach growled angrily. Since plunging into the darkness, he had lost all sense of time. He knew their progress had been laborious, but he had no clue how long they had actually been walking or how deep they had come. Suddenly, he felt someone approach and was relieved when he saw it was Furna, even though her scaly face took on a slightly more monstrous appearance in the flickering light.

"Just when we thought it was going to be easy," she whispered and motioned at the entrances spilling off the chamber.

"Think Igne can make sense of it all?"

"Only one way to find out." Furna tilted her head toward the apprentice mage. "We're hoping you can tell us which way to go."

"I can try," replied Igne, but her tone didn't fill Rowan with confidence. As Igne was starting to lift her claws to her temples, they were disturbed by a high-pitched wail that filled the cave and echoed between the rocks.

"By the Shining Ones, what is that?" asked Rowan. He gripped the hilt of his sword, and the gathered crowd fell into silence. The noise grew in intensity and swirled around them. Each time Rowan tried to place the origin of the sound, it seemed to change direction and appear in a different place.

Suddenly, a shape burst out the gloom to Rowan's right. A small goblin - even smaller than Rowan had seen before - ran into the cavern, flailing its skinny arms. Rowan was surprised to see pale skin, which took on an almost orange hue in the flaming light, and large black eyes that swivelled wildly as it raced toward them. The goblin didn't seem to notice the humans and salamanders as it barrelled forward, but then, just as it was about to crash headlong into Igne, it stopped running and skidded to a halt.

It tilted its head slowly upward as it stared, in terror, at the salamander. Rowan was about to tackle the goblin, but it let out a sharp squeak before quickly turning on the spot and disappearing down another tunnel. Its squeals of terror quickly disappeared and, once again, the cavern fell into silence.

"Was that a scout?" asked Igne.

"Scouts don't normally run around screaming," replied Furna. "The whole point is to *not* be seen."

"And why wasn't it green?" added Berusk.

"Screaming or not. Green or not. All that doesn't change anything," said Rowan, gruffly. "Igne just needs to tell us which way to go and then-"

Before Rowan could finish his sentence, the cavern filled with new noises. It was a bizarre mix of high-pitched voices and rushing feet. However, this time, it was clearly not the noise of a lone goblin.

"Weapons at the ready!"

Rowan planted his feet firmly on the ground and bent his knees; bracing himself against whatever was about to emerge from the dark. He breathed deeply, and then the cave erupted into madness.

Pale-skinned goblins emerged from hidden openings all around them. Most appeared to be in a blind panic and didn't even notice Rowan and the others before it was too late. The first groups to make it through the maze of stalagmites desperately tried to stop colliding with the humans and salamanders, but the remaining goblins slammed into them, forcing them forward and into battle.

Rowan kicked viciously at a goblin that stumbled too close. He heard the crack of its long nose breaking, and it fell to the floor howling. Another leapt half-heartedly at Rowan, eyes closed and claws scrabbling wildly. This time, Rowan plunged his sword into the monster's chest and watched its pale face go slack. He didn't have much time to remove his blade before a further couple of goblins - both pushing each other toward Rowan - came at him. He bashed one over the head with the pommel of his sword, and its black eyes rolled backward into their sockets. Rowan stamped on its neck, just to be sure. The other was dispatched with a quick slash of Rowan's sword, which opened a savage-looking wound across its chest. It stumbled backward squealing before toppling into the pool. Dark blood dirtied the previously clear water.

Rowan was already breathing heavily, and sweat was pooling underneath his armor, making his shirt sticky. Farm-life had made him weak. Yet, he was determined to keep fighting, and a fury drove him onward. The memory of the numerous goblin attacks on his home spurred his blade, and he felt a rage growing in his gut. Another attacker lunged clumsily at Rowan. This one was armed with a small rock. It ducked under Rowan's sword and hammered the rock onto Rowan's glittering breastplate. It made a small, useless clanging noise before pinging out of the goblin's grip and skittering across the floor. The goblin looked up meekly and shrugged its shoulders before Rowan thrust his blade through its slack-jawed face.

More goblins were pouring into the fray, and Rowan noticed that some were now armed with rusty weapons and makeshift shields. Several were using farming equipment, like sickles or even spades, and had pot lids for bucklers. A few had simple mining equipment clutched into their small hands. It almost annoyed Rowan that the goblins expected to best them armed with such crude weaponry. He couldn't believe he had lived in fear of attacks from these weak creatures back on the farm. How had they been overwhelmed by vile imps armed with rusty blades and cooking implements? It was ridiculous. He had become weak since leaving the army, but these monsters were no match for the might of a Basilean soldier! Glorious battle hymns of the Hegemony soared through his mind and lifted his spirits.

Thou hath felt our sword... thou hath felt our strength... thine eyes have seen the glory... O, Basilea!... O, Basilea!... thy enemies doth fall.

He roared and ripped a wooden barrel lid from the grasp of an approaching goblin. Without the makeshift shield, the goblin turned and tried to run away, but Rowan quickly surged forward and booted his foe to the ground. It squirmed in the dirt while Rowan planted his boot on its back and then slowly drove downward. The beast went limp. The tide was starting to thin, but Rowan was only just beginning.

A pair of goblins approached armed with 'spears.' Rowan almost laughed at the crude nature of the weapons: a couple of kitchen knives strapped to the end of broom handles. He batted one away with the flat of his sword as the goblin loosely jabbed it toward him. The other he managed to grab with his gauntlet before lobbing it across the cavern. Both goblins looked at each other in fear before bickering and pushing against one another while trying to escape. Rowan made two quick slashes and watched in satisfaction as two more goblins fell to his sword. He turned to find more attackers but, as he spun round, a goblin climbed up a nearby stalagmite and leapt onto Rowan's back. Its weedy claws grasped uselessly around his neck, scratching slightly at his bare skin as it tried to get a grip. Rowan reached behind and pulled the struggling goblin off him. Without thinking, he marched toward the pool and plunged the wriggling attacker under the water. Growling, Rowan held the body down under the water until eventually, with a final shudder, the thing went limp.

A hand clamped on his shoulder and Rowan wheeled round angrily, blade at the ready and shouting at his would-be attacker. Furna leapt backward quickly from Rowan's well-aimed slice. He glowered at her for a moment, convinced it was another foul monster ready to attack him. Furna eyed him, warily, keeping her own sword close.

"They're gone," she said, calmly. Rowan's breath came in rasps, and his heart was thundering in his chest. He noticed that Furna was looking at him curiously. Was it respect... or fear drawn across her face? Before she could speak further, Rowan dropped to one knee and rammed his sword into the ground. Under his breath, he began muttering prayers to the Shining Ones, thanking them for guiding his weapon. When he was done, Furna offered him her claw and pulled him back up.

"You fought... *well*," said Furna, although there was a hint of something else in her voice. Rowan looked over her shoulder and, even in the dim flickering light, he could see the others were looking at him too. "We certainly weren't expecting anyone to break into song."

"I was *singing*?" asked Rowan. His breathing was finally coming back under control.

"All 'doth this' and 'thine that'," chuckled Furna. "Very inspirational, but you might want to work on your harmonies."

Rowan gave her an awkward smile and tried to get his breath under control. With the cavern now silent, he took a moment to survey the carnage around him. The bodies of goblins were everywhere. Some had blackened skin, where the flaming swords of the salamanders had cleaved through skin and bone. Others bore more simple wounds from those of the humans. Rowan turned over the body of one with his boot to get a closer look.

"Bring over that torch," he told Furna.

He crouched down. The goblin was dressed in filthy, tattered rags - possibly an old potato sack - with a crude wooden breastplate that appeared to have been made from an old shop sign. Rowan was surprised to see how pale the skin of the goblin was. In fact, it was almost white, which meant the black saucer-like eyes appeared like gaping holes against the light tones of its face. Once again, he wondered how such scrawny little beasts had caused him and Mary so much misery. Here in the dark, they looked like the stuff of fairy tales, not terrible beasts that came in the dead of night and brought ruin to anything they touched.

"Anyone injured?" he asked. There was a small shout toward the back of the crowd of humans. Rowan worked his way over and found Brenwin, a young lad of just a dozen summers, if that, laying with a nasty slash across his stomach. Rowan had tried to tell the boy to stay back on the farm, but his father had insisted and said the experience would make a man of him. Inspecting the wound, Rowan was concerned he wouldn't make it to manhood if the injury was left to fester in the lingering gloom.

"Osian, go with Elis and get your son back home. That cut could turn nasty."

"I'm fine," gasped Brenwin and struggled to pull himself up. Rowan gently placed a hand on his chest.

"I'm sure you fought well, Brenwin," replied Rowan and looked across the nervous face of Osian, before leaning in closer to Brenwin. "Between you and me, I need you to help your father out of the tunnels. I think he may have messed his breaches when he saw those goblins."

Brenwin stifled a laugh before accepting Rowan's hand and allowing himself to be pulled, slowly, to his feet. He clutched his side, and Rowan could see he was struggling not to cry out in pain. The lad would turn into a fine man... if he survived, considered Rowan. Before they disappeared back up the tunnel, he grabbed Brenwin's father.

"If he dies, it's on you," he hissed. "I said he should have stayed back at the farm. He has proved himself more of a man than you, that's for sure."

Osian simply grunted in response and followed Elis and his son back up the way they had come. Rowan watched them go and prayed to the Shining Ones to keep them safe.

"Igne thinks she's found the correct way," came Furna's voice and snapped Rowan from his own thoughts. He turned to see Igne breathing heavily and pointing a trembling claw at one of the dark exits.

"It's harder than I thought to tell the path with all these tunnels," she added, meekly.

Rowan clapped a hand on her shoulder.

"It's harder for all of us," he replied gently. "Lead the way..."

With a determined nod, Igne headed into the shadowy path. Rowan was impressed to see that, unlike the other salamanders and their flaming swords, Igne had conjured a small nimbus of light around her claws. The ball was the color of fire and swirled like molten magma. Occasionally it would flicker slightly, if Igne stumbled or stopped for a moment to check they were on the right path. Rowan also noticed it gave off a little heat and spread some welcome warmth through the damp, cold air.

This time, their progress seemed quicker as they headed ever downward into the very bowels of the earth. Rowan kept his weapon drawn at all times but, despite a few echoing shouts or screams drifting up the path, they didn't encounter a single goblin on their journey. He thought it odd they had encountered little resistance but was pleased they hadn't been forced to fight in the confines of the tunnels. He knew that such close combat often saw men injuring their fellow fighters, just as much as they wounded the enemy.

Up ahead, Rowan noticed, once again, that the passage was opening up into a bigger cave. This must be the center of this infernal nest, he hoped, and gripped his sword tighter. The tunnel opened into a much grander cavern that towered above them. Rowan could only just make out the ceiling above, which was dimly lit by glowing crystals and the salamanders' flaming swords. He had a sort of begrudging respect for the effort it must have taken for the goblins to dig out this mighty expanse.

The rocky floor was covered in filth and rubbish. Pieces of bone, which had clearly been snapped by eager claws and sucked dry, were mixed with broken weapons, bloody patches, pieces of clothing, and other, more indescribable, detritus. It was then that Rowan noticed the awful stench of the place, and his senses recoiled at what some of that other filth might be. Shaking his head, he scanned the cave to see if they were about to encounter more goblins, but it was completely empty. A bizarre stillness had settled on the place, although Rowan could feel it must have normally been a site of intense activity and chaos.

In the center, he spied an elaborate throne sitting atop a stone mound, while cages lined one side of the grand hall. More tunnels stretched off from this main chamber, and Rowan was confident they had found the heart of the foul den. Yet, there wasn't a goblin in sight.

"It looks like it's been abandoned... and recently," said Furna as she approached Rowan.

"They must have heard us coming," replied Rowan. "Down here in the dark, their senses are much keener than ours... but, even then, they have managed to leave so quickly."

Furna growled, angrily.

"Every time I think we have these pests cornered, they slip through my damn claws. This is a wild scorchwing chase."

Rowan detected more than a hint of sadness in her voice. He knew how much catching the goblins had meant to Furna. It was almost like she had something to prove to herself, and the more the goblins eluded her grasp, the less she believed she was capable of achieving her goal. He felt some sympathy with her.

"Something tells me they're not coming back to this place," stated Rowan. "It feels... empty, somehow."

He was disturbed from a shout to his right. A few of the farmers were digging through a mound of what Rowan assumed to be rubbish.

"Rowan! You need to look at this," came an excited shout, followed by laughter from a few of the other farmers and more spirited voices.

He walked over and was surprised to see a farmer called Aeron holding a fine silver tray and staring at it in disbelief.

"The greenskins took this from my home on a raid last year," explained Aeron. "Look, it bears the crest of Primovantor."

Rowan tooked the proffered tray and could indeed see the crest. He was about to say that surely it couldn't be the same object, when another man claimed he too had found a family heirloom. With that, the pile of 'rubbish' was alive with men digging through the dirt to uncover treasure. There were shouts of joy and excitement as they found golden trinkets, coins, and gems. Even the salamanders began to sort through the mound and emerged with glittering rings that caught the dim light in the cavern.

"It's a treasure trove!" exclaimed one man.

"We're rich," echoed a salamander, and there was more deep-throated laughter.

Rowan simply stared at the pile, mystified.

"Why in the Shining Ones name did they take all this? Why cause all that misery and pain, to just shove it in a heap?"

"What does a goblin need with gems and gold? It isn't like they can trade for goods," answered Furna. "It was the weapons and food they really needed. If they couldn't eat it or use it, it must have been thrown away."

A laugh escaped Rowan's lips.

"They have been sitting on a fortune but raided our villages and farms for pots, knives, and Shining Ones know what else to use as clumsy weapons. They could have raised a mighty host with just a portion of this lot."

"Well, let us just be thankful the goblins didn't realize that!"

Rowan looked again at the pile. Admittedly, it wasn't all grand treasure. Amongst the items, he could see broken toys, ornaments, wooden trinkets, books, and more. Even so, there would be more than enough to share among the farmers. Perhaps they would even have enough to start their own settlement with defenses to stop the goblins, should they ever return. Plus, there would be plenty left for the salamanders to buy a grand ship.

"You can finally head home," said Rowan, with a smile.

* * * * *

Something about the words surprised Furna. Over the past few weeks during their pursuit of the goblins, the Three Kings had seemed a long way off. Even when they first entered the cave and saw the goblins had deserted, she had felt the chances of them ever getting home slipped ever further away. But now, she was standing in front of a hoard that contained enough treasure to buy a frigate, let alone the simple ship they required for what remained of her crew.

Yet, her spirits refused to lift. She should have been laughing and joking with the rest of the party, but the image of Hr'zak's head splitting open as that foul beast clamped down its awful jaws kept flashing through her mind. It was joined by the screams of her crew that had been ripped apart by those ancient, living trees as they had pursued the goblins. Her eyes burned with fury.

Deep down, she knew that she was angry with herself, rather than just the greenskins. She was angry at her hubris that had led to the shipwreck in the first place. She was angry that she had betrayed the trust of her crew. She was just... angry.

Now, presented with more than enough means to buy the ship to return home, she found herself dissatisfied. It felt as though her mission wasn't complete.

"Igne?" she turned to the smaller salamander, who was admiring an amulet carved with intricate elven script. "Can you still sense where the goblins went?"

For a moment, Igne looked confused, before she she must have seen the fire burning in Furna's eyes. Igne quickly pocketed the amulet and then held a claw to her temple before closing her eyes. After a moment, she snapped them back open and pointed to the pit near the throne.

"Down there," she uttered.

Furna realized that Berusk had been watching them both with interest.

"Surely you can't be thinking of going after the goblins still?" he asked. "Look at all this plunder! There's enough to buy a fleet here. You've got to let it go."

"What about Hr'zak and the others?" replied Furna.

"We lost many more on the sea. Are you going to start battling the waves next?"

She knew Berusk was right. She was being stupid and acting like a hatchling. But there was something about the way the goblin had sneered at her when he unleashed the slasher, and she still remembered the preening screech of that older goblin as he blasted her with that unnatural prod. Furna twitched involuntarily when she remembered the arcane lightning surging through her body.

"I have to do this," she stated. "I have to get revenge!"

"You *have* to get us home," growled Berusk. "You're acting like a damn fool!"

Furna realized the conversation had attracted the attention of the other salamanders. They were watching her keenly.

"Let her go," came Rorsha's voice. He was casually turning a glorious ruby around in his claws as he spoke. "She's washed up. As a captain, she destroyed our ship, killed half our crew, and sent us on this reckless path to catch a handful of worthless greenskins. Do you really think we'd get enough to buy a ship by selling a couple of goblins? Trusk must be turning in his grave."

"How dare you speak about your captain like that!" roared Berusk and drew his sword. The humans quickly darted out the way as they saw the salamanders squaring up for a fight. Furna laid a claw on his shoulder.

"No, Berusk, he's right. I'm no longer fit to be the captain."

Slowly, Furna lifted the battered tricorn hat off her head and handed it to Rorsha. The first mate grinned as he placed it, almost ceremoniously, upon his scaly head.

"Furna, please..." rasped Berusk softly, but Furna simply shook her head.

"Captain," said Furna and saluted Rorsha. The rest of the salamanders gave sharp salutes, apart from Berusk. Rorsha leaned in closely to Furna.

"Now you'll see how a real captain leads their crew," he whispered before turning to the crew. "Kill the humans and take as much loot as you can carry. We'll buy a whole fleet to take back to the Three Kings!"

"No!" shouted Furna, but a few of those salamanders loyal to Rorsha had started to ready their swords.

There were confused looks among Rowan and the other men as the salamanders spoke in their own harsh, guttural language, but many had begun drawing their own weapons when they sensed the atmosphere in the cavern change.

"What's happening?" asked Rowan, nervously. Rorsha ignored him.

"What are you waiting for? Your *captain* has given you an order!"

"That dragon's scale brew has warped your mind," growled Berusk. This time, his blade roared into flames as he prepared to leap at Rorsha.

"The only thing that's warped here is your bizarre sense of loyalty," barked Rorsha. "She owes you nothing. You're like a hatchling cuddling up to a clutch warden. It will be a mercy to send you to Kthorlaq's embrace."

Rorsha drew his own blade, and the pair started to circle each other.

"Wait, Berusk, this is my fight, not yours," said Furna. Berusk started to argue, but Furna silenced him with a sharp shake of her head. She drew her cutlass.

"Isn't this touching?" chuckled Rorsha.

"If I win, the crew's still yours, but leave the humans alone," she hissed. "Just promise me you'll get everyone home."

"I'm the captain, I'll do as I damn well please once I've beaten you."

With that, Rorsha darted forward and viciously slashed his sword toward Furna's waist. She darted backward and parried with her cutlass, sending echoes clanging around the cavern. Rorsha came at her again, wildly swinging his weapon and forcing her to parry again and again. Furna could see the wild look in his eyes and recognized the touch of dragon's scale brew. Somehow, he had been drinking again. Furna knew that Rorsha wasn't bad, but the pressures of their long journey and the effect of the brew had taken their toll. Under any other circumstance, he would have made a great captain, but his thoughts were clouded.

Rorsha lunged, but the blow was clumsy, and Furna had plenty of time to lean out of the way before delivering a stinging punch to Rorsha's scaly snout. He thrashed his tail angrily in response while dark smoke curled from his nostrils, and he surged at her once more. This time, she was ready. As he swung his sword to slash at her neck, she twisted around and deftly caught the hilt of his weapon with her cutlass. With an almost casual flick, she sent it soaring skyward before it landed with a crash in the pile of rubbish and treasure.

He looked at her in disbelief and started to dash toward his blade, but he was too slow. Furna sprang at him and delivered a crushing uppercut that sent him reeling backward. She followed it up with another powerful backhand that sent him sprawling into the dirt. His captain's hat skidded across the ground. While he struggled to pull himself back up, she pinned him back to the floor with her foot and placed her cutlass at his throat.

"This isn't you, Rorsha," she said and fixed him with her gaze. "I know there's a good salamander in there. I would have never made you first mate if I didn't think you had the heart for it."

Rorsha struggled for a moment, growling. The other salamanders and villagers watched in complete silence.

"I know you just want to get home - we *all* want to get home, but the humans have done nothing wrong. You would have grown to regret that order."

Rorsha stopped struggling and looked back up at Furna.

"I'm just so tired," he mumbled, "and so cold. Can't you feel the chill? The cold seeping into your scales. The dwindling fires."

"All the more reason for you to get the crew back to the Three Kings. Killing the humans would do nothing to help that and, deep down, you know that too. We're corsairs, not pirates, Rorsha."

"I yield," he said, but Furna didn't remove the tip of her cutlass from his throat.

"Do I have your word you'll leave the humans alone?"

"Yes," he muttered.

"And you'll get the crew home?"

"You have my word."

Furna sheathed her cutlass and offered Rorsha her claw. After a moment, he took it and allowed himself to be pulled up, before marching over to retrieve his own blade.

"You should have killed him," muttered Berusk.

"He isn't evil, Berusk, and he will ensure the crew gets home. We all make mistakes. Remember that time on Axe Island?"

Before Berusk could answer, Rowan slowly approached the two salamanders.

"What was that all about?" he asked, cautiously. Furna saw an odd look in his eye. The slight mistrust that some humans had when dealing with the other races of Pannithor.

"He said my mother was a frog," answered Furna, speaking in the common tongue once more. She hoped her hollow laugh was enough to convince Rowan.

"Nothing for me to worry about then?"

"The only thing you need to worry about is getting all that treasure home. The crew will just take enough for the ship. The rest is yours to split." She looked over and saw men already filling their pockets. "Although it looks like you may have to be quick to make sure there's some left."

"And your hat?"

This time Furna sighed a little. "I'm trusting Rorsha to get the crew home. I have my own path to go. My own fight to fight."

"She's being ridiculous," grumbled Berusk.

"I know there wasn't much fighting here, but I'd like to return the favor," said Rowan. "I never would have plucked up the courage to even enter this place if it wasn't for you. Let me come with you."

Furna shook her head.

"Thank you, but this is my fight, and if anything happened to you, I would live in fear of Mary tracking me down for revenge."

They both laughed, and Furna gave him a salute.

"Captain," she said.

"Once a captain, always a captain," replied Rowan and returned the salute.

Furna turned her attention to the gaping pit below the throne.

"You're sure that's where they went, Igne?"

"As sure I can be, Captain."

"Please, just Furna now." She gave Igne a kind smile.

With that, she took a running leap into the pit and landed heavily among the broken bones and rusty weapons. She let her eyes adjust to the gloom for a moment before seeing the open portcullis ahead. A dark corridor disappeared into the distance, and she gritted her fangs against the rotten smells that drifted from the tunnel. When she was about to head into the shaft, she realized with frustration that she had nothing to light the way. Her cutlass wasn't made from the same obsidian as the flaming swords used by the other salamander. She cursed her haste.

While she was looking around in the filth for something to use as a torch, she was disturbed by sounds of others entering the pit. Furna turned to find Berusk, Igne, and Rowan sliding down the rocky walls.

"Did you really think we would let you go alone?" asked Berusk.

Despite herself, Furna gave her companions a wide grin.

"You don't have to do this," she said, but her words couldn't hide her relief.

"It would be two minutes before I killed Rorsha if you left me alone with him," rumbled Berusk.

"And you'll never find the way without me," added Igne.

"I thought you may miss my wonderful singing. *O, holy land! O, pious land! I stand before thee! Mine soul aflame!*" Rowan's hymn bounced around the pit.

"Please, in Ktholaq's name, I'll only let you come with me if you stop singing," laughed Furna. "Seriously though, you don't have to do this, particularly you, Rowan - this isn't your quest."

"Mary nursed you back to health, she probably cares more about you than she does about me now! I'd hate to return without knowing what your fate was."

Furna shrugged.

"Let's go goblin hunting!"

CHAPTER TWENTY-TWO

"In the gobs' name, just keep running!" screeched Grogger. Their dash through the pit had been desperate, and Grogger had kept shouting to keep the hordes of underminers charging through the darkness. Although his vision had been quite specific that he may have died in the cavern, he wasn't sure how much time he would have to make his escape. The salamanders could be hot on heels or potentially days away. Still, he didn't want to risk it. They needed to cover as much ground as possible.

"The mighty king sounds scared," said Grukhar with a smirk.

"Shut the snoz up! No one asked you," spat Grogger. "Just concentrate on getting us out of here."

"We're close," hissed Grukhar with a grimace as she carried on running.

Grogger hoped that Grukhar's determination to save her own skin meant she wouldn't try to betray him immediately. Still, he made sure that he kept close to Ug as he lumbered down the tunnel alongside them. Every so often, he would cast Grukhar a suspicious glance, expecting her to produce a hidden blade from somewhere and slit his throat. So far, the attack had not come - but he knew it would, and then he would be ready.

In between the multitude of thundering feet, his sharp ears caught the sound of running water. Grogger hoped that Grukhar wasn't leading him to a waterfall where she would push him to his death. Instinctively, he moved closer to Ug and hoped the troll might protect him. After all, he had saved Ug from the cavern troll... even if he had volunteered him for the fight in the first place.

Before he had time to ponder whether he should just kill Grukhar now, they emerged into a much larger tunnel. Through the center of the passage roared a mighty underground river that splashed and crashed against the rocky walls of the cavern. A path had been carved alongside one edge, and moored to it were three massive barges.

Grogger was amazed the boats could float due to the fact they appeared to be constructed from random pieces of wood nailed together. He recognized the doors of human homes, tables, and even what appeared to be the remnants of a trebuchet. Each of the barges creaked and groaned as the harsh current of the river pulled against the scrappy ropes that held them in place.

"What happened to the fourth one?" Grukhar muttered to herself.

Grogger looked along the path and saw that one mooring was empty. A piece of rope trailed into the water, and he spotted the prow of a sunken barge. He recoiled in horror.

"You expect me to go on one of those?"

"If my glorious king would prefer to turn back and fight the scalies, then I would be happy to fight. Just give me back my grogging pick," snarled Grukhar and held out a claw.

Given the choice between the possibility of his vision coming true and taking his chances on the barges, Grogger knew what he would prefer. After all, he hadn't seen himself drowning in the dark.

"All aboard the boats!" he shouted. Grukhar started to walk off, but Grogger quickly grabbed her arm. "You stick with me. I don't want you sending me off on some boat you know that's going to sink."

Grukhar gave him a wicked smile before pointing to the second barge.

"I supervised the building of this one myself," she replied.

Grogger pushed and shoved his way through the underminers as they fought to clamber aboard the barges. Although the boats were big, he wasn't sure how they were all going to fit on. As more goblins piled onto his barge, he was sure he felt it beginning to sink under the weight.

"Cast off! Cast off!" he cried impatiently and was pleased to see Gritter and Klunk cutting the ropes. Kackle just managed to leap onto the craft but almost threatened to tumble back into the current until Gritter thrust out a claw and pulled the wiz aboard. However, more bodies were piling onto one side, and he could feel the deck tilting precariously toward the rushing water. "We're going to capsize! Stop them getting on the boat! Shove them off if you have to."

With that, a furious scrap broke out between those trying to push their way onto the barge and the passengers already aboard that were trying to stop them. Grogger heard numerous splashes and screams as desperate underminers were pushed or pulled into the freezing water below. Ug was scooping up goblins that were clinging to the side of the boat and tossing them into the river. They quickly disappeared without a trace.

Painfully slow, the ropes holding the barge in place gave way, and it started to drift into the current. The bow was now too far away from the path for goblins to make the jump, but a few more frenzied individuals tried to make it anyway, only to find the embrace of the freezing torrents. Finally the last rope snapped with a sharp 'twang,' and Grogger's barge moved precariously away, accompanied by the ragged cheers of the goblins. In front, the first boat was already moving ahead, but behind him, the third was in complete chaos.

Like him, the goblins on the remaining barge had quickly realized that the weight of the never-ending underminers was threatening to capsize them. Fights were breaking out on the deck as groups fought among themselves to stop others leaping onboard or threw some individuals overboard that were already on deck. But it simply wasn't enough. Eventually there was a loud cracking sound, as the sheer weight of bodies began to crush the crudely built structure. Some goblins plunged into the water, hoping to swim to the other barges, but the currents were so strong, they were quickly carried away screaming. Others clung desperately to the shards of the barge, perhaps hoping they would float to safety. However, they also quickly felt the chill grasp of the water. Grogger watched the last few disappear, howling as they went, before shrugging and turning his attention to Grukhar.

"Where does this go?" he asked.

"No idea," answered Grukhar. "Never been on 'em. Sent some scouts on a boat once, but they never came back."

"They never came back?" Grogger struggled to hide his shock.

"Nah, so I guess it must go somewhere, otherwise they would have just come back and told me it didn't go anywhere," explained Grukhar. Grogger shook his head in disbelief.

"Or it could go to a massive waterfall or lead us straight into beardy mine, you stupid snoz! They probably didn't come back because they're dead!"

"No one calls me a snoz," seethed Grukhar. "Call me that again and I'll kill you."

"Threaten me again and I'll get Ug to throw you overboard," snapped Grogger and leaned in close to Grukhar. "I asked you to help me escape, and now that we're on the barge, your usefulness is getting less and less by the moment."

Grogger gave her one last disdainful look and stomped off to the back of the barge to think. As he went, underminers bowed low and thanked him for saving them from the salamanders. A few even kissed his feet as he passed. Irritated, he swatted them away.

"He shouted at me," squealed one with excitement.

"He touched me!" yelled one after Grogger slapped its puckering lips.

"He *kicked* me!" said another, proudly, and showed off the mean bruise that was blossoming on its cheek.

Eventually, he shoved his way to the stern and sat grumpily on an upturned box. While he was pondering his predicament, Magwa and Jo'os joined him. Jo'os immediately curled up near Grogger's feet. He reached down to tickle his ear but quickly snapped his hand away when he saw Magwa watching him.

"Jo'os senses something in you," croaked Magwa. Grogger noticed he was leaning more and more heavily on the prod as they had progressed on their journey.

"He's probably just hungry," retorted Grogger, grumpily, but he felt a swell of pride at the thought that this mighty beast appeared to respect him. Magwa simply grunted.

"Magwa has been wondering why we left that cavern in such a hurry. Surely with all these goblins, Magwa thinks you could have faced whatever was coming down those tunnels."

Grogger was about to tell the nosey old goblin to mind his own business when he decided that perhaps he may know something about the visions.

"I had another vision," whispered Grogger.

"Ah, a vision that showed us escaping?"

"No. A vision that showed me - all of us - dying."

Magwa's brows rose in surprise, and he stroked his chin with a dithering old claw.

"So this vision did not come true?"

"Well, no, but it showed me what might have happened if we stayed in the cavern."

"And what of the other visions?"

Grogger hated it when the senile old gob spoke in riddles like this. The years had withered his mind like an old weed that had been in the sun for too long.

"Just spit out what you mean, you old snoz."

"You considered the other visions would come true? Grogger with an army. Grogger as leader. Grogger as *king*.Yet this one did not come true. Does that not worry you?"

"Why should it? The vision helped. It told me what to do."

"What if the other visions are not true?"

The thought hadn't occurred to him, but now that Magwa said it, his mind was wracked with doubt. What if the visions were showing him what *could* happen, rather than what *would* happen?

"Well, we better make snozzing sure they do come true then," he hissed. Magwa watched him coldly while Jo'os snored at his feet.

"Magwa has no doubt that Grogger Split-tooth will be a king. As Magwa said, Jo'os can sense your greatness."

For a moment, Magwa shut his eyes, and Grogger was convinced he had fallen asleep. He looked around and wondered, just for a moment, how easy it would be to grab the prod and simply push him overboard. Jo'os was asleep and probably wouldn't even notice. Without realizing, Grogger slowly started reaching a claw toward the prod but quickly snatched it back when Magwa's eyes snapped open. Magwa eyed him for a moment before speaking.

"In one vision, you rode a giant machine, yes?"

Grogger nodded. It was the first vision he had experienced after drinking that awful concoction by Kackle. The drink that had started him on this bizarre path. Had he really believed the visions would come true? Did he really think he would become king? King of all the goblins? He shook off the doubts. Of course, he was destined for something special. He looked around at the thin, scrawny-looking underminers as they bickered among themselves or threw up due to the rocking motion of the barge. He was better than all these. Better than that idiot Bung and his useless cronies. Better even than Magwa.

Originally it had all been about getting the army to take out Bung. Petty revenge for the way Bung had mistreated him all these years. But with each vision, a growing sense of ambition had blossomed inside Grogger. Even finding the dagger - whatever the Abyss it was - added to that sense that he was destined for something special. He was never meant to be a simple scout, heading out to spy on human settlements and report back to some dim-witted biggit. He was meant for greater things. He was meant to be a king. *The* king.

"It was some sort of massive mincer," said Grogger. "A huge thing."

"Then you will need someone to build it, and Magwa knows just where to find them. As long as this river doesn't take Magwa too far."

"You know a *lot* of goblins," added Grogger, suspiciously. Magwa let out his mad, high-pitch laugh. It shook his frail body and caused his ears to wobble. Jo'os stirred in his sleep and the gathered underminers looked across nervously before going back to in-fighting or violently vomiting.

"You are right, Grogger Split-tooth. Magwa has lived far too long and met far too many goblins," answered Magwa, in between fits of laughter. "Perhaps though, the gobs have placed me here to help you, and when you are king, Magwa can finally join the rest of my pack."

Once again, Grogger wondered just how long Magwa had been alive. There were so many stories about him, so many legends passed between the clans. He doubted Magwa would even remember when he crawled out the spawning pool.

"The last bunch of misfits we met wanted to kill you," groaned Grogger, "so you'll excuse me if I don't get excited about another tribe that you've met before."

Magwa wagged his claw, dismissively.

"No, no, no. This is very different, *very* different. These are a tribe of gadjits called the bodjits. They just want to build! Great machines that shake the earth. Flying machines!"

"Flying machines?" snorted Grogger. "Only dragons and birds can fly."

"It's true," came Kackle's voice as he pushed through the throng of underminers. "The old boss Graf sent countless clan members to negotiate with them, but they always refused. They didn't care about joining a clan or anything. Just wanted to be left alone. Odd bunch, really."

The fact a wiz called the bodjits odd was mildly disturbing to Grogger. After all, it was normally the magic users of a clan that slowly went mad as their mind was overwhelmed by their attempts to master arcane sorcery. Yes, the so-called gadjits liked to experiment with all-manner of wild contraptions, but they would typically blow themselves up or accidently launch themselves from a new catapult design before they started to lose grip of their senses.

"Imagine that, great Grogger! The first goblin king to have an army of flying machines," said Magwa, excitedly. Grogger rolled his eyes and looked across the deck at the underminers. Some of them stopped fighting or clutching their stomachs long enough to notice he was glowering at them.

"He's looking at me!" swooned one underminer wearing, what looked like, a child's dress.

"He looked at me first!"

"The king that didn't fight!"

"The king that ran away," joined another.

"All hail the king!" came several shouts.

For all their faults - and they were numerous - he had to admit the underminers seemed loyal to him. He tried to ignore the fact they had turned extremely quickly on Grukhar, given the chance, and instead focused on how devoted, at least for now, they seemed to him. He certainly had the numbers to start an army, now he just needed all the complicated machines that came with a great goblin force.

"How far until we get to these bodjits?" Grogger asked Magwa.

"Magwa thinks this river will lead us very close. Very close!"

"How *convenient.*" Grogger couldn't help but shake his suspicions about Magwa. Why was he helping him?

"The gobs look down on you, Grogger Split-tooth. They have great things planned for us all."

As he considered, once again, the visions he had seen, Grogger realized how incredibly tired he was. He couldn't remember the last time he had slept, and a sudden exhaustion threatened to overwhelm him. Goblins didn't need a lot of sleep, but the small amounts Grogger had managed to snatch in between running, fighting, and trying to stay alive were catching up with him. He felt his eyelids drooping, but just before he closed them for a final time, he spotted Grukhar staring at him, menacingly. His eyes snapped open.

"You lot," he shouted to a group of nearby goblins.

"He's speaking to us!" Screamed one and fainted. The others grovelled quickly toward Grogger while he tried to contain his disdain for the wretched idiots.

"I'm going to have a snooze. Don't let anyone come near me... especially Grukhar."

"It is our honor, your majesty." The small group of goblins formed a protective semi-circle around Grogger. One had somehow caught a fish and was swinging it, experimentally, like a club. The gentle rocking motion of the barge helped Grogger quickly drift off into a fitful sleep, imagining that at any moment he would wake to find Grukhar's pick poised over his face.

* * * * *

Furna, Igne, Berusk, and Rowan charged through the tunnels. In the glow of Igne's magical ball of flame and the light from Berusk's sword, there was evidence of the goblin's hasty escape everywhere. Scraps of food, rusty weapons, and even occasionally the odd trampled body were littered along their path.

"We just missed them," hissed Furna, angrily. "If I hadn't spent so long recovering from that damn fall, we could have caught them."

"A few hours or even a day wouldn't have made a difference," huffed Rowan. "The greenskins must have somehow received warning that we were coming. They cleared out before we even got close."

Furna knew that Rowan was right, but she was still furious with herself. Once again, she had let the goblins slip out of her claws. Deep down, she knew that her continued disappointment with herself was the reason she was pursuing this pointless quest. She should have swallowed her pride and gone with Rorsha once they found the treasure. But here she was, running blindly down a tunnel and ready to be greeted by Kthorlaq knew what.

Looking at the others, she was both glad and disappointed they had chosen to join her. Disappointed because she was dragging them into her madness but glad to have the assistance she would no doubt need. After all, she had failed to catch the goblins when they were just a clawful of them. Now it looked like there was a damn army.

Up ahead, Berusk suddenly raised his claw to bring them to a halt. "Hear that?" he rasped.

Furna tilted her head. The sound of rushing water echoed off the clammy walls.

"A river?" asked Igne.

"An escape route," grunted Furna. "These goblins have more lives than a damn gur panther." She nodded for them to continue, and they carried onward. As they ran, she quickly cast a glance at Rowan. He was breathing heavily as he jogged along, and Furna realized that life on the farm must have made him softer, compared to his days in the Basilean infantry. Of all of them here, this was certainly not his fight, and she wondered why he had chosen to come. However, she quickly realized it was the same reason as her: revenge. The way he had fought the goblins in the cave was clearly a man driven by fury. Fury at the life he and Mary had never been able to live because of the goblins and their interminable raids. In some ways, she doubted if it even mattered whether these were the same goblins that had ransacked his farm time and time again; he just needed to feel like he was doing *something*. He just needed some justice.

The sound of rushing water was getting louder by the moment before the tunnel suddenly opened up into a large underwater river. A small path clung to the righthand side of the cavern wall, seemingly threatening to topple into the raging torrent at any moment. Furna quickly scanned her surroundings and noticed the crude pieces of rope that were tied to wooden poles hammered into the ground. She walked over to one and ran the moldy rope between her claws.

"Boats," she groaned. Every time she seemed to be getting close, the goblins had yet another means of escape. At this rate, she wouldn't be surprised if they sprouted wings and flew into the sky when she finally grabbed hold of them. Her thoughts were disturbed by the sound of high-pitched squealing and she noticed, with disgust, one of the pale green goblins was desperately clutching to a barge pole sticking out of the water. The wretched creature was completely bedraggled and dripping wet. It would occasionally reach out a trembling claw to Furna before quickly grabbing back onto the pole as it threatened to lose its grip.

"Where have they gone?" shouted Furna to the miserable wretch.

It responded with a series of incomprehensible shrieks in its own squeaking tongue. She tried one more time.

"Can you speak the common tongue? Where have your horrible little friends gone?"

Once again, she was greeted by more irritating wails and moans. With a flash, she whipped a pistol from her holster and shot through the barge pole. The gunshot sounded like cannonfire as it ripped through the cavern, followed by the crack of the wooden pole. The lone goblin fell into the water with a pathetic splash, and its desperate pleas for help were quickly carried away by the currents. Furna reloaded her pistol before placing it back in her holster.

"It might have been more use to us alive," said Berusk, flatly.

"You heard the stupid creature, it couldn't speak a word. And as soon as we weren't looking, it would disappear up a dark hole or we'd find a knife between our shoulder blades," replied Furna, with a growl.

"Good riddance," added Rowan and spat into the rushing water.

"Look, it's pretty obvious where they've gone," said Furna and pointed at the path that hugged the river. "We follow that and see where it goes."

"We could be under here for weeks," said Berusk and slapped his tail angrily against the floor. "We've got no idea how long this damn thing is."

"Actually," interjected Rowan, with a slight cough, "the River Wharke isn't too far from where we first entered the caves. I wouldn't be surprised to find that this comes out there. It's only a few hours' march."

"See, Berusk," said Furna cheerfully and clapped him on the back, "only a few hours' march. And look at all the great scenery you've got to enjoy." She spread a claw around the gloomy underground network of tunnels and stalagmites.

"Is it too late for me to go back with Rorsha?" grunted Berusk.

"We both know you'd already be squabbling like hatchlings," she replied with a wink, then turned to the former mage. "Igne, are you still able to feel that prod?"

"I am, but it's getting fainter. The river must be carrying them pretty fast."

"No time to lose then. Let's go," said Furna with a cheerfulness she really didn't feel and set off walking along the narrow path. Despite her comments to Berusk, she wasn't relishing spending more time in the damp and dark. She just hoped the underground river would be easy to navigate, because if Igne was losing the touch of the prod, then it would make it much harder to find their way through the network of tunnels.

After they had been walking for a while, she fell into step with Rowan.

"Before we go any further, I just want to make sure you know that you don't have to do this. I know Mary brought me back from Kthorlaq's embrace, and for that I'm eternally grateful, but I don't expect you to watch over me forever, Rowan."

"That's only part of it," he sighed before looking at her for a moment. "How long have you been part of a crew?"

The question caught her slightly unawares. "Almost as long as I can remember."

"You're more like me than you know," chuckled Rowan. "Well, imagine not having that crew around you, suddenly you're all alone and left to deal with the world. I grew up an orphan, after my mother left me outside a sisterhood chapel. The sisters said I must have been born out of wedlock and she didn't want the disgrace. Happens more than you think... even in the holy land of Basilea. Then when I was too old for it to be deemed decent to live among the sisters, I was enlisted straight into the army."

"How old were you?"

"I'd estimate I was about eleven, perhaps twelve, summers. Either way, it was too young to become a soldier. Things you have to do, monsters you have to face... it's no good for a young lad." Rowan went quiet for a moment and the pair continued to walk in silence through the oppressive shadows. Eventually, Rowan gave a slight cough and continued. "Even so, I was always surrounded by others. Always part of a regiment, a battalion... an army. Someone at my elbow in the shieldwall or sharing an ale in the mess tent after a long campaign."

Something suddenly occurred to Furna.

"If you joined when you were so young, how come you only rose to the rank of captain? Surely with such a long military career, you would have climbed through the ranks?"

"Someone lowborn like me can only climb so high," muttered Rowan. "The generals and dictators of the Basilean army tend to be chosen from the noble families of the Hegemony."

"Wealth won't protect you on the battlefield," hissed Furna as a whisp of black smoke trailed from her nostrils.

"If you've got enough wealth, you never end up anywhere near the battle," replied Rowan, sadly. "I guess, eventually, I grew tired of watching my friends and brothers die screaming around me and started to look for companionship of a different kind, which is when I met Mary. She was a healer attached to our company, and I found myself spending more and more time in her field tent, even when I wasn't injured. We both talked about how we wanted a different life, away from the blood and mud of the army. Before I knew it, I'd swapped a sword and shield for a scythe and plough.

"We arrived at that farm so full of hope. So full of excitement, but it all quickly turned to ashes. It seemed that every time we planted crops or bought some new livestock, the raiders would come under moonlight and rip our world apart. It was like they were sent by the Abyss to spite us. Each moment of happiness, snatched away in their foul, green claws. And each time, it was left to Mary and I to pick up the pieces. There was no willing soldier to plug the gap in the shieldwall. We were alone. I was alone."

Furna realized that Berusk and Igne were both listening to Rowan speak. Igne, in particular, seemed captivated by his words. For the first time, Furna considered just how young Igne was compared to her and Berusk. Of course, for one so young, a life on the ocean must seem full of adventure and excitement; but she wondered how long that sense of wonder would last. Perhaps Igne would have been better training with the mage priests back on Three Kings than risking her life on each voyage across the seas. Furna was quickly snapped out of her own thoughts when she realized that Rowan had begun talking again.

"I know I don't have to do this, Furna. I know this is really your fight but, for once, I want to take back control. I don't want to be the one cowering in the darkness waiting for unseen attackers or feel useless. I want to be the one that they fear. The one they run screaming from. I want to hold my head high and say that even when I was left alone, I didn't give up. I kept up the fight."

Furna guessed that, deep down, she always knew Rowan's reasons for joining her. After all, it wasn't too dissimilar to her own reasons for tracking down the goblins. Since her ship had wrecked off the coast of the Successor Islands, she had been struggling to take back control. Struggling to prove to herself that she was worthy of the title of captain. Somehow, the desire to catch the goblins had become irrevocably fused with that desire. Now it was the only thing that drove her. It didn't matter about getting home. It didn't matter about the ship. It just mattered that she could prove to herself that she was capable of catching those little green bastards.

"Your fight is my fight," she said to Rowan and shot him a toothy grin.

"Just don't tell Mary I've become a soppy sod in my old age." The pair's chuckling was stopped abruptly by Igne hushing them to be quiet.

"There's something up ahead." She hissed and quickly dimmed her shimmering ball of light, plunging them into the grasping darkness.

To their left, the underground river still raged, but the path they were walking along had started to turn a corner and, thankfully, widened a little so they no longer had to walk in close pairs. Although they couldn't see what lay in wait, there were definitely whispers of what sounded like an angry, high-pitched conversation. Furna brought them to a halt.

"More goblins?" she asked.

"I'm not sure," said Igne, while straining to catch the snippets of chatter.

"Whatever it is down here, I doubt it's good."

"Shall we wait? See if they clear out?" suggested Berusk.

"Ha! Getting timid in your old age, Berusk?" whispered Furna. "It doesn't sound like there are many of them, and I don't want to lose any more time than we need to."

The small group continued to listen for a moment. The conversation continued to grow in volume, but the rushing torrent beside them stopped Furna being able to tell exactly what it was. Although it sounded similar to the high-pitched chatter of the goblins, it was faster and somewhat sing-song. It rose and fell in volume and pitch as the conversation clearly became more heated. Suddenly, there was a loud splash when what sounded like a body hit the water, followed by more excited chittering and a scream that grew fainter as it was swept down the river.

"Perhaps we just wait for them to throw each other in?" said Berusk, gruffly. Furna ignored him.

"Igne," hissed Furna, "can you send your ball of light ahead of us?"

The younger salamander nodded eagerly.

"Right, when I say, shoot your ball of magic round that bend. Hopefully they'll be blinded by the light and we'll have the advantage... even if it is only for a moment. Ready? Now!"

Igne's ball of light blazed into life and shot around the corner. Even Furna had to shield her eyes from the roaring flames. From further down the tunnel, they heard squeals of surprise and perhaps pain as the brilliant light bathed the tunnel in its magical glow.

"Let's go!" Furna charged down the tunnel with her pistols drawn. However, rather than goblins, she was surprised to see around a dozen large rats, almost the size of men, and standing on their hind legs. They were dressed in filthy rags, and their fur was even dirtier. Some were shielding their eyes from the blinding light while others were chittering wildly and pulling rusty-looking blades or spears from their holsters.

"By the Shining Ones," she heard Rowan whisper behind her. "It's true."

Shaking off the sense of confusion, Furna aimed and pulled the trigger on her pistol. The head of the rat closest to her exploded in a shower of gore, splattering the fur of its neighbor. Suddenly the rotten smell of burning fur assaulted Furna's nostrils, and she realized that Igne was zipping the ball of light between the rats and setting them on fire. A couple jumped into the cooling river, only to be washed away, while the others rolled desperately in the dirt in a futile attempt to put out the magical flames.

Just ahead, Rowan was fending off two rats armed with crude spears. Rowan almost casually swatted away their weak blows before smashing his shield into the face of one. There was a crack of bones and a squeak of pain before Rowan followed up with a deadly jab of his blade. The rat fell limp to the floor. Its partner dropped its spear to the floor and turned, ready to dash back down the tunnel, but Rowan was too quick. He leapt on the creature's back, knocking it to the ground and plunging his sword into its back.

Furna spotted another rat trying to make its escape and took aim with her second pistol. In the gloom, it was tough to aim, but she trusted Kthorlaq would keep her aim true. There was a loud crack as she pulled the trigger, and Furna grunted in satisfaction as the bullet tore through the monster's back and it toppled into the river. She looked around for another target but was surprised to see the fight was over. Rowan was cleaning his blade and muttering prayers, while Igne was breathing more heavily, clearly tired from the exertion of using the ball of light as a weapon.

"I didn't even get chance to draw my blade," said Berusk with a huff. He walked up to a dead rat and pulled on its fur to raise its head. "What are these monstrosities?"

"A rumor," replied Rowan.

"Not often I encounter rumors in underground passages," said Furna. "Perhaps you can enlighten us a little more?"

Rowan gave one of the lifeless corpses a kick.

"Some of the soldiers said they had seen giant rats when fighting out in the east. Great hordes of furry beasts, accompanying the dwarfs that worship the Abyss. But they were wretched things that had to be whipped into battle by their twisted masters. Yet when the battles were over, there were never any bodies. Some said the other rats would eat their dead, but most said it was a trick of the Abyss. An illusion so repulsive that it sent men mad."

Furna inspected one of the stinking bodies close to her. Nearby was the semi-eaten leg of a goblin. She noticed there were other limbs and even a head. All bore teeth marks.

"Looks like they were eating the goblins that were washing down the river."

"At least we don't have to worry about the goblins having more allies," added Berusk.

"We do have to worry if this plague is spreading west," muttered Rowan. "The goblins are bad enough... but giant rats? May the Shining Ones give me strength."

"Throw their bodies into the river, just in case others come this way, and let's move on," commanded Furna and lobbed a body into the churning currents. She was surprised by how light the ratman was, and she could feel its bones under the malnourished skin. It hardly made a splash as it fell into the water. The horrors spawned by the Abyss never failed to amaze her, but there was something particularly rank about these latest creations. She gave an involuntary shudder before recovering herself as others splashed into the torrent.

"Right, let's move on. We've got goblins to catch!" she said. "Why am I getting a sense of deja vu?" chuckled Berusk.

CHAPTER TWENTY-THREE

Grogger was flying. The wind whipped his ears as he soared to almost touch the clouds. Underneath him, the ground zipped by. Fields, houses, even castles were like playthings to him. He smirked as he imagined he was a dragon, able to blast them all into oblivion with a ranging torrent of his fiery breath. He closed his eyes for a moment and listened to the howl of the wind.

Then he heard another sound. The sound of battle. There were screams, the clash of weapons, and the crack of gunfire. He looked down and was surprised to see flames raging below him. Had he somehow breathed fire like a dragon? Among the flames he saw goblins running and howling with fear. From up here, they were like insects, scattering from the fire as it crept toward them. Insignificant insects.

Then he realized, with horror, that the dying goblins were screaming his name. Angry, violent howls of terror that were all directed at him. They were dying because of him. With a start, he noticed that he was starting to descend. He was dropping quickly toward the ground and the furious crowds of goblins that were baying his name. Now he could feel the warmth of the flames as he got closer to the madness below. He wasn't sure what he was more afraid of – the rampaging fire or the blood-thirsty mob. Grogger began to scream.

He woke with a violent start, and his eyes darted around. For a moment, he could still feel the heat of the flames on his skin and hear the roar of the goblins. It took him a few seconds to realize he was sitting back on the barge. The underminers closest to him were looking at him with wide eyes. Some were muttering and pointing.

"You were screaming," said Kackle, and Grogger realized he was standing next to him. Just like the underminers, there was a look of fear and confusion on the wiz's face.

"Just a bad dream," replied Grogger while trying hard to resist the temptation to look for scorch marks from the flames. Grogger hoped it wasn't a vision, because this one hadn't ended well for him.

"What are you all gawking at?" he shouted to the crowd and threw a nearby piece of wood at them. The goblins quickly looked away, although Grogger was sure he could still hear some muttering. One dashed out to grab the wood and proudly held it to its chest as though it were some sort of holy relic.

Grogger leaned back and, for the first time, noticed the night sky above him rather than the stalagtites of the caves. Glittering lights shimmered in the cloudless black, and he wondered if it was true that each of them was a former goblin king or queen. Goblin rulers tended to come and go very quickly, which explained why there were so many. It was often said that only the best leaders would be rewarded with their own light in the night sky. Grogger sneered slightly at the thought. The shining things weren't great goblin leaders, they were all failures. All sent up to the heavens to look down on a world they had failed to change. A world they had failed to conquer. It was a punishment, rather than a glorious reward. Forced for eternity to be reminded of their short-comings. Well, he didn't plan on joining then. He had plenty more to do down here!

"Where are we?" he asked Kackle.

"We came out the caves not too long ago," answered the wiz. "Magwa is up front trying to find out where we are. He keeps mumbling that we're close."

Grogger jumped off the barrel he had been resting on and strode off to find Magwa. The nightmare had left him feeling uncomfortable, and he hoped the old gob would have some good news.

He was surprised to find Magwa and Grukhar talking to each other. His mind raced at the thought that the two were plotting against him. Instinctively, he reached toward his dagger as he neared the pair of conspirators. Magwa turned to him.

"Ah, Grogger Split-tooth, we were just talking about you," said Magwa with a smile.

"Plotting my demise?" replied Grogger with a hiss. He was surprised when Grukhar burst out laughing.

"Quite the opposite," she said. "Magwa has been telling me about why he thinks you will be the king to unite the clans. And why I shouldn't be trying to kill you for taking the underminers from me."

The answer caught Grogger off guard slightly, although he kept his claw on his dagger.

"Magwa sees great things for Grogger Split-tooth, and Magwa does not need visions to know this."

"And you believe him?" Grogger asked Grukhar.

"I think he's mad as a bag of mawpups, but I'm willing to wait before I kill you. Call it a test." Grukhar flashed him a toothy grin.

"I don't need a test from anyone, least of all a test from you."

"Then maybe I'll kill you now?" Grukhar's golden pick suddenly appeared in her claws.

"How?" said Grogger with a gasp and drew the dagger. He noticed, with disappointment, that it wasn't singing to him.

"Magwa gave it to Grukhar while you slept," he explained. "This is her test. If she fails, Jo'os will pass his own judgment."

Grogger's mind raced. Part of him knew he should kill Grukhar because she was a threat to his rule, but there was something stopping him. Almost like Magwa and his decision to support Grogger, he sensed that Grukhar would play her part in his future. He just hoped that part wasn't to kill him. Without pulling his eyes away from Grukhar, he slowly placed the dagger back in its scabbard.

"I still don't trust you," growled Grogger.

"I still don't like you," snapped Grukhar but put away her pick. Their angry glares were interrupted by Magwa's mad cackles.

"You squabble like goblings," he laughed. "When you stop arguing, Magwa has good news."

"More potential assassins you plan to give weapons to?" scoffed Grogger, and Grukhar quickly shot out her tongue.

"Magwa said stop arguing!" screeched the old goblin and banged his prod on the rattling deck of the barge. A crackle of lightning snaked up the hilt and around Magwa's claw. A wild look entered his eyes. "Magwa has said you will be king, Grogger Split-tooth, not a petty scout watching his back for blades. Do not make Magwa regret that decision. Do not make a fool of Magwa!"

More lightning coursed around the prod, and Magwa's eyes glowed an unnatural blue. Grogger could feel the crackle of magic in the air. He saw that Jo'os' hair had begun to stand on end as the static soared around them, and the nearby underminers had started to back away.

"Do you think Magwa is a fool, Grogger Split-tooth? What about you, Grukhar Rockcrusher? Magwa has watched kings rise and fall. Laughed as kings died in the dirt and never even lifted a claw to help. Now Magwa helps Grogger Split-tooth and he acts like a spoilt gobling, constantly worried about grasping at life, instead of seeing what he could become! The gobs have willed you to live. The gobs have willed you to do something great. Do not make Magwa out to be a fool!"

He thudded the prod once again and, in an instant, the magic swirling around the barge disappeared. Grogger realized his jaw hurt from clenching his teeth so hard. Even Grukhar looked like she was ready to jump off the boat. Magwa's furious face suddenly broke into a wide, slightly unhinged grin.

"And now Magwa's good news," he said and pointed to a mountain. "That is where we will find the bodjits."

With the location in sight, Grogger quickly commanded the barges to be docked on the banks of the river before the current carried them too far away. With numerous shouts and arguing, the barges were slowly steered over to the side of the river and hit the grassy banks with a shuddering thud.

"All ashore!" shouted Grogger, and hundreds of goblin charged onto dry land, clearly thankful to be away from the potentially deadly torrent of water. A few underminers were even kissing the mud, in between thanking Grogger for leading them to safety.

Grogger was the last to leave his boat and he leapt onto land, ready to start issuing more commands. However, as he hit the ground, there was an ominous cracking behind him. He turned to see bits of wood snapping off the barge and tumbling into the water. There was a large snapping noise, and the whole barge broke in two before being quickly swallowed by the river. Grogger shot Grukhar a dark look.

"I thought you supervised the building of the barge yourself?"

"Didn't say I knew anything building boats though, did I?" she replied with a shrug. "I live in a cave, not a grogging river."

Once again, Grogger considered why he was keeping her around. However, he didn't fancy another admonishing from Magwa, so he would let her live... for now.

"Lead the way Magwa!"

* * * * *

Although the mountain that Magwa had pointed out to Grogger hadn't looked that far away, the march to the bodjit's location took longer than he expected. Leading such a large number of goblins was tougher than Grogger had realized. He kept having to stop to deal with small squabbles or make sure that a group hadn't just wandered off after seeing something interesting in the distance.

Their surroundings made Grogger nervous too. Normally he was used to scurrying through mountains or trees under the cover of darkness. But here, in the shadows of the mountains ahead, the ground was ominously flat and grassy. There were no trees to cover their progress or caves to quickly duck into at the first sign of trouble. They were dangerously exposed in the sparse grassland... and daylight was coming.

"How long until we get there?" Grogger asked Magwa and tried to hide the hint of fear in his voice.

"It has been long since Magwa was here, but it is near those mountains," he pointed a wavering claw into the distance.

Grogger started at the mountains again and sighed when he realized they didn't appear to be getting any closer. However, not too far on the horizon, he did spot numerous trails of smoke drifting upward into the increasingly light sky. A human village, he thought, with a growing sense of panic. Out here, they would be sitting mawpups for any humans that wanted to take them out.

"We're heading straight for a grogging village!" said Grogger to Magwa. He grabbed Magwa and pointed a claw at the smoking homes.

The old goblin stopped for a moment and stroked his chin.

"Hmm... Magwa doesn't remember a village. Do you, Jo'os?" The huge mawbeast looked up at the mention of his name and gave a small growl. Grogger rolled his eyes.

"How long ago were you here?"

Magwa's eyes glazed over slightly as he considered the question.

"Jo'os was only a pup, so however long that was."

Grogger let out an exasperated sigh and decided he needed someone to scout out the village, rather than marching straight into a potential deathtrap with hundreds of ill-equipped goblins. He considered his options for a moment before deciding there was only one person he could trust: himself.

"Gritter, you head back to the remaining barge with the underminers. Dismantle the boat and make whatever defenses and weapons you can." Grogger was expecting some sort of argument from the former maw-beast handler, but he just nodded before scuttling off and shouting at some nearby goblins to follow him.

"Magwa, Klunk, Ug, Kackle, and..." Grogger hesitated for a moment while he considered what to do about Grukhar. Sending her back with Gritter and the underminers was a potentially dangerous option if she decided she wanted to take back control. But without the underminers protecting him, would she try to kill him? He decided to take the risk. "Grukhar, you all come with me to scout this village."

Once again, Grogger felt the thrill of command surging through him. He loved the sensation of power as he watched the goblins following his instructions without question. Even the previously petulant Ug seemed willing to do whatever Grogger commanded. There was no doubt in his mind that if anyone could unite the clans, it was him. He was destined to do this.

* * * * *

Compared to marching with the underminers, Grogger and his small warband made quick progress toward the village. Even with the sun now blazing in the sky, Grogger didn't feel the sense of unease he had while trundling along with all the goblins in tow. Despite the exposed grassy plains, he hoped that five greenskins, a troll, and a mawbeast would not attract that much attention. Jo'os also appeared to be enjoying the wide open surroundings. Occasionally he would dart off and re-appear with a rabbit in his gaping jaws. Typically he would drop the rabbit at Magwa's feet in exchange for a rough scratch behind the ears but, occasionally, he would bring a rabbit to Grogger, which drew envious glares from Magwa.

Grogger turned his gaze to the village in the distance. Although the houses were still too small to make out properly, he was surprised to see that all of them had large plumes of thick, black smoke billowing from their chimneys. And even from this distance, his sharp ears caught the banging and clanking of machinery.

Suddenly something else caught his attention, a shape was rising up from the village and heading skyward. His eyes grew wide in fear.

"A dragon," he hissed. "It's a snozzing dragon!"

Grogger immediately threw himself onto the ground and was quickly joined by the others. Even Ug pressed himself into the grass and nervously watched the shape as it flew over the houses. Grogger's mind raced. Of all the dangers he had expected to face on his quest, he hadn't expected to encounter a dragon this soon. He had hoped to face such a formidable beast with an army safely in front of him, complete with rock throwers and sharpstick throwers to take out the monster, while he remained at a very safe distance. The answer was simple: they would just have to find a different route to the bodjits. One that didn't go anywhere near a snozzing dragon!

Then, just as Grogger was about to tell them all to turn back, he realized that Magwa was cackling to himself. He cautiously turned his head to see that Magwa was still standing, with an arm resting across Jo'os' neck. His body was shaking as he laughed.

"Magwa never thought they would actually get it to work."

"Get down," rasped Grogger. "The dragon will see us!"

Grogger grew angry as Magwa let out a shrill laugh in response.

"That is no dragon, Grogger Split-tooth, that is the flying machine Magwa told you about."

He looked over at the shape again and noticed that, unlike the graceful flight of a dragon, the flying object was sort of bouncing through the sky. Just as it looked like it was going to crash toward the ground, it would lurch back upward and the process would continue. It never got much higher than just skimming above the rooftops, and even then it appeared that it struggled to maintain that height. Then it dropped out of the sky like a stone, and there was a loud crash.

"Perhaps not working that well," laughed Magwa.

Grogger leapt back up and tried to regain his sense of dignity.

"You're telling me that's a machine?"

"Magwa said the bodjits had flying creations, did he not? But last time Magwa was here, they would not work."

"What are they called?" piped up Klunk, with a sense of wonder in his voice.

"Winggits," replied Magwa, "and just imagine an army that used them, Grogger Split-tooth. Who needs a giant contraption when you can fly through the air?"

A wicked grin spread quickly over Grogger's green face. Once again the mad old goblin had come through. He congratulated himself for not killing Magwa and just stealing the prod. There would always be time for that once he had the army and now flying machines. Dusting himself off, Grogger started running toward the village with his small warband in tow.

The village itself was nestled in the foot of the mountain range that stretched across the horizon. As he got closer to the houses, he realized that what must have been a former human village was almost unrecognizable. Each of the houses had been 'upgraded' by the inventive bodjits. Some had massive cogs that burst through the roof and turned with an awkward grinding noise, others had rickety towers that tumbled upward and looked like they might fall over at any moment. But all had some things in common: smoke that billowed from numerous chimneys sprouting from their ramshackle roof, and the furious sound of hammering. The occasional explosion shook the village, which often sent parts of the buildings toppling toward the ground. With each boom, Grogger tried to hide his nervous jolts.

After one particularly loud boom, he watched as an object was catapulted skyward. Grogger watched it zipping through the sky for a moment before realizing, with horror, that it was heading straight for them. Before he had time to dash for cover, a large rock smashed down just a few lengths away from him. Grogger nervously looked at the village to see if more projectiles were heading his way.

"Do you think they aimed that at us?" he asked Magwa.

The old goblin shrugged and kept on walking. "Perhaps we should ask?"

Despite occasionally stopping to check for objects potentially hurtling at them, the warband was quickly approaching the settlement. Now Grogger could see the village was nestled in the valley at the foot of the mountain range. A rickety fence closed the gap between the mountains, although Grogger doubted it would stop Ug, let alone a rampaging army. In the center of the fence stood a metal gate. It appeared to have been made from old shields, swords and other random objects all clumsily melted together. It was clearly the work of goblins, thought Grogger.

"Do they *live* in that village?" Grogger asked Magwa.

The thought of living above ground sent a strange chill through Grogger. Being up here in the open, exposed to the elements and under the blinding rays of daylight, made Grogger deeply uncomfortable. Even now, he longed for the safe embrace of a gloomy cave. After all, it was much easier to sneak up on a foe and stab a dagger in their back when it was pitch black.

"When Magwa met them last, they were in the caves. This is... *new.*"

Eventually the goblins arrived at the gate. Grogger looked up at the metal structure and quickly recognized the weapons and shields of numerous armies: Basileans, dwarfs, goblins, even orcs. He shuddered at the thought of trying to take a shield from a menacing orc.

"Now what?" asked Kackle.

"I guess we knock?" replied Grogger and hammered the hilt of his dagger against the gate. It made a loud clanging noise that echoed through the valley but nothing happened. He was about to knock again when a small hatch in the gate shot open.

"Go away!" said a reedy voice, and the hatch snapped shut.

Grogger glowered at the hatch before banging again.

"My name is Grog-"

Before he could finish, the hatch opened once more.

"I said go away!"

Grogger was considering asking Ug to smash down the stupid gate when Magwa gave a small cough behind him.

"Maybe Magwa could try. It has been a long time since Magwa met the bodjits, but they may remember Magwa."

"Be my guest..." replied Grogger, with a gracious wave of his claw toward the gate.

Magwa shuffled up to the hatch before giving it a quick rap with his prod. Small sparks of lightning shot off the tip and cascaded up the metallic gate.

"Magwa demands…"

The hatch was thrown open almost immediately.

"Did you say Magwa?" asked the same reedy voice.

"Yes, Magwa, and-" The hatch was snapped shut once more. This time, Grogger could hear a multitude of voices chattering inside the village. He turned to Magwa, who responded with a confused shrug. They were both startled by the sharp bang of the hatch as it opened once more.

"Magwa Howlclaw?" asked a different voice.

The aging goblin paused for a moment before answering.

"Magwa once had that name, yes. Magwa has had many names, over many moons."

The hatch closed again, but this time it was quickly followed by the sound of gears grinding together. Grogger jumped backward as the gate began to swing open, throwing up dust and dirt as it scraped along the ground. The hinges screamed in protest, and Grogger wondered how long it had been since it was last opened. Indeed, he wondered if it had ever been opened. Once open, Grogger was greeted by the sight of three small goblins.

Each of the greenskins was dressed almost identically. A thick leather apron protected their body while goggles filled with thick glass protected their eyes. The glass magnified their normally beady red eyes, making them unusually large. They constantly twitched fingers, which were hidden inside black leather gloves and dipped into pockets lining their large belts that were filled with odd tools and contraptions.

"I am Grogger Spl-" before Grogger could finish, the three goblins pushed past him and dashed at Magwa. Jo'os began to growl and prepared to pounce, but Magwa quickly calmed the beast with a wave of his claw. Grukhar stifled a snort of laughter at Grogger's surprised expression.

"We are so glad you are back, Magwa Howlclaw," said the goblin with the reedy voice.

"Things have gone well in your absence," added another. "And I see that Jo'os has grown very mighty. His armor will need to be bigger!"

"His armor?" asked Magwa, but the bodjits ignored him.

"The plans you left were difficult but not impossible," said the third goblin.

"Magwa's plans?" The aging goblin was clearly struggling to work out what was happening.

"But everything is ready for your army King Magwa," finished reedy-voice with a delighted smile.

"*King* Magwa?" screeched Grogger.

CHAPTER TWENTY-FOUR

Grogger wasn't sure what was irritating him more, the eager smiles of the three goblins as they gazed upon Magwa or the raucous laughter of Grukhar.

"I am in the presence of two kings," said Grukhar between fits of giggles. "Who should I bow to first?"

"*Two* kings?" asked one of the bodjits, and looks of confusion passed between the inventors.

"Yes, yes," snapped Magwa, irritably. "There will be time to explain later. For now, remind Magwa... what *were* Magwa's plans?"

"Of course, King Magwa. Follow Wrencher and we can show you." The bodjit pointed to the goblin with the reedy voice who grinned manically.

"This way, this way," said Wrencher and almost ran into the village. The group followed and the metal gate noisily slammed shut behind them. Grogger fell into step alongside Kackle.

"Did you know about this?" he hissed.

"Know about what?"

"Don't play stupid," growled Grogger. "You knew this was going to happen. You must have seen it in your infernal bones. You and Magwa, working together and making a grogging fool out of me! How long have you been planning this?"

"No, no, I swear..." Kackle was quickly cut off by Grogger's dagger appearing at his throat. Grogger briefly closed his eyes in delight as the dagger started to sing to him once more. He had missed its haunting melodies.

"You have taken me for an idiot," said Grogger with menace dripping from every word. He pressed his dagger harder against Kackle's neck, causing a small trickle of blood to run down his claw. "I do not like being made to look like a fool."

"I swear on my life that I am not plotting anything," pleaded Kackle with a look of horror on his face. He weakly attempted to push Grogger away while stretching his neck to avoid the dagger.

Grogger struggled to ignore the singing. It felt like the dagger *wanted* him to kill Kackle. Grogger shook his head as he considered Kackle's desperate pleas. A goblin's life was the most precious thing a goblin had, so to hear Kackle swear against his own life gave Grogger second thoughts. The dagger's song took on a more angry tone as Grogger slowly eased it away from Kackle.

"You believe the visions then?" asked Grogger, suspiciously.

"There is something special about you. Something that I have never felt from another biggit... or king. Something I do not even sense from Magwa. The old snoz is powerful, yes, but he is not meant to be king. *You* are meant to be king!"

Grogger placed the dagger back into its scabbard, where it gave one final angry blast of song.

"If the time comes to choose, I hope you remember whose side you're on," said Grogger.

Ahead of them, Wrencher had stopped outside what looked like an old village hall. However, it had been extended numerous times by the bodjits, so it was now much bigger than a barn. The extensions were clumsily added on and looked like they may have collapsed at any moment.

Outside the rickety structure were gathered more bodjits, all dressed in similar garb to Wrencher and his two assistants. Grogger heard excited whispers about 'King Magwa,' and his blood boiled furiously.

"We hope you will be pleased with the results, King Magwa," said Wrencher and opened the doors to the village hall with a flourish. Grogger quickly pushed past Wrencher and barged into the building.

The hall was lit by dim lamps that lined the walls but, even in the patchy light, Grogger could see the glimmer of row upon row of war machines. He recognized rock throwers, sharpstick throwers, mortars, war trombones, modified mincers, and, what he assumed, must be the strange winged contraptions that he had seen flapping in the sky. The sight stunned Grogger into silence. There would be no stopping a goblin force armed with all this. He *had* to have it. He *must* have it! He noticed the others had entered behind him.

"What do you think, your majesty?" asked Wrencher, excitedly.

"This... this is all for Magwa?" The old goblin sounded confused but strangely excited. Grogger noticed an odd glint in his eye and his breathing came in quick gasps.

"Of course!" replied Wrencher. "Sometimes we wondered if you would ever come back, but we continued to build, regardless. Has the war begun?"

"The war?" replied Magwa.

"Against the beardies!"

A few of the bodjits spat on the floor at the mention of beardies.

"Yes, Magwa, tell them all about the war," said Grogger with a smirk. Magwa shot him a filthy look.

"How long since Magwa was here?" he asked.

"Many, many moons," replied Wrencher. "It would have been Thunk that you gave the plans to, and he in turn gave the plans to Thump, who passed them on to Clomp, but he told us all about the great war. The battle to destroy all beardies in the dwarf mountains and take back our home. The war to kill Golloch, the big beardy king."

More bodjits spat at Golloch's name.

"Our home?" Magwa was gazing at the various war machines and running his claw through Jo'os' thick mane. Grogger noticed, with a great deal of apprehension, that the old goblin had a grin that was growing with each new war machine he spotted.

"Yes, yes!" chipped in one of the other bodjits. "You told us all that the dwarf mountains were the true home of the goblins, but those filthy beardies had tricked us and stolen it."

"And now you have the tools to kill as many beardies as you want, King Magwa," added Wrencher.

From outside the hall, Grogger heard the bodjits chanting Magwa's name. Although he had to admit that he was pleased the welcome from the bodjits was warmer than that of Grukhar and the underminers, he was becoming concerned about the increasingly far away look on Magwa's face.

"Worried you're not the only one who fancies becoming king?" whispered Grukhar with a slight snigger.

"Magwa, perhaps you should explain why we are *really* here?" asked Grogger, but the old goblin didn't appear to be listening. "Magwa?"

Wrencher nervously looked between Grogger and Magwa.

"Is there something wrong, King Magwa?"

"No, no, Magwa just needs. Magwa must..." his voice trailed off slightly as he walked toward a mincer. The spikes on the machine's powerful drill shimmered in the dull lamplight. Magwa slowly, almost gently, began to stroke the metal.

"Magwa, remember..." started Grogger but was quickly cut off.

"Remember what, Grogger Split-tooth?" snapped Magwa. "That you came to Magwa with nothing? That you destroyed Magwa's home? That you want Magwa's prod?"

Grogger raised his claws in protest and quickly shook his head.

"Magwa is no old fool. Magwa sees the way you look at the prod."

With that, he banged the magical artifact on the floor and sent lightning crackling up into the ceiling. A few pieces of smoking wood crashed down.

"On the barge, you said..."

"Magwa says a lot of things, Grogger Split-tooth. But without Magwa, you would have nothing. No dagger. No underminers. No machines. No army. And what sort of a king has *nothing*?"

Grogger stood open-mouthed as Magwa continued to rant. Of all the goblins he thought he would be betrayed by, Magwa was the last goblin he expected to stab him in the back. A low growl formed in the back of this throat.

"Why shouldn't the great Magwa be king? Magwa has lived longer than any goblin. Seen more than any goblin. Killed more than any goblin."

Magwa held Grogger's increasingly furious gaze.

"What has Grogger ever done to deserve to be king?" asked the old goblin before coughing up a large, phlegmy ball of spit. "There is only one king here, and his name is Magwa!"

Before he knew what he was doing, Grogger whipped out his dagger and leapt at Magwa, ready to slash his throat open. In a flash, Magwa jabbed the prod at Grogger, and arcs of magical lightning criss-crossed through the air in his direction. Grogger quickly ducked and rolled under the deadly magic, which crashed into a rock thrower behind him. The war machine exploded and showered the room in splinters of wood and metal.

Grogger darted sideways to hide behind a mincer as Magwa let loose with his prod once more. The powerful magic drilled a hole right through the ramshackle machine and exposed Grogger's hiding place.

"Jo'os, kill him!" screeched Magwa and pointed a quivering claw at Grogger.

The massive creature remained still and stared at its master, a look of confusion playing across its bestial face.

"What are you waiting for?!" howled Magwa. "Magwa said kill him!"

Somewhat reluctantly, Jo'os let out an almost mournful howl before bounding straight at Grogger, who was still hiding behind the mincer. Grogger clambered on top of the machine to try and give himself the height advantage over Jo'os. He tightened his grip on his dagger, which was now singing glorious hymns of battle. But even that didn't cheer Grogger's spirits. He had come so close to becoming king. So close to becoming something special. But then Magwa had snatched it away, like a petulant gobling. It was just like all the other times when someone else had stopped Grogger from achieving greatness. And now here he was, about to become a meal for Jo'os while Magwa would leave with a ready-made army.

He braced himself ready for Jo'os to leap and expected to feel the sharp agony of his razor sharp teeth as they chomped on his green flesh - but the attack never came. Just as Jo'os was about to pounce, Ug slammed into the mawbeast and sent it skidding across the floor. Jo'os quickly recovered and charged at the troll, dodging a clumsy punch before clamping its jaws around Ug's thick, green leg. Ug roared in agony and started thumping Jo'os' head but with little effect. The beast held tight. Now, with blood streaming down his leg, Ug clutched his rock-like hands around Jo'os' jaws and began to pull them apart. Slowly, ever so slowly, Jo'os' gargantuan jaws loosened their grip, and Ug jerked his leg free. With a satisfied grunt, Ug lobbed Jo'os across the room and sent him smashing into a sharpstick thrower. The machine collapsed on top of Jo'os, who remained motionless.

"Jo'os!" screamed Magwa and spun round to point his prod at the troll. A massive bolt of lightning sped at Ug and knocked him flying across the room. He crashed through the thin walls of the building, scattering the bodjits who were gathered outside. Grogger looked up nervously as the impact sent shockwaves through the structure. Pieces of ceiling tumbled down and thudded onto the floor. If the fight continued any longer, the whole place would collapse, he thought to himself.

Grogger hoped Jo'os' injuries may distract Magwa, but another jolt of lightning quickly told him this was not the case.

"Grukhar!" shouted Grogger. "Deal with the old grog."

He looked around to see where Grukhar was and noticed her lolling casually against a catapult. She shot him a sickly smile.

"This is your fight," she replied. "I don't give a snoz who wins. Although my gold's on the ancient gob with the magical staff that fires magic stuff."

With Grukhar's shrill laughter ringing in his ears, Grogger desperately looked around for Kackle and Klunk, but they were clearly hiding or had run away at the first sign of trouble. Another bolt of lightning slammed against the mincer and knocked him onto his back.

"You've killed Jo'os! You've killed Jo'os!" screamed Magwa. "And now Magwa will kill you!"

Grogger scurried across the floor as a shaft of arcane energy caused the mincer to erupt into pieces. He quickly threw himself into the dirt as a piece of drill whirled just inches from his head and slammed into a nearby bolt thrower. There was no way he could beat Magwa in a straight fight. As soon as he got close, he'd be blasted back to the Abyss.

"Wait, King Magwa!" hollered Grogger and hoped to buy himself some time. No more lightning bolts erupted through the air. "Remember what you told me. About watching your pack die. All the pups that came and went."

Grogger slowly started creeping toward a nearby war trombone - a cunning plan forming in his wicked, little brain. He risked peeking from behind a rock thrower to see what Magwa was doing. He was relieved to see his betrayer staring sadly at the wreckage that hid Jo'os' lifeless form.

"If you were a king, there would be hundreds of pups. Thousands of pups!" shouted Grogger, and he was pleased to see Magwa's prod starting to droop. "All those followers dying while Magwa still lives."

"Magwa *still* lives," muttered the old goblin.

Grogger tucked himself behind the war trombone and carefully pushed his claw inside the gigantic, trumpet-like barrel of the massive, metal gun. He was delighted to find it was already loaded, and he could feel the sharp nails, pieces of metal, and whatever else the bodjits could find to shove into the device.

Slowly, he wheeled the war trombone around so that it was pointing directly at Magwa. Finally, he checked the fuse and the chamber that held the explosive black powder. Everything appeared to be in place. Admittedly, he had never fired a war trombone, but how hard could it be? He had seen them used in battle and *most* didn't immediately explode. He squinted down the barrel one last time and was pleased to see Magwa, muttering quietly to himself, in the sights. It was now or never!

"And the first to die under King Magwa's reign is Jo'os! You killed him, Magwa. Your only friend. Dead! Dead because of you."

Grogger watched eagerly as Magwa's head snapped up. He could almost feel the rage coming off Magwa in great waves. With a loud scream, Magwa swung the prod around and fired a great blast of energy straight at Grogger. The crackling blue lightning struck the war trombone, but it didn't shatter into pieces. Instead, the metal absorbed the magical energy, and

Grogger smiled as it traveled down the barrel, straight to the chamber full of black powder. He held the mighty gun tightly and hoped his plan would work. There was a loud boom, and the random pieces of metal shot out of the trombone with a roar. Grogger was thrown backward by the recoil and thumped his head against a nearby mincer.

Slightly dazed, he just about saw the shards of ammo blasting at Magwa but was surprised to see the older goblin react with a remarkable turn of speed, considering his age. Magwa threw himself to the floor as the razor-sharp debris soared safely over his head and ripped into the various machines behind him. There was an almighty crash as a sharpstick thrower collapsed.

At first, Grogger was disappointed the blast hadn't immediately killed his intended target, but then he noticed with delight that when Magwa had dived to the ground, his prod had skidded across the floor slightly. This was his chance! Shaking off the stars that were still dancing across his vision, Grogger pulled himself up and dashed toward Magwa, scooping up the prod as he went. In the heat of the moment, Grogger had momentarily forgotten the dangers of holding the ancient artifact, and he winced slightly as his claw clutched around the hilt and recollections of the underminers being electrocuted suddenly flashed across his memory. But... nothing happened. His claw closed around the prod, and he wasn't immediately roasted by arcane energy. Instead, he could feel power soaring through him. Grogger let out a high-pitched, slightly manic laugh. This was yet more proof he was meant to be king. More proof that he wasn't destined to die at the hands of a mad, old snoz.

Brandishing the prod, Grogger marched over to Magwa who was still laying face down in the dirt. With a sharp kick, he rolled Magwa over.

"I want you to see this," hissed Grogger. "I want you to see when I *beat* you!"

Magwa held his stare and smiled before letting out a short, sharp whistle. Out the corner of his eye, Grogger caught movement in the wreckage that had hidden Jo'os' previously still body. The mawbeast was slowly emerging from the pile of wood and metal.

"I'm not beaten yet," coughed Magwa.

Grogger pressed his foot firmly onto Magwa's chest and kept the prod pointed at his neck. Nervously, Grogger's eyes darted between Magwa's leering face and Jo'os' mighty form. Magwa whistled again, and Jo'os snapped its head in their direction. A thunderous growl filled the creaking barn.

"Call him off or I'll kill you," rasped Grogger.

"Kill Magwa and he'll kill you," laughed Magwa.

Grogger wondered how he could get the prod to fire its eldritch energy. Perhaps he could get one blast off before Jo'os tore his throat out, or maybe he should just run away with the prod? His mind raced with the options, until a sharp bark brought his attention back to Jo'os.

"Save Magwa, Jo'os," screeched Magwa.

Grogger expected Jo'os to leap over, but instead, the beast appeared to be intently watching them. It was breathing heavily after the fight with Ug, and its breaths came in deep grunts. Its eyes flicked between Grogger and Magwa. Eventually, it gave a sharp grunt and started padding over toward them. Grogger readied himself and prepared to use the prod to fend off Jo'os.

"What are you waiting for? Kill him, Jo'os! Kill him!" howled Magwa.

But Jo'os didn't pick up pace or leap at Grogger's throat. Instead it slowly - and somewhat anxiously - crept toward Grogger with its head bowed low and tail between its legs. Grogger realized he was shaking with fear as Jo'os came ever closer. The prod trembled in his claws, and Grogger could sense Magwa chuckling beneath him. This time, there would be no Ug to save his life.

Grogger felt the sweat dripping from his long, green nose as Jo'os got within striking distance. He tried to firm up his grip on the prod, ready to defend against the beast; but the attack never came. Instead, Jo'os, almost nervously, crept up to Grogger and nuzzled his snout against his side and let out a low whine. The beast's large, brown eyes looked up at Grogger as it snuffled beside him. Grogger took one claw off the prod and reached out to Jo'os - almost expecting it to be snapped off at any second. Then, gently, Grogger began stroking Jo'os' matted fur. He let out a sigh of relief, realizing that he had been holding his breath for the past few moments. Something swelled in Grogger's chest, and his mind reeled with joy at what was happening. Magwa had stopped chuckling.

"Jo'os knows I'm the alpha now!" laughed Grogger and began tickling the mawbeast behind the ears. "He senses it too. He senses a king!"

"You win," said Magwa, quietly, and Grogger realized with revulsion that the old goblin was actually crying. "You win, Grogger Split-tooth."

"What do you say to your *king*?" asked Grogger with a barely disguised smirk.

"Kill Magwa," he sobbed.

"What?" The response surprised Grogger. He had expected denial. He had expected pleading. He hadn't expected this.

"Jo'os was the first of Magwa's pack. Now Magwa has nothing." Magwa pressed his wrinkled neck against the prongs of the prod. "Do it!"

Grogger knew he should kill Magwa there and then. The prod was his. Jo'os was his. The army would be his. But he hesitated. Just like his reluctance to kill Grukhar, there was something that stopped him plunging the prod through Magwa's neck.

"Do it!" screamed Magwa. "Do it, please!"

"No," replied Grogger. "Your life belongs to me now, and I'll decide when I kill you."

Suddenly a commotion near the entrance disturbed Grogger. He looked over to see Wrencher and a small number of bodjits running into the barn, armed with smaller, handheld versions of the war trombones. They were all pointing the blunderbusses at Grogger.

"King Magwa, we're here to save you!" said Wrencher, proudly.

"There is no *King* Magwa," hissed Magwa. "There is only one king here. Destined to be king of all the goblins."

"Who?" inquired a clearly confused Wrencher.

"Meet King Grogger Split-tooth," answered Magwa.

"Who?" asked the bodjits.

"Me! Me, you snozzing idiots!" shouted Grogger. "The one with the grogging great prod and his foot on Magwa's chest."

The bodjits lowered their weapons.

"King... *Grogger?*"

"And I'll be taking all these nice war machines!" said Grogger with a wild grin.

There was more commotion at the entrance, and Grogger readied himself to face more foolish bodjits. A small goblin dashed into the room.

"We've spotted some scalies! They're coming to the village!" There was more than an edge of panic in its voice.

"Why can't they just leave me the grog alone?" snarled Grogger. "We need to end this here, otherwise they'll be chasing me forever."

He stepped off Magwa's chest and held out a claw.

"Help me take care of the scalies and maybe, just maybe, I'll kill you afterward."

For a moment, Magwa just stared up at Grogger, and he almost expected him to swat the claw away but, eventually, Magwa grasped Grogger's claw and pulled himself up. The pair glared at each other before Grogger passed him the prod.

"Don't make me regret this," snapped Grogger.

"Magwa is beaten," he replied and looked at Jo'os with a frown. "There is nothing left for Magwa to fight for."

"Let's kill some scalies," screeched Grogger.

CHAPTER TWENTY-FIVE

CHAPTER TWENTY-FIVE

Furna eyed the village suspiciously. At first, she had hoped it might provide some refuge from the last few days of traveling, but as they neared, she noticed there was something *off* about the houses. Many looked like they were about to tumble to pieces, whereas others had strange contraptions attached to them. The realization that this wasn't about to be some safe haven just added to her exhaustion and hunger.

She didn't know how long they had traveled through the cavern but, eventually, they had emerged into the open air and almost stumbled directly into the goblin camp. It appeared that the goblins had begun to dismantle the barges to turn into some sort of makeshift fortress. However, she didn't think it would stand up to a strong wind, never mind marauding attackers. The strange, pale-skinned goblins swarmed all over the structure, adding seemingly random pieces of wood or metal to the fort. Occasionally they would stop and nervously look skyward. Furna realized they were probably not used to life outside of the caves they had abandoned.

Thankfully, the goblins seemed so busy making whatever it was they actually thought they were making, that Furna and her small warband had managed to sneak past without being spotted. Due to the fairly open plains, they had crept low to the ground and prayed to Kthorlaq - or the Shining Ones in Rowan's case - that they wouldn't hear the high-pitched screech of a goblin guard. But no shout came and so they continued onward, constantly asking Igne if she could feel the pull of the magical implement they had been following.

Now they were approaching the village and something, Furna wasn't sure what it was, told her that this was it. This is where they would finally end this. It wasn't about catching the wiz now. It wasn't even about gathering the money to sail back to the Three Kings. It was about revenge. Pure and simple. Since encountering that damned wiz, Furna had experienced nothing but trouble. The loss of members of her crew with those cursed trees, having to watch Hr'zak get ripped apart by that terrible beast, even the behaviour of Rorsha. It could all be blamed on the blasted goblins. And then, on top of all that, the story of Mary and Rowan had stirred something inside her. Unlike her, they didn't want a life of adventure or swashbuckling. They had wanted to settle down. Perhaps start a family. But the greenskins had spoiled all that. Everything they touched, they ruined.

"There's something not right about that village," said Rowan as he came up beside Furna.

"I think that's where they might be," she replied. "I think this is where we end it. One way or the other."

"At least they've left the others near the river," grunted Berusk. "I wouldn't have fancied facing all that lot."

"You're losing your fighting spirit," laughed Furna, although it felt like a hollow jest. She knew her own fighting spirit was dwindling like the fire that normally raged inside her. With each failed strike against the goblins, she could feel the flames cool that little bit more. She dreaded to think how Berusk must feel. In the cave, she had noticed him shivering and heard his teeth chattering. Now, back in the open, he had warmed up; but occasionally, his normally bright, yellow eyes had a distant, glassy appearance.

"So, what's the plan, Captain?" asked Berusk.

Furna had to admit that she hadn't thought that far ahead. In fact, in many ways, she hadn't expected to catch up to the goblins at all.

"Igne, does it feel like they're inside that village?"

The younger salamander had been strangely quiet since joining Furna on her mission, and she wondered if Igne was having second thoughts. There had been numerous times that Furna had thought about telling her to turn back and find Rorsha but, selfishly, she needed her to follow the pull of magic that surrounded the goblins.

"I can sense the prod in there, so if they've stayed together, then that's where they are."

"And there was nothing back at that camp?" asked Berusk.

"No, the prod wasn't there," replied Igne.

Furna turned her attention back to the village. The ramshackle fence that guarded the perimeter was too high to scale but looked like it might be smashed through quite easily. With the rest of her crew here, she may have been able to hack it down; but with only four of them, she was struggling to come up with an effective plan.

"If only we could knock part of that fence down," sighed Furna.

"I may be able to help with that," suggested Igne, helpfully.

"I doubt your fireballs would do much damage to that," said Berusk with a huff. Igne shot him a sideways glance.

"It's something a bit bigger than a fireball."

* * * * *

Grogger snatched a telescope from a bodjit and pressed it to his eye. He was standing on a platform that leant precariously against the village's perimeter fence. With each gust of wind, he could feel the structure wobble ominously, and he had to stop himself grabbing onto something in a panic.

"Where the snoz are they then?" he snapped in frustration.

He scanned the horizon while the bodjit nervously tried to point out where they had last seen the salamanders. Thankfully, the sun was just starting to set, which he hoped would give the goblins the advantage if they chose to fight now. He wasn't sure how well a scaly could fight in the dark, but he most certainly could wield a blade.

"This grogging thing's not working," he grumbled. He was about to strike the stupid bodjit over the head with the infernal thing when his eye caught some shapes on the plain. It was the scalies... and a human. However, he was confused to see only four of them. He moved the telescope left and right, expecting to see the rest of the salamanders they had fought in Magwa's former home.

"How many did you see?" he asked the bodjit alongside him.

"Three scalies and a human, your majesty," replied the goblin, bowing slightly with every word. Grogger was pleased to see the bodjits were very quickly coming around to the idea that he was in charge. That was one of the good things about goblins, they were quick to accept change... it was just later when they tried to stab you in the back that the problems started.

"Are you sure there were no others? Like a big gang of them or anything?"

"No, your cunningness."

Grogger snapped the telescope shut. His mind raced with the possibilities of what happened to the rest of the scalies. In his vision, he'd clearly seen lots of them entering the caves and slaying whatever goblin they could find. And the man was new too. There were no humans in his vision, and that made him nervous. Had the vision been wrong?

"How many are there?" shouted up Magwa. His voice had a sullen tone, since losing the fight with Grogger, yet he appeared to have fallen in line.

"Just three and a man. There is no sign of the others."

"Could the rest be at the camp?" asked Grukhar.

Of course, the camp, thought Grogger. It was likely the scalies had stumbled across the other goblins and were busy fighting the underminers. Or more accurately, killing the underminers. He doubted Gritter would have the leadership qualities to lead the underminers in an assault against a group of hardened salamanders, even if they did have the advantage of more fighters. It would be a slaughter.

On the other claw if, for some reason, the underminers managed to win or there were no other scalies, they may provide some handy backup against this small group. Four hundred or so against four was the sort of odds that Grogger liked. He turned to the bodjit.

"Is there any other way out of here, apart from the great big gate?"

"Yes, your sneakiness, there are tunnels under most of the houses. They all lead to various parts of the plains."

This was all good news, thought Grogger, but it left him with a bit of a dilemma. He needed to know what was happening or had happened to the underminers, although he wasn't sure who to send. He doubted he would ever see Magwa again if he sent him onto the plains. He wanted to keep Kackle here, just in case his magic came in useful and Klunk... well, Klunk was Klunk. Unless he needed someone to blow up the underminers, it was probably best to keep him close. He could potentially send a bodjit, but they seemed extremely skittish and nervous, even for goblins, so he predicted they would leg it at the first sign of trouble. That left Grukhar. Potentially the least trustworthy of the bunch. However, he knew the underminers would listen to her, and she seemed keen to kill the scalies, just as much as him. He just hoped her lust for killing salamanders was more than her lust for killing him.

"Grukhar, go with this weedy bodjit and find out what's happening with the underminers." He watched her face for any hint of potential betrayal.

"Yes... your majesty," she replied and gave a half-hearted salute, like Grogger had seen some humans do. He really did not trust her, but he was left with little choice. If the underminers had been slaughtered, it would set back his army plans.

"You... you... you... want me to go out... there?" stuttered the bodjit. "I might get killed."

Grogger rolled his eyes.

"Let me make this decision easier for you. You *might* get killed out there or you will *definitely* get killed when I throw you off this platform and get Jo'os to eat you."

Behind his goggles, Grogger could see the bodjit's eyes grow wide with fear before he started nodding eagerly. After that, he quickly jumped down from the platform and ran to Grukhar.

"This way," he mumbled and sped off toward one of the nearby houses.

Grukhar gave Grogger a mean-looking smile and waved her claw. With that, she turned and followed the bodjit. Grogger watched her go and hoped he hadn't just made a terrible mistake. Shaking off the awful sense of self-doubt, he pulled out the telescope once more. The salamanders had stopped walking toward the village and now appeared to be gathered around a small fire. He continued to watch them for a moment while he hatched a plan to kill them once and for all.

* * * * *

"Are you sure about this?" asked Furna. The glow of the campfire danced off her scales as the sun began to set on the horizon. Instinctively, she moved closer to the fire, keen to feel its warmth. She noticed that Berusk was edging nearer too and gazing into the shifting flames. His tail lashed against the ground as he basked in its glow.

"I hope she's sure, because that fire is going to ensure that if they haven't seen us already, they'll definitely have seen us now," said Rowan, nervously. He kept looking between the fire and the gate, as though he expected a horde of goblins to charge out of it at any moment.

Furna ignored him and leaned in closer to Igne. She placed a heavy claw on the apprentice mage's slim shoulders, and she could feel the tension bunched up underneath the scales.

"You don't have to do this," whispered Furna. "We can find another way in."

"The archmage always said I was one of the best he had seen, you know," muttered Igne. "Said I had a natural talent and could manipulate the planes of magic unlike any hatchling he had seen. But I didn't want a life of reading dusty scrolls, while practicing my incantation techniques. I would watch the corsairs setting off on their adventures, and I knew that was what I wanted to do. I wanted to be out on the open seas, not reading about the oceans in a book."

Igne went quiet for a moment before looking into Furna's eyes.

"But now, if I'm honest, I think I've had enough of swashbuckling and treasure hunting. I'm ready to go home. I will study whatever the archmage can throw at me. So, the quicker I get us into that village, the quicker you can do what you came here to do, and perhaps we can catch up with Rorsha, then get home."

"I'm sorry," mumbled Furna.

Inge laid her claw across Furna's.

"Don't be sorry, Captain. I wouldn't swap my time in your crew for anything else. It's been an honor to serve on your ship."

With that, Igne focused on the fire and began to mutter under breath. Furna backed away as Igne barked and rasped the ancient tongue of the salamanders. Although Furna didn't understand most of what was being said, she recognized that Igne was repeating the same phrases over and over again. With each incantation, the wind began to whip around them, and Furna noticed the flames of the campfire begin to leap and dance in time to the words. Occasionally the fire would sputter, as though it were about to blink out of existence, and Igne would re-double her efforts. Her claws shook as she drew invisible symbols in the air.

Furna was about to interrupt and promise to find another way in, when the small blaze erupted into a column of fire that swirled into the sky.

"Well, now they've definitely seen us," muttered Rowan before Furna hushed him to be quiet.

The column of flames quivered and shook with each new incantation, and slowly but surely, the raging fire began to take shape. First, two arms formed before being quickly joined by a simple but unnatural face that shifted and morphed into different appearances.

"A fire elemental," gasped Rowan as the towering body of flame let out a crackling roar. He backed away from the living inferno and shielded his eyes.

Even Furna had to shield herself from the blazing heat of the elemental and she covered her eyes from its molten glow. She wondered how Igne, sitting so close to the monster, could stand the stifling temperature. Underneath the magical beast, the ground cooked and split under the curse of its molten touch. Grassy clumps erupted into flame as the elemental slowly started to move around.

Igne pointed at the gate of the village, and the elemental gave an almost imperceptible nod. As it advanced, everything it touched exploded into fire, which only served to feed the all-consuming hunger of the elemental. Their lives may be short, but they burned with a fury like nothing else on Pannithor.

Furna grinned. She'd like to see the goblins stop this.

* * * * *

Grogger groaned. How was he going to stop a grogging fire monster?! He watched in horror as it advanced slowly but surely toward the rickety fence of the village. He doubted the scruffy bits of wood and metal would stand one punch from the might of an elemental.

"They've got a snozzing fire elemental!" he shouted down to the other goblins at the bottom of the viewing platform. "Any ideas how we stop it?"

"What about a really, really big bomb?" suggested Klunk, hopefully. "I mean, like a really *massive* bomb!"

"Do you think highly flammable explosives are going to stop or help a magical creature that literally feeds on flames? I mean, it actually eats fire! Just think about it for a moment, Klunk!"

"But, but it's a really *massive* bomb, boss," came the dejected response from Klunk.

Grogger considered just killing Klunk now to save him the trouble later. He had to be the stupidest goblin he had ever met.

"Any other brilliant ideas, or do I have to do all the thinking round here?" asked Grogger. "Anyone?"

"I still have the summoning spell," mumbled Kackle.

"Speak up, Kackle, I can't hear you properly up here."

"I said I still have the spell. The spell to summon the water elemental."

Grogger allowed himself to feel a slight sense of relief. Perhaps it wasn't completely hopeless! He quickly formulated a plan in his cunning brain. If Kackle could keep the fire elemental busy, it meant he could deal with that pesky scaly that was in charge. Without a leader, they would all run away - just like a goblin would in battle. Meanwhile, Ug and the others could deal with the rest. He even had an idea to keep Klunk busy. His mind raced as he worked out the chances of them surviving the attack. Although he thought some of them might die, he was pretty confident that he could make it out alive, at least. Then he could run back to the camp, find Grukhar and the underminers, then return to take care of whatever was left behind. It was snoz proof!

"Start chanting that spell or whatever it is you need to do!" shouted Grogger.

He saw the wiz was looking slightly nervous.

"It nearly killed me last time... and everyone else," replied Kackle.

"Well, mumble the magic words properly or use more blood or whatever it is you need to do. Sacrifice one of the bodjits if required. Just get me a water elemental!"

Kackle sighed and began to rummage through his various hidden pockets and up his long, flowing sleeves. Eventually, he produced a crumpled piece of parchment and waved it sheepishly at Grogger.

"I think this is it," he said with another sigh. Grogger shot him a wicked smile. Being a king really did suit him.

* * * * *

Cautiously, Furna followed behind the elemental. She tried to stop herself staring at the lava-like creature to at least give herself a small portion of night vision. The sun had almost completely set, which meant they would have to fight the goblins in the dark. Something she didn't relish. Occasionally she would look toward the fence, expecting that at any moment the small, black arrows of the greenskins would start flying toward them. But nothing came.

"Why aren't they shooting?" she mumbled under her breath.

"My thoughts exactly," echoed Berusk. "They *must* have seen us by now."

Unlike Furna, Berusk was edging ever closer to the elemental. He almost seemed to be basking in its furious heat. Occasionally, Furna had to grab him to ensure he didn't just stumble into the torrent of flame.

"Could Igne have been wrong about them being in there?" asked Rowan, who was keeping well away from the elemental. Furna thought he would boil in his armor if he got too close. Even from this distance, she could see the beads of sweat trickling down his face. Occasionally they would drip off his nose and make a small pinging noise as they hit his breastplate.

Furna looked back at Igne. She could just make out her crouching form in the dim light. They had been forced to leave her near the original spot of the campfire. She needed all her concentration to bind the elemental to its current form. Alone on the plain, she looked dangerously exposed, but Furna wasn't sure what else she could do. She needed Berusk and Rowan to help her deal with whatever was behind the gate. Assuming there *was* something behind that gate.

"She hasn't been wrong yet, and I trust her not to start getting it wrong now," said Furna and hoped her lack of confidence wasn't betrayed in her shaky voice.

Her eyes were drawn forward as a noise came from the village. It was hard to make out underneath the cracking and fizzing of the elemental as it burned everything in its path. She cocked her head and strained to listen.

"Do you hear that?" she asked Rowan and Berusk.

"Hear what?" replied Rowan.

"I can't hear a damn thing with this walking torch in the way," grumbled Berusk.

Furna paused for a moment to listen; the elemental kept advancing toward the gate. She couldn't quite catch the sound, but it was almost like the noise of a river... or a waterfall. But they were no longer anywhere near the river that had carried the goblins to safety. She listened again. Now it was unmistakably the sound of rushing water.

"I hear it," said Rowan. "It's like the fountains in the City of the Golden Horn."

"Why would a bunch of goblins have a load of fountains?" asked a confused Berusk.

And with that, the plains erupted into chaos. The gate to the village exploded open, spilling wood and metal everywhere, as what appeared to be a wave crashed onto the plain behind the wreckage. With a sudden sense of dread, Furna saw the wave had a face. It turned toward her and bellowed. Chunks of soggy mud and grass fell from its gaping maw.

"Great," said Rowan, "now *they* have an elemental too. What's next? A dragon?"

The Basilean let out a hollow laugh that quickly turned to a groan as he saw a shape emerge from inside the village and flap skyward into the night sky. Its bat-like wings were briefly lit by the glow of the moon before the light was extinguished by a passing cloud, and it disappeared into the night sky.

"You had to say it, didn't you?" said Berusk. "You just had to say it!"

"Well, next I'll wish for a bloody regiment of men-at-arms to come and help us, seeing as I appear to have developed magical powers," replied Rowan.

"Let's ignore whatever that was and get inside that gate!" shouted Furna. "The elementals can do whatever they do."

At the sight of the water elemental, its fiery cousin began to shift and morph. Even from her safe distance, Furna could feel its temperature intensify to a furious white heat. Now the ground beneath it didn't just catch fire, it was actually melting. Rocks turned to liquid magma, which the elemental absorbed. Its fists became broiling lumps of molten lava and a sort of protective shield of rock formed over its shifting face. Furna wished she could see the toll this must be taking on Igne and prayed to Kthorlaq that she would be safe. There would be time to check on her later.

In the raging glow of the fire elemental, Furna could see smaller shapes emerging from the ruins of the gate. She snarled as she recognized the goblins they had been chasing. Admittedly they weren't all there, but it was enough for her. She couldn't see the wiz that had caused all this mess and guessed that it must be controlling the water elemental. Roaring Kthorlaq's name, she charged at the goblins.

* * * * *

Grogger almost couldn't believe it as he had watched the water elemental forming before him. Despite the visions, the weird singing sword, and even Magwa's lightning prod, he still found it hard to believe in magic sometimes. He was more of a practical goblin. He preferred to rely on a cold dagger to slit an enemy's throat than hope he could utter the correct incantation.

Kackle was clearly struggling to control the watery creature though. Goblins weren't typically skilled in the ways of magic, and Kackle was no different. His normally bright green visage had turned a pale and sickly hue, while sweat poured profusely from his forehead. The effort of controlling such a powerful magical creation must have been huge, Grogger thought idly, before considering that it was most certainly going to kill the wiz. *Ah well*, he thought, there would be plenty more wizzes when he had his army. They would flock to Grogger like flies.

His thoughts of grandeur were interrupted as the water elemental demolished the gate and charged onto the plain. Small streams and puddles cracked through the surface as the ancient magic pulled up hidden water from underground rivers to feed the elemental's desire to live. Its desire to fight!

With the gate destroyed, it was time to deploy the next part of his scheme.

"Klunk!" he bellowed. "Take off!"

Although the banggit had initially been disappointed that his massive bomb plan wouldn't come to fruition, when Grogger explained his new plan, a crazed smile had quickly spread across Klunk's eager little face. Klunk would sit in the winggit and throw his bombs down onto the scalies below. The bodjits had nervously explained that the winggits were designed to spot enemies, rather than actually engage in the fight, but Grogger had quickly dismissed their fears. He may not be able to capture a dragon, but he could still cause chaos from the skies.

He watched with curiosity as the winggit was loaded into what appeared to be a huge sharpstick thrower. A large group of bodjits struggled against ropes as they slowly pulled it backward until they were greeted by a loud 'click'. At the rear of the flying machine sat a bodjit alongside two levers, while its feet were firmly planted on a set of bellows. It gave the levers an experimental couple of shoves and seemed happy when the bat-like wings of the contraption moved up and down. Next it pressed on the bellows, which also seemed to move the wings.

In the front of the winggit, Klunk was surrounded by explosives. Grogger had to admit that in the short time between announcing his plan and executing it, Klunk had appeared with clawfuls of bombs, fireworks, and grenades. He had loaded them all into the winggit with a wild look in his eyes before squeezing himself into the seat. A few bombs toppled out and onto the floor, causing nearby bodjits to dash for cover in case they exploded. As he watched the explosives hit the ground, a terrible thought occurred to Grogger, and he grabbed the nearest bodjit.

"How often do these things actually survive take off?" he asked and pointed at the winggit.

"Nine times out of ten, your curiousness," replied the bodjit eagerly, and Grogger breathed a sigh of relief. Those odds were certainly in his favor. The thought of the winggit crashing while packed full of Klunk's high explosives had sent a shiver down his spine. With that much ammo, Klunk could probably take out the entire village.

"The take off is fine, it's the flying that's the problem," added the bodjit with an almost helpful tone. "That's when most tend to smash into the ground and shatter into pieces, killing everyone inside, destroying whatever they land on, and crushing anyone unlucky enough to be underneath the wreckage."

A cold sense of dread threatened to overwhelm Grogger as the bodjit pottered off. He was about to shout over to Klunk when the bodjit in charge of flying the winggit gave two claws up and rammed some goggles onto its head. Grogger could hear Klunk cackling. With that, the bodjit began furiously pumping its legs on the bellows while pulling the levers in a mad frenzy, causing the cloth wings to flap frantically. This was quickly followed by a loud 'twang' when the bodjits cut the rope that held in the winggit in place. The crude flying machine was immediately launched skyward at a momental pace, and Grogger was slightly alarmed to see various bits of wood and metal fly off the winggit as it was propelled into the air. He could still hear Klunk howling with laughter.

He watched in horror while the machine appeared to lose its initial momentum from the launch and started drifting, inexorably downward. But, just as he was looking for somewhere to take cover, the fierce flapping of the wings finally started to take effect, and the contraption bobbed through the air across the plains. Klunk's cries of 'wooooooooooo' drifted into the night sky. Grogger gave himself a satisfied nod and prepared the next part of his plan to kill the scalies.

"Ug and Magwa, let's go," he screeched before giving a whistle that snapped Jo'os to attention. The mawbeast bounded alongside him. Grogger was aware that Magwa was watching him keenly. He revelled in the legendary goblin's jealous stares. It didn't matter about the prod now, he had Jo'os under control, and that was better than any magical trinket.

Stepping over the remnants of the gate, Grogger was delighted to see the elementals were already engaged in combat. As he watched, the water elemental launched a ponderous punch at its target. The fire elemental blocked with a molten arm, causing the liquid fist to instantly boil and turn to a large cloud steam. Yet the cooling effect of the water solidified the magma of the fire elemental, and a large lump of steaming glass fell to the ground and shattered. Both elementals roared in anger and began to circle each other warily.

Now Grogger looked over to the plains to see his true enemy. He recognized the leader of the scalies and noticed, in passing, that it was missing its hat. The scaly was being flanked by another lizard and the human.

"Ug, you take the big scaly!" shouted Grogger. "Magwa, deal with that human. Me and Jo'os will kill the leader."

The troll grunted in response and headed toward his target. Ug had found a large piece of metal in one of the bodjit's workshops and had rammed it into a piece of wood to create a makeshift claymore. He swung it, experimentally, as he started running at the salamanders. Magwa, meanwhile, was more reluctant to engage the foes. He nodded, sullenly, at Grogger before thumping his prod on the ground. Out here on the plains, the lightning crackled upward into the sky. Dark clouds formed around the magical energy, and there was a rumble of thunder, followed by a zig-zag of lightning. In the brief flash of light, Grogger spotted the winggit clumsily gliding above them.

"This is it!" screamed Grogger and leapt onto Jo'os' back. At first, the mawbeast was surprised by its new rider and bucked slightly underneath Grogger, but he grabbed a claw around Jo'os' grubby mane and held tight. Eventually Jo'os calmed down and Grogger gave him a quick kick to head in the direction of the salamanders. Jo'os let out an almighty howl and galloped forward.

With his long strides, Ug was the first to reach the enemy. As he approached, Grogger saw his old enemy – the salamander he had first encountered back in the woods – silently moving his scaly lips before his sword burst into unnatural flame. It was just in time, as Ug's savage claymore swung in for the kill. The salamander knocked the powerful but unskilled blow aside and pressed in to gain the advantage. Grogger's confidence floundered slightly as he noticed Ug watched the trembling flames of the blade with a hint of trepidation. The troll's natural regeneration abilities were hindered by fire, and if the salamander could land a decent blow, Ug wouldn't be able to regenerate the wound.

Growling, the salamander unleashed a flurry of blows that Ug struggled to parry. Ug was only saved by the fact his claymore was so large, making it hard for his foe to reach around to the troll's unprotected body. But the scaly attacker kept on coming, clearly determined to end this quickly. Unfortunately, in his desire to finish the fight, he failed to spot a savage kick from Ug. The blow knocked him spinning, and he struggled to keep a grip of his sword. The flames flickered slightly as the dazed salamander gathered himself.

Ug was quick to try and gain the advantage. Holding the claymore in both powerful hands, he brought the sword down in a strike that Grogger thought would have easily cut his opponent in half. The salamander just managed to roll out of the way, as the weapon slammed into the ground and showered the pair in mud. Grogger's sigh was met by a bellow of frustration from Ug.

This time, it was the salamander that worked to press the advantage. Gripping his sword, he charged at Ug, making sure the troll was focused on the crackling flames. But, instead of trying to hit Ug with his blade, he quickly spun around and used his thick tail to take out the troll's legs. The monster fell to the ground with a heavy thud and the seemingly unkillable salamander prepared to deliver the finishing blow.

For a moment, Grogger considered riding over to help him. Instead, he leapt off Jo'os and drew his dagger, ready to face the salamander leader.

"Jo'os, help Ug," he shouted and pointed at the prone troll. The mawbeast whined slightly, perhaps worried about its new master. "Go!"

With a shake of its mane, Jo'os sped off in the direction of Ug. Grogger turned his attention to his intended target. She had drawn her cutlass, and for a moment, the pair simply circled each other, warily. Above them, lightning tore through the sky, and Grogger wondered if a storm was coming or Magwa had started fighting the human. In the brief flash of lightning, Grogger saw the anger raging in the eyes of his opponent. *Good*, he thought, *anger will cloud her judgment and dull her skill*.

"I've been waiting for this," grunted the salamander in common tongue. Grogger struggled to understand the rough growls, but he got the jist and let out a cruel laugh.

"Waiting to die? I make it quick," he answered skittishly. His quick tongue struggled around the slow language of the humans. He wasn't sure if the scaly had understood, so he resorted to sticking up two claws. This time, the reaction was immediate, and her eyes blazed while she swung her tail angrily from side to side.

While the pair circled each other once more, Grogger took a moment to see what was happening around him. Hopefully Jo'os could deal with Ug's attacker and then quickly aid him instead.

The bigger salamander quickly advanced on Ug as the troll struggled to pull himself up. Just as he was about to plunge the sword into Ug's chest, Jo'os pounded into him. The flaming sword scraped across Ug's chest, causing it to blister and burn. Ug roared in agony but remained otherwise unscathed.

Jo'os' impact threw his target backward but, somehow, the salamander kept his balance and prepared to face this new beast. They both issued low growls as they sized each other up. Occasionally Jo'os would leap in and snap his mighty jaws, only to be fended off by a well-timed swing of the salamander's flaming sword, forcing Jo'os to return to a safe distance and shake its filthy mane angrily.

Grogger was pleased to see that Ug was finally struggling to one knee and preparing to enter the fight once more. He snickered slightly at the thought of his old enemy attempting to face off against Ug and Jo'os. That fight would be over in a matter of moments. Ug thudded the ground with his imposing fist, either in anger or pain. Either way, Grogger spotted Ug's beady eyes were locked on the salamander.

The sky lit with lightning once more and Grogger briefly turned his attention to Magwa and the human.

The mad shrieks of Magwa mixed with the crackles and pops of magical energy blasting from his prod. Magwa's eyes glowed blue as lightning rippled around the rod and down its claws. The human dodged another volley of magic and quickly ducked behind his shield, bracing himself for another. Every time he tried to get within striking distance of the goblin, the prod erupted into life and shot out another burst of eldritch power.

Grogger almost could not believe the uncanny, somewhat terrifying, abilities of Magwa. In the past, when he'd seen magic users conjuring spells or using magical artifacts, they began to tire, but that didn't appear to be affecting the goblin. If anything, with each blast he seemed to be getting stronger, and the plains echoed with rumbles of thunder.

There was another boom to his right, but this time it wasn't thunder. The ground near Magwa and the human erupted in a blinding flash, as something hit it from above. Distracted by the explosion, the soldier almost didn't notice the arc of lightning soaring toward him, and he only just leapt aside in time. Magwa's unhinged cackles cut through the momentary silence.

Magwa banged the prod into the dirt, sending a bolt of lightning zig-zagging upward. The winngit carrying Klunk and his array of explosives was briefly lit by the arcane magic, before being enveloped in darkness once more. More grenades rained down.

Explosions rocked the ground, and the man leapt sideways to avoid getting covered in mud that was thrown up by the salvo. Alongside the grenades, Grogger's keen eyes picked out rockets launching from the winngit. *Just how many explosives had the crazy snoz squeezed into the contraption?* thought Grogger.

A rocket bounced off into the distance before exploding with a deafening boom and showering the area in colorful sparks. Another richocheted off the ground and sped toward the human, only for him to bat it away with his shield. It was followed by another shot of lightning from Magwa's prod that screeched just above his target's head.

Grogger tried to snap his attention back to the fight with the salamander leader, but he was somewhat distracted by the songs of his dagger. It didn't matter that he didn't know the words or the fact that the occasional vision of the fiery pits of Abyss flashed across his consciousness. The songs filled him with a violent joy, and with each jab and thrust of his dagger, the singing reached an almost ecstatic crescendo. It seemed to tell him when to duck, when to weave, or when to block. He almost laughed at how easy it all was. The dagger - or whatever it was that powered the dagger - wanted him to win. He didn't even care *why* it wanted him to win. He could think about that after he'd cut the salamander's throat.

His opponent's cutlass flashed at him again and he almost casually knocked it aside. The glowing green runes of the weapon gave his face an unnatural glow as he sneered at his opponent.

"Slow, slow, slow," he laughed and grinned at the obvious frustration of the salamander. He stuck out his tongue while rolling under another strike that would have killed most other opponents. He was unbeatable! He just hoped the other members of his gang were equally as skilled.

The salamander fighting with Ug and Jo'os was clearly starting to tire. Grogger had heard that the stupid lizard-things relied on the sun to warm them. But now the sun had set and the temperature of the plains had dropped dramatically. To Grogger, it appeared the salamander had become sluggish. Even its magic flaming sword appeared to be weakening too. It spluttered and threatened to extinguish with each labored swing. Perhaps sensing his opponent's weakness, Jo'os had redoubled its efforts. The mawbeast circled around his mark and leapt in with small nips and bites. They weren't enough to kill the salamander, but they were enough to wear him down. He tried to swat Jo'os away with his tail, but the mawbeast just leapt over it, as though it were a game. Grogger realized it was only a matter of time before the cold slowed the salamander down completely and Jo'os would be able to finish the job.

For a moment, the scaly hung his head and breathed heavily as though exhausted. As Jo'os leapt in for another nip, he quickly spun round and slammed his fist into the beast's face. The salamander smiled to himself when he heard the creature's howl of pain, and Grogger grimaced. Jo'os scrambled backward, whining with blood streaming from his mouth, but the salamander didn't wait, he quickly followed up with his sword raised. Jo'os let out a little whimper, as it struggled to pull itself back up, clearly dazed from the force of the blow. The flames on the salamander's sword seem to grow brighter, briefly lighting the battlefield around them, as he raised the blade to deliver the final blow.

But the death strike never came. Ug crept up on the salamander and grabbed him from behind before wrapping his muscular arms around his captive's neck. The salamander dropped his sword in surprise and quickly resorted to clawing at his unseen foe, but as quick as his sharp talons tore through the green flesh of the troll, the wounds quickly healed back up. He tried lashing his tail against the monster, but it had little effect. Instead the vice-like grip grew tighter and tighter. Grogger noticed with glee that Jo'os had leapt back up and was staring straight at the salamander. The goblin beamed with pride as it dawned on him that the Jo'os had pretended to be injured to distract the stupid salamander.

Ha! Outsmarted by a mawbeast, thought Grogger with a sense of smug satisfaction.

The salamander started to thrash violently against Ug, but it was pointless. The thick, trunk-like arm continued to inexorably crush his foe. Then, for a moment, it looked as though the salamander may break free, and Grogger grunted in frustration.

Ug let out an almighty roar and lifted the struggling salamander above his head before smashing him down onto the ground. Splayed in front of the troll, Ug pressed one of his enormous feet on the salamander's neck. Even from where he was fighting, Grogger heard the gruesome snap of the scaly's neck. With a roar of satisfaction, Ug picked up the limp body of his kill once more, before throwing it, unceremoniously, down to the ground. Ug bellowed and thumped his chest in celebration.

One down, thought Grogger.

* * * * *

Rowan heard the commotion but fought to ignore it. He had his own problems to deal with. Not only did he have the lightning bolts to avoid but, occasionally, random projectiles would be lobbed from the sky and explode just a few steps away from where he was standing. It was clear that whatever the flying machine was, it was following his movements and trying to blast him back to the Shining Ones. A plan popped into his head. Whoever was chucking bombs at him clearly didn't have much idea where they were aiming, so perhaps they wouldn't notice if he got close to his foe.

First he had to make sure the contraption was following him, though. Breathing deeply, he began to sing.

Thou hath felt our sword... thou hath felt our strength... thine eyes have seen the glory... O, Basilea!... O, Basilea!... thy enemies doth fall.

The Shining Ones shall follow thee... they protect our souls... from up on high they gaze below... and guideth one and all.

Above the sound of his singing, Rowan was aware of a creaking sound somewhere in the sky. Another projectile exploded beside him. He ignored the shower of mud and continued advancing toward the goblin with the infernal staff. This time, a burst of lightning forced him to roll out the way, but he didn't stop. He needed to take out that damn goblin.

Now he ran, continuing to sing at the top of his voice. He just hoped the flying machine would be able to keep up. Rowan saw, with some satisfaction, that the goblin with the prod was clearly alarmed that Rowan was coming straight at him. It grabbed the prod with both claws and fired a quick succession of shots that veered wildly off target. He prayed to the Shining Ones that his unseen assistant would be more helpful, as he stopped dead in his tracks.

He realized he must be blessed by the Shining Ones as two grenades detonated in rapid succession ahead of him. The first one created a blinding flash that forced the goblin to cover its sensitive eyes, whereas the next blast knocked it flying. Its magical prod, which had caused Rowan so much trouble, flew out of its claw and, for the first time, Rowan realized that the air had been pregnant with a static charge while the prod was being used. There was a final rumble of thunder above him, and then it felt like the plains could breathe again, without the lightning constantly constricting the atmosphere like an angry snake.

Rowan looked over at the prone body of the goblin and spat. With that pest out of the way, he could help the others. His satisfaction soon turned to horror when he saw the bellowing troll standing over the limp form of Berusk. He whispered a quick prayer to the Shining Ones to guide Berusk's soul back to the Three Kings before turning his attention elsewhere.

Furna clashed weapons with another one of the goblins. He cast a quick glance over to the elementals, but there wasn't a great deal he could do to help there. The pair of magical creations were locked in a wrestling matching that sent clouds of broiling hot steam in the air, while the ground below them was a bizarre mix of molten rock and muddy puddles that bubbled and hissed due to the constant heating and cooling.

However, there was one thing he needed to take care of before he could help Furna. Looking around on the ground, he located the prod. Rowan was surprised to see intricate elvish carvings spiralling around the hilt. There was a delicate beauty to the curling elvish letters, and he wished he could understand what they were saying. But this was no time to get distracted, and he quickly scooped the prod up. When he grasped his gauntleted hand around the hilt, he felt a surge of energy so powerful that he almost dropped it in shock. Yet, he held firm and used his other hand to steady his aim.

Now, turning his eyes to the sky, he listened out for the telltale flapping of the flying machine. Then he spotted what looked like a fuse being lit. He aimed the prod and prayed that *something* would happen.

"May the Shining Ones guide my aim," he whispered.

A golden light erupted from the prod and sped skyward. Unlike the crackling energy of the lightning, this was a glorious shaft of pure power that hurtled toward the flying contraption. Rowan was almost sure he could hear the hymns of the Elohi as the surge cleaved through the night sky. The pilot of winggit desperately tried to maneuver out of the way, but it was impossible, the golden beam tore through the machine like paper and continued upward into the heavens.

Rowan was thrown several feet backward by the force of the angelic burst and almost knocked senseless. The prod was torn from his grip, landing hidden somewhere in the grass, and the golden light winked out of existence, returning the night sky to darkness. Although, not quite complete darkness. What looked like a burning comet was plummeting toward the plains, and Rowan realized with some satisfaction that it must be the flying machine. As it hit the ground, there was an almighty explosion that shook the earth beneath Rowan's feet. A huge ball of flame tore upward, and Rowan could hear the impact of pieces of machinery being thrown from the blast.

With the flying device out the way, it was time to help Furna. Just as soon as his head stopped throbbing.

* * * * *

Grogger didn't even bother to turn around at the sound of the explosion. He knew it must be that idiot, Klunk. He only hoped that whatever chaos the banggit had caused had somehow managed to kill the human, which left him to deal with the remaining salamander.

"Just us," he quipped and was delighted to see the salamander's snarl of anger.

"This ends now!" roared his opponent and fought with renewed vigor. Now, even with the help of the dagger, Grogger was struggling to block the lightning fast strikes of the cutlass. One thrust sliced open his arm and he screamed in pain while trying to keep hold of his precious dagger. He parried a few more attacks, but the shooting pains from his wound threatened to overwhelm him. No matter how quickly he moved, it seemed the salamander was faster. He panicked as he saw the fire burning in her eyes. She was going to kill him. She was actually going to kill him! All this for nothing.

He gritted his teeth against the pain and considered the best way to retreat. If he could make it back to the village he could seek refuge in one of the workshops and send the bodjits out to deal with the salamanders. Or just wait for Grukhar to return with the underminers... if she ever returned. He suddenly considered the awful possibility that the other salamanders could have killed the goblins, leaving him with no back-up.

After some serious consideration, he decided to do what any good goblin would do in this situation... he legged it. Turning his back on the salamander, he ran as fast as his little green legs could carry him. His injured arm screamed in protest as it pumped furiously to propel him forward to the village. Grogger concentrated on the gate. If he could just get to the gate, then he would be safe. He could hear his furious foe giving pursuit and imagined that the last thing he would feel before being struck down was the hot breath of the fiery creature on his neck. The nightmarish idea forced his legs to go even faster.

However, something glinting in the grass caught his eye and his heart leapt. It was Magwa's prod! He had no idea where the aging goblin had gone, but that was definitely his prod. A brilliant plan popped fully formed into his cunning brain, and he changed direction, heading straight to the prod. He just hoped that the salamander's eyes wouldn't be as keen as his in the dark.

Once he was close enough to the prod, he pretended to trip and landed heavily in the dirt, making sure he kept the artifact within close reach.

"Mercy, mercy, mercy!" he pleaded and held up his claws before throwing the dagger to one side to show he had given up. He knew he wouldn't be needing that.

The salamander stopped in her tracks and looked at him with contempt.

"You have a sick sense of humor," she sneered. "After all of this. After all that's happened, you dare to beg for your life."

"No more trouble. No more trouble," came Grogger's reply, and he hoped she didn't notice he was slowly creeping closer to the prod.

"You have the nerve to ask for mercy when you gave no mercy to Hr'zak. No mercy to Berusk. I just pray to Kthorlaq that Igne will be still alive after I finish with you. Otherwise, you'll pay for her death too."

Grogger was surprised to see the salamander put away its cutlass and pull out a pistol instead.

"I've used my blade to kill more honorable creatures than you," it hissed. "You deserve to be shot like a rabid dog."

Grogger's face fell at the pistol. He wasn't sure the prod would be quicker than a gun!

"Wait, *wait...*"

* * * * *

Rowan finally came to his senses and surveyed the battlefield. The wreckage of the flying machine still blazed in the distance, and occasionally fireworks would shoot out with a whistling sound or a small explosion would rock the plains. The elementals were still locked in their eternal struggle, but both appeared tired. They were much smaller than he remembered, and he guessed the powerful magic was starting to dissipate.

Furna! The thought of her safety suddenly jolted him to alertness, and he scanned around to see where she was. He was surprised to see her not too far away, and his heart leapt in excitement when he saw she had cornered the goblin leader, who was grovelling on the ground. He just hoped Furna would end it quickly and they could check on Igne.

Then he noticed something else – the goblin was slowly moving away from Furna. He wanted to cry out, to tell her to end it quickly, but his throat was hoarse, and he only managed a weak rasp. His heart sank when he realized why the goblin was still moving while pleading for his life - he was trying to reach the magical prod that Rowan had foolishly dropped.

With his muscles screaming in agony, Rowan pulled himself up and charged at the goblin, just hoping he could reach them in time.

* * * * *

Grogger could see the salamander was about to press the trigger when they were both distracted by the foolish human running toward them. He was shouting and pointing at the prod, but Grogger didn't care; a moment's distraction was all he needed. He leapt at the prod and felt a surge of power run through him as his claws gripped around it. In one fluid move, he flipped around ready to shoot his foe, but the human barged into him. Grogger struggled to keep a grip on the prod as they tumbled through the dirt.

"Rowan! Move out of the way, I can't get a clear shot!" roared the salamander.

Grogger and his attacker stopped rolling in the dirt, and he was delighted to see that somehow, he had ended up on top of the human. In a flash, he used his free claw to produce a hidden dagger from his boot and rammed it into a gap between the plates of armor. Right near where Grogger hoped a human's heart might be. The man howled in pain and his grip went momentarily limp.

Grogger spotted the salamander trying to take aim in the confusion, but it was too late. Grogger stabbed the prod in her direction, and a bolt of lightning zig-zagged straight at her. She managed to pull the trigger, but the shot went well above Grogger's head. Then he watched in amusement as the stupid creature dropped her pistol and felt toward the smoking hole that been torn through her chest, before collapsing in a lifeless heap.

The human writhed underneath Grogger and tried to grab Grogger's neck with shaking hands, but it was no use. Grogger spat in his face before delivering a vicious blow to the man's face with the butt of the staff. With his final assailant now removed, the goblin howled a scream of delight that echoed across the plains.

CHAPTER TWENTY-SIX

Rowan awoke to find himself in what he assumed was a dark cave. But, as his one open eye adjusted to the gloom, he saw shelves lined with empty ale caskets and realized, with some confusion, that he must be in a cellar. He struggled for a moment when he noticed his legs and arms were tightly bound, but he quickly stopped when awful pains shot through his body. His face, in particular, felt like it was on fire; and when he ran his tongue along the inside of mouth, he noticed raw gaps of missing teeth.

In the dark, he heard excited chittering and realized, with some horror, that he was not alone. He recognized the dim shapes of several goblins talking - or rather arguing - in the corner. He assumed they would be debating the best way to kill him, and he sent his thoughts up to the Shining Ones to protect Mary when he was gone.

One of the goblins turned around when they heard him muttering prayers. With revulsion, Rowan realized it was the awful leader of the greenskins.

"I'll kill you," he tried to shout, but his mangled face and mouth ensured it only came out as a muffled cry. Grogger let out a high-pitched laugh in response.

* * * * *

After he had shot the salamander, Grogger had quickly gathered his gang and prepared for an attack from the rest of the pirate crew. Jo'os and Ug seemed mostly unharmed by the encounter, although Ug had a wicked scar across his chest that was struggling to heal. He had occasionally picked at it, as though he was confused why it wouldn't repair itself. Magwa, on the other hand, hadn't fared so well. The impact of the blast had shattered one of his legs, and Grogger had found him limping along looking for his prod. For a moment, Grogger simply considered putting the old goblin out of his misery, but he felt that Magwa's work wasn't quite finished yet. Instead, he handed him the prod and let him lean against Jo'os as they returned to the bodjits.

Back in the village, Grogger found Kackle collapsed in a heap. At first, Grogger had assumed he was dead but, upon closer inspection, discovered he was simply exhausted from summoning the water elemental, which had now evaporated. With a start, Grogger remembered the scaly mage and quickly ordered Ug to find them in the plains. He hoped they would be in a similar state to Kackle.

For a while, Grogger told the bodjits to prepare for an attack from the rest of the salamanders... but the attack never came. As the sun began to creep ever upward on the horizon, Grogger's heart swelled at the thought he had won – particularly when Ug returned with the prone form of the mage slung over his shoulder and the rest of the underminers, including Grukhar and Gritter, in tow not far behind. Meanwhile, most of Klunk's smoldering body was found in the remains of the winggit. Grogger had not bothered to ask the bodjits to look for the arm and leg that were missing.

Now he was debating with Grukhar, Gritter, and Magwa what to do with the human and salamander.

"I say we get a mawbeast to eat them, starting from the toes," said Gritter, excitedly.

"Why does a mawbeast get to have all the fun?" asked Grukhar. "We could chop them up ourselves and feed them to a mawbeast." She let out a demented cackle.

"Magwa thinks we could put them in a rock thrower and see how far they fly!"

Grogger rolled his eyes. This debate had been going on for ages, and he was getting bored. He almost thought about stabbing the prisoners and getting done with it all. But where was the fun in that? His ruminations were disturbed by a shout from the human.

"You'll never win. Evil must always be punished," shouted the man in between wheezing coughs. "The Shining Ones will smite you. Smite you and all your stinking, spiteful kind."

He tried to spit but only managed to cough up a loose tooth.

Grogger's skin bristled at the mention of the Shining Ones, but the part about him never winning forced a furious bile to rise in his throat. He stomped over to his prisoner.

"Pull him up," spat Grogger. Ug loomed over the prisoner from behind. The troll roughly grabbed his hair and yanked him upward, causing him to scream in agony. Ug stopped when the man's ruined face was level with Grogger's.

"What you say?" Grogger knew his skittish tongue was mangling the human words, but he was too angry to care. He took out his frustration by giving the captive a vicious slap across the cheek.

"You won't win," moaned the man. "Hundreds of your kind come and go. You bring pain and suffering, but then 'poof,' you're gone. Never to be seen again. No one knows who you were. No one cares what you did. Nothing. You're all nothing."

The human tried to give a harsh laugh, but all that erupted from his chest were more painful-sounding coughs. Grogger's body shook with rage. Nothing! *Nothing!* He was far from nothing. He was going to be the king of the goblins. The king of *all* the goblins.

"Kill him, boss, kill him!" shrieked Gritter. "No one talks to you like that. Whatever he said, it sounded real bad. Didn't understand a word of it, but must have been bad!"

Grogger whipped out his dagger and pressed it to the man's neck. The blade sang and Grogger's eyes rolled upward as he prepared to slice the stupid human's throat wide open.

"Do it," laughed the broken soldier. "The Shining Ones will welcome me and make sure my name is remembered in the halls of Basilea. Who will know your name? No one. No one!"

Grogger stopped and looked into the half-open eye of his captive. His green face cracked into an awful smile, and he leered viciously. Grogger had devised a much better use for the human.

"Ug, follow me and bring the man," laughed Grogger and disappeared up the stairs of the cellar. "I have an important task for you, human!"

"What about the salamander?" asked Grukhar.

"Kill it," said Grogger, absent-mindedly. He left Grukhar and Gritter arguing in the cellar about which one would kill the salamander first, while Ug noisily dragged the prisoner up the steps by his hair.

Outside of the tavern, the village was a bustling hive of activity. Underminers and bodjits were busy moving war machines out of the barn and into the streets of the village. Other goblins were piling up weapons into a large mound of metal and wood. There were hundreds of greenskins everywhere that Grogger looked. He beamed with joy. There must be hundreds, possibly thousands, of goblins that had started flocking to the village already.

"See this," said Grogger and pointed to the bustling forms. "My army. Grogger's army!"

The man tried to turn away, but Ug grabbed his chin and forced him to look back at Grogger, who pressed his long, green nose up against the human's face.

"Name is Grogger! My *name* is Grogger! Say it!"

The man clamped his mouth shut.

"Break one of his fingers," spat Grogger and was greeted by a yelp of agony as Ug snapped a little finger.

"Say it!" screamed Grogger and showered the foolish human in spit.

He screams were only greeted by an agonized whimper.

"Break another," yelled Grogger. The man shrieked before going limp. Grogger slapped him across the face to try and bring him around.

"Grogger! Say it!" he delivered another stinging blow to the semi-conscious captive's face before screeching. "Say it! Say it! Say it!"

"Grogg...er," mumbled the man and drifted in and out of consciousness.

"Again!" screeched Grogger.

"Grogger," he sobbed, and this time, Grogger nodded with satisfaction.

"Go back to humans. Tell Grogger is on way! Tell the *king* is on way. Understand?"

The human nodded before passing out.

Grogger was pleased to see Grukhar and Gritter emerging from the tavern. Both were covered in blood and grinning wildly.

"Good, I have a job for you two," said Grogger. "Take the human as close as you dare to a city and leave him there."

"You aren't going to kill him?" asked Gritter with a look of confusion.

"No," laughed Grogger. "He has a far more important job than just dying. He is going to tell the world that Grogger is coming. That the lands of men will fall under the rule of Grogger Split-tooth! That the goblin king is finally here, and no one will stop us!"

Nearby goblins broke out in spontaneous and rapturous applause.

"Long live the king! Long live the king! Hail to Grogger!"

EPILOGUE

"We found him outside the city gates," said the night watchman.

Captain Dwight looked at the sorry figure lying on the bed. He was covered in cuts, bruises, and his fingers bent at odd, painful angles. A scruffy, matted beard covered his face, and parts of his shaggy mess of hair appeared as though they had been torn out. Underneath the soiled armor, he was dangerously thin, and Dwight was surprised he was still managing to even breathe.

"Was it the smell that attracted you to him?" said the captain and held his hand against his nose. "Where did you say you found him?"

"He was in the woods near the north gate," replied the watchman. "Tompkins thought he saw movement at the edge, so we went to investigate. Found him near some dead rabbits. They looked like they had been eaten."

Captain Dwight shuddered. What an awful man. He appeared to be a vagabond that had, somehow, managed to steal the armor of a Basilean soldier. He didn't have time to deal with all this now. They had to prepare for the visit of Lord Darvled later that week, and he wouldn't like seeing filthy scum like this roaming around the city.

"Throw him in jail and we can interrogate him after Lord Darvled's visit."

Suddenly, the man's remaining eye snapped open, and he grabbed Dwight's arm. His grip was like a vice, and no matter how much the captain struggled, the man remained latched on.

"The king is coming," said the man and his voice rose to a manic, shrill laugh. "King Grogger is coming, and he will kill us all!"

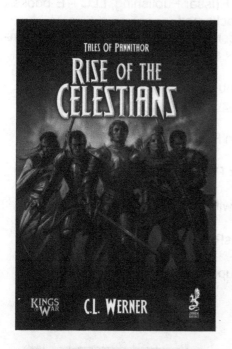

TALES OF PANNITHOR
RISE OF THE CELESTIANS

KINGS OF WAR

C.L. WERNER

TALES OF MANTICA
DROWNED SECRETS

BEN STODDARD

KINGS OF WAR

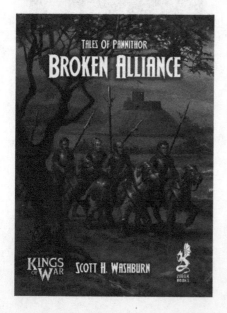

TALES OF PANNITHOR
BROKEN ALLIANCE

KINGS OF WAR

SCOTT H. WASHBURN

TALES OF PANNITHOR
HERO FALLING

KINGS OF WAR

MARK BARBER